KAYNDO

Book 2: Ring of Despair

By: Terri Luckey

****

I dedicate this to my late mother who always encouraged and indulged my love of books.

Logo by Diverse Pixel (**www.diversepixel.com**)

Kayndo 'Ring of Despair'

By Terri Luckey
© 2015 Terri Luckey

ISBN-13: 978-0692464076
ISBN-10: 0692464077

This is a work of fiction. Names, characters, places and incidents are either the product of the author's imagination or, if real, are used fictitiously.

Cover by Diverse Pixel (http://www.diversepixel.com)

For more information about the book contact:
www.terriluckey.com

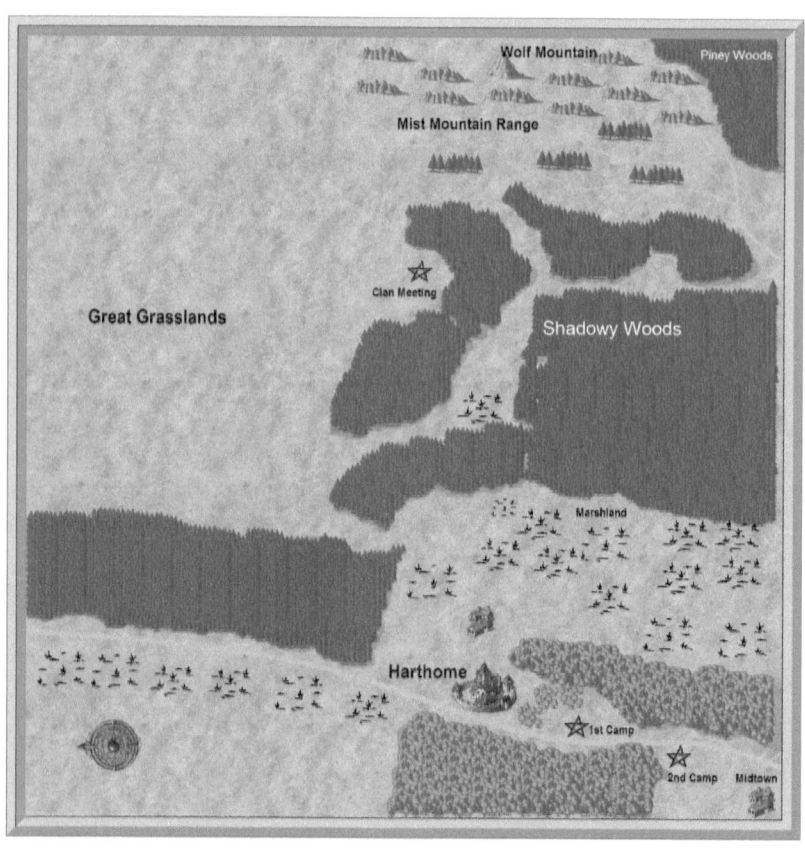

TABLE OF CONTENTS

-Prologue-

Tib stood hidden in the shadow cast by the threshold of the doorway of one of the unused castle rooms. He let other servants go by and waited for Maydlan's creamy, heart shaped face to appear. Good. She walked alone. Her strides were hurried as she drew closer. He stepped out into the hall. She paled and threw a hand to the center of her chest. He hadn't meant to frighten her. He pulled down his hood to reveal his sandy hair and hazel eyes.

"Your Royal Highness," she said in a breathless whisper.

"I told you to call me Tibalt if we're alone." He held out the tiny slip of folded paper. "I found this note. I believe it belongs to you."

Scarlet flushed her cheeks and contrasted sharply with her shiny, black hair. She was so pretty and only two years older than Tib. Why was she so interested in Varian, who was twice their age?

Her hands trembled as she took the note from him. A mouse scurried out from a crack between the stones in the castle wall and ran across her shoe. She squealed and dropped the note. Before Tib could react, the mouse grabbed the note in its mouth and disappeared in the wall again.

Stupid mice were always invading the castle. "I'm sorry, Maydlan. I'm afraid it's going to be part of a mouse nest now."

"Did you read it?" Her voice quaked.

Usually, Tib let the staff believe they should be cautious around him. But he didn't want to scare her more, so he winked. "Lucky for you, Father just reamed me about respecting others' privacy, especially if I wanted them to consider me a friend. Is there a reason to be concerned about losing the note?"

Her hand flitted to her throat. "No." She lowered her hand and spoke firmly. "Thank you, for respecting my privacy."

She wasn't only pretty, but nice too. When he left, would

Maydlan care? Shouldn't he find out? What did he have to lose?

He touched her arm. "Maydlan, if you get tired of Varian, let me know."

She drew back fast as if his hand was on fire. "I'm a servant, and you're a prince."

"Not for long." The countless lessons were a waste. He needed a companion to be king. "What animal companion would choose someone who doesn't want them?"

Maydlan's mouth formed an O. "I'm sorry."

"For what? I don't want the job. I just hated to disappoint Father."

Her chin quivered. "No, I'm sorry I didn't know that before I gave someone else my heart."

"Oh, then I'm sorry too." Tib stood to the side and waved her on.

1

Shattered Illusions

"Kingdoms falter when they lose their heart, so Pericards can't fail to protect our king."~ Blake

Footsteps drummed against the castle's stone floors, reverberating as if an entire army moved through the halls. Tib quickened his pace. The king had little time to waste, especially on his fifteen-year old son. And this was his last day to convince Father not to send him away to the wolf clan. Tib glanced back.

Varian, the first visitor from the Eastern continent to their kingdom of Taluma, walked behind him, sandwiched between two rigid Kagards. Was it the soldiers' padded clothing that made their strides so stiff? Varian's mouth parted into an arrogant smirk above his pointy beard. He lifted his brow as if to say, "Why hurry?"

When they came to the plain wooden door, Tib gave himself a quick perusal. He brushed off a strand of his sandy-colored hair from his sleeve, then moved into the long meeting room with its undecorated stone walls. Chairs and two plain square tables furnished the room.

Father sat behind the table at the other end. His eagle companion, Seemo, perched next to him, and Pericards stood at attention around the two. The Pericards black uniforms and the hands already resting on their swords set them apart from the Kagards. No empty chair on Father's side for his son. So he wouldn't be welcomed over there. Just like anyone with a report to make.

Tib bowed. "My King."

The light from the oil sconces on the wall picked up the red tints in Father's hair as his green eyes inspected him. Father's lip turned up a smidgeon in a tiny smile. "The change to punctuality is appreciated."

Seemo ruffled his feathers. It grated on Tib. Father's bird companion was always welcomed close. He had plenty of time for the eagle, even after it had bitten Tib. And—the even bigger irritation—Seemo would reveal any deceit.

"You may come forward too, Varian," Father commanded.

Varian pursed his lips. He and his guards bowed, then moved up to join Tib.

Father pointed toward some chairs on their side of the table. "You may both sit. What have you learned, Tib?"

Tib plopped down. The table's width kept several feet between him and Father. He took a breath before starting, "The weapons of the ancients don't take much skill to use. Not like a bow or sword, and they'll rip a hole through flesh and even bones. These things are much better than anything we have." Father gave him a sharp glance. Had he revealed too much? If Father ever learned he knew more about the ancients than their weapons, he'd be in serious trouble.

"Your task was to determine these weapons' weaknesses, not tell me how great they are." Father's rebuke stung.

Tib just told him the truth. How was it his fault if Father didn't like it?

Father's gaze turned to Varian. "How do we defend against them?"

Varian shrugged. "You can't."

"Everything has weaknesses." Father's tone sharpened. "If you're serious about aiding us, you'll reveal them."

Varian's normal haughty air faded. He threw his hands up, startling his guards, but his palms were empty. "I am, sire, but I don't know of any."

The sides of Father's mouth turned down. "Search harder."

"I will."

A clatter came from behind Tib. The servants carried in trays of covered dishes and placed them on the other table. The scent of cinnamon, garlic, and onion wafted through the air. Tib's stomach rumbled. Roasted duck maybe? Baked apples?

"Have you learned our beliefs, yet, Varian?" Father asked.

"I have. You believe after the ancients burned our world, Kun sent JoKayndo to teach you to care for His creation and keep it balanced." Varian used a lecture tone, but at least it didn't hold derision. "Those rules are called the Vita. Your clanspeople regulate that balance, and some have animals that mind-speak. If that balance is in peril, you believe Kun will send a Kayndo to restore it."

"Good. I know you don't believe in Kun. You don't have to believe, but you must respect *our* beliefs. If you want to join us, you'll need to swear loyalty to me, to Taluma, and to keeping the Vita." Father's tone softened. "Are you willing?"

Varian waved his hands in another of those flashy gestures he loved. "Yes."

Really? He'd do it? A loud clang startled Tib. One of the servants, Maydlan, had dropped her tray. Red flushed her cheeks and stood out against the flawless white skin and lustrous black hair. Had she been staring at Varian and not paying attention? Why was she so enamored with him? She scurried to retrieve the spilled apples covered in cream. Tib's stomach rumbled again.

Father's eyes raked Varian. "Then give me your oath, now, with Seemo judging if you speak truly."

Quick footfalls slapped behind Tib. He looked over his shoulder to see Maydlan running toward him, brandishing a knife.

What? Tib froze. Cold, icy fear stabbed his heart. *I'm going to die.*

"Watch out!" Varian shouted.

Father leapt across the table, tackling Tib. Plates fell and shattered. Tib's chair toppled. Rough stones pressed into his back as Father's body pinned him to the floor and blocked his vision.

"Get her," someone shouted. Screams pierced the air. Another crash. "She threw the knife!"

Father's body twitched above his. Seemo shrieked. Who did it hit? Father or the eagle? Tib struggled. He couldn't get free, but Father's shoulder moved a little, enough for Tib to crane his neck to see around it.

Seemo was diving at Maydlan, his talons clawing for her eyes.

She threw her arms up to fend the eagle off. Varian smashed a fist into her throat. She grabbed her neck and a horrible sucking filled the air. Pericards tackled her. She flopped on the ground underneath them.

"Get her hands and feet," a burly Pericard shouted.

The clump of people stopped moving. Her gasping had quieted. Was she dead? The Pericards rose, then backed up to reveal her lying with only the whites of her eyes staring at the ceiling.

"Help the king," the burly Pericard bellowed. "Shield him and the prince." They swarmed in to form a protective ring around them, cutting off most of Tib's view with their legs.

Father shifted and slid off Tib to sit in front of him. A knife protruded from his back and blood seeped around it.

Oh no. Just how badly was Father hurt? And why did Father protect Tib? Did he really care? What if he died? Tib's heart lurched.

Someone was screaming among the servants. Someone else sobbed. Tib's hands shook. He wanted to scream too.

"Stay alert. Expect more attacks," the Pericard ordered.

More? Tib's heart skittered. His illusion of safety behind the castle's walls with the Pericards guarding them lay shattered like the plates. Shivers racked his body.

2

Earning a Fringe

The strong eat, the weak die. To survive we must fight ~ Jaycee

Goosebumps rose all over Dayvee's six-foot frame. Must be his nerves or the chill among the pine trees in the mountain range they called home. He grabbed another handful of the damp, crumbled leaves and moss from his pouch. The rough texture scratched as he rubbed it over his flesh and buckskin clothing. He even coated his hair. At least it was cut short.

Then, he worked it into Jaycee's thick, gray coat. He'd grown so close to the wolf he trained for the prince. Someday, he'd have to hand him over. A fist squeezed his heart, so he pushed the thought aside.

The scent of decaying leaves and mint filled the air and hid their scent. Better than the stink of a dead carcass like the companions preferred. That odor might be appealing to their enemies today. As their best tracker, his uncle was going first with his five trainees, and they couldn't risk alerting the treacherous hyenas. They'd already attacked Dayvee and his father before.

"We'll fight in pairs and watch each other's back." Codee's tall, muscular frame cast a shadow as he came closer. His gray-blue eyes settled on Dayvee. "I'll take you."

His uncle? Cackles. Elayni might need his protection. Dayvee's stomach jiggled as if grasshoppers jumped inside. To defy Codee wasn't an option if he didn't want to be left out.

Under his dark-brown shock of hair, Brando's deep blue eyes pierced Dayvee. "I'll cover Elayni's back." He grabbed his forearm. "You can trust me not to let my family be hurt."

"Me too." Elayni tucked a golden-lock behind her ear.

He returned Brando's forearm clasp. "I trust you."

"Geno, you have Chayla's back. And from here on in only signals." Codee raised his index finger. The signal to follow in a line.

Dayvee fell in behind Codee with Jaycee. Codee's single, smooth brown braid fell over the back of his rucksack and barely swayed as he and his wolf companion, Wilee, glided through the trees. It would have been nice if Dayvee had inherited his grandmother's hair like Codee. It would be better than his yellow hair from his father and grandfather— with that annoying white streaked cowlick in front that refused to be tamed.

The sun moved to mark mid-day, and the rays soaked in as Dayvee trailed his uncle. Sweat dampened the band across his forehead as he climbed a brush covered slope. Should he take the time to remove his coat? Maybe later.

When they came down the other side, the brush thinned, and Dayvee slipped in the soft footing. The ground leveled, stopping his slide before he fell. Whew.

Codee pointed to prints in the mud. Four toes, wider than a wolf's, but not quite as long. The triangular-shaped pad lay closer to the toes too. Crisp edges. Fresh. And they crowded the ground. Weren't the hyenas concerned about covering their trail? Maybe they felt safe in such large numbers? Dayvee's stomach churned as they followed the tracks through the valley.

Hah. Jaycee's thought penetrated Dayvee's mind. *We'll show them how safe they are.* As Jaycee's excitement rose, adrenaline spiked through their bond to Dayvee. Intoxicating. As if he had drunk Razi, but without the mind-numbing effects.

The wall of rock on their left side ended, but the prints continued beyond it. Codee stopped and raised the palm of his hand, signaling them to wait. He flicked a finger toward a stand of several trees packed close together. Must want the trainees to use them for cover.

Dayvee glanced at the others. Brando shot him a crooked grin. Elayni's light-blue eyes danced. Chayla's auburn head of hair lifted to show him her tiny mouth set in a firm line. Determined? Crinkles formed above Geno's thick brows. Concerned? The trainees' wolf companions' ears stood erect, and their normal glide held a bounce. As excited as Jaycee.

As Codee and Wilee crawled forward on their bellies around the wall of rock, Dayvee slipped behind a white pine. He struggled to keep his emotions in check. So much harder with Jaycee's surging too. Could there be a greater life than his...that of a Calupi?

Now if only he could change his father's mind. Maybe today, he'd be able to convince their alpha leader, Leeto, his son wasn't weak. If only Dayvee had thrown his weapon at the condemned like everyone else. Nero tried to murder them. He deserved the ring of death sentence. But Dayvee couldn't do it. If he didn't show Leeto he deserved high-status, he wouldn't gain respect, and Elayni's parents wouldn't approve of her life-mating him when they finished their training.

Whispers assaulted Dayvee's mind from nearby animals—a squirrel, a rabbit, a badger, a hawk, several other birds, some mice. *Hello, Kayndo.*

Dayvee wasn't a Kayndo yet, even though they didn't seem to care. He ignored the whispers and tried to shut them out. The gift Kun gave him to mind-speak to every animal, and not just a bonded companion, made it difficult to focus sometimes. But maybe he should use it. Did they need to kill the hyenas when he could just ask them to leave?

Don't. Jaycee's cold nose nudged his hand. *They're hyenas. They'll just keep returning until they learn a lesson. Your father and the others are coming up now.*

Leeto, the fourteen Calupi, and twenty wolves with him were difficult to spot with their willful cover of dirt and leaves. The two neighboring wild packs sent three wolves each. It would be different having wild wolves fighting with them. But with all those prints, they might need them.

Wilee says we're to move forward now, Jaycee sent.

Dayvee crept out from the trees and dropped to his belly. His heart thumped against the ground as he slid over the damp grass and patches of mud. At least it didn't hold a covering of snow anymore.

The moisture seeped through his clothing. He almost rounded the wall when a whoop-whoop sounded, and then those cackles.

His mouth dried and he froze. Those cackles haunted his dreams. Did they know they were here? Was he crazy? He could die.

Seize the moment. Jaycee's usual response when Dayvee showed concern about what might happen in the future. He shouldn't have stopped. Didn't everyone tell him he worried too much?

He forced himself to worm forward through the foliage, past the stone cliff. A thick odor cloyed the air, like burning bugs, and made his eyes water.

The stink of trouble. Hyena scent.

He blinked a few times to clear his vision and squinted to see. Several holes dotted the ground. Must be their dens. Among the brown grass, he spotted them, short ears on top of wide faces, the bodies painted with black patches. They lay everywhere basking in the sun or gnawing on bones. At least fifty. Dayvee shuddered. His fingers found the hilts of his weapons.

Leeto howled. The signal.

Dayvee leapt to his feet and ran after Codee toward the nearest hyenas. As Codee knifed one, Dayvee turned around to cover his back. Hyenas sprang forward and circled around them. One drew its lips back to expose its teeth and lunged toward Dayvee.

His heart raced as he flung his nails. They buried into the hyena's neck, but it kept coming. He kicked it in the chest and pushed it back. The hyena's teeth clicked together and missed him by an inch.

Dayvee stabbed it in the side of its head with his tooth. He pulled his weapon free in time to meet another jumping at him. His slash missed the hyena's eyes, and its teeth locked onto Dayvee's leg. Pain jolted him as warm blood sprayed his pants.

He plunged his tooth into the back of the hyena's head at the base. It released its grip and fell dead at his feet. Dayvee's wounded leg stung. Tender, but far from debilitating.

Jaycee battled another hyena at his side. He reached over to help, but Jaycee's teeth tore into the hyena's neck and ripped its throat. The body thudded as it hit the ground. A whoop whoop signaled the hyenas retreat. They raced away.

This is fun, Jaycee sent.

More like petrifying. When Codee and Wilee gave chase, Dayvee turned, and ignoring the pain in his leg, ran after them. Codee threw his nails and hit one's shoulder. Dayvee stepped to the side long enough to cast his. It bounced off the hyena's forehead, but the hyena dropped to the ground. Blood pooled around it. Barely pausing to retrieve his weapon, Codee slashed the hyena's throat and raced toward another.

Dayvee grabbed his nails and followed. His breath came fast and his heart pounded. Jaycee's anticipation of their next clash sent energy surging through Dayvee, and he caught up.

Codee released his nails and hit a hyena in its knee. It balanced on three legs and sprang at them. Wilee met the charge and took it to the ground, clamping his teeth down on its neck. When he drew back, the hyena didn't rise.

Luko says to stop. Leeto wants a few to escape so hyena clan receives our message about what happens to those who invade here and attack us.

Exhilaration poured into Dayvee. They'd defeated their enemies. His heart still pounded at his escape from those jaws of death. Every breath he drew, sweet. The breeze playing on his face, a caress. The warmth from the sun, pure bliss. What a life he lived.

Jaycee's thought crashed into his mind. *Howl with us.*

Dayvee's victory howl erupted from deep within him and spilled out to join Jaycee's and everyone else's. Calupi ran together to celebrate their accomplishment and slap each other's backs. Brando and Elayni raced up. Red flushed her face, but she seemed fine. Leeto's rare smile as he and Luko joined them sent Dayvee's spirits soaring even higher.

Leeto called out, "Does anyone have any serious injuries?"

No one claimed one, and Dayvee wasn't going to either. He refused to limp as they trotted back to the hyena dens.

A soft whimper came from one of the numerous holes that littered the ground. Dayvee's breath caught as a pup wobbled out. Must only be a few days old. How could the hyenas leave a pup? Wolves would either carry their pups away in their mouths or die to protect them.

Dayvee's elation crashed. He wouldn't kill a defenseless pup. The wild wolves moved over to ring it. They'd kill the pup and any others too. Wouldn't Leeto do something?

The hyenas killed the wolf pack that lived here, so the two nearest packs will split this area. It's their decision, Jaycee sent.

It didn't seem right. Dayvee wouldn't watch. He stalked around the cliff. Jaycee trailed him. He climbed up to a protruding ledge on the cliff. It made a good place to sit. The sun had burnt off most of the mist to give him a grand view of the mountains that rose around him. The crisp scent of the pines dotting them filled his nostrils. Other trees showed buds now. Wouldn't be long before they, too, turned green.

A sharp twinge of pain shot through his calf. Clambering up to the ledge must have aggravated his wound. He better check it.

Wilee trotted around the bend, then Codee. If Codee saw his bite, he'd tell Leeto. Dayvee would take care of it later.

Codee craned his neck up at him. "Leeto's not happy with you."

He shouldn't have let himself slump. His entire life, he'd strived to please Leeto, but he seldom did. "That's nothing new. I can see how killing adult hyenas protects the pack, but pups can't endanger us. And what about the Vita? We're to keep the balance above everything else."

"That's what we did." Codee's mouth formed a serious line. "Hyena clan never received consent from the council for hyenas to move north." He cupped a hand over his eyes to shield them from the sun. "Why do you think they're so overcrowded and desperate to move?"

"I don't know. Hyena clans vow to keep the Vita, too, so the packs they monitor shouldn't be out of balance." A burst of color drew Dayvee's gaze. The blue cup-shaped Crocuses announced spring's arrival as loudly as any drum.

"No," Codee said. "But maybe they don't hold their vows as seriously. They should be asking their wild packs to cut back on litters so no one suffers starvation. Letting them overpopulate *our* territory, too, will harm the Vita."

Some baby birds opened their beaks wide in a nest on a branch of a nearby cedar tree. "I couldn't watch them kill defenseless pups, even if Leeto thinks I'm weak."

A snort came from Codee. "You've seen worse. They can't survive on their own, so a quick death's more merciful. Don't you care what Leeto wants anymore?"

Why had Dayvee foolishly believed that, with his father's admission of love for his son, he'd change and stop treating him so harshly? After replaying that conversation, he caught it. Leeto hadn't *really* confessed he loved Dayvee. He said he *would* love Dayvee. Leeto believed he'd love Dayvee in the future, not now. Leeto's love still needed to be earned. But Dayvee was tired of trying to gain the impossible. "I thought I was doing what Leeto wanted before. That turned out badly. Maybe I should try pleasing me now."

"Packs don't work like that. We follow our alpha, and that's not you. Do you want to live in a town?"

A Calupi life was the only one Dayvee wanted. "I gave my vows, and my feelings haven't changed."

"Then act like it. We're ready to leave. Are you coming?"

"Yes." He wasn't that far up, maybe six feet. He jumped down, and his wounded leg gave. His knees collided with the ground. Pain ricocheted through him, but he scrambled up.

Codee handed him a red fringe. "Each Calupi who fought earned one of these for risking their safety to protect the pack."

"Thanks." Dayvee attached the red fringe to his tooth pouch, taking off a brown. That made six red. Pride surged in him. Maybe he could gain high-status. Codee's and Leeto's weapons' pouches were out of room for red fringes. But the forty they displayed generated plenty of respect from other Calupi.

He and Jaycee followed Codee and Wilee around the cliff. Dayvee didn't see any pups. The dens had been filled, and only the trainees waited. Leeto led the other Calupi off in the distance. Codee raised his finger in the air. At his signal, Dayvee and Jaycee lined up.

Codee shifted his rucksack higher on his back. "I think we can take another trail and beat the others to Wolf Mountain. I hope you don't disappoint."

Dayvee's body dragged. He needed more sleep, not a race. Did Calupi always have to turn everything into a competition? Leeto never allowed easy, but since Codee took over their training three months ago, they had been pushed past exhaustion. The groan Dayvee had been biting back escaped.

"Not happy?" Codee glanced back.

"Dayvee's never happy when he hasn't had enough sleep." Why did Brando reveal that? Codee and Leeto didn't need reminders of his weaknesses.

"That's too bad. I expect him to keep up." Codee broke into a lope.

Dayvee concentrated on his footing so he didn't stumble too much. A haze filled his vision. He blinked a couple of times. Was that a tree branch overhanging the trail? He ducked, but not fast enough. It slammed into his forehead. He staggered and then sprawled to the ground, landing amidst a patch of plants with green clustered leaves. Small, white flowers with yellow filaments rose among them. Bitter cress. These leaves would be good to eat.

He put his hands on his knees to sit up, couldn't garner the energy, and his vision blurred. He wiped at his eyes. His hand was bloody. Must have come from his pant leg. Blood soaked it and the white flowers around him. But how much was the hyena's?

Jaycee sniffed at Dayvee's injured leg. *I feel weak, also, so I informed Wilee you're hurt.*

Sorry. I forgot it affects you too.

Footsteps raced up. The others ringed him. Grim faces revealed their concern. Codee leaned down. "Where are you injured?"

Dayvee pointed to his calf. Codee yanked Dayvee's boot off and blood poured out of it. "Cackles," Codee exclaimed.

Why did he have to be the only one who got hurt? This would be more evidence of weakness. "I couldn't dodge and let the hyena get you."

His uncle slid his tooth up Dayvee's pant leg and cut the seam. "You could have yelled a warning so I'd move."

"Now you tell me."

Codee poured water over the bite, grabbed bandaging from his pack, pressed it against the wound, and clamped down. Pain rocketed up Dayvee's leg. He bit his lip to keep from crying out.

"Why didn't you inform us you were hurt?" Codee pulled a strip of hide around the bandaging tight.

Dayvee choked off a scream, but it mangled his answer. "I didn't think... it was serious."

Two Codees shimmered as he tied the ends of the strips together. "Next time you're injured, you tell me regardless. That's an order."

Dayvee's vision swirled. "I'm dizzy."

"You lost a lot of blood, but you better not see Kun," three Codees answered. "That's another order."

Could Codee give orders to Kun? Darkness claimed Dayvee.

3

Difficulty

"The more difficult a challenge, the better. It keeps us sharp." ~ Leeto

Tib's heart raced at the footfalls thudding behind him.

His senses screamed at him to check. A glance over his shoulder revealed only Pericards following him through the castle's halls. They must be amused by Tib jumping around at every sound, but he couldn't relax his guard. Three months ago, Tib foolishly believed he wasn't vulnerable. Father paid the price when he shielded Tib and was stabbed. Why had Tib ever believed that Maydlan was sweet?

Tib had been kept guarded ever since, but the Pericards failed to keep them safe before. He didn't feel any more secure, and he missed his privacy. At least his trip to stay with a wolf pack had been cancelled. Thank goodness. He came to Father's chambers, and the stationed Pericards moved to allow him access.

As he entered, the heavy tapestries on the walls and the drapes hanging on the windows rippled in the breeze. Seemo ruffled his feathers on his perch near the bed. The open window must be for the eagle, but it chilled the room too much. Amidst the blankets piled on the mattress, Father appeared small. He used to fill more of the bed, before the infection from the knife wound ravaged his body. Captain Blake stood at the bed's foot while Mother sat beside it with her tawny hair in disarray. Black rings shadowed her eyes.

A heavy pit formed in Tib's stomach. Father was injured because Tib stood frozen and didn't act. "How is Father?" he asked.

"Better." She tucked his blankets around him. "He's much stronger, even more than yesterday. Carsan came earlier to give him medicine and said he still shouldn't move much."

Tib's heart leapt. Father was finally beating the infection.

Father's eyes opened. "Water," he rasped.

Mother tipped a glass of water to his lips, but most dribbled down his chin. He must still have problems swallowing.

"Tib." Father's voice sounded hoarse. "I'm giving you the authority to act in my place."

Tib hated listening to whining petitioners complaining about mostly imagined problems in their kingdom of Taluma. "But you're better."

"Not enough to focus for that long. My advisors will help you."

"Can't mother do it?"

She took Father's hand. "I'm not leaving him. Besides, I haven't had your preparation, and I never liked politics."

Maybe Tib got the whole not liking politics thing from her, but he didn't share her interests either. She loved puttering around her garden.

"If something were to happen to me…" Father's voice trailed off.

Tib's heart twisted. "No, you're getting better."

Father ignored his outburst. "You have the knowledge to succeed me." He coughed. Mother gave him another drink.

According to the Vita, kings had to be chosen by a companion. Tib shuddered. "You know how I feel about a companion."

"We're going to resolve that. Taluma and I need you." Father wheezed. "I just wish I knew if Maydlan worked alone. But I can't figure out why they'd target you before you're chosen and it's certain you'll be king. Could you have offended her?"

"I don't know. I thought she was a friend. At least, I wanted *her* as a friend. I even told her if she got tired of Varian to come find me."

Father's eyebrow shot up. His gaze turned to his guard captain. "Blake, have you learned anymore?"

"No sire. Varian claims the last note he sent Maydlan was a goodbye." Those gray eyes gave Tib a steely look. "He says he told her not to wait for him since he didn't know how long you'd have him locked up. Varian thinks she must have blamed you and wanted you to lose someone too."

"I hope it was that, and she acted alone." Father coughed again.

"I don't trust him." Blake's hand went to the hilt of his sword.

"I know, but if he were involved, why shout a warning and kill her? None of it makes sense." Father raised his head a little. "You'll keep Tib guarded."

"Yes, sire."

Pericards knocked at the door. "Drako's here, Your Majesty."

"Send him in."

The immense wolf came in first, then the tall wolf clan messenger in his buckskin clothing. His sharp cheekbones and chiseled chin swung to take in the room, then his liquid brown eyes stopped on Father and widened. He should have seen Father a few days ago. He was much better today.

"Sire, I came as asked." Usually, Father asked clanspeople. They might be Taluma's subjects, but they had their own council and laws. And Taluma's cities were more dependent on the clans than the clans were on them.

"Blake, let him through." Drako came nearer to the bed. Father reached a thin shaky hand out to give him a paper slip and a message tube. "Once you read it, can you make sure whoever needs it, gets it? Use our pigeons for those who should receive it in a hurry."

Drako opened the message and scanned it. Tib's curiosity burned, but it had a way of getting him in trouble, so he refrained from asking. His mother's knitted brows made him suspect she didn't know either. Blake might, but you couldn't tell anything by his frozen mask.

"Sire, I can't send it completely by pigeon since their location's kept hidden, but I can get it close enough to be delivered today or tomorrow."

Must be going to one of the clans. Many of them kept their homes hidden, so it left a lot of possibilities.

"That's fine." Father wheezed. "Since we need Tib too much for him to leave now, could a Calupi come here and teach him about wolves and the pack?"

Oh no. Since he couldn't go to wolf clan, Father would bring them here. Tib glanced again at the giant wolf, Juno. The wolf's mouth parted to let Tib glimpse those huge teeth. A chill ran up his spine.

Drako rolled up the message. "I'll do it, Your Highness, but I have to meet up with our council members first. It shouldn't take more than a week to return."

Father grabbed Drako's forearm in the clan arm clasp. "Thanks."

"I'll do what I can, but I'll need him alone, and he'll have to obey my orders."

"Blake, keep Tib's obligations to a half day. Drako will have him for the rest. Tib, I expect you to do whatever Drako tells you," Father commanded.

Was Tib supposed to let Juno eat him? Perhaps feed him a few fingers at a time? "Yes, Father."

Drako and Juno strode to the door. Drako glanced back at Tib. "I need to send this message, but I'll meet with you in the library before I leave."

A Pericard outside in the hall stuck his head in. "The healer's here."

Carsan with his head of gray hair usually kept an unruffled calm, but he backed up quickly to let Juno and Drako out before entering. "Sire, the medicine's effectiveness will wear off soon, and I need to clean your wound again."

What took him so long to give Father medicine that helped? The attack wasn't yesterday.

"Tib, you need to meet up with Drako, then you can hear petitions. The rest of you leave too." Father waved his hand weakly. "No one in until Carsan leaves."

They all filed out, even Tib's mother. "I'll be right outside the door."

When the door closed, Tib asked, "Why is Carson treating him alone now? You were with him before."

"Your Father doesn't want me to see him in pain." Did pain increase when someone got better? "Go. Don't keep Drako waiting."

One thing for sure, Tib would be in pain if Juno attacked him. And he wouldn't even have Pericards to protect him.

#

Dayvee drifted half-awake and made the slow ascent from deep sleep to full consciousness.

The familiar scents of wood smoke, soil, and minerals filled his nostrils. He was somewhere in the caves of Wolf Mountain—his home. Was it night or morning? He forced open his eyes. A few embers still glowed in the fire pit. Lamps hanging on the walls cast enough light to show him the rough texture of the pitted stone.

With over a hundred rooms in the cave complex that stretched for miles, each was still unique enough to provide him a map. He picked out the fluted pillar formation, the dark striation on the wall, and the room's half moon shape—the common area of the training dens. The shelves that held the trainees' things confirmed it. Jaycee raised his head from across Dayvee's foot. *Good morning.*

Morning, Jaycee.

He pulled open his bedroll to check his leg injury from the hyena hunt. No blood soaked the clean wrapping.

Geno and Chayla slept a little ways away. Elayni lay at his side. Her long lashes under her eyes grazed her high cheek bones. Golden hair fanned loosely around her head. The impulse sprang up in Dayvee to kiss her, but he resisted it. Her pert nose wrinkled. She must be waking.

Brando rested on his other side. His eyes were open. He must have caught Dayvee staring at Elayni. Did he mind? He knew Brando had feelings for Elayni, too, just not how deep they ran. If Elayni had to choose between them, surely she'd choose Brando.

His friend's deep blue eyes sparkled with merriment. "A little extreme. Letting a hyena bite you to sleep."

Dayvee chuckled. "Jealous?"

Brando fired a punch at Dayvee's shoulder. He rolled and let Brando's fist hit the ground. Another miss in the game the two of them played to improve their reaction time. "We had to pull you on a travois."

Dayvee's stomach grumbled. *I'm hungry too,* Jaycee nudged him.

A little twinge came from his leg wound when Dayvee stood and put his weight on it. Not enough to impede him. Scuffling sounded as the other trainees rose, too.

He threw some meat in Jaycee's bowl as the others did the same for their companions. Dayvee grabbed a mixing bowl off the shelf. "Brando, Elayni, what do you want for breakfast?"

Jaycee's muzzle rose from scarfing the meat. *Codee's here.*

Codee strode into the room. "How's your leg, Dayvee?"

"Just a twinge."

"Kwutee stitched it while you were still unconscious. He'll see you again this afternoon. Grab your rucksacks. We're heading out."

"We haven't even eaten," Dayvee grumbled as he set the bowl back on the shelf.

A glint came into Codee's eyes. "Tired of trail food already?" He turned and put his index finger in the air.

Dayvee grabbed his rucksack as he and Jaycee took their place behind Codee. "What will we be doing today?"

"This morning, stealth. I keep hearing you behind me. And this afternoon Kwutee and Tayro will teach you how to treat injuries. You should learn not to ignore yours."

So, Tayro was working with their healer as his apprentice again? Dayvee would have to be careful. He and Tayro had never been friendly, and he'd tried to poison Dayvee once.

Don't worry. I'll be watching him, Jaycee sent.

Thanks.

Codee led them out into the cave's corridors. The gray-headed Miko shuffled by carrying oil to fill the wall lamps. Other than Miko, no-one was moving around.

Two Calupi's stood with companions beside the cave's mouth, but they were in shadow. Normally, there weren't two guards stationed at an entrance. Both lowered their heads to Codee.

The white fringe that marked an omega drew Dayvee's attention. Omegas received the worst chores until they gained enough red to cancel the white. Only one person currently wore a white fringe since he'd endangered a pack member. What was Tayro doing there?

Codee pointed to the end of the line, and Tayro fell in with his companion, Topay, as they filed past the guard. So Tayro wasn't working with Kwutee. He was rejoining their sub-pack. They pushed carefully past the pine boughs hiding the mouth of the cave.

Even though the horizon only held a gray cast, Dayvee blinked as his eyes adjusted from the cave's dimness. Why couldn't Codee even let the sun come up?

Codee led them toward the creek. The creek ran free of ice, now, and none of the large stepping stones they placed in it had washed away. They crossed without getting wet.

The sky lit in a blend of orange, pinks, blues, and yellows as the sun rose. Dew from the trees and grass sparkled as they reflected the light. Dayvee goggled at the beauty Kun painted.

Codee came to a halt. "When you track animals this morning, try to get within an arms length undetected before you strike. Elayni with Geno. Brando, Chayla, and Tayro will go together. Dayvee with me. Those partners aren't debatable."

Dayvee's friends disappeared into the pine forest with their companions. There must be a reason Codee separated Dayvee and Jaycee from the other trainees, but he didn't like it.

Codee pointed to the left to a track. Four small toes with nail marks above. A small triangle shaped pad. A fox. "We're going to track it so you can talk to it."

That's why. No one but the leaders knew about Dayvee training to be a Kayndo.

"I don't want to talk to animals while I hunt them." Dayvee'd rather not do it at all, but he and Jaycee followed Codee and Wilee under the pines. The smell of decaying leaves mixed with pine, and a hint of flowers made a heady bouquet for a Calupi who loved the forest.

"So don't hunt, just talk, or are you going to keep hiding from it like a turtle?"

What an insult. "I'm not a turtle. You don't have any idea what it's like."

Codee knelt and felt another track, fresher. His voice hushed, "Tell me."

Dayvee whispered too. "So you can tell Leeto?"

"That's not a request." Codee rose and began walking again.

A moss covered log blocked their path. Jaycee leapt it as Dayvee stepped over it. "Fine. Get it out of your head it's a gift. It's not pleasant. At first I had to want to talk to animals. Now it's stronger, and the whispers are always there. You know what it's like to have Wilee speak in your mind?"

"Yes."

"That's like a shout, but now imagine behind his voice, ten, twenty, or fifty whispers wanting your attention. And if you acknowledge any, they turn into a shout too. Sometimes I think if one more invades my mind, I won't find my own thoughts, and I'll go crazy."

Codee stopped and faced him. "So how do you handle that?"

"I try to block it out. Ignore the whispers. If too many shout at once, I can't understand them anyway, and I end up with a huge headache."

"When I have several people shouting at me at once, I sort through them, figure out what's most crucial, have the others shut up so I can hear, then do it again and let the next speak. You have to learn to do the same."

"It's a lot harder in your head."

"What's Leeto say about difficult?"

Dayvee let out a heavy breath. "It'll never be an excuse he accepts."

"See the fox den over there? Codee pointed.

A hole in a rise, partially covered by brush. Dayvee nodded.

"Go speak to it while I wait with our companions."

Dayvee walked to the den and focused on the whispers to find one. *Hello, are you home?*

The fox poked his head up. *Hi, Kayndo. Did you need me?*

He wasn't Kayndo yet. *I'm just a Kayndo in waiting.*

Ask if you can use his body, Jaycee sent.

Can I do that with other animals?

I don't know. Find out.

Dayvee turned back to the fox. *Can I share your body?*

The fox's puzzled thought came, *If you can, Kayndo, you are welcome.*

Dayvee let the strong desire fill his mind to join the fox in his body. A lightheaded feeling of disorientation hit him as he peered at himself. His green eyes looked glazed and his white cowlick above his forehead stuck out from his otherwise blonde hair.

A movement drew the fox's gaze. A squirrel's whiskers twitched in a distant tree. Amazing. Details of his surroundings jumped out at Dayvee in crisp clarity, but the colors seemed different—more muted like pastels. Rustling sounds came from behind him in the den. This fox must have a family. Strong odors assaulted him—the fox, the trees, Jaycee's and Wilee's scent, his own, Codee's, and several he wasn't sure of.

Dayvee let the desire to return to his own body fill his thoughts. He was back looking at the fox. The dizzy sensation returned as he re-orientated to the new perspective. *Thank you for allowing me to do that.*

You're welcome, Kayndo.

As he trotted back to Codee, Dayvee mulled it over. Incredible to experience how an animal's senses differed from his own. This was one Kayndo gift he didn't mind.

No, it's not a Kayndo gift. Jaycee sent. *When Nero abused you, a voice told me to share my body with you. Maybe Kun. Talk to Kwutee.*

Codee put a hand on his shoulder. "I want you to speak to animals every day now."

Evee's asking everyone for help. Elayni got tossed by an elk, Jaycee sent.

Dayvee's heart fell to his toes and a lump rose in his throat. *Take me.* He ran all out after Jaycee, leaving Codee behind with Wilee.

Dread squeezed a fist tight around Dayvee's gut. How bad?

She got knocked unconscious. They've got the elk on three legs and are keeping it away.

If anything happened to her. *Brando's there now. He killed the elk. Elayni's coming around.*

Thank Kun!

Tayro wants to check her, but Brando doesn't want him near her.

Dayvee burst into the clearing behind Jaycee and took in the scene. The elk on the ground in a pool of blood. Elayni crumpled on the edge by a tree. Brando knelt beside her, with Evee and Bruno nudging her feet. Geno and Chayla looking on with their companions. Tayro standing back with Topay. He ran to her, pushing by Geno and Chayla, fell to his knees next to Brando, and grabbed her hand. "You okay, Elayni?"

Her light blue eyes blinked a couple times. "Yeah, I'm fine. Just got knocked out for a second."

He scrutinized her. Torn clothing. Her pant leg and arm wore blood.

"You're bleeding!"

Elayni sat up slowly. "I think they're just scrapes."

"Let me treat her, Dayvee." Tayro's head was down. He sure had changed. The haughty attitude Dayvee had come to expect from him was gone, but should he risk letting him touch Elayni? Tayro's head lifted a little. "I helped her before." He took a couple steps closer.

Dayvee shook his head. "But I don't trust you now."

Brando leapt up, "Tayro, I warned you to keep your distance." Tayro took several steps back. Bruno's hackles rose as Brando pointed. "Stay there. You're already on my list to be taught better than to endanger my family." He shot Geno a glare. "And how come you let Elayni get hurt?"

"It wasn't his fault." Elayni's long eyelashes fluttered. "I got too close. Geno threw his nails, too, and tried to distract it. Good thing it already shed its antlers."

Dayvee wrapped both his arms around her and gave her a hug. "Don't scare us like that again."

"It wasn't intentional," she mumbled into his neck.

Dayvee's breath caught, and his heart raced at the touch of those soft lips on his skin. He released her reluctantly.

Brando came over and hugged her too. "Codee shouldn't have put you that close and separated you from your family. Do you think that would have happened with us?"

When Brando let go, Dayvee clasped his friend's forearm. "I'm glad *you* got here fast. Thanks for taking care of it."

"Enough!" When had Codee arrived? Well, it was the truth. "Elayni, I'm going to look at your injuries," Codee barked. "Tayro, you can stay and advise me, but I'll do the handling. The rest of you cut up that elk."

Dayvee went to the elk, slid his tooth across its belly, and gutted it. Brando helped him pull the organs out.

Tayro, Codee, and Elayni moved back toward them.

"I told you I was fine. Just a little bump on the head and a couple scrapes." Elayni pulled her tooth and kneeled beside them to help.

Dayvee grabbed her arm. "I think you should rest and let us handle this."

"Don't act like I'm incapable." She shook off his hand. "I'm Calupi, so this is nothing."

"Right." Codee gave her a chin tilt. "Now, why isn't everyone else working?"

Geno's feet shuffled. "I didn't want to get blamed if one of them cuts themselves."

Tayro motioned to some green plants with brown stripes on their leaves, Jack in the Pulpits. "They want me to keep my distance, so I'll gather these." The corms were good to eat if dried for several months, but if not, they could be toxic. Unease sent a chill through Dayvee. How did Tayro plan to use them?

"We're not in *Dayvee's* family." Chayla pointed toward him. "He doesn't want us, but we don't deserve that." She sniffed. "We're not strangers. We stood with him too."

Geno moved closer to Chayla and wrapped an arm around her back.

Jaycee sent, *You shouldn't have three omegas, just one.*

Had Dayvee been treating them like Omega? He hated it when he'd been excluded when they were with Nero. Then they ignored him. He should have tried again, especially since they stood with him.

"You better stop hurting Chayla..." Geno said threateningly, and Graydee's hackles rose.

Bruno's warning growl split the air. "Or what..." Brando stood. "I'd love a fight if you want to challenge me."

"He won't need to challenge you. I will if you're attitude doesn't change." Codee's gaze switched to Geno and Chayla. "You're not sheep, but Calupi, so it's okay to demand the respect due you. Still, everyone needs to do their share of the work."

Geno and Chayla went to the top of the elk across from Dayvee and his friends. Tayro finished gathering and went over to the head. Codee pulled his tooth, grabbed the front leg of the elk, and cut around the muscle to remove it. He paused and pointed his tooth at Dayvee. "And you aren't related to Brando and Elayni. You have real families."

Brando snorted as he returned to cutting. "Shouldn't a *real* family notice a lost child, or one who ran away? We're a *better* family. We chased away the dark for Dayvee, not you."

"Enough Brando." Dayvee's gut churned. Why did he reveal *that*?

"Sorry. But it's not even a problem anymore. Codee doesn't need to tell Leeto."

That rabbit was in the hole. Dayvee threw some meat in his rucksack so hard blood splattered. "He'll tell."

"As long as Leeto's alpha, his interests will come over yours." Codee put Wilee's rucksack on his companion. The pouches full of meat hung over the wolf's sides.

Growls rang out from their companions. Jaycee's head swiveled to the tree line. *A bear.*

Dayvee's heart raced as he jumped to his feet.

A mama bear with two cubs moved around the thin tree trunks. Her sides appeared sunken and the cubs did too. She must be fresh out of hibernation, so she'd be desperate to eat. She opened her mouth and bellowed at them.

Jaycee pressed next to him, growling as Dayvee threw his rucksack on. He signaled by raising his three middle fingers, then pulled his nails. Brando drew his nails and moved to his side with Bruno, Elayni slid to their rear with Evee to form their fight triangle. That was better. He could protect them easier now.

"Everyone fall back," Codee ordered. "We don't need the rest enough to fight her for it."

What? Calupi hardly ever retreated. And they didn't normally give up their meat to the predators that came after it. But Codee had ordered it. Dayvee elbowed Elayni softly. She and Evee took slow steps as Brando and Bruno backed together with Dayvee and Jaycee.

The other trainees scrambled to retreat as the bear approached. Would she attack them?

4
Underappreciated

"Respect is gained by proving your value." ~ Leeto

Tib let his gaze wander as the Mayor droned on. The ornate throne with carvings and red fabric stood empty beside him as a silent rebuke for causing Father's injury. He refused to sit in Father's spot. Not that anyone would want him to.

There weren't many watchers today. Nothing important was going on anyway.

The sun from the castle's tall windows above played over the thick Kwin rugs in colorful patterns. Father's advisors were at the side of the room, with Varian sitting a little apart. No one wanted Varian freed, much less made an advisor, but Tib had insisted on both. At least Varian sided with him. The only one, and he deserved to be here. He had killed Tib's attacker, Maydlan.

One thing he and Father had in common now. Tib was always cut off. Blake and five other Pericards surrounded him.

This should be the last petitioner of the day, thankfully. If he did make the changes Varian suggested, he would see fewer. Tib interrupted the mayor's spiel. "I can agree to allow Portia to expand and assign more Kagards, but it will mean new land leases, and your current ones will also be raised to cover the expenses."

Portia's mayor spluttered. "Portians wouldn't agree to that, Your Royal Highness."

"You shouldn't get something for nothing. From here on out, if your city wants something, be prepared to pay for it, including Kagards or seeing me."

"Your Royal Highness," Blake's rigid face wavered. "Kagards are distributed based on need. If you do this, poorer cities and towns will have none."

Reed, the willowy Botanee advisor, rose so quickly he knocked over his chair. "Portia shouldn't expand. The marsh would be impacted... Your Royal Highness."

Slow again to add the honorific. Why did Tib even bother? Father's advisors argued about every decision Tib made, and so did the petitioners. They didn't want him here, and Tib didn't want to be here.

"Fine. Things will remain the same. You may go, Mayor." The mayor bowed and backed out.

A Kagard rushed in carrying a message tube. "An urgent message for you, Captain."

Blake met him at the rope, removed the message from the holder, and glanced at it. "Your Royal Highness, I need to discuss this with you and your advisors. Alone."

Tib waved his hand. "Clear the room."

When the last man filed out, Blake fingered the hilt of his sword. "Kagards spotted another ship near where Varian's sank."

Another ship? Could the king from Varian's continent already be invading?

Varian jumped up. "Just one?"

"Yes. It sported a black and green flag, but it moved back out to sea."

Varian sat down again. "That's King Nolan's flag, but there'd be more if he were invading." He rubbed his fingers across his chin. "He must be scouting the lay of the land. You have to make the ancients' weapons, or you're going to be slaughtered."

A shiver ran up Tib's spine.

Blake's frozen countenance slipped, and his lip turned down just a tiny bit. "Those weapons would contaminate us."

Varian threw his hands out. "The contamination from the ancients' stuff is long gone, and if you make your own, they wouldn't be the ancients'."

"It's against the Vita." Reed crossed his arms. "Prince Tibalt, your father wouldn't approve."

Maybe not, but Tib had to do something. Invaders were coming.

What else had any chance against them? "Father gave me the authority to make the decisions until he's better, but I'll talk to him."

#

Relief poured into Brando at their escape. As they moved around the pines to the cave, he reached out to Bruno. *Are you sure that bear didn't follow us?*

Yes.

He ducked inside the cave's entrance with the other trainees and paused to let his eyes adjust to the dimness. The familiar scents of burning wood, terra, and minerals assaulted Brando.

We're home, Bruno sent. Like the comfort of a blanket on a cold night, warmth enfolded Brando. He must be sharing Bruno's emotions again. Their home didn't bring comfort to him. Only a handful welcomed him here after his mother died, and his father earned the name 'tiger' by leaving to work alone. As the tiger's cub, Brando received a begrudged place at the bottom of the hierarchy. His refusal to accept it painted a target on him.

Codee stopped and knelt to undo and slide off Wilee's rucksack. "Dayvee, what is the law of the pack?"

A foot softly slapped stone, keeping an arrhythmic beat—a sure sign Dayvee was nervous. "To protect the pack and defend the Vita."

"The pack, not a few. You're not waiting for my orders, and when that bear came, pack-mates were left out of your defense. Everyone should have acted as one."

Geno looked up as a little brown bat unfurled its wings, then he turned to Codee. "We don't even know his signals."

They hadn't made it very far inside before Codee criticized Dayvee. He was acting like Leeto. And, of course, the other trainees couldn't wait to rip at someone's flanks. Brando repressed a sigh. Did they always have to mess up his efforts to keep his family happy and safe?

Codee took off his own rucksack to stand it next to Wilee's on the floor. "You broke the law."

"I'm sorry." Dayvee hung his head. "You're second. I should have waited for your decisions. Mine are always wrong anyway."

Bruno nosed Brando. *Doesn't Dayvee know how often he gets it right?*

I try to remind him, but he only dwells on his mistakes because Leeto pounces on them.

"You're not always wrong." Codee bent to stuff meat from his rucksack into Wilee's. "Your defense strategy was accomplished quickly. If it included everyone, I'd be impressed." He straightened. "I can help you avoid bad decisions, but not if you won't wait or listen." He held out Wilee's rucksack to Dayvee. All of you go to the storage room and put the meat away, then come to the ceremony room." Codee and Wilee turned and took the other branching.

Elayni moved up beside Dayvee. Brando joined them so they and their companions could walk together. The others trailed them as they strode through the caves corridors of pitted stone in shades of tan and gray. Dripping water and the soft murmur of voices filtered through from somewhere.

Why did Codee want them in the ceremony room? Must be fight training. Excitement surged into Brando. He liked the challenge of fighting in the ring and the respect it earned him. Bruno bounced at his side.

As Brando weaved in to miss a jutting protrusion from the wall of the corridor, Dayvee signaled by putting his thumb on the outside of his fist asking Brando to go easy. Hadn't Brando already made the mistake of hiding their training and skill? Dayvee didn't even know his own abilities and was beaten by his doubts in his last fight.

"There you go, again, using signals that exclude us." Chayla's tiny feet stomped.

How cute. Her flushed cheeks drew Brando's attention to her sparkling almond eyes, auburn hair, and tiny freckles smattered across her pixie nose. A stunning combination. But were Chayla and Geno friends or foes? They had stood with and against them. Brando couldn't trust loyalties that flipped easily.

"Why would we want someone for our next alpha who doesn't care whether we get hurt?" Geno's voice echoed around them.

Was Geno like so many others, jealous of Dayvee because he'd be the next alpha? Brando ducked so he didn't hit his head on a low spot.

"I do care whether you get hurt, but I don't care about being alpha." Dayvee's sad tone rang with sincerity. "I'd rather just be Calupi."

Tayro's steps shortened as the grade sloped down steeply. "You wouldn't have done all those extra things for Leeto if you didn't care about the alpha position."

"I never had a choice. I was born into the wrong family."

Tayro's tone softened. "You should have just told Leeto you weren't interested."

"If Leeto wants someone to do something, he finds a way to motivate them," Dayvee declared.

Maybe if they wanted Leeto's esteem like Dayvee did. Leeto's opinion didn't concern Brando since he didn't respect it. "Dayvee's going to be a great alpha, and he cares about you, but I'm not sure he should. Did *you* care when *we* were excluded or mistreated?"

"Yes." Chayla sniffled. "We only held you back from helping Dayvee to protect you."

Chayla wanted to protect him? Brando smiled to himself. She probably would do it for anyone. Chayla was way too cute and would have too much status as their history writer to be interested in him, a tiger.

Bruno brushed his leg. *You're not a tiger. You're Calupi.*

Not very many think that.

Elayni pressed close to get around a rock chimney on her side. "Our family's received way more wrongs than we gave."

That sure was true. They arrived at the lowest and coldest den in the complex. Dayvee pulled back the hide covering the entrance. "We all made mistakes, but we shouldn't keep repeating them. I don't want to exclude those in our sub-pack."

Brando only wanted to let those he could trust get close. It was easy to hurt those close to you. The families they were born to did it all the time. "My family holds three people."

Dayvee's breath blew out.

He wasn't happy with him.

They jumped down with their companions a few feet into the storage room. They ducked to squeeze through the tight, narrow part, then the room widened to reveal a seven foot ceiling. Baskets hung down with edible plants and flowers, dried fruits, roots, and nuts. Shelves lined the dark-gray walls and were filled with rolled pelts, smoked meats, nuts, grains, honey, jams, and even beverages. The largest casks crowded the floor.

They found the empty casks for raw meat to be smoked this evening, and Dayvee dumped the meat from Wilee's rucksack into one. Tayro and Topay moved up to join him.

Did Tayro want to try and harm Dayvee again? Brando cut him off. Bruno growled as Brando raised his fist. "Stay farther away."

Tayro and Topay retreated.

"Brando, I can fight my own battles." Dayvee removed his own rucksack. "Tayro doesn't need to be near me to use his weapons if he wants to hurt me. You told me not to hate. What's going on with you?"

Was Brando letting himself fall into the hate trap again? No, he was thinking clearly and wasn't consumed with getting even. "I don't hate him." Brando finished storing his meat. "But they're not your battles alone, they're ours. And he likes poison, so he'll need to be close to use it."

Dayvee released an exasperated sigh.

Tayro and Topay went over to another cask, and Tayro dumped his meat. "I wish I could take back what I did to you both. But if you repeat my mistake and cling too tightly, Brando, you'll lose everything too."

Did Tayro think he would relax his guard? Brando rolled his shoulders. Wasn't happening. "I'm not making the mistake of letting others harm my family again."

Dayvee folded Wilee's rucksack up and put it inside his. "There were too many."

"Maybe." Brando fired another punch at Dayvee, and he ducked under it. Another miss. "Maybe not. But either way, it came too easily."

"You don't have to make them family, but let's at least be friends with those in our sub-pack and include them." Dayvee's green eyes pleaded with Brando. "Don't we have enough problems without creating more?"

Brando could give it a try. "All right, Geno and Chayla, but you better like pranks because friends get them. And I won't agree to Tayro. He can work with us if he keeps his distance, but that's it."

Elayni chewed her lower lip. "I'd agree to Geno and Chayla if they stand with us every time and don't call Brando names. They want in, so they better understand we're a package deal."

Dayvee glanced at Tayro. "I'd like to call you friend, but they're right. You have to earn our trust." He went over to Chayla and Geno. "I'll use the pack's signals if you're willing to forget the past and join us as friends?"

"I'm willing, but I'd rather you teach us your signals." Chayla put her emptied rucksack back on. "And I don't trust Tayro either. So if he tries to hurt you again, I'll stand with you against him and anyone else."

"I agree with what she said, friend." Geno's face crinkled into a smile.

Dayvee stuck up his right pinky. Brando stuck up his, and so did Elayni.

"Right hand with pinky up, fingers curled in means we approve, or yes. Left hand with pinky to the side and fingers curled out means no, we don't approve." Dayvee hugged Chayla and clasped Geno's arm. "Welcome, friends."

Elayni hugged both Geno and Chayla. After slapping Geno's shoulder, Brando folded his hands around Chayla and her rucksack to give her a hug, then slid his surprise beneath the flap.

Dayvee led them out of the room back into the cave's corridor. "I hope you do earn the right to be called friend, Tayro. Friends mean more to me than status."

"I *do* want to be your friend. I give you my word, Dayvee. I won't harm you."

Dayvee might believe it, but Brando wasn't about to trust *his* word.

Chayla's scream pierced the air. She had dropped her rucksack, and his frog jumped away.

"Brando!" Elayni hollered.

Brando cracked up. Everyone else joined in, including Chayla. Even the wolves cocked their ears to show their amusement.

Dayvee laughed so hard he held a hand to his belly. "I'm willing to make the sacrifice if you need to stop pranking an old friend to concentrate on the new."

Brando dissolved in laughter again. He finally got control. "Sounds like you might be underestimating me."

"Never."

Only Dayvee and Bruno held such faith in Brando, and it scared him. He put on a confident act to keep the tormenters at bay. Elayni saw through it. What would happen when Dayvee did and learned his faith was misguided?

It isn't, Bruno sent.

A few turns later and they arrived at the ceremony room. The overhanging stalactites glistened as they caught the light of the lamps. In the center of the large cavern, stones outlined a circle on the floor— the ring. Leeto stood near it with Luko. Leeto and Dayvee did look alike with their blond hair, rugged faces, and tall, muscular bodies, but Leeto had blue eyes to Dayvee's green, and his stance shouted confidence. No one could doubt he was alpha.

Leeto pointed at Dayvee, Brando, and Elayni, then the sand-covered floor in front of him. Brando walked over with Dayvee and Elayni. Dayvee signaled with a flattened hand, wanting them to let him handle it. Dayvee and Elayni lowered their heads. Brando wasn't about to do that. Bruno pressed against him. *You should lower your head to your leader.*

Dayvee elbowed him. Brando turned his head to Dayvee and lowered it. *I do. I follow Dayvee, not Leeto.*

A tick spasmed in Leeto's jaw, but he turned his gaze on Dayvee. "Are you still afraid of the dark?"

"No." Dayvee's foot tapped furiously.

"What about dark caves?"

Dayvee slumped. "I don't think so. I didn't want to go back in the one I was trapped in, but I spent enough time there."

"Do you remember your first lesson on fear?" Leeto asked.

Silence answered him. They were only seven years old, but Dayvee must remember. Brando would never forget the bloody palm prints in the trees from Dayvee clinging too tightly while he climbed them for three days.

Finally, Dayvee gave Leeto a bitter, "Yes."

"Are you afraid of heights now?"

"No," Dayvee whispered.

"So you knew how to defeat this fear." Leeto's tone filled with contempt. "You should have faced it. Now what do you have to do?"

"Go back in the Nowhere tunnels until I can tell you I don't fear them anymore?" Dayvee mumbled.

"Yes, after dinner. Don't take anyone or anything in. Not even Jaycee or torches. Go to the end of the North one, then come out and convince me, or you'll do it again."

Brando couldn't contain himself any longer. "You don't have to do that. We can leave."

"I can do it," Dayvee said.

Leeto crossed his arms. "I want my sub-packs cohesive, but the chains binding you three are too tight. So I'm separating you before one goes off the cliff and takes the others."

"No." Dayvee's head raised, and he snarled at Leeto. "You can't do that."

"There can only be one leader at the top." Leeto uncrossed his arms. "That's me. Not you. I'll decide what you trainees need." He stuck his finger in Dayvee's chest. "You can suggest, but don't ever tell an alpha what to do."

Dayvee's head dropped. "I'm sorry. What do I have to do to get you to reconsider?"

Leeto's chin jutted out obstinately. "Two things. You let anger control you, so what's the first?"

"Swim twenty laps today to remind me to keep my cool." Dayvee was always swimming or running for Leeto. No wonder he was so fast at both.

"Yes. And second, you'll have to prove being stuck together doesn't hurt you."

Dayvee's eyebrow arched. "How?"

"Since you trainees wanted to fight earlier, you'll get the chance. We'll bind you three, tying your hands together. If you can defeat the others, I won't separate you now." He flipped a hand at Codee. "Do it."

In the rope challenge, they fought with ties around their ankles, but to fight with their hands bound with each other? It would be impossible to fight very well like that. Brando wouldn't bet on their odds. Leeto must want to deliver a painful lesson.

"I'll fight bound." Dayvee stuck his hands out. "Let Brando and Elayni fight normal."

What if Dayvee opened his stitches? "No." Brando pointed to Dayvee's leg. "He was injured yesterday. Let me be the one bound."

Leeto lip twitched. "None of you have to fight bound if you agree to separate."

They all shook their heads.

Leeto harrumphed. "Then, you'll learn being stuck together too tightly isn't helpful."

"Put your hands in front of you." Codee wrapped one end of a rope around Brando's wrists a couple times, snugging them together, and knotted it. Then, Codee tied Elayni's wrists and Dayvee's on the same short line with only a few feet of rope between each. "If you're so good at fighting, it shouldn't matter if we even the odds a little." He pointed to the ring.

A little? Brando matched his steps to Dayvee and Elayni's as they moved into the sand covered ring. Their companions left them to watch from outside it. Pack law prevented them from taking part in fights between Calupi pack mates.

The other trainees followed them in and took up positions on that side of the ring. Dayvee whispered, "They'll probably split and come at us from different directions."

The tight bindings chafed Brando's wrists. "We can't block or punch very well like this. We'll have to use our feet to knock them from theirs before they divide."

The other trainees whispered together too.

"How should a wolf or Calupi meet a challenge?" Leeto barked.

Brando recited the answer with the others, "Growls for growl, teeth for tooth, nails for nail, wounds for wound."

"What will a wolf or Calupi do who doesn't want any respect?" Leeto asked.

"They don't fight," the trainees spouted. "They roll over and show their neck."

Brando would much prefer to take a beating over contempt.

"You can punch, kick, and wrestle." Leeto lifted an arm over his head.

Brando lowered his head so his neck couldn't be easily reached, then dug his feet into the sand to find purchase to spring from.

Leeto dropped his arm.

They lunged forward.

5

Motivation

"An enemy will find any weak spot and use it to destroy us all. ~ Leeto

All Dayvee's instincts screamed they were in for a thrashing and to flee, but he matched strides with Elayni and Brando as they ran with their hands bound together toward the other trainees. Chayla, Tayro, and Geno dropped to the sand covered floor, and lying back, craned their necks.

What were they doing? Dayvee pulled to a stop with Brando and Elayni and asked, "Why are you rolling over?"

"I told you I'd stand with you." Chayla winked. "I'm not standing, but I'm with you."

Tayro crossed his arms over his chest. "I gave you my word I wouldn't harm you. I won't fight you bound and injured."

"To think we're so incapable we need bound opponents is an insult," Geno growled. "So put your hands on our necks."

"I never thought you were incapable." Dayvee glanced at Elayni and Brando. "Should we?" They gave him a nod. Dayvee hesitated. "I don't like asking them to roll over for us."

"You didn't ask." Geno tilted his head back farther to expose even more of his neck.

"No, but it could cost you, so thanks." Dayvee bent and ran his bound hands across the other trainees' necks signifying the kill.

"Codee, remove their bindings," Leeto ordered. "Dayvee and Brando can fight each other."

Codee came into the ring and untied them. Dayvee rubbed his wrists. "I don't want to fight Brando. I'll roll over."

"You'd need to fight if one of you challenges the other." Leeto hollered. "And I won't have Calupi rolling over when we stand together to face threats. You need more motivation."

Dayvee groaned to himself. What would Leeto do now?

"There are some boulders out front." A corner of Leeto's lip turned up. "They need to go up above our entrance to defend against attackers."

"We can't climb that path carrying boulders," Dayvee sputtered.

Codee's eyes glinted in amusement. "Not easily. You'll have to work together. Eat lunch, then see Kwutee. When he's done, you'll carry boulders."

...

Dayvee came to the hide-covered doorway of the keeper's den with Jaycee. Kwutee opened it. "Where're the other trainees?"

"They were going to wait until you finished with me to come for our healing lesson. Jaycee will tell Bruno when you're ready."

"That's fine. Clunee and I are making paper."

Paper was too important to mess up, so Kwutee and Clunee usually completed the last steps alone. Everyone helped gather fibrous plants like milkweed, cattails, nettles, carrot tops, cornhusks, and dandelions. "Do you want me to come back?"

"No. You can help if you'd like." Kwutee motioned him in.

"Sure." Dayvee moved inside with Jaycee. He took in the wall mural of the giant white wolf, JoKayndo, with several wolf companions bringing Kun's message to the first Calupi.

"Hello, Dayvee." Gray hair covered Clunee's head, and his gnarled fingers clutched a pot. It must be difficult to write their histories with those fingers, but Chayla would soon be aiding him.

Dayvee lowered his head. Older Calupi deserved respect for their wisdom. "Hi."

Kwutee and Clunee's companions, Keeno and Chugo, nuzzled Jaycee and Dayvee to greet them. The cave floor was bare. Kwutee's colorful floor rug was rolled back, and an untreated hide with small holes was stretched over a drying frame, with pots below it to catch the water.

"What needs to be done?" Dayvee asked.

Clunee turned his pot over on the hide stretched over the drying frame. "We've cut, soaked, cooked, rinsed, and mashed the plants. All that's left is turning the pulp and spreading it."

As Dayvee flipped more pots, Clunee and Kwutee spread the pulp. When a thin layer of pulp covered the entire hide, Kwutee placed another hide dampened with water over it.

Clunee pulled on the hide, stretching it tight. "I'm glad we stored enough dried plants. Our supply won't last until spring."

Seems like a lot of work. Why do you need paper? Jaycee asked.

Dayvee placed another flat rock on top to press the pulp between the hides. *We can't pass our memories at death to our pack mates' minds like you do, so our history needs to be written down. And we write messages if we don't want them shared.*

"That's enough rocks." Kwutee held up his palm. "Now it just needs to dry a few days before we cut the sheet into smaller ones."

Clunee rubbed his hand over the small of his back and straightened. "I'll ask Franko to barter for more from the Botanees. They're the paper masters." He and Chugo left Kwutee's den.

Kwutee pointed his staff at Dayvee. "Pull off your pants and bandage and sit on the bench."

Dayvee did. He shivered as Kwutee poured cold liquid over his bite.

"No sign of infection. Any problems walking?" Kwutee asked.

As if Codee would ever let them walk instead of run. "No."

After Kwutee re-bandaged him, he handed him the flask. "Keep pouring this over it for a week. Then we can remove the stitches."

"I wanted to ask your advice." Dayvee grabbed his rucksack and stowed the flask inside. "But I don't want Leeto to learn about this."

"As long as it won't hurt the pack, I'll keep your confidence."

Dayvee pulled his pants on. "All right. When Nero tortured me, I prayed to escape the pain. Then I left my body and I saw, heard, and felt what Jaycee did from his. Can you tell me anything about that?"

Kwutee's black eyes pierced him. "It's called body hopping, and it's very rare. I've spoken to a couple clan members who did it.

Keepers believe two things are needed—a real close bond and a dire situation. When the emergency ends, so does the ability."

What? That can't be right. "My crisis is over, and I just did it with a fox I'm not bonded with."

"I've never heard of anyone doing it without a bond, but maybe when you prayed, Kun gave you that gift. If it will help you, use it, but carefully. If you're consciousness is absent from your body too long, the heart stops, and you won't draw breath." Kwutee's forehead wrinkled even more. "Why are you keeping this from Leeto?"

"You both say abilities should be used to benefit the pack. If I think this will help us, I'll try, but I don't want him expecting more from me. I can't satisfy him now."

"I won't reveal it." Kwutee shifted to lean heavier on his staff. "Now, I'd like to ask you to do something—give Tayro a real chance." Did Kwutee have a soft spot for his former apprentice? "I know your friends usually do the rejecting, but you've gone along with it."

Maybe Dayvee should explain. "Brando and Elayni are the only ones who spoke out against Leeto when he treated me harshly. Nero tried to tear their loyalty from me and couldn't. So they've both earned mine."

"Adults know not to confront an alpha in front of the pack. That would be considered a leadership challenge, but almost all of them risked Leeto's wrath and met with him privately to offer *advice* about you." What? Maybe it was Dayvee's pack, too, like Leeto claimed. Kwutee harrumphed. "Tayro has faults, but great potential too. He could be a valuable friend, so will you try?"

"Hmmm." Tayro did act as if he changed, but for how long. "I promise I'll give him a chance, but he has to prove himself and not just to me."

"I think he will, and you won't regret it." Kwutee waved at the door. "Now, call for the others. Tell Bruno yourself. Abilities *do* need to be used."

· · ·

Dayvee's shoulders and back ached as he struggled with the other trainees to carry the last boulder up the steep dirt path that wound up the mountain. Jaycee's tail waved as he and the other wolf companions bounded ahead of them.

A grunt came from Brando on his left. They stood the lowest at the back of the boulder and held the most weight. "Dayvee, I'm sorry about Leeto sending you into the tunnel."

"Just try to avoid talking to either of them about me."

Brando's crooked smile appeared. "I'm going to think of a prank to teach them a lesson."

Elayni rolled her eyes at Brando from the boulder's left side. Chayla's sweat streaked face peered over the right side. Geno and Tayro slid each foot carefully as they backed slowly at the front. Tayro huffed out, "Does Codee always tell on you? I thought you were really close."

Dayvee's heart pinged, and he drew a deep breath. "I respect him, but we're not nearly as close as we used to be a few years ago."

Elayni's shoulder's sagged, the strain showing. "Is it still too thin to be talking about?"

Brando had warned him to care so much about Codee and Leeto would only get him hurt. Dayvee didn't listen. It cost him a rip in his heart that might never get a thick scab. "They should know. He led me to believe I could confide anything to him." His hands were sweating inside his gloves. "Every confidence was betrayed."

Elayni's mouth pursed. "Each of us has something that matters a lot to us. For Brando, it's deciding who gets to be family. Me, I don't like being left behind. Dayvee doesn't want Leeto learning more about him. And that's why we've been using signals Codee doesn't know."

"You're in our sub-pack now." Dayvee's biceps stung as if they were on fire. "You should get a request, too, so think about what matters to you most for a few days and let us know."

A wolf howl that ended in a yip pierced the air. An alert, but not an alarm. There was no way they could pull their nails without dropping the boulder. Dayvee couldn't see anything with his back to the cave.

The wolves were up higher, so they should have a good view. *Jaycee, what's happening?*

Outsiders approaching.

Do you think they'll be a threat?

No. They're with one of our Calupi patrols.

Geno's eyes scrunched. "They have two bears with them, so it's Ursans." Since Geno and Tayro were walking backwards, they could see something of what was happening below.

Tayro craned his head. "Maybe it's your adopted brother's family, Dayvee."

Made sense. They were one of the few that weren't Calupi that knew their location.

Tayro and Geno stopped moving. "Most everyone came out of the cave, but Leeto and Codee are going alone to meet them," Tayro reported. "Codee and Leeto are clasping arms with the two Ursans, and the patrol is leaving. Looks like they're handing them something. I think a message tube."

Another pain stabbed Dayvee's shoulders. "Okay, let's keep going so we can get done."

Tayro and Geno took another few backwards steps. "Huh," Tayro's brow pinched.

"What?" Dayvee asked.

"Leeto's pointing toward us."

Dayvee wanted to turn around but didn't dare.

"My legs are shaking and my arms are slipping." Chayla's side of the boulder tilted. "I'm going to drop it."

Dayvee was closest. "Hold on, Chayla." Dayvee kept one hand under his side and scooted his other arm farther underneath to wrap beneath hers too.

An ache traveled from Dayvee's shoulders all the way across his back as more weight settled on him, and he fought to right the boulder. Heat flushed his face with the effort. He couldn't let it fall. They could get hurt, and so could the pack below.

#

Codee sighed to himself. Leeto didn't appreciate the Ursan's interference, especially with Dayvee. Unfortunately, these weren't just any Ursans, but Bunjee's father and his uncle Santo, here on official business. Santo sat on the Ursan Council, and their great uncle presided over the Clan council.

Leeto probably regretted following Kwutee's advice and informing the council they had a Kayndo in waiting. And this was just the beginning. With the king so ill, everyone had to be told.

Luko's ruff raised as Leeto spoke softly. "There's no reason for Dayvee to be consulted. I make the decisions."

"Your decisions are the problem." Even though Santo's tone was heated, his voice was hushed. Maybe he realized Leeto didn't want to be overheard. "Your pack representative was questioned, so the council knows everything. Stop risking his safety."

The messages crumpled in Leeto's hand. "I don't tell Ursans how to teach your leaders. He'll be an alpha whether he's ever a Kayndo or not."

"Do you think you can just produce another if something happens to him?"

Wilee nudged Codee. *The trainees are in trouble.*

I didn't think it would take this long. Codee turned to Leeto. "Should I go help them?"

"Not yet," Leeto answered.

"Then I will." Santo took a step toward the mountain.

"Don't interfere." Leeto put a hand on the hilt of his nails, but he didn't pull them. "They're Calupi. Their arms would need to break before they let the boulder fall on their pack."

Santo stopped, but his bear companion, Shakree, huffed. "I was going to wait to give this to you alone, but I can't now." Santo handed Leeto a white piece of hide with writing on it.

A rebuke from the Calupi council. That could cause their ranking to plummet. Codee glanced over his shoulder at their pack's drawn faces. Yeah, they noticed. Leeto read it and passed it to Codee.

Wolf Clan has received a sanction of ten percent of lease earnings due to your pack's negligent behavior in safeguarding the future Kayndo. If more harm comes to him, we might never live down the shame, and Wolf Mountain Pack won't. His safety should have been given the highest priority as soon as you learned he had the Kayndo gifts. Rectify it.

That wouldn't just hurt the pack, but all of wolf clan. A portion of all leases was divided so each clan received them, but they'd give a bigger percentage now.

"We're to escort Dayvee to the clan meeting where the council is selecting more guards for him." Santo rested a hand on Shakree's shoulder. "Now, let us go to him."

"They're not in trouble, anymore, since they shifted to aid each other." Leeto hung his head. "I apologize for any wrong I committed, but he's a clansman, and if you guard him, he'll feel trapped and break free. There's only one way he might be able to tolerate it."

Leeto was right. Codee's skin crawled at any type of confinement.

"How?" Santo asked.

"Doing the same as when he was younger. He'd tell you he roamed these woods freely, but he didn't. The wolf he loved most was with him, nudging him out of trouble. We planned to send the pack mates he loves with him. Let us assign them to guard him."

"I'll inform the council, but they'll have to approve them. And you better get him down from that mountain."

"Go, Codee," Leeto ordered.

Codee raced up the familiar trail with Wilee. His burning lungs warned him he couldn't keep the pace at this grade much longer. Leeto's lessons must be as difficult on him as the trainees. *Wilee, ask Luko to find out if Leeto wants me to inform the trainees of the first message.*

He says yes, and tell them they're being assigned.

Codee reached them and grabbed the boulder near Chayla to help. "There's only a few more feet." As they moved forward together, he issued the warning Leeto wanted them to hear. "A pack is strong, but we can be brought down by one weak link. When you help your friends' slack or do it yourself, our entire pack suffers." They reached where the mountain curved back above the cave's entrance and leveled for a little bit. Their companions already waited there. "Now set it down gently."

Dayvee's sweat streaked face broke into a smile. "Woo. We did it." They slapped each other's backs.

Codee gave them a chin lift. "Well met."

Dayvee peeled off his gloves. "Who's down there? Is it Bunjee's family?"

"Yes, they brought several messages for us."

Tayro wiped his brow. "They must be important to be carried by pigeon part of the way."

"They are. The king's infection has spread and will probably take his life. They want Jaycee to be sent immediately to Harthome for the prince."

Dayvee's eyes misted. Jaycee pressed against him.

Codee had warned him about getting too close to a wolf he only trained. He put a hand on Dayvee's shoulder. "You have to harden your heart now."

"Will they... be taking him?"

"No." Codee dropped his arm. "Wolves are miserable alone. A sub-pack will leave tomorrow morning and remain with him. It could help Jaycee if the one who knows him best offers the prince advice. And young Calupi might find it easier to adjust to the city, so Leeto's giving you six the assignment."

Dayvee's mouth hung open. "But we're not even done training."

"You will be by the time you arrive. It will be a long rotation, probably a year, so it's voluntary. If any of you don't want to go, we'll select another."

All of the other trainees were looking at Dayvee. He brushed his fingers over Jaycee's head. "I have to go if it means Jaycee might receive better care."

"Then I will." Brando grinned crookedly. "I wonder if the prince likes frogs."

Elayni's eyes rolled. "They'll need me to keep them out of trouble, so I'll do it."

Chayla removed her gloves. "I think Harthome might give me a lot to write about, so I'll go."

Geno moved closer to Chayla. "Me too."

Tayro studied the ground and mumbled, "It can't be any worse."

Codee gave them a terse nod. "Okay. We have a sub-pack. Eventually, you'll need to decide who will lead it, but take your time and consider carefully. *Wilee, can you tell Dayvee the council is informing every clan of our Kayndo in waiting so they can prepare. The pack will be told tomorrow, so he might want to tell his friends first.*

Wilee went to Dayvee and along with Jaycee, he pressed against him in a show of support. Wilee sent, *He's not happy about everyone learning, but he knew it was coming.*

Codee waved his hand toward the trail. "Go eat dinner now. I'll let you know when Leeto's ready for you to go in the tunnel, Dayvee."

"He's having someone fill it with surprises, isn't he?"

"What do you think?"

"He'll be trying to find another weakness." Dayvee and Jaycee turned and went down the trail with the sub-pack and their companions.

6

Cohesive

Two howls are better than one. ~ Jaycee

Dayvee laughed to himself. Brando wanted to complete one last prank before they left, and the other trainees wanted in. Dayvee whispered, "Codee's close by." Then he raised his voice so it would echo. "I've got to go take Leeto's test."

"We'll be there to help soon," Brando exclaimed.

Dayvee wasn't really allowed to take anyone into the Nowhere tunnel, not even Jaycee. He had to prove to Leeto he didn't fear dark caves, anymore, so he turned down the corridor alone. When he reached where the lamps stopped, he sucked in some air and courage and continued on. Nothing to fear. This wouldn't be like being trapped for days in the other cave. He'd be okay. When he reached the North Nowhere tunnel, he pulled back the hide covering and stepped inside.

Total blackness swallowed him. His heart didn't pound. His breathing wasn't turning ragged. He trailed his hand against the rough wall. His senses heightened, and he picked out the soft flutter of bat wings. He couldn't take Jaycee inside, but Leeto didn't say he couldn't receive aid from the animals already there.

A rattle split the quiet and panic crashed through him. His heart thumped so hard it rocked his chest. Rattlesnake bites could be deadly.

Please don't bite me, Dayvee sent.

I won't bite you. I'm a bull snake, and I don't belong here.

Dayvee released a heavy breath. Leeto planned well. Bull snakes sounded like rattlers when their tails struck a bed of leaves. *I'm sorry. I'll release you, but would you like to help me first?*

How, Kayndo?

The snake hissed in amusement as Dayvee explained. He needed to hurry, so he reached out to a bat in the tunnel, *Can I share your body.*

#

Codee didn't enjoy informing Leeto that Dayvee was going to defy his orders, but it was his job. Dayvee must be petrified of dark caves to risk having his friends help him. Codee moved with Leeto and their companions through the cave's corridors using a hunter's caution. *Wilee, will you ask the other companions not to share we're following?*

Wilee nudged him. *I told them.*

Codee peered around a stone outcropping as the trainees' reached the last lamp before the North Nowhere tunnel, then disappeared beyond the light's reach.

Leeto stopped and took torches from the barrel. "We know where they went." He lit two, then handed one to him.

Codee lifted the torch as he and Wilee followed Leeto and Luko into the tunnel. Now to find the trainees.

The sound of crashing rocks reverberated around them. A cave in. Dust billowed. Codee's heart raced. He fell to his knees and covered his head. When the rumbles stopped, he looked up to pitch black. The dust had put their torches out. The scuffling must be Leeto, probably retrieving his fire kit from his rucksack. A rattle sounded.

Codee froze. "Stop!"

"I wouldn't be sure that's a bull snake." Dayvee's voice echoed around them. "I can give surprises too."

"Where are you, and what are you talking about?" Puzzlement infused Leeto's words.

"I'm outside the tunnel. Welcome to our motivation training." More than one laugh rang out. "You and Codee should enjoy lifting rocks too."

"That isn't funny." Leeto's retort reverberated.

Brando's guffaws sounded defiant, but Elayni giggled nervously. "We never thought your motivation training was funny," she said.

Codee let menace seep into his voice. "I hope you've learned to fight well. You'll need it when we call the rest of the pack to free us."

"And admit your trainees got the best of you?" Chayla's voice wavered. "What will that do to your respect?"

So it wasn't just three trainees involved this time.

Leeto's tone sharpened. "Dayvee, you defied me and failed the test."

"No one was in the tunnel except me and now you, but I'm out. I followed your orders and passed your test. Ask Luko to judge. I don't fear dark caves anymore."

"It's not possible. To make it to the end and back would take a few hours."

"I did it." Dayvee answered confidently.

"Luko says you spoke truth, but how?"

"Telling you everything wasn't in your orders."

"We lifted boulders all afternoon." Geno's voice cracked. "You should be able to handle these rocks."

"We won't lift any," Leeto snarled. "*You* will until you free us, and that's an order you shouldn't defy. The pack wouldn't hold this against us, but you."

"We could go to another pack or form our own," Dayvee threatened. "But we'll free you since you were never trapped. Light your torches. The snake is your bull snake. We just pranked you."

Gales of laughter filled the tunnel. He and Leeto lit their torches and walked back to the entrance. It was true. Only pebbles littered the floor. Codee craned his neck and lifted his torch. Two hides were roped to the ceiling, but one end hung down. Dayvee must have dumped the pebbles, then the dust, to simulate a rock fall. Clever.

Brando pulled the hide covering the tunnel entrance aside. "You sounded awfully worried about doing your own motivation training."

The trainees clasped their arms around each other's waists and laughed at their leaders' expense.

The bull snake slithered past Leeto. "You should go to the training rooms before I forget you're trainees, but there will be a punishment."

Dayvee picked up the snake and draped it across his neck. "We knew that, but you shouldn't *forget* two things. What Codee tells you about me might not be right, and Brando's a genius at pranks." The snake's tongue forked out. Dayvee ran a finger across his head. "I'll release him." All the trainees moved away together.

Leeto should be pleased. Dayvee obviously led them. Not one scurried away until Dayvee left. Leeto slapped Codee's back. "Well met. I knew giving them a common enemy would work. They probably grumbled about us all the way up that trail, but they're certainly cohesive now."

Leeto probably wouldn't let him ease up, but Codee had to try. "Yes, but if you keep driving a wedge between us and Dayvee, he may not want to come home."

"Clay made sure he knows and loves every bit of this mountain so he'll come home. And without that wedge, he wouldn't challenge us for leadership. I already messed up telling him I loved him."

Codee shook his head. "Why don't you just step down?"

"He has to take the leadership, or he won't gain as much respect."

"Do you really want him to leave with only harsh memories of you? If he becomes Kayndo, he may not survive."

"We've never had a Kayndo trained by us. He should survive." Leeto clasped his forearm. "But his guards need to ensure it. Can I count on you?"

Codee returned the clasp. "Always."

#

After a quick stop to release the snake, Dayvee returned to the training rooms with his friends. His back burned from everyone slapping it. He wiped his eyes from laughing so hard. "That was the best prank ever." He grabbed his bedroll out of his rucksack and spread it out near the hearth. "I didn't like sleeping alone when we were with Nero, so I'll welcome anyone that wants to join me."

Elayni put her bedroll on his right side, and Brando placed his on Dayvee's left. He smiled at them. Chayla and Geno rolled theirs out away from them. Tayro spread his even further away.

Jaycee grabbed Dayvee's bedroll and took off. Dayvee made a leap for it but missed. Was Jaycee pulling another prank on him? Brando cracked up laughing and made a grab for his bedroll, but he was too late. Bruno got to it first. Now, all the trainees chased wolves carrying bedrolls. Jaycee circled the room and took Dayvee's back to where he started as the other wolves all converged there.

Dayvee laughed. "Our companions are right. We're a sub-pack and should be sleeping together. Geno, Chayla, and Tayro, would you please join us?"

Chayla's nose scrunched, and it made her freckles stand out. "What about Brando?"

Brando grinned. "I'm okay with you and Geno, and I'll be all right with Tayro if he stays on the end."

Dayvee sighed. He promised Kwutee he'd give Tayro a chance. How could he get Brando to? Their companions dropped their bedrolls and moved away.

Chayla was so petite lying between Brando and Geno that only a little of her reddish-brown hair showed. She popped up and gave them a shy smile. "This is better."

There were no big spaces between them now. "I agree." Dayvee lay back. Their companions had clumped together below the trainees' feet. *Thanks, Jaycee.*

You're welcome.

Dayvee kept tossing. Tomorrow everyone would learn he was a Kayndo in waiting. Some were already jealous he was an alpha's son. How much worse would this be? The sub-pack should learn first, but he couldn't find the words to tell them. And how was he going to deal with losing Jaycee? It would tear a hole in his heart like when his mother's companion, Clay, had died.

There was no way he was going to sleep tonight, even if Leeto let them. Cackles, he forgot to swim his laps today. Leeto would ask him tomorrow, but he didn't want to go to the pool room in the cave.

Jaycee, who's guarding the main entrance?

Miko.

Perfect. "Psst. Anyone sleeping?"

Brando's head shot up. "Na, I can't."

Elayni had taken her braid out, and those beautiful golden tresses spilled around her arm as she propped her head on it. "Me neither."

"Let's get out of here and have a fun night before Leeto decides on some punishment for our prank."

Brando grinned. "The family's way overdue for a fun night." He stood. "Are you thinking of taking a plunge?"

Dayvee rose too. "Yes, and I want to include the sub-pack."

"They might not want to, but I'm okay with sharing." Brando rolled his bedroll up.

"Me too." Elayni slid out of hers, then gave him her breathtaking smile. "But it'll be cold."

"Share what?" Chayla's almond eyes sparkled.

"You'll see. If you trust us." Dayvee stuffed his bedroll in his rucksack. "We won't be back until sunrise. If you want to come, wear what you would for swimming. Take dry clothes, a towel, gloves, your sleeping rolls, and rope. Make sure it's not frayed."

Everyone hurried to gather their things. Geno stuffed his towel in his rucksack. "Are we going swimming?"

"Not exactly. Put your boots in your rucksacks, too. Barefoot is quieter. No talking until we get past the communal room."

Jaycee, can you warn us if anyone comes?

Yes.

The trainees softly padded through the corridors until they came to the West Nowhere tunnel. Before the lamps ran out, Dayvee grabbed torches from the barrel on the floor. "Everyone take a few." He lit one. *Jaycee, you and the other companions are going to have to meet us on the mountain. You can't go out this way.*

When everyone had a torch burning, he led them to the tunnel entrance. He pulled the hide back and waved the others in.

"Nowhere tunnels only have dead ends, so what are we doing here?" Geno asked.

"This one has something else. Our own bolt hole." Elayni stumbled over the rough patch of stone at the entrance, and Brando steadied her before Dayvee could.

"You're kidding," Geno exclaimed.

"No." Brando dropped his arm from Elayni. "Dayvee found it when he was lost. He couldn't reach it, but we solved that problem. You're the only ones outside of us that know."

Tayro's eyes widened, but he followed Chayla and Geno in. "It should be guarded like the other entrances," Tayro said. "What if an enemy uses it?"

Brando snickered. "They'd fall a long way and die."

Dayvee closed the hide and led them down the left branching into the maze of the West Nowhere tunnel. Their voices quieted as they climbed the steep grades. A pillar formation rose at his side, a darker shadow sprawled across the floor just beyond it. Their torches weren't enough to illuminate it. He pivoted and put his arm out to make sure they stopped. This is one of the bottomless pits, so you need to rope in."

Chayla's voice cracked. "You don't expect us to go over that, do you?"

Brando chuckled. "No, we're going inside it."

"No way." Geno backed a couple of steps.

Elayni pulled her rope out of her rucksack. "Dayvee would never want anyone to get hurt. You'll be safe as long as you follow his instructions."

Her confidence in Dayvee swelled his heart.

Brando looped his rope. "Leeto would ask if you're rabbits or Calupi. A little risk adds to the fun, but you can always go back, and we'll do it without you."

"Are you claiming *you* weren't afraid your first time?" Geno asked.

"I was petrified," Dayvee admitted. "Brando told me I had to trust myself and my family. To stop thinking and leap. And that if my torch went out, he'd be behind me with another. So do you trust us?"

"I'll do it." The light of their raised torches revealed Chayla's head, but her short body was in the dark, making it appear as if she didn't have one.

"I'll go." Geno took a couple steps forward to rejoin them.

"Me too," Tayro said.

"Then do like we do." Dayvee propped his torch on top of the stone pillar that rose at the side of him. He made loops at each end of his rope and knotted it. "Get your ropes out and tie in. Leave ten feet between your knots." He slid one loop around the formation, gave it a strong tug to test it, then stepped into his other loop. "Everyone double check someone else's knots and ropes." He tested Elayni's while Brando did his. Chayla tested Brando's.

The rough rawhide encircled Dayvee's fingers as he drew on his gloves. "We go one at a time. I go first. Brando will go last and keep a hand on the ropes just in case. Ready?"

Brando raised his gloved hand and placed it on Dayvee's rope. "Go."

Dayvee grabbed his torch in one hand, the rope in the other, and jumped. The rope dug into his arm pits as it caught. He swung himself over to the pit wall. When he found the opening covered with brush, he scooted some aside. Moonlight spilled into the pit. He poked his head through the opening. The spray of the water made the ledge damp.

He found a crack in a stone that seemed fairly dry to lodge the torch in. Then he hauled himself onto the ledge. Stars twinkled so close, as if he could reach out and touch them. The clouds partly obscured the moon. It gave him enough light to see the ledge, although the mountain above and below lay in dark shadow. The scents of the crisp night air, with the water and pines below, filled his lungs.

He placed his rucksack back where it should keep dryer, then stuck his head back in the opening. "Send the next." Elayni swung down. He caught her and helped her through, holding on to her hand longer than he needed to. His heart sped up. Seemed like forever since he had time alone with her. Codee never partnered her with Dayvee like Nero had. He released her hand. "Stay at the back."

As each arrived, he helped them through. "We're on a ledge, so stay near Elayni." Their gasps as they took in the view of the stars filled him with warmth. He did right bringing them.

When all but Brando had come through, Brando hollered, "I'm sending the ropes."

"Everyone reel yours in." Dayvee coiled his around his hand and elbow. "Put them in your rucksacks, and place your rucksacks over by mine."

Dayvee tossed one end of his rope onto the rock that protruded above and tested it. "I'm sending the rope up." He threw it inside the hole.

"I caught it." Brando usually did on the first try.

Dayvee grabbed his end with his gloves. The rope tightened as Brando dropped below him. He hauled on the rope until Brando's hands reached the ledge, and he sprung up onto it.

"How are we getting back?" Tayro asked.

"There's a trail we'll take to the other side in the morning." Elayni waved her hand. "You know where the creek comes out of Wolf Mountain in back, and it falls to form a pool?"

"Yes. But that's high up."

"Both are below us now."

Dayvee grabbed the rope hanging from above and tested it again. "We drop to the pool by running off the ledge with this rope and letting go after we count to three. If you don't want to do it, we'll take you down the trail to the pool."

Brando took his rucksack off and put it in the pile. "The pool's deep. It's safe as long as you wait to take the plunge until you're far enough out from the mountain."

"What if we let go too close?" Tayro asked.

"Don't." Brando's tone turned serious. "You could hit one of the protrusions and die."

"You can barely see." Geno's voice trembled. "Why do you do it at night?"

Dayvee tied a large knot in the rope to help them hold on. "During the day, someone might climb up after us and find our bolt hole. Miko's companion will alert him we're out here. He'll inform Leeto, but no one will come."

"I... I don't swim like a fish like you, Dayvee," Chayla's stutter revealed her fear.

"Who does?" Brando moved to the back of the ledge, closer to Chayla. "I can't beat Dayvee in a swim race."

What good did that do Dayvee? Calupi didn't compete in swimming, except for fun. "Chayla, I'm going first so I'll be there if anyone gets in trouble."

Brando came over and extended his hand for the rope. "Let me go first."

The moon moved behind the clouds, and the night thickened around Dayvee. "It was my idea. I'll take the most risk."

"Why is first more risky?" Tayro had his back pressed against the stone of the cliff. Did he fear heights?

"If something like a log got washed into the pool, the first will land on it." The torches flickered and dimmed as Brando's voice filled the mist shrouded ledge. "We usually check the pool before we go, but we haven't been here since last fall."

A stab of fear pricked Dayvee's gut. What if something was down there? This was his last opportunity to plunge before they left. And he loved it. Here, he was free. He didn't have to prove himself to anyone. No one could even see him when it was this dark. "We'll know soon. Brando, go last and count everyone off."

Brando exhaled heavily. "All right."

Dayvee grabbed the knot on the rope and ran.

Then he was flying off the ledge.

"One, two, three."

He let go of the rope.

7

Plunging

"Letting those you love face danger is much harder than jumping off a cliff yourself." ~ Dayvee

Free from the ledge and rope, Dayvee plummeted, and his exhilaration soared. He tucked in his elbows and spun himself, twirling faster and faster. He drew up his knees and somersaulted. Flipping once, twice, he straightened, stretched out his arms, and plunged into the water. It parted, and the cold stole his breath. He turned and kicked for the surface.

His head broke from the water. "Oh yeah!" He abandoned himself to the joy of the moment and let himself fall back, laughing as he floated weightless. The stars twinkled above, and the moon had come out from the clouds. Their reflection lit up the pool around him.

Nice view isn't it. Jaycee's thought flooded his mind.

I was beginning to wonder if you had trouble finding it.

No. We've been busy cleaning branches from the pool.

Dayvee never asked, but still the wolves helped him, and swimming wasn't their favorite thing to do. Gratitude flooded him. *Thank you. Was it bad?*

It would have hurt.

"How's the water?" Brando shouted down.

Dayvee turned over and swam beneath the ledge. "Cold but worth it. Lower the rucksacks to me, and I'll light the fire and torches."

"Your dive was amazing," Geno yelled.

Since the moon came out of the clouds, it revealed his dive. Cackles.

Elayni laughed. "He doesn't like us watching. Don't stop,

Dayvee. We'll turn around next time."

"You should have turned around last time." Dayvee caught the rucksacks and climbed from the pool to untie them. "You can haul up the rope." He moved to a level area nearby where they had their fire ring and their stacked wood. "Who wants to go next?"

"I'll go." Elayni's voice was raised, but it wasn't necessary. The voices above drifted to him easily in the stillness of the night.

"One, two, three." Elayni plummeted above him, tucked her knees, and hit the water, creating a big splash. "Yes!" She was laughing as he took her hand, and she climbed from the pool. Her laugh was infectious and warmed him. His heart raced with her hand clasped in his. He didn't want to let go, but he needed to get the fire going to warm them.

He built the fire and lit it as Elayni stuck torches in the ground by the pool's edge so everyone could see it easily.

"Any of you others want to try plunging?" Dayvee called up.

"I'll do it." Chayla's small voice shook.

"If you want to wait, I'll go with you and make sure you don't get hurt," Brando offered.

"Yeah, I'd like that," she said.

Was Brando sweet on Chayla? Geno acted as if he were interested in her too. All the Calupi their age were probably considering lifemates since they'd be able to pledge soon. Dayvee had sure been thinking about life-mating Elayni. He'd much rather Chayla be the one to snare Brando's heart.

"I'll go." Geno swung out on the rope. "Ohhhhhnooo!" Then the splash. Geno's head popped up. "This is what you do for fun? It's freezing."

"Yeah. Didn't you like it?" Elayni asked.

"No." A broad smile stretched across Geno's face. "I loved it."

Next, Tayro dropped. When his head broke the surface, he shook the water from his hair. "Wow." He swam over to them.

Brando's voice drifted to them. "Just hold on to my neck, Chayla."

As Brando and Chayla plunged, a small scream escaped her. Then her laugh peeled out. They hit the water and bobbed back up.

"Yes!" Brando's fist pumped the air. He held one arm around Chayla as he swam to the edge. "So, what did you think?"

"It's terrifying." Chayla giggled. "But really thrilling at the same time. I wasn't sure whether I wanted to laugh or cry."

"You picked the right one." Brando helped her out.

"Can we do it again?" Chayla asked.

Brando chuckled, then pointed. "The trails over there, and there's a knotted rope to help us climb it. We usually go back together."

"Everyone want to go?" Dayvee asked. All their heads bobbed in agreement, so he moved to the trail and grabbed the rope. The others followed him.

When they got close to the ledge, Chayla asked, "How long have you been doing this?"

"We were eight when Dayvee fell off the ledge." Anguish filled Brando's voice, even though it happened long ago. "We thought he'd die for sure." Brando shook his head as if he could shake the memory out of it. "Then we heard a splash and him laughing. Next thing we know, he's hollering for us to jump too." Brando's tone lightened. "So we did, and we kept right on plunging ever since."

"Can you do those twists and flips like Dayvee?" She asked.

Dayvee grabbed another knot and hoisted himself onto the ledge. "No, his are better. How do you think I learned?"

Brando chuckled. "I think yours are better."

Dayvee reached for Elayni's hand and lifted her over. "Go farther back."

Elayni scooted away from the edge and rose to her feet. "They both are amazing, just different. Dayvee dances with the stars. Brando's are like a controlled tornado."

Brando hauled himself over, then helped Chayla. She let go of his hand and moved back. "Will you show me?"

"Sure. I'm not shy like Dayvee."

No, and surely Chayla would be impressed. Dayvee always was. After they helped Geno and Tayro up, Dayvee handed the rope to Brando. The moon free of clouds gave them plenty of light. "You can go first."

Brando grabbed the rope, raced for the edge, then jumped. "One, two, three. He dropped and wrapped his arms around himself, then spun through the air. His body knifed and flipped completely over, then he spun again, reached his arms above his head, and plunged into the water with barely a splash. No shout came.

"Brando!" Only silence answered Dayvee.

#

Wilee's cold nose nudged Codee, tearing him from his dreams. *Leeto's coming.*

Did he ever sleep? Codee rose. Jolay peered out from the hides. "Is something wrong?"

"Probably nothing. Go back to sleep." Codee entered their communal area and lit a few more lamps.

They're here, Wilee sent.

Codee drew back the hide to his den and met Leeto's stern visage. "What's wrong?"

"They're up at the pool again," Leeto frowned. "This time with all the trainees."

Codee sucked in a breath, and his heart leapt to his throat. He calmed himself. Dayvee knew what he was doing up there. Leeto and Codee had both hidden to watch him before. His diving was breath taking. Even when he was much younger, he and his friends had never been hurt. "Maybe we should give him one last night. He'll have some good memories to take with him."

Leeto never paced, yet he was pacing the room. "Probably another of Brando's ideas. Dayvee holds too much trust in him, and his influence is hurting us. I'm still not sure I want Brando going with."

Codee would try to change his mind again. "They're as close as brothers. They might join another pack if you split them, and I planned to put Brando in charge of the ring since he's the fiercest."

"He could pose a challenge to Dayvee's leadership." Leeto turned at the hearth and came back toward him. "We're real brothers, and you can't tell me you haven't considered challenging me."

Codee sighed inwardly. More than once.

"Dayvee has to learn. Too much trust will bring down an alpha and kill a Kayndo, so tomorrow we tame the tiger." Leeto stopped mid-step. "Cackles."

"What's wrong?"

"I just had Luko call Dayvee to order him back. He's not answering."

#

Panic gripped Dayvee. Brando still hadn't said anything. Another voice shouted in Dayvee's mind again. Luko's. That wasn't who he needed. He ignored it and reached out to Brando's companion. *Bruno, is something wrong with Brando?*

No, he just lost his shorts when he hit the water, so he's putting them back on before surfacing.

Finally Brando's holler came, "Yes!"

"Great dive." Dayvee cracked up laughing. "But I guess you're shy after all."

Brando's laughter pealed out and filled the night. "Maybe a little."

Luko's trying to reach you, Jaycee sent.

I'll respond now. Luko?

A knife of pain lanced through Dayvee's head as Luko's shout filled his mind. *Leeto wants you to stop diving and come back.*

Dayvee rubbed his temple. Why should Leeto care now? It must be because Dayvee took the other trainees. Elayni and Chayla were both running their hands over themselves to generate warmth. Geno was jumping up and down. Everyone must be freezing. They needed to warm up.

Tell him we'll stop diving, but we need to warm up around the fire, not hike the mountain at night. We'll come down in the morning.

To defy Leeto meant Dayvee could expect at least a tongue lashing, probably in front of the entire pack, but it couldn't last too long. He was leaving. His attention turned back to the other trainees. "Okay, this is the last one. Want to do it together so we can get down faster?"

"Yes, but how do we do that?" Geno asked.

Dayvee moved the brush back over the opening to hide it. Then removed the rope. We can't use this, or we'd fall on each other. He threw the rope over the side. "We just hang on to each other's hands and run. When I yell, jump out as far as you can. Ready?"

"Yes." They said together.

"Grab hands." They did. "Run." Dayvee drove his legs faster for more speed. "Jump!"

He pushed off and flung himself out, dragging the others farther. They stopped moving sideways and dropped. He didn't twist this time. Just let himself plummet, down, down, until his feet hit and the water parted, stealing his breath again. He kept their hands in his as he kicked for the surface and broke through. They all came up around him laughing.

"Everyone else should go warm up in your bedrolls around the fire. I have to swim laps for Leeto."

When Dayvee finished, he dried off and sank into his bedroll. Chayla scooted closer to Brando. "You should have shared this place with us sooner."

"Wouldn't have done any good. No one down there cares whether we're hurt, but I doubt your parents would have let you come."

"Probably not." She sighed. "I couldn't have lied and said there wasn't any danger."

"You never were in danger. I went with you the first time, and Dayvee wouldn't have let you jump short, but who would believe us?"

Tayro pulled a stick out from under his bedroll and threw it in the fire. "Leeto cares about Dayvee. He wants him to be the next alpha."

Elayni crossed her arms. "Have you been sticking your nose out of the den at all? Jonesee and Franko are lousy fathers, but I'd take them over Leeto."

"Like fight training today." Brando sat up. "Couldn't you tell he wanted Dayvee to get hurt?"

Shouldn't Dayvee defend his father? His love for him cried out, yes, but it was hard to defend actions he didn't agree with. "Leeto believes he's helping me."

Brando raised one eyebrow. "No one should want that kind of help. Do one of your impressions of him, Elayni."

Elayni stood and drew herself up. "Dayvee, if you did something stupid and received injuries, you should suffer to learn better. Don't expect any slack from me while you heal."

"Wow." Chayla pulled her bedroll up further to her neck. "You've got his voice and mannerisms just right."

Elayni sat back down, and Brando tousled the hair on the top of her head. "Always. There isn't a voice or animal she can't imitate."

Dayvee needed to tell them. His heart thumped harder in his chest. "I have something important I need to share with you."

Elayni pushed Brando's hand away and smoothed her hair. "What is it?"

"Everyone else will learn tomorrow." A deep breath helped calm Dayvee's nerves. "I should have shared this with you sooner, but I didn't want to be treated any more differently than I already am." Stop rambling and tell them.

Elayni took his right hand. "I don't care what you tell me. I'll support you."

Brando clasped his left forearm. "I don't believe you have anything to be ashamed of. With you it's probably something great like you're a Kayndo."

Dayvee gasped. "You knew?"

"No. Wow. I just put out the best thing I could think of. I can't believe it. You're really a Kayndo?"

"A Kayndo in waiting. I have the gifts, but I may not be needed, and I really hope I'm not. It isn't a good thing, no more than an alpha's son is."

"What do you mean it's not a good thing?" Brando lay back, put both his hands behind his head, and chuckled. "I won't have to search for frogs anymore."

All the others were smiling. They weren't upset at him. Relief charged through Dayvee. He laughed. "I'm not calling frogs for you."

Chayla had propped her head up on her arm, but her body lay hidden beside Brando. "Is that how you passed the test?"

"Not exactly. I body hopped."

"What?" Elayni asked.

"I can share an animal's body and feel, see, and smell what they do. So I went with a bat to the end of the tunnel and back." Elayni chewed her bottom lip. A sure sign she wasn't satisfied with Dayvee's answer. "Maybe your companions can explain it better."

He settled back. Stars plastered the sky. Would this be the last time he ever saw this view? He'd strived so hard to be able to claim Wolf Mountain as his home, and he hadn't wanted to leave it. A lump rose in his throat. Was it right to ask his friends to come too. What if they didn't come home?

Dayvee had to keep that from happening. "I don't think any of you should go with me tomorrow. If I have to become Kayndo, it will probably mean war. You could die."

"I'm going." Brando kicked Dayvee's bedroll. "I'm not missing the fun and don't even think about sneaking off 'cause I'd follow."

"What happened to never leaving me?" Elayni sniffled.

Oh, no. Was she crying? Dayvee couldn't look. Elayni's tears tore him up, and he'd agree to most anything to stop them. "I was hoping you'd choose to stay, so I wouldn't be leaving you."

"I'd follow too," she choked out.

"I'm going," declared the other trainees.

Five wolves lifted their heads at the trainees' feet as they shouted in Dayvee's head. *We're going.*

Pain shot into his temple, so Dayvee rubbed it until it subsided. "I was afraid that's what you'd say." He made an effort to burn this moment in his memory to carry with him. The stars, the crisp scent of the mountain air, the wood smoke, and the fire crackling and popping, his friends' even breathing around him. "We better get some sleep. Codee plans on leaving early, and I doubt he'll allow us any slack tomorrow."

Brando snorted. "Like we expected that to happen."

Dayvee closed his eyes and whispered his prayer. "Kun, please let us come home safely, and if not me, at least let my friends."

8

Honored

"To slink is taking the easy path. Calupi prefer holding their heads high on the difficult trail." ~Leeto

The ceremony room erupted with foot stomping, hand clapping, and wolf howls as Dayvee and his friends entered with their companions. Apparently, Leeto had already made the announcement. The pack's pleasure filled Dayvee with joy, but his embarrassment rose. He didn't do anything to deserve their acclaim, and he didn't want to become a Kayndo. Kwutee and Leeto stood in the middle of the ring and motioned the trainees to join them.

Leeto's face held no expression as Dayvee and the others stopped in front of him. He slid an arm around Dayvee's back. What was Leeto doing? Calupi often hugged, but not Leeto. His father's arm had only been across Dayvee's back a few times. Whatever this was, he better not relax. It could only be a precursor to the criticism he'd receive for their prank and for defying Leeto's order.

Leeto turned him and signaled the others to face the pack too. "These Calupi and their companions—Dayvee and Jaycee, Elayni and Evee, Brando and Bruno, Geno and Graydee, Chayla and Cato, and Tayro and Topay—will be leaving today. His voice echoed through the chamber. "Codee and the traders will accompany them to the clan meeting, then they'll go alone to Harthome to take up duties as either the castle's first sub-pack or Kayndo and his first warriors."

Kwutee hit his staff on the ground. "Would Wolf Mountain pack like to honor them and show them our support?"

"Yes!" The pack answered with one voice. Whistles, applause, and foot stomping thundered through the room.

Leeto held up a hand and the pack silenced. "If Dayvee becomes Kayndo, will any of the Calupi and companions at Wolf Mountain answer his call?"

"We will!" It boomed as if every Calupi had answered. The companions howled their agreement.

Leeto squeezed Dayvee's shoulder. "It might be hard for me to find any willing to stay." He gave Dayvee a gentle shove and dropped his arm, his signal for Dayvee to speak to the pack.

If Dayvee could just forget Leeto's presence, he might not feel as if he teetered on a cliff edge. The pack wouldn't want to see the boy his father claimed wasn't good enough, or the Calupi they'd seen Andee best in a challenge, but a Kayndo. How could he give them a living legend from the stories they all knew by heart?

He couldn't convince himself he was good enough to be Kayndo. How would he make them believe it? The silence grew heavy with their expectation. Wasn't the Kayndo a leader? Dayvee had scrutinized Leeto his entire life, so surely he could pull off the alpha act as well as Elayni. This wasn't the time to shirk.

Dayvee drew himself up, put his shoulders back, and lifted his head. He projected his voice and made it strong. "I am overjoyed to have *your* support." Then his mind went blank. What else was there to say? Leeto and Kwutee had already told the pack about him. Leeto gave him a chin lift. Must have been enough.

Leeto moved up beside him. "Kwutee, say the prayer so we can feed them before they leave."

"Kun, we thank you for the bounty you've provided us. We would ask that you give these young Calupi your aid and strengthen them for the challenges ahead so they always remain faithful to you and the Vita."

Leeto slapped Dayvee's back and motioned to the tables set up. "Since we honor you and your companions today, you'll go first."

Dayvee's eyes had to be as wide as his friends'. The pack must have worked for hours. Far more than a normal breakfast, dishes crowded the table with aromas that set his mouth to salivating before he tasted a thing. He might as well enjoy the feast before Leeto harangued him.

Dayvee filled Jaycee's bowl before stuffing his own with nut and berry cakes, poured honey over them, and crammed some sausages and rice pudding on the side. Eating it all might make it difficult to walk when he left.

Leeto came over to where Dayvee sat eating with his friends. "Jonesee just made it back. He'd like Brando to meet him in his family den."

Brando jumped up. Both he and Bruno bounced with excitement as they rushed out. Leeto moved off, and he and Codee left the room. Maybe Leeto wanted to give Codee last minute instructions.

Other Calupi crowded around them. Dayvee shoveled his last bite in and rose to greet them. He lifted his head to keep the Kayndo facade. No one wanted to see the real Dayvee with all his doubts. His friends also stood. One by one, the pack came to clasp Dayvee's arm. "I'll answer your call," echoed in his ears.

What if he told them the truth? Maybe they shouldn't. Dayvee didn't know anything about being a Kayndo. Instead, he reiterated, "I'd be honored to have you."

Tobee hobbled over to Dayvee. His misshapen bowed legs only allowed him to walk with that strange gait. Most of the pack pointedly ignored him. Some of the women would talk to him since he helped with the children, but Tobee could never gain any status or stop slinking. He had no respect. At twenty-four years of age he should have a companion, but his parents didn't think he could pass the tests, so he never took them. He wasn't Calupi. Tobee's head hung down tight against his chest. "I hope you come back safely."

Pity welled up in Dayvee. He couldn't refuse to acknowledge him. "Thanks, Tobee."

That drew some frowns from Calupi who didn't approve. Oh well. At least he earned the frowns. Better than the admiring looks bestowed on him because of the Kayndos in the stories. No one knew if Dayvee was going to be one yet. And he certainly would never be like those. He wasn't anything close to a hero.

#

Brando came to the familiar hide-covered doorway with Bruno. Should he knock? No, this was their family den, even if he hadn't been in it for years. If Jonesee wanted to finally act like a father and meet with Brando before he left, he could do this. He pushed back the hide covering the doorway and walked in.

There were only a few lamps lit, but they cast enough light to reveal the rug on the floor that used to be bright, the wall mural with his mother's companion painted on it, and the shelves containing cooking utensils his mother used. One of Brando's first wood carvings sat on the table, and pillows lay scattered. A thick layer of dust coated everything, and the hearth with no fire announced it was no longer a home. A lump filled his throat.

Jonesee and his companion stood at the side of the hearth. Wow, Brando stood at least three inches taller than his father now. There were other changes since he had seen Jonesee a few years back. His face, so similar to Brando's own, was leaner and held more lines, and his dark-brown hair had a few gray hairs sprinkled in. Living without the pack must be exacting a toll.

Jonesee's lips were clamped tight together. Not even a hint of a smile greeted Brando. What kind of goodbye was this?

A rustle warned Brando of the hide being pulled back. He pivoted around. Leeto, Codee, Andee, and Pako came in with their companions. What were they doing here? Wait a minute. With Jonesee it made five Calupi, a quincee. The pack used a quincee to deal with problems where there could be trouble. His heart sped up. Refusing to submit to the leaders made Brando the problem, and he couldn't even fight Leeto or Codee since he promised Dayvee he wouldn't.

Bruno's growl split the air. Five wolves stalked toward Bruno as he sent, *Luko's ordered me to desist and not to betray the leaders by sending a message to the others.*

Brando sent back, *Don't take on impossible odds, Submit.*

Bruno lowered his head, but Brando couldn't. He refused to give into panic. Leeto's gaze fell on Brando, and he got hit by his intense magnetism. Dayvee had it too. The spark that kept your attention riveted to them. Brando resisted the pull. He wouldn't fawn over

Leeto.

Jonesee's head was lowered. "Brando, lower your head to your alpha and second."

He couldn't submit to Leeto's leadership. Not when Leeto continued to harm Brando's family. Surely Leeto wouldn't break pack law and hit a pack mate outside the ring. These weren't kids. "I lower my head when someone deserves my respect." Brando raised his head higher and squared his shoulders. "The best fighters in the pack this time, Leeto. And still five against one? Should I feel honored?"

Jonesee's brow rose. "What are you talking about?"

Figures. Jonesee didn't even know, although Brando spent weeks healing from his broken ribs. Only one way to find out if he'd care. "Yesterday was four years to the day from when Leeto sent another quincee after me, only then it was kids."

"It was only supposed to be one kid," Leeto retorted. "But he was afraid of a tiger's claws." He glanced at Codee, then his tone and demeanor softened. "Maybe it wasn't my best decision, but you were hurting Dayvee and yourself by running the opposite direction than the pack." Leeto's blue eyes locked on him. "There's no reason we have to be adversaries. If you'd just turn around and run with us, we'll make sure Dayvee succeeds. Isn't that what we both want?"

The sharp desire rose in Brando to please him. Why? He no longer hated Leeto, but he sure didn't care for him.

You said you respected his fighting, Bruno sent. *Strong leaders are needed for a strong pack.*

It was true. Packs needed to be strong to thrive. Could Brando forgive Leeto for everything he'd done? The memory surfaced of Dayvee slamming his own head into the wall when he failed to satisfy Leeto. There could be no justification for how Leeto repeatedly crushed Dayvee.

Brando looked away from the pull of Leeto's eyes. "I'm not hurting Dayvee. You are. No matter how much he accomplishes, you still criticize him."

"When no other trainee can match him, and I'm still demanding more, the pack knows I'll make him into our best alpha ever. They won't settle for anyone other than him to ensure our future." Leeto shook his head. "But you're harming everything we've accomplished. You've got him and the other trainees rolling over, doing pranks, and defying our authority. It has to stop before it spreads further. Then there will be no authority and that hurts the entire pack."

Jonesee's shoulders fell. "I didn't teach Brando to respect authority, so it's my fault."

Didn't sound like Brando could expect any help from Jonesee. That wasn't anything new.

Leeto clasped Jonesee's forearm. "Not entirely. Dayvee agreed to do what I wanted if I left Brando alone. Dayvee paid the price, but Brando never learned."

So that's how Leeto motivated Dayvee. Brando didn't like being used like that.

Leeto turned back to him. "If you'll just agree to follow your alpha's instructions, your status and Dayvee's will rise, but if you refuse, I can't let you rejoin him."

"You can't stop me."

"That's where you're mistaken. I'm alpha. Not you. Not Dayvee. If you won't cooperate, I'll bind you. Surely you realize you can't best us all."

"You'd break pack law?"

"We don't need to strike you to bind you. But if you refuse to submit and fight us outside the ring, then you've broken pack law, and we will fight back."

Brando looked at Jonesee. "And you'd help him?"

"Whatever he decides. He's our alpha and I trust him," Jonesee declared. "But even if he's wrong, we're never going to find a perfect alpha. Calupi leaders make decisions we don't agree with. But the pack needs to support them when we agree, and even when we don't."

"You shouldn't support the pack over your family."

"Even if you challenged Leeto and won, the pack wouldn't follow you. Leeto's a good alpha and they know it. If you want status, you need his support, not mine."

"You should still support your family, regardless. But you don't, and that's what drove my mother off a cliff."

Jonesee flinched. Did it really bother him? Why should Brando care? Jonesee has to know it would hurt Brando to be separated from Dayvee and Elayni. Jonesee always hurt him. This was the last time Brando would let him. "I don't have a father. Neither does Dayvee, and he'll figure it out too."

Leeto took some strips of leather out of his pouch. "You have two choices. Both involve not telling Dayvee and giving me your word to submit to my authority. You can go with Dayvee, now, if you'll do what we tell you and report everything to Codee."

After Brando made the mistake of revealing Dayvee's former fear of the dark, Leeto had to be wondering what else Dayvee was hiding from him. He must want to use Brando to learn more about Dayvee and to manipulate him.

"You really think I'll act like Codee and betray Dayvee's trust forever?"

"I'll limit the vow until he learns. It won't do me much good after that."

No, because if Brando did it, Dayvee would probably never trust him again.

"What's the other choice?"

"Leave on rotation with Jonesee. He'll finish training you. After a year's time, if you prove you can submit to authority, I'll let you return and assign you to Rodnee. But you won't rejoin Dayvee."

"What if I decide to do neither?"

Leeto held up the leather strips. "After Nero, I'm not about to let another foe hurt us from within. If you won't follow your alpha, then Frozen Platte Pack in the north is in need of members. They're willing to give you a chance and see if a tiger can learn to submit. Andee will take you, but he won't remove your bindings until you give your word not to come back."

"And how will you keep Dayvee from finding out and coming after me?"

"He doesn't have the time. If he goes after you, I'll send Jaycee with others. Do you think he'll put your needs over Jaycee's, the packs, and the Vita? Typical of a tiger to even want that."

Rage burned like an inferno inside of Brando and sent the blood pounding in his ears. He couldn't let it consume him. He drew some huge breaths. "You don't know him. He'd do it." The choices were impossible. Tears came to Brando's eyes, and he couldn't stand it. Leeto would consider it weak.

Brando fought to get himself under control. He ran his fingers over the dust on the table. Dayvee needed to go with Jaycee, or he'd blame himself if something happened to that wolf.

Maybe Brando should just agree to go on rotation with Jonesee. It was only a year. Leeto couldn't keep him away from Dayvee forever. But what if Dayvee or Elayni needed Brando, and he wasn't there?

There were two exits from their den. Three Calupi stood behind him. Two in front. Could he get around them and reach one? If Leeto didn't want Dayvee to know, any pursuit would end when he reached Dayvee.

He had to try to escape.

I'll be on your heels, Bruno sent.

Brando darted forward.

9

Paths

"If you're headed in the wrong direction, turn around and take the correct path." ~ Kwutee.

Miko finally moved away. Dayvee must have spoken to everyone in the pack. But where had all his friends disappeared to? Elayni was moving out the entrance with her father, Franko. The rest of them were probably spending some time alone with their families too. Dayvee had been mistaken about talking to everyone. Codee's new life mate was heading toward him now.

Jolay's shiny black hair, light complexion, and large green eyes were so striking. Why did he get tongue-tied and clumsy when Elayni or Jolay focused on him? They both were so beautiful, articulate, and graceful. Did he have to always show them he wasn't?

As Jolay clasped his forearm, Dayvee unglued his tongue. "I'm sorry about taking Codee from you again."

"Don't be. When you consider a life-mate, make sure they're willing to sacrifice for the pack, or you'll both be miserable." Jolay lowered her voice to a whisper, "Just appreciate what Codee gave up and don't crush him."

Huh? She should ask Codee to stop crushing Dayvee. "What has Codee given up?"

"The second's job is the hardest because they give up their own dreams and desires to support those of the alpha. Codee was offered the alpha position if he'd stay with my father's pack. He turned it down."

"Why?"

"He said his obligations weren't done here yet."

"Helping Leeto."

Her laugh tinkled out. "Not Leeto, you. He can't show it because he's second, but you're all he talked about."

Did Codee really care so much for Dayvee? If so, he was sure good at hiding it. Leeto and Codee strode back into the ceremony room. Dayvee's friends all entered behind them.

"Everyone finish your goodbyes," Leeto ordered. Jolay left Dayvee to go to Codee as Leeto, Milay, and Bunjee came over. Leeto gave Dayvee a hug that almost lifted him off his feet. "Remember who you are, and what I taught you. Meet and beat every challenge."

Bunjee, with eyes shining, hugged him next. "I hope you become Kayndo. I want to answer your call, but they probably won't let me since I'm not chosen yet."

Dayvee couldn't put on an act with Bunjee, so he spoke honestly, "I hope I don't become Kayndo. That could mean war." Dayvee tousled Bunjee's hair. "I'd rather see you at the next choosing when I come back for another companion."

As Milay hugged him, she said softly, "I know you consider Clay your mother, and she earned the title. Just remember that wolf was *never* wrong, and she believed in you."

Yes, Clay earned it. Supposedly Milay had been depressed after his birth. She rejected him. Clay nursed him on wolf's milk with her own two pups. Both pups had died, but Dayvee thrived. Clay's love for him had been constant.

When Milay moved back, Jaycee retreated a few steps as the alpha wolves, Luko and Skylay, came forward to press against him. Dayvee brushed his fingers over their heads. Luko sent, *Clay would be very proud of her pup.*

Did she know? Is that why she raised me and gave her life for mine.

Luko nudged him with his nose. *She knew Kun had a plan for you, not what it was. She did what she did because she loved you.*

I miss her so much.

She hasn't left you. Luko's tail wagged. *Her love and ours is going with you. Just search your memories, and you'll find it.* Luko and Skylay dropped back beside Dayvee's parents as the other wolves in the pack came over to nose him. He touched each of their heads. He'd miss them as much as any person they were leaving behind.

Codee signaled by lifting his hand, then he walked toward the entrance. The traders moved after him, each pulling a travois behind them. Dayvee and Jaycee followed with the other trainees.

The entire pack came outside and waved, shouting parting messages. "May Kun go with you and keep you safe," were Leeto's last words.

What had happened to Leeto's condemnation? Did he think Dayvee was sharp enough now? Was he finally proud of him? Dayvee better stop deluding himself. He just answered, "And also with you."

Then it hit Dayvee like a punch to his gut. Leeto never ignored anyone defying his orders. He must believe Dayvee might never return. That convinced Dayvee the trail he was on might drop him over a cliff. He pushed the unease aside and ignored it.

However it went, as the castle sub-pack leader or the next Kayndo, he wouldn't see Wolf Mountain and them for a long time. He wiped a tear away as a slow drizzle started. More rain. Yuck. He glanced over his shoulder as the pack faded from view. At least he wasn't going alone.

Wait, what was wrong with Brando? His head hung low. Bruno was almost slinking. Why did Brando's face look funny?

Dayvee and Jaycee dropped back beside his friend. "Look at me."

Elayni turned around, and she and Evee came to them too. Brando's head sunk even lower, and his shoulders hunched forward.

Dayvee grabbed Brando's arm and stopped walking. The other trainees moved up around them.

Elayni took Brando's chin in her hand. "Lift it, Brando. You know we won't move until you do."

Brando raised his head a little. His nose was swollen and held a bump. His headband was wet and clung to his head, revealing another lump. Dayvee reached out and pulled his headband farther up. A purple knot lay below. They had been in the ceremony room. Brando wasn't in the ring there. Surely no one would break pack law and hit Brando outside of the ring.

"How did this happen? Did Jonesee do something to you?" Silence answered Dayvee. Oh no. Not that again. Twice before, Brando had stopped talking. When his mother disappeared and after those kids ganged up on him. Was it rain dripping from his face or tears? "Brando, talk to me. If you don't, we're going back so I can challenge your father."

"Don't call him my father," Brando choked out. "He's nothing to me, and I just tripped and fell."

Bruno's tail hung down low. He shared emotions with Brando. Why was Bruno so sad if Brando just fell? Dayvee released his breath heavily. Calupi didn't lie, and there were plenty of places in the caves where it was easy to trip, especially if someone was upset and not watching where they were going.

Elayni wrapped her arms around Brando and hugged him. "What did Jonesee say?"

Brando's whole body shuddered. "I'm so stupid to think for a minute he wanted to be a father."

"You're not stupid." Elayni dropped her arms and released him. "Tell us."

"I can't talk about it." Brando picked up a stick and sent it flying to the side of the trail.

Dayvee squeezed his shoulder. "Is it too thin?"

Brando's shoulders sagged, but he nodded once.

Tayro shifted his feet. "I could give you a compress that will help with the swelling."

"I don't want it, and I told you not to come too close," Brando retorted.

Tayro and Topay retreated several steps. Codee and Wilee dropped back, leaving the traders. "Is there a problem here?"

Brando's head dropped. "No problem."

Whatever Jonesee did to him, it stole Brando's fire. He never submitted to a pack leader that easily. Dayvee wanted his friend back. "I'll challenge Jonesee."

Brando's head lifted. "It's my problem." His head sagged again.

"Leave it."

"It's not your problem, it's ours."

"It won't solve anything."

"You don't have time for challenges," Codee barked. "Jaycee's needed in Harthome, now, so move." He pivoted and walked off with Wilee.

Brando and Bruno plodded after Codee without waiting for the rest of them. The others turned to Dayvee. He sighed. "We'll go, but if any of you can cheer Brando, I'll do your share of the chores tonight." Dayvee broke into a trot to catch up.

"What if more than one of us does?" Chayla slipped on mud, and Geno put a hand out to steady her.

"I'm willing to do all of them to bring back Brando. So anyone who gets him to laugh or even smile, I'll do yours."

They caught up to Codee and Brando, who walked behind the last travois with their companions. Apparently, Codee was going to let the traders lead while he stayed back with them.

"I know something." Chayla and Cato ran up to Brando. "Can I hug you?"

"I don't need pity hugs," he mumbled.

"How about a not doing chores hug?" she asked.

"What?"

"Dayvee says he'll do our chores if we cheer you."

"I already hugged him," Elayni said. "Do you think yours are better?"

"Maybe." A shy smile peeked out from Chayla. "Can I, Brando?"

Brando's head lifted a little, and he stopped. "All right, but I don't think it will work."

Chayla stood on tip-toes, reached up, and wrapped her arms around him. After a second, she released him. "You didn't smile."

"Sorry."

She shrugged. "I tried."

"Codee, what will we do at the clan meeting?" Elayni asked.

"You're going to meet the Kwin there. Leeto leased horses for you to ride to the capital."

His friends' concerned faces must mirror Dayvee's own. "But we've never ridden horses."

"You'll learn and travel faster. Taluma needs a chosen prince if the king dies."

The lump rose in Dayvee's throat. He'd soon lose Jaycee. He pushed those thoughts away. If he dwelled on it, he wouldn't enjoy the few days he had left with the wolf.

"Some of us haven't been to a clan meeting." Elayni sloshed through a puddle. "Can you tell us what to expect?"

Brando's head lifted more. The three of them had always wanted to go to a clan meeting. Elayni might get a smile from him yet.

Codee's braid swung as he glanced over his shoulder. "We quarter Taluma and hold one in each territory—North, South, East, and West. All the packs, pods, herds, and flocks send delegations to theirs." He pulled his straps on his rucksack and shifted it higher on his back. "You'll see some you never knew existed."

"What else will we see?" Elayni pulled a hood over her hair.

"There will be merchants, storytellers, musicians, food, games, and competitions. But we won't have time for you to see much."

"Couldn't we spend at least one night there?" Brando asked wistfully. "I'd be willing to give up a night's sleep. I bet Dayvee would for that."

His friends' expectant faces turned to Dayvee. "You'd be right." Dayvee had pleaded with Leeto to allow him and his friends to go with Codee for the last one, but it hadn't worked.

"Sorry, but there will be others." Codee and Wilee moved around a tree limb that protruded over the trail.

Geno sighed. "Not for five years."

"You'll have to settle for the pack meeting next year," Codee replied.

"We've all been to pack meetings." Elayni chewed her lip. "They're every two years, and it's only wolf clan."

"Yes." Codee shot back. "But next year you'll be able to compete."

That brought a few smiles, but not Brando's. Most Calupi

probably dreamed of winning a competition for their pack. Pack meetings lasted two weeks, but it felt like one long celebration with all the contest winners and couples that held life-mate ceremonies there. Would Elayni want to do a life-mating ceremony at the pack meeting? Dayvee would prefer fewer people, but he'd do it for her.

"I bet I could learn lots of new stories at a clan meeting," Chayla proclaimed.

Codee shrugged. "It can't be helped."

Should Dayvee tell them Codee wouldn't be swayed? That would only disappoint his friends and spare his uncle. Dayvee reached for a thorn branch to hold it back from snagging him or Jaycee. Wild roses. Kwutee urged them to eat rose hips often. They helped fight colds and fatigue. "Codee, these are full of rose hips. We can gather them and catch up."

Codee gave him a chin lift. He approved.

Dayvee grabbed a pouch from his rucksack. A shout rang out—Brando's. A frog jumped out of his rucksack. The chagrined look on Brando's face did it. Dayvee laughed so hard his side hurt. The other trainees joined in, and their wolves wagged their tails in amusement.

Brando finally snorted and a chortle escaped. "Dayvee?"

When Dayvee got control, he answered, "Not me."

"Who?" Brando asked.

"Me." Chayla's voice wavered. She and Cato stood underneath the vines to avoid the thorns while she collected the hips. It kept her out of the rain too. Sometimes small could be good.

Dayvee put another handful of hips in his pouch. "You won't have any chores tonight, Chayla."

"Sorry, Elayni, but her hug was better." Brando let out a hollow laugh, nothing like his normal guffaws. Still, it was good to hear.

Elayni rolled her eyes. "You're like most of the men in the pack now."

Brando grabbed branches carelessly to tear off the hips, as if he wanted the thorns to scratch him. "What are you talking about?"

"Your nose has a bump."

"Cackles." Brando put his hand to his nose and gave her a weak chortle. "My beautiful nose is gone."

"All right, Elayni. I'll do your chores too." Dayvee put his pouch back in his rucksack. "We have enough. Let's go."

When they caught up to Codee and the traders, Dayvee caught Elayni craning to see her parents, Franko and Tinay.

"You could walk with them," Dayvee suggested.

Elayni's red lips pursed. "They haven't even looked back once, only forward to their next trade like always." She released a deep breath, and her fingers entwined in his. "I'll stay with those that cared enough not to leave me."

His heart sped up, and his hand felt really warm where she held it, even with the rain. Was it sweating? "I don't want to leave you."

"Thanks. I'm okay, but Brando needs to cry. He won't, so I'm afraid he'll explode."

"Yeah, I know." Dayvee released her hand and went with Jaycee back to where Brando and Bruno plodded. He grabbed Brando's arm, pulled him to the side, and waved the others on. "What can I do to help?"

Brando's fists curled. "Release my vow."

"Not yet, my ferocious friend."

"Then I'll have to settle for Tayro."

Dayvee's hair, headband, and clothes dripped rainwater, sending a chill through him. "If you want to punish people that made mistakes, you can start with me. I made the most."

"It's not the same. You never planned to harm anyone."

"But it did. A companion's dead that helped me because I didn't handle things right." Tears came to Dayvee's eyes. Why did he let that happen? Maybe Brando wouldn't notice with the rain. He strode faster. The others came back into view.

Jaycee nudged Dayvee with his nose. Sympathy came through their bond.

"I'll *try* to use restraint with Tayro, but you *have* to stop blaming yourself." Brando called out, "Come here, Elayni. Dayvee needs cheering up."

Cackles. Did Brando really have to point out Dayvee's weakness

---

to Elayni? She and Evee dropped back. Brando broke into a trot with Bruno to rejoin the others as Elayni grabbed Dayvee's hand. "Are you okay?"

The touch sent a spark racing through him, and his spirits lifted. Those light blue pools that were Elayni's eyes fixated him.

"We won't be training much longer," he said.

"No, we won't," she whispered.

Dayvee wanted to kiss her and leaned in, her mouth so irresistible. His lips met hers. The spark set a fire off inside him. Flames roared. They demanded he give them more fuel, and nothing would please him more. He wrapped his arms around Elayni and brought her closer, deepening the kiss.

Brando comes, Jaycee warned as fast footsteps pounded.

Dayvee tore himself away from those soft lips. Brando and Bruno loped toward them. The others weren't in sight.

Brando gave them a wink. "Feeling better?"

Dayvee's lack of breath mangled his answer. "Yes... I am."

"Good. Codee sent me. He wants you."

Dayvee glanced at Elayni. "Shall we?"

She nodded, then dropped his hand and took off at a run, laughing. "Evee and I will beat you back."

"We going to let her?" Dayvee asked Brando.

One corner of Brando's lip twitched, almost a smile. He really was fighting his good nature. "Let's go."

Dayvee and Brando matched their strides. Jaycee and Bruno loped alongside them. When they caught up with Elayni and Evee, they raced neck and neck until they were almost to Codee. Dayvee and Brando hung back so she'd win.

She laughed as they slowed to a fast walk behind Codee. "I told you I'd win." Her blue eyes sparkled.

Brando kicked a stick off the trail. "Don't get too excited. We let you win again."

Red flushed her cheeks. "Did you really?"

Dayvee ripped his attention from her to focus on Codee. "You needed me?"

Codee's eyes glinted, and a corner of his mouth turned up. "Just didn't want anyone lost too long."

"We weren't lost."

"Sometimes it's not obvious when you're losing the trail." Codee frowned, and his eyes pierced Dayvee. "You have to slow down to take the correct path."

True, Jaycee sent.

Dayvee nodded once. Correct path or not, it would have been nice to finish the kiss. He glanced at Elayni. She gave him a full smile that lit her face and showed her dimples. He tripped over a tree root, but quickly caught his balance. Why did his body betray him and become so clumsy around her?

Brando drove a punch at Dayvee that he dodged. "Might want to watch where you're going."

Codee looked back over his shoulder. "Dayvee, I want you to hunt for deer, but you need a refresher, so not the first. We're going to be trotting, so you'll have to really run. I expect you to meet up with us when we get to the grasslands."

Dayvee blew out his breath. "That doesn't give me enough time."

"I think you can do it."

Geno's heavy brows lifted. "What?"

"It's a patience lesson," Dayvee explained. "Codee says a good hunter needs it, so I can only kill the third deer I track down."

"Patience is also needed for life. Now go," Codee ordered.

Dayvee broke into a run with Jaycee.

. . .

At midday, Jaycee and Dayvee rejoined the others as they cut onto the grasslands. The rain had stopped. Now, sweat soaked Dayvee's clothes, and he had nothing to show for his effort.

Codee's face was stern. "How many?"

"Two deer."

Codee flicked his finger, and Dayvee rejoined his friends.

Brando whispered, "At least it's not scary rabbits anymore."

Dayvee chuckled as the memory surfaced of sitting for hours by a rabbit hole at age eight for his third rabbit. His friends came, but

Dayvee wouldn't leave to tell Codee he failed. Brando found the other entrance, and Elayni imitated a fox's bark while Brando stuck a stick in and knocked it around. When the rabbit barreled out, jumping in Dayvee's arms, he had shrieked and dropped it.

Jaycee nudged Dayvee. *An injured lease wolf is calling for help, and we're closest.*

The traders stopped. Their companions must have alerted them too. Franko trotted back to Codee. "What do you want to do?"

"The trainees and I will go. We'll catch up with you later." Codee and Wilee loped off to the east, deeper into the grasslands. Dayvee and Jaycee raced after them with the other trainees.

A horse pulling a wagon appeared. Boards with small gaps between crossed the wagons sides, but the back stood open. The horse slowed and stopped, and a burly man climbed down with hair almost the color of carrots. "I'm Brett. I'm glad you're here. The wolf gets worse by the hour."

"What happened?" Codee asked.

"We were attacked by a bear." Brett rubbed the back of his neck. "She got mauled when she defended us."

Codee gave him a nod. "We'll take a look."

Brett pointed to a hide blanket in the back of the wagon. The trainees followed Codee as he climbed into the wagon and pulled the hide off. Their companions waited on the ground. A black wolf lay cloaked in several bandages.

Codee glanced at Tayro. "You probably have more healing knowledge than me. See what you can do for her." He pointed to Dayvee. "Help remove the bandages."

Codee dropped off the back of the wagon. "Did you go into a bear's cave?"

"No, it came barreling into our camp. We tried to drive it away, but it kept coming. With the wolf's help, we were finally able to kill it."

Dayvee unwrapped some of the bandaging on her head. The wolf stirred and opened her eyes to slits. Tayro came up beside him to unravel the bandages on her body. Her eyes popped open, and she snapped at Dayvee, barely missing his hand. Dayvee and Tayro drew back. The wolf bounded onto three feet. Her hair rose. She growled. Dayvee backed with Tayro a few steps but couldn't go farther. They were hemmed in by the other trainees.

Jaycee and the other companions had their front feet on the back of the wagon, trying to jump in as the trainees scrambled to get out. The wolf charged at Dayvee, opening her mouth to reveal her teeth.

10

Revealed Messages

"Secrets are like moles. They give you a shaky footing and surface sooner or later." ~ Codee

Tib had to convince Father the ancients' weapons could aid Taluma against the invaders. When he came to Father's chambers, the Pericards stationed there moved to allow him access.

As he entered, the heavy drapes rustled. The window still stood open for that blasted eagle, and it chilled the room too much. The giant bed swallowed Father, and only his face lay uncovered. It appeared almost skeletal—one-third its former size.

Mother hovered over him. Her ready smile never appeared anymore, and the shadows under her eyes grew gloomier by the day. Father's illness had exacted a heavy toll on her.

"How is Father?" Tib asked.

"He's not doing as well as the last few days, so I sent for Carson. How was your morning?"

"The same. They don't listen to me. You should do it."

She wiped a damp rag across Father's brow. His eyes never opened. "He gave you his authority. You only have to do it until he gets better."

Father needed to hurry up and recover, and then Tib would tell him he didn't want to be king. To choose another.

A Pericard opened the door. "Drako's returned, and the healer's coming."

"Good. Send them in." Mother said.

A tingle ran up Tib's spine as Drako entered with the giant wolf, Juno. Drako wanted Tib to spend time alone with the wolf.

Mother shook Father's arm. His eyes opened. "Drako's here."

Father's mouth contorted, but nothing came out. His mouth twisted again, and he weakly croaked, "Drako…glad to see you…tell."

"Sire, I received a message back. The prince's companion and his sub-pack are on their way here."

Great. Tib would have to deal with even more wolves.

"Long?" Father asked.

"They'll lease horses at the clan meeting, so it shouldn't be more than three weeks, Your Majesty."

"Gud. Tib ne wuf to be king."

Tib shook his head. "I'm not ready for a companion yet."

They gray-headed Carson entered as dignified as ever. Father stammered out, "Tell."

Carson's rigid posture softened. "I've done all I can. The king knows he doesn't have long to live."

Mother's sobs pierced the air. "No."

"The medicine you gave him before helped." Tib ordered, "Give him more."

Father's labored breaths filled the room.

Carson wouldn't meet Tib's gaze. "That was only a stimulant to clear his head and give him energy, but I warned him it would speed the infection's onslaught." Carson sighed. "He insisted he had things that needed done."

"Tib, I'm hadeen yus Talum now." Father mangled the words but Tib understood. "Tak car her. Proms me, fallo the Vita."

"Just live." Tib wiped at his tears with his sleeve. "Please. I'm not ready."

Father's lips lifted in a small smile. "K…Kun." And then nothing.

The room became so very quiet. No labored breaths filled it. Carson bent over Father then turned to them. "I'm sorry. He's gone."

Mother threw herself over Father's chest, and her muffled sobs broke Tib's heart. He wanted to join her. He fought to hold back the despair that threatened to enfold him, and the tears that kept escaping. A prince wasn't supposed to lose control. But everything seemed broken. Father gone with so much left unsaid.

He didn't even get the chance to tell Father he loved him or ask him if he loved his son. It was cruel not to let them say goodbye.

Tib rounded on Carson. "You had three months to heal him, and instead you hurry his death. Get out. I don't ever want to see you again."

Carson hurriedly left the room.

Then Tib turned his attention to the Calupi. "Drako, what did his message say?"

"The king has very little time to live. Bring the prince's companion and arrange to hold the choosing so my son can become king."

"You sent that to strangers, then sat me down and talked, but never shared my father was dying. How could you do that to us?"

"I only did what the king asked."

"You're not welcome here. Leave."

"I can't. I agreed to train you, and you agreed to do it. I know you're hurting, but you still need to keep your word and act honorably."

"You're lecturing me about honor when you deceived me and my mother?" He pointed to the Pericards. "Go, before I ask them to remove you." The Pericards drew their swords.

Drako moved toward the door with Juno, then looked back. "I hope you change your mind for your sake and that of Taluma's." They strode out.

Tib turned to the Pericard captain. "Blake, I know I can't fire you, but you need to stay out of my sight. I can't believe you had me listening to petitioners drone on while my Father drew his last breaths."

"I told him I'd keep you guarded, and we just followed his commands. It wasn't my counsel to keep it from you. I *am* sorry for your loss and mine. He was my friend too."

"What friend lets someone he's supposed to protect take something to hasten his death? And you don't have to guard me personally, so get out!"

Blake pivoted on his heels and left the room. Tib went to his mother. "Please. He's gone now. You have to get up." She stood, then buried her face in Tib's chest. He patted her back. "I need you. I don't know if I can do this on my own."

"I'm sorry." She threw up her hands. "I just can't." She ran from the room, crying.

The Pericards opened the door. "Varian's here."

"Let him in."

"Tib, I came as soon as I heard. Whatever I can do to help, just ask."

"I really don't know what to do. I feel so lost." He choked. "I just want Father to get up."

"First, you need to give yourself permission to grieve. It's okay to sink down in that chair and let me take care of everything else." He turned to the Pericards. "What are your burial customs for a king?"

Tib did as Varian suggested, plopped in the chair, and let Varian and the Pericards talk. He put his hands over his face. He never even got to ask Father what he should do about the invaders. It was a scarier world, now, and Tib had to face it alone. His tears dripped through his fingers as he grieved for his father and the life he used to know.

#

The wolf with bared fangs lunged closer. Dayvee steeled himself for the bite. Tayro threw his nails and caught the wolf in her throat. She gasped for breath. Her eyes rolled back, and she collapsed, dead.

"Why'd you kill her?" Dayvee shouted at Tayro. "We could have calmed her down."

"She had rabies." Tayro's face paled. "Even a small bite would have meant your death."

Dayvee took in the tell-tale white foam at her mouth. A shiver ran up his spine. Rabies. No medicine would help that. If he'd been bit, he'd soon be raving and shut away to die alone. Remorse rose. "I'm sorry. I shouldn't have yelled at you."

"It's okay." Tayro shrugged.

"No, it's not." Relief at his escape flooded Dayvee. "Thanks for saving me."

Jaycee leapt in the wagon. *Sorry. It's our job to assess sick wolves. We didn't realize she was crazed until she attacked.*

So that's why guilt was pouring through Dayvee's bond. *You can't assess an unconscious wolf.*

Codee's mouth set in a grim line. "Everyone out. We need to go back to the creek and wash off the disease. Even if you didn't touch her, you may have brushed against something she drooled or bled on." He glanced at Brett. "I suggest you do the same."

A short walk took them to the creek. As Dayvee waded in, the cold stole his breath, and goose bumps rose all over him.

When Dayvee washed Jaycee, he shook, spraying Dayvee. *Thanks.* After they climbed out, Dayvee changed, thankful for his spare clothing's warmth. He packed his wet clothing to hang over the fire when they camped.

Codee turned to Brett. "You should probably burn the wagon and body."

Brett sighed. "I agree."

"You weren't at fault, so you can lease another wolf if you want."

"I do." Brett pointed at the wagon. "She proved her worth."

Codee took a rolled up cloth, a small container of quick-drying dye, and a sharpened bone from his pack. He used the bone dipped in the dye to write on the cloth. "We'll let you know when one's ready."

Brett drove the wagon to a muddy area, free of grass, and unhitched the horse. Dayvee and his friends helped pile wood around the wagon. Brett lit a torch and threw it on the wood. The wagon caught, and soon, flames leapt in the air. Codee led the trainees and their companions away.

On the grasslands, they didn't need to follow a trail, so Dayvee and his friends walked abreast. The companions raced ahead to scout. Tayro plodded behind them. Brando dropped back and clapped him on the shoulder. "Since you protected my family, I've taken you off my list."

Elayni went to Tayro and hugged him. "It would have been awful to have Dayvee get rabies." She grabbed his arm and pulled him up between her and Geno.

Codee stopped and turned to Tayro. "You recognized the danger and acted quickly to protect a pack member, so you earned a red fringe. That makes two red, so you can swap them to get rid of the white now."

Mist came to Tayro's eyes. "Thank you."

Dayvee recalled his own relief at losing a white fringe reminder to protect the pack. Too many enjoyed teaching the wearers a lesson—omega treatment. Tayro took off his white and red fringe and handed them to Codee, who gave him two brown.

Codee pointed to a coyote's track. "There're lots of animals here. Practice speaking to them, Dayvee, and our companions too."

Brando's face scrunched. "When you use your gifts, do you learn all our thoughts?"

All his friends turned concerned faces on Dayvee. Chayla touched her companion's head. "Cato says you asked them not to reveal anything we wouldn't want to share."

"I wouldn't want Jaycee revealing my confidences."

Elayni grabbed his arm. "Thanks."

"You'd do the same for me."

Brando's face turned beet red. They all looked embarrassed.

Codee cleared his throat. "If Dayvee becomes the Kayndo, those who support the Vita will answer his call and take his orders. Any who want to aid him need to be willing to follow his lead."

"We already chose Dayvee to be our sub-pack leader. We'll follow him." Brando slid his boot sideways to scrape off some mud.

"What? When?" Dayvee asked.

"When Kwutee was treating you."

And you didn't think you should share that with me?" Dayvee smoothed his cowlick. "It better not be because my father wants it."

Brando let out a derisive snort. "It had nothing to do with Leeto. It was obvious to us."

Elayni slipped on another patch of mud, but recovered. "If Brando led, we'd be in trouble. I'd run us ragged, Tayro lacks trust, Geno's not a thinker, and Chayla's too shy."

Brando slapped Dayvee's back. "You'll lead us well."

"But you know I've made mistakes—more so than any of you.

I'm not sure I'm the best choice."

"That's okay," Geno declared. "We are."

"They'll never find a leader who doesn't make mistakes. Leaders aren't Kun. Mistakes are the best teacher." Codee leveled a hard look at Dayvee. "Will you accept the burden of the sub-pack's leadership?"

His friends nodded. They believed in Dayvee. "I'm still not sure, but I'll accept and try not to let them or you down."

"Congratulations." Codee clapped his shoulder. "Just so no one's confused, Dayvee leads your sub-pack, but my authority exceeds his as second-in-command of the pack. If we both give you orders, mine are followed first." They resumed walking.

"Do one of your impressions, Elayni," Geno said.

"Who do you want this time?"

"Do Kwutee."

Elayni's face wrinkled and she shuffled, bent over. "Treat others the way you wish to be treated."

"Yup, that's Kwutee." Chayla chewed on her thumb nail. "I wish I could make my voice sound like someone else."

"You can write." Elayni drew herself up. "Each Calupi can benefit the pack if they work hard with whatever gifts Kun blessed them with."

"No more Leeto." Brando shuddered. "I feel like he's looking over my shoulder." They laughed.

As they moved off the grasslands, their companions rejoined them. The trail narrowed so they went to single file, and their voices dwindled. Dayvee's eyes turned gritty as fatigue swept in. Such a long trek on too little sleep.

A root snagged his foot, and he stumbled again. Every one of his friends had tripped often in the last hour. Were they having trouble picking up their feet too? Codee led them back west and then cut north. A gobble alerted them to a turkey. Codee glanced over at Dayvee and Brando and tilted his head toward the noise.

Dayvee crept toward the sound with Jaycee, Brando, and Bruno. He pulled his nails. When he picked out the turkey standing in front of a bush, Dayvee flipped his thumb to signal Brando. One after another their nails bit deep in the turkey's neck and detached the head from the flapping body. Fresh meat for dinner.

Codee gave them a chin lift when they caught up. "Well met. We'll camp at some caves ahead and catch up with the traders in the morning."

The ground sloped down and then flattened. Yellow pines grew predominantly until the woods opened up before a rock cliff face marred with jagged lines. The companions raced forward and disappeared inside the cave closest to the ground, then popped back out.

"Wilee says it's empty. We'll use that one to shelter tonight." Codee ordered, "Gather wood."

Dayvee brought a bundle of branches back. He laid it down and rummaged through his rucksack. Miko gifted them with several flasks of oil before they left.

Dayvee poured the oil into a bowl along with some water. When he threw in a piece of bark with the wick, it floated, so he lit it. Dayvee wasn't afraid of a dark cave, anymore, but he'd learned better than to enter one without a careful scrutiny. He carried his contrived lamp into the entrance.

Bumps and fissures pocked the walls of gray stone. Five strides across and four back measured the cave's size. Just enough room for them all to lie huddled together inside. Codee stuck his head in. "Yes, that's how I remembered it. Build the fire outside and leave room between to get in and out. The heat will still come in to keep us warm enough, as long as it doesn't rain and douse the fire."

Dayvee set the lamp in a cranny. "Maybe one of the other caves is larger."

"No, I've explored them before. They're just as small and involve climbing."

Dayvee took off his rucksack, spread his bedroll out, and withdrew his fire kit. After starting the fire, he and Brando plucked the turkey and cleaned it. Tayro placed some of the meat on skewers with chicory bulbs. He mashed their rose hips and heated them with a little water to make a sauce to dip the skewers in. Rose hips were so tasty it wasn't difficult to eat them like Kwutee urged them to.

When they finished eating, Codee ordered, "Dayvee, set out snares."

After Dayvee and Jaycee returned, he hung his clothes to dry, then sat with the others by the fire. He kept yawning. They couldn't have slept but an hour or two last night, but he couldn't regret the plunging. The sun hadn't set yet, but Dayvee was ready to seek his bedroll. His head kept falling to his chest, and his eyes kept closing. He'd sleep a few seconds and snap awake to resume braiding the rope he worked on.

Codee rose and grabbed the water bags. "I'm going to fill these." He walked away from camp.

"I know what I want my request to be." Chayla put down the scrap of hide she'd written on.

Dayvee forced his eyes open and lifted his head. "What?"

"Whether you become Kayndo or not, I want to write our story, so I need everyone to tell me their feelings each evening about the day's events."

"I can't make everyone, but I agree to tell you mine." Dayvee turned his gaze to Geno. "Have you decided your request?"

"Yes." Geno's hands flashed as he mended a broken strap on Chayla's rucksack. "I know I'm a year younger, but I want to be counted as important too, so will you let me watch your back?"

Dayvee hated to refuse him, but to be asked to guard a leader's back was the second highest honor a pack member could receive in a fight, right after taking loved ones to safety. Those duties were usually assigned to a leader's most trusted—their second and third—and those positions were already taken.

Geno's dark brooding eyes crinkled. "I know I won't be your second or third. I'm not asking for the the title or the job, just the one duty."

Almost like he read his mind. Dayvee usually let Elayni take his back. Brando liked to fight on his left side since he was left-handed. Maybe Dayvee should change it. If the enemies were many, he couldn't see Elayni behind him.

He raised a brow to Brando, who was whittling on a piece of

wood. Brando lifted his pinky. He was okay with it.

"I'll fight at your front." Elayni's dazzling smile revealed that cute dimple that stole his heart.

"Pfft. That's never going to happen. You chose me to lead." Why did his friends keep glancing at each other as if he had said something wrong? The leader always took on the danger first. Red sprinkled all of their eyes. With their exhaustion, maybe they weren't thinking clearly.

"When we form the ring, Elayni can fight at my right, Brando my left. Tayro and Chayla can fight behind them, and Geno, you can take my back.

Geno came over and clasped his arm. "I won't let you down."

Dayvee returned the clasp. "I know you won't." He turned to Tayro. "So do you know your request?"

Tayro put down the bowl with the plants he'd been shredding. "I don't want to watch pack mates suffer when I can help. I want you to let me treat you."

"I can't speak for everyone else, but you can treat me," Dayvee answered.

"If you trust me, most everyone will follow." Tayro picked up his bowl and returned to popping heads off flowers. "Brando, I'm really sorry about helping deliver that message. I hope one day you'll forgive me."

Dayvee's gut twisted. "What message, Tayro?"

Tayro's mouth dropped open. "You never told him?"

Brando shook his head. Elayni's face wrinkled in puzzlement.

Dayvee put down his rope. "I don't think we should keep secrets that affect our sub-pack from each other. Tell me, so I don't have to order someone to do it."

"I only kept it from you to spare you." Brando's pine shavings stopped flying. "When they ganged up on me, they said the leaders didn't think a tiger cub's place was beside the next alpha."

For four long years, Dayvee had been kept in the dark. "What leaders, Tayro?" Dayvee demanded.

"The older kids said it came from the alpha, but I didn't hear Leeto say it."

"Do you know, Brando?"

"I've always known."

Dayvee's heart ached. It came from Leeto. There was no leader Brando thought less of. How could Leeto do that? "No wonder you quit talking to me. Everything you went through was my fault."

"No, never yours, always his. And I didn't quit talking because I blamed you. I quit talking because hate consumed me like it did you. When I realized how much it was hurting me, I let it go. Now will you finally release me, so I can fight them on their terms?"

Heat blazed through Dayvee. There was absolutely no way he'd defend Leeto's action this time. But Dayvee needed to be the one to call him on it. "Not yet."

"But why?" Brando slammed his knife into his pouch. "Why train so hard if you're never going to let us use it?"

Codee and Wilee walked out of the woods. "Good question, Brando, but don't worry. I'll let you use it. Everyone up for fight training."

Wilee joined the the trainees' companions where they sprawled nearby in a clump, resting. Why couldn't their Calupi rest? A groan escaped Dayvee.

Codee's mouth set. "You need to be ready to meet danger, regardless of when it occurs. You can wrestle, punch, and kick, but no interference."

Dayvee stowed his rope in his rucksack. "If something came at us, now, I'd probably lie down and hope they'd get it over with." An exasperated breath escaped. "We can't fight when we're too tired to move."

"That's too bad, since if you fight well, I might be persuaded to let you sleep." Codee paired them up—Elayni and Chayla, Brando and Dayvee, Geno and Tayro. "Okay, go."

There was no way Dayvee was going to fight Brando, but he'd wrestle him. Too bad Brando excelled at wrestling. It wasn't long before Dayvee lay looking at the sky with Brando pinning him. What would Codee say if he fell asleep now?

"Stop." That wasn't Codee's voice. It sounded like Leeto again.

"With me, Dayvee. Everyone else take a break."

Jaycee and Wilee joined them as Dayvee followed Codee a short distance away. Codee turned and faced him. "You should have learned better than this when you fought Andee. You're not even trying. When Leeto and I compete, he might win, but he has to work for it. Brando needs competition."

"Then don't put me against him."

"All right. If you won't fight Brando and show me some blood or bruises, I will. He'll suffer, but he'll improve his skills. Your choice."

Dayvee hated it when Codee acted like Leeto. His father would want Dayvee to pay for a poor performance. But it was his failing, not Brando's.

Jaycee's ruff rose as Dayvee glared at Codee. "Brando won't fight you or Leeto without my release, and I'm not giving it."

"Then he'll take blow after blow until you do."

"No. To hit someone who doesn't fight back is abuse. You can fight *me*."

"I'll fight you both unless you win."

Dayvee did a fast scrutiny to ascertain his footing. Mostly flat ground. No rises, holes, rocks, or sticks. Only grass, pine needles, and leaves. Codee must have cleaned this area for a fight when he sent Dayvee to set snares. He planned this, and there'd be no avoiding it.

Codee came at Dayvee then with a fast punch thrown at his face.

11

Resolving Problems

"Problems are like mice. When you thwart one, another comes along."
~ Codee

Tib wasn't happy with Blake. Varian would know what to do. He hurried to meet with him.

Varian answered Tib's knock. "I'm enjoying the new room. Come on in."

"You deserved it." Thick rugs, tapestries, and sconces softened the stone walls and floor. A large bed and several ornate chairs furnished it, and a fire crackled in the hearth to dispel the chill. Father had the room prepared for Drako, but he wouldn't be needing it now.

Varian flipped a hand toward a tray. "Would you care for anything?"

More of the kitchen staff than Maydlan must have befriended Varian. His movements weren't hindered anymore, but they still brought him trays. Tib grabbed an apple bar. "I bet you found lots of good metal in the ruins."

"A little. Not near enough for our needs. Too much of it's rusted and would be hard to get out, transport, or melt down." Varian held up a mug.

Tib shook his head. He didn't care for the thick, bitter brew Varian called coffee that was popular on his continent. "On the east and south side the ruins have been swallowed by the woods. I bet I could find more if I wasn't stuck here."

"How was your morning?" Varian asked.

"It wasn't good." Tib took a seat in a chair. "Some clanspeople came with their animals." He shuddered. "One had a bear."

Varian sat in the chair opposite him with his cup of coffee. "You shouldn't have to deal with those animals." His face wrinkled in distaste. "I'd ban them from Harthome."

Tib swallowed a bite of the apple bar. That was a good idea, and it would keep any from attacking him. "Blake won't order the Pericards or Kagards into the ruins since they believe it risks their souls. Stupid superstitions."

"You're running out of time." Varian sipped noisily from his cup. "Why do you put up with that?"

"The Kagards and Pericards answer to Blake. They give their oaths to him." Tib finished his apple bar.

"How do they get paid?" Varian asked.

"The Kagards collect the land leases, and the treasurer distributes it."

"Who does the treasurer answer to?"

"My father. I guess me, now."

Varian drained the rest of his cup. "Make your soldiers understand that. Tell them if they want to be paid, they give their oaths to you and do as you say." He smiled. "Otherwise, throw them in the dungeon, and replace them."

Tib wiped the crumbs off his pants. "I could just dismiss them."

Varian's smile faded to a grimace. "And let them turn others against you? Just lock them up long enough to get the guns made. Then you can release them." He put a hand on Tib's shoulder. "If you don't stop the invaders, they'll kill them. Soon, they'll thank you, so why argue now?"

Would his father have approved? Probably not. But what choice did Tib have? Did he have time for arguments when King Nolan wanted to conquer the world? Taluma would fall just like Varian's kingdom had if they didn't prepare.

"I'll think about it." Tib made a face. "Now, I need to go deal with the petitioners again."

Varian dropped his arm and shook his head. "They *are* insufferable. If you want, you can go to the ruins, and I'll see them for you."

"Can I do that?"

"Sure. Just like your father did with you. Appoint me regent and give me your authority when you're absent."

It would be nice if Tib didn't have to listen to their bickering, and he could find the metal easier than Varian. He knew those ruins well. "I might take you up on that, tomorrow."

"I hate to add to your worry, but you should read these notes." Varian handed him two slips of paper.

Tib scanned them. *Go back to your continent, or we'll kill you.*

You got in our way last time, you won't the next. Leave before you die.

Tib jumped up. "Do you know who they're from?"

"No, they were slipped under my door. The writing doesn't even look the same. But someone might try again to kill you."

Tib paced the room. His anxiety increased. Would they attack him again? Or Varian? "I'll assign you Kagards. I don't want to lose you."

"Tib, the Kagards don't like me since I'm not afraid of the ancients' things. The threats might be from them. If you want people to guard me, let me choose them."

"That's fine. Hire whom you want. I'll let the treasurer know."

Tib hurried from the room and through the halls. He kept jumping at the Pericards footfalls behind him.

#

Dayvee sidestepped and Codee's fist sailed past his left cheek. Fury at his father and uncle fueled him, his muscles tensed and burned with desire to be unleashed. He'd show Codee what fighting Andee taught him. *Hit hard! Hit now! Hit with everything!*

Dayvee plowed his fist into Codee's stomach. His uncle bent, and Dayvee jabbed Codee's nose. His head snapped back, blood flowing from his nostril. Codee's arm rushed forward. Dayvee dodged but not fast enough. Codee's blow connected—the pain was as if splinters flew into Dayvee's eye. *Punch back! Punch back*! He pounded, ducked Codee's fist, threw a punch into Codee's eye,...*there, how's it feel...* then sidestepped Codee's kick.

Jaycee and Wilee watched from outside the ring. Other animals whispered to Dayvee. He tightened his focus to him, Codee, and Jaycee. The rhythm of the fight flowed through his mind and body, his training kicked in, and his thoughts and movements became almost instinctual. Lock onto Codee. Keep pounding. Draw back. Arms up to block. Don't let anything connect. Codee fired punch after punch. Dayvee avoided them, easily, like in the game he and Brando played.

Circle him, Jaycee sent. *Keep searching for an opening. Any weakness.*

No one would abuse Dayvee's friends. He didn't care if it was Leeto in Codee's skin. The wolf side found a weakness.

Dayvee swept his foot into Codee's knee. The joint buckled, and Dayvee drove his fist into his uncle's face, hitting his right temple. Codee fell. Dayvee jumped on him. He reached for Codee's throat, but his uncle threw his legs up and flung Dayvee off. They both leaped up. Dayvee's heels rose, and his weight shifted. His body had returned to his fighting stance without thought.

Codee's eyes sparkled. He and Leeto *did* enjoy fighting. Dayvee would teach his uncle there was nothing to like. Dayvee and Jaycee appraised Codee for a weakness. They'd find another opening. The nape of Dayvee's neck heated. A growl surged to the back of his throat as he stalked Codee.

His uncle unclenched his fists and held his hands up palms out. "Okay, that's enough. I'm not going to fight Brando. That was a test to see if you could be motivated to fight hard. You passed."

It took a second for it to sink in. Dayvee dropped his fists. His concentration relaxed, and he took in his surroundings. His friends ringed them. When had they come?

"Well met." Codee chuckled. "For a moment there I thought you might beat me."

"You just didn't give Dayvee time, or he'd have won." Brando's eyes met Dayvee's. "Sorry, Codee told us it was a test, and we couldn't interfere."

Dayvee gave him a nod. He understood.

Codee's eyes twinkled as they fell on Brando "You were right."

Elayni put a hand on her hip. "Brando?"

Heat surged through Dayvee. Why had Brando been talking to Codee again? He took a breath to keep his tone civil. "What were you right about?"

"Codee asked if you'd fight hard if he threatened me. I told him you're ferocious when you defend your family." Brando wagged his eyes. "But I warned him not to try it unless he wanted to lose."

Dayvee released another breath heavily. "You *really* need to quit talking to Codee."

Brando gave him his impish grin. "I was hoping you'd release me, but either way, you needed to learn you don't have to take Leeto's dung anymore."

Beads of sweat dotted Codee's forehead. "What we need is everyone's best effort. If you train your body to always hold back, when the threats are real, you *won't* fight fierce, and your friends *will* die." Codee tilted his head toward their bedrolls. "You can all bed down now. He glanced at Tayro. "Do you have something for Dayvee's eye? I'm afraid it's going to be black."

"I'll make a compress to help." Tayro scrutinized Codee. "You might want one too. I'm afraid both your eyes are going to be black, and your nose is swelling."

After putting the compress over his face, Dayvee crawled into his bedroll. A few frogs croaked. They must be through hibernating. Their calls lulled him.

Before sleep claimed him, he said a quick prayer to thank Kun for his escape from the rabid wolf. What would have happened if Tayro hadn't joined their sub-pack? He couldn't imagine a worse death.

. . .

Dayvee and Jaycee were last on guard duty. The sky had lightened. Sunrise wasn't far off. He fed Jaycee and cooked some grain into gruel for breakfast. It shouldn't be long before everyone woke. Coughing broke the quiet. It came from Geno again. Was he getting sick? Geno's eyes cracked open to slits.

You better do it soon, Jaycee sent.

Dayvee contained his mirth as he set his plan into motion. *Now.*

A dozen frogs croaked in Codee's ear. He leapt up with a yell.

The trainees' eyes shot open as the frogs jumped away from Codee.

Dayvee released his laughter, and it spilled out into the morning. Jaycee cocked his ear in a wolf laugh. His friends joined in.

Brando held his stomach and wiped tears from his eyes. Finally, Brando was really laughing. "Almost as funny as mine, Dayvee, but you should have shared so I could have watched Codee's reaction from the beginning."

Codee gritted his teeth. "Dayvee?"

"You keep saying I need to talk to animals more, and I was just checking to see if you'd be ready to encounter danger."

Codee threw his shoulders back. "Do you want to lift boulders?"

"I was following your instructions. If you want to punish me, fine—but only me. No one else knew, except for Jaycee."

"If you and your friends agree not to pull any more pranks on me, I'll let that one go." Codee filled Wilee's bowl with meat. "But if you don't, all of you can lope all the way to the clan meeting."

"Dayvee's pretty fast. Do you think you could keep up with him?" Brando and the other trainees rose to feed their companions and eat.

"Just try me."

"Is everyone willing to stop pulling pranks on Codee?" Dayvee asked.

"Not forever, but I'll agree not to prank him until we arrive at the clan meeting." Brando grabbed a bowl of gruel.

The other trainees' stopped eating to give him a nod. "All right, until the clan meeting. "Will you accept that, Codee?" Dayvee stowed his and Jaycee's bowl in his rucksack.

"Agreed."

Dayvee put out the fire, as everyone gathered their things, and cleaned up their camp. Then Codee led them away from the caves. "I'm going to have you work on your skills. The traders are going to teach you about trading, so we'll work on leading now. Since you've chosen Dayvee to lead, he'll start, but each of you will have a turn and learn something about it." He beckoned to Dayvee. "Come up front."

When Dayvee and Jaycee joined him and Wilee, Codee said, "You'll be making the decisions. But if we face a dangerous situation,

I'll step in. Just keep taking us north. I'll let you know if we need to pick up another trail."

As they left the plains and climbed a foothill, the trees became more numerous, and the trail narrowed. Codee and Wilee dropped behind Dayvee and Jaycee. As they traveled, the sun's rays warmed the crisp air. A dogwood tree still held a few delicate white petals with pink dimples on the end, but most lay like a carpet underneath. The three tear drops of a deer track crushed some as it trod over them. Must have been nibbling on the blooms.

Dayvee kneeled and touched the print. The sides felt damp, so it was fresh. "We have plenty of rations and need to hurry, so maybe this isn't the time to hunt."

Codee gave him a head tilt. "I agree."

They came to a patch of yellow flowers above shiny, heart-shaped leaves. March Marigold. Tayro stopped. "These are good for coughs. I want to gather some to help Geno, if he'll trust me?"

Graydee cocked his head, revealing Geno's uncertainty. Dayvee sighed inwardly. It might be really difficult for Geno to trust Tayro with March Marigold. It was edible, like spinach if boiled several times and leached, but poisonous if not prepared properly.

"You can treat me." Geno finally answered.

"Okay," Dayvee said. "You and Tayro collect them, get some for us to eat, too, then catch up."

. . .

The clouds in the sky grew darker and opened. More rain. The slow, but steady fall chilled Dayvee and turned the damp ground to mud, splattering his pants as they moved through the woods.

Jaycee's coat lay flattened, making the wolf appear a little smaller, but not much. *The traders are close.*

Dayvee caught movement ahead where the trees ended at a clearing. The trader's stopped and waited for them to catch up. Codee had Elayni leading now. She straightened her posture. Was she still trying to get her parent's recognition and approval?

Brando and Bruno trotted beside Dayvee and Jaycee through the thinning trees. Brando's shoulders still hunched as he plodded along, slinging mud. Maybe he needed to get his mind off his own problems with Jonesee. Dayvee whispered to him, "I think Elayni's going to get her hopes crushed again."

A frown creased Brando's face, then it lifted, and his mischievous crooked grin appeared. "Thanks, Dayvee. This is a great time to cross Franko's name on my list." His feet picked up, and his gait increased.

"No, I didn't mean for you to do that." Dayvee couldn't let it happen. "Do I have to order you not to?"

Brando and Bruno jumped over a log. "How long do we have to keep taking them treating us like dung?"

"We don't have time for challenges." Dayvee and Jaycee weaved around one side of a tree as Brando and Bruno went around the other. "Codee would send you back to the pack, and we need you."

When they reached the traders, Franko moved around Elayni and Evee to Codee and inclined his head toward Wilee. "He filled our companions in on your trouble." Then Franko went over to Tayro and clasped his arm. "Well met."

A big smile crossed Tayro's face. "Thanks."

Franko hadn't even acknowledged Elayni. Her face fell as Codee and Franko passed her and walked up together to lead the entire group.

"We should try to make Elayni happy. Let me talk to Franko," Brando whispered. "We might not have another chance."

Codee looked over his shoulder at the trainees. "Franko is going to teach you now about what the traders do."

Franko's voice rose above the slow patter of the rain. Everyone bunched close together as he explained how to examine goods, avoid being tricked, and get the best bargain.

Dayvee flashed Brando the signal for retreat. He and Brando snuck to the rear with their companions. "Just talk?" he asked softly.

"Yes. Franko isn't going to challenge me, but he can't know I won't."

Dayvee would like for Elayni to have some happiness. "All right. What can I do to help?"

"Distract Codee, and don't jump in if things unravel."

Dayvee stopped his tapping foot. "You should know better. I'll have your back, but do you think that will happen?"

"No." Brando's sheepish smile peeked out. "But there have been a few times when I was wrong."

Hopefully this wasn't one of them. They crept up to rejoin the others.

"Each of you will help the traders pull a travois." Codee motioned to Franko's. "You'll act as if you're selling the load. When you come to an agreement, you'll try to buy the load. Afterwards, they'll give you advice. Then switch, and go to the next trader until you've tried to purchase and sell goods to each."

How could Dayvee distract Codee when he couldn't lie? Did he need to? The truth would get his attention. "Codee, can I talk to you, alone?"

Codee nodded once and turned to the other trainees. "Just keep following the traders. We'll be right back."

Jaycee and Wilee came, too, as Dayvee and Codee dropped behind the others. "You shouldn't put Brando with Franko and Tinay if you want friendly."

Codee slipped on some wet grass and caught himself. "They're on his list too?"

Dayvee's feet sunk in a puddle, and some of the water came into his boots. "I'm not saying."

"How many are on this list?" Codee asked.

Dayvee's boot's squished at every step. "I think four, since Petee and Chancee were exiled, and Tayro was removed."

"So Elayni's parents, me, and Leeto?"

"You'd have to ask Brando. I don't have any say over it and can't get names removed."

"So why isn't Jonesee on his list?"

"His list isn't about who hurt him, but his family. If I had say over it, Jonesee'd be on it."

"I can't make exceptions." Codee's eyes narrowed. "He needs to learn to be friendly with everyone in the pack."

"I know we all serve the Vita, but there's more than one path. Do you think Elayni's parents acted irresponsibly when they left her nine months of every year?" Codee didn't answer. "Brando and I both do, and he'll tell them sooner or later."

"He's trying my patience." Codee wiped rain from his face. "If he formally challenges or accepts one, he'll go home."

"You hurt Elayni!" Brando's shout rang out. "One of you should have stayed."

Brando's baring his teeth. Jaycee's cocked ear told him the wolf was laughing. They ran forward.

Everyone else had spread out to ring them. Dayvee wormed himself between Calupi to push to the front. Brando stood toe to toe with Franko.

"It was selfish to make her fend for herself." Brando's fists were balled, but Bruno wasn't growling from where he watched with the other companions. "Why have a child if you don't want one?"

"You don't have the status to challenge Franko, trainee," Julee yelled. He was Franko's second, and if he believed Brando was going to break the law and hit Franko without a merited challenge, he might jump in. Franko's entire sub-pack could follow. If Codee approved, they might go as far as to give Brando a harsh lesson and call it fight training.

Dayvee might need to spring to Brando's aid any second.

12

Losing Control

"If you believe you can control everything, you're lying to yourself." ~
Kwutee.

Tib was wet, cold, and miserable. The rubble in the ruins was harder
to sort through in the rain. The twisted metal and concrete weighed
even more when sodden. The gloomy forest around him reflected his
mood.

Of course, it could be worse. He could be stuck listening to
petitioners and arguing with his advisors. Thankfully, Varian was there
to deal with them. Tib had given Varian the authority to be his regent
and speak for him when he was absent. Varian knew what they'd face
with the invaders, and what they should do to prepare. That was the
most important thing. And Varian seemed to enjoy it. Tib sure didn't.

Tib wore gloves, but he still used a stick to poke through the
rubble. Aha, a lead pipe. They could use that. He worked it out from
the mess and threw it in the pile he'd collected to take to the cart.

He grabbed at another, but it wouldn't give. He yanked at it
harder. The pile shifted and slid, bringing rubble down on him. He
jumped back, retreating until the pile settled. Another close call. He
had only collected enough for a few more weapons, and they needed
hundreds. It would have to be enough for today. It was getting late, and
he wanted to get dry. He grabbed the armful and made his way out of
the ruins to the cart where the Pericards waited. They wouldn't be
happy if they knew how Tib risked himself, but they wouldn't enter the
ruins.

This would go much faster if Tib had help. He needed to do as
Varian had suggested and replace them. The kingdom didn't have time

for their superstitions if they were going to be ready to meet the invaders.

#

The Calupi around the ring jostled Dayvee for a good view. The taut bodies of men and wolves alike signaled to Dayvee they believed there'd be a fight. How long before they jumped in?

They stood on wet grass and mud in the meadow they clustered in, but there weren't many rocks. Slick footing, but not impossible. Brando's jaw was set, and his fists were clenched as he glowered at Elayni's father.

How far would Brando push this? Dayvee checked Bruno. The wolf's ruff wasn't up. He turned back to Brando. His heels touched the ground. They had spent a lot of hours perfecting their fighting stance. If Brando planned to fight, he'd be in it.

Elayni stepped into the ring and sidled in between Brando and Franko. She put her hand on Brando's chest. "Don't do this. Back away."

Only a pack leader could enter once a fight ring was established, but it wasn't really. The Calupi and wolves standing in a circle weren't a ring of stone. Of course, if Codee called it fight training, they didn't have to have a ring. But Codee wasn't admonishing Elayni for interfering.

"I'm done retreating," Brando declared. "They should learn how much they hurt you."

Codee yelled, "Back up, Brando!"

Brando didn't move. Elayni grabbed his rucksack and tried to pull him away. Brando slid his arm from his rucksack and let her have it.

"Please, it's done." A tear ran down her cheek. "I don't need them now."

Brando's eyes softened. He reached his finger out, wiped her tear, then leaned in and kissed her forehead. "No, you don't. You have me and Dayvee...but they should still learn."

Dayvee's stomach knotted. In Brando's mind, did he just kiss a friend, or the girl he wanted to life-mate? Better worry about that later. Would Codee let Dayvee enter the ring? If things fell apart, he wanted to be as close as he could get. He strode to Brando's side and pretended to admonish him. "This isn't a good time for a challenge. The traders need to get to the clan meeting, and injuries could make that harder."

Franko's face twisted. "You're right, Brando. We hurt Elayni, and I *do* know it. Our skills as traders benefitted the pack, but one of us should have stayed." His eyes locked with Elayni's. "I'm sorry. We *do* love you."

"You have a little time to make it up to her," Brando snarled. "I don't think you can, but I suggest you try."

Elayni dropped Brando's rucksack, went to Franko, and hugged him. Brando grabbed his rucksack and winked at Dayvee. "Come on."

Dayvee and Brando moved back with their companions. The ring opened and let them out, then disintegrated as Codee hollered, "Franko, lead them to the river. We'll catch up. Brando and Dayvee, follow me."

"Just a second, Codee. I need to collect on a bet, and I might as well give you more to yell about." Brando caught up to Chayla, who was already moving away with the others. She spun around. He grabbed her, leaned down, and kissed her on the lips. "Mmmm. Best winnings, yet."

Chayla's face flamed as Brando trotted back to Codee and Dayvee. "Okay, now you can yell."

Codee snapped, "You defied my order, Brando."

"No," Brando grumbled. "I was just slow following it."

"This wasn't the time for confrontations, but you lose control too easily and let your emotions rule you."

Dayvee shuffled his feet to fight the chill. "Brando was very much in control, and he had my permission. Elayni needed Franko and Tinay to acknowledge her before she left."

Wilee's stiff posture told him Codee still seethed. He turned his anger on Dayvee. "There're better ways to get the same result than calling out a leader in front of everyone."

Codee and Leeto never seemed to have any qualms about criticizing Dayvee in front of everybody. Maybe Dayvee should have tried something else first, but what Brando did worked.

Codee turned back to Brando. "You still disregarded *my* order, but you better not be slow to follow *these*." He shook his finger at him. "Don't even think about getting too friendly with Calupi girls until a life-mate ceremony, and the only time you can be unfriendly to anyone is if I okay it. Do you understand?"

Brando's eyes narrowed. "Yes, I think you're really worried about being on my list. You should be."

"I'm out of patience with you." Codee took his rucksack off. "I'd like to give you some fight training, right now."

Bruno and Wilee both stiffened. Brando flung his own rucksack a few feet away and balled his fists. His legs spread to the width of his shoulders, and his heels lifted as he balanced on the balls of his feet. Now, Brando was serious. "If you can get Dayvee to release me, I'd love for you to learn better than to hurt my family."

"Why do you think I asked him to come?"

Codee and Brando turned eager faces on Dayvee. Their readiness was clear in their tense bodies, like coiled snakes ready to spring. Brando had tightened his abdomen, and his biceps stood rigid.

Dayvee crossed his arms. "You both know we don't have the time for fights or injuries." Brando's heels fell to the ground.

Codee released a heavy breath. "Lucky for you, he's right."

"You're the one with a lucky reprieve, and you better stop hurting my family." Brando stomped to his rucksack, grabbed it, then broke into a trot to catch the others. Bruno trailed him.

"I haven't done anything you haven't." Codee shouted after him. What did he mean by that? Codee glanced over at Dayvee. "Are you going to protect him forever?"

"Brando and I did the same training. Why are you so certain I'm shielding him?"

"If you're worried about me, don't be." Codee smirked. "I've watched him fight."

"It always shocks me when people underestimate Brando, again and again." Dayvee shook his head. "You only saw what he wanted you to."

#

It warmed Brando to hear Elayni's laughter resounding over the sloshing of the nearby river. She rose from where she sat with the adults on the other side of the fire and practically skipped over to where the sub-pack spread their bedrolls out.

"Do you mind if I sleep over with them?" she pointed to her parents.

"Of course not." Dayvee waved her off.

She took her bedroll around the fire while the rest of the sub-pack got into theirs. Their companions curled up together at their feet.

Dayvee turned away from watching the stars to face Brando. "You did good, my brilliant friend."

Guilt pressed down on Brando. The weight was too difficult to bear when Dayvee believed in him so much. He couldn't even lift his head. "Tell Codee that."

A crash startled Brando, and their companion's heads popped up. Embers streamed into the sky from a log that had fallen apart in the fire.

"I did. But we aren't supposed to be kissing girls before a life-mating ceremony, and you kissed two in front of everyone. What did you expect?"

Brando had held a secret crush on Elayni for years, but she only wanted Dayvee. Brando tried to stop thinking of her, but she kept invading his mind. Lately, Chayla's face had been crowding her out. His kiss on Elayni's forehead wasn't much. His body never even responded to it. But when he kissed Chayla, it was like a sucker punch to the gut. It let out all his air and left him reeling. Now, he wanted more. "I don't regret that."

Geno turned a glare on Brando. Did Chayla's affection belong to another, too? But Chayla hadn't acted like his kiss wasn't wanted. Her lips also moved. Maybe this time he was in the running. Who was he fooling? It was a bet. She wouldn't really be interested in the one the pack called tiger.

"So what was the bet?" Dayvee asked.

Chayla propped her head up on her arm. "I told him if he confronted Franko, it would turn into a fight. He bet me a wood carving of Cato against a kiss that it wouldn't."

"I should have warned you to never bet against Brando." Dayvee chuckled. "He doesn't lose."

#

The next morning, the cold drizzle still fell and chilled Dayvee. The mountains rose above him on both sides, but gray skies obscured the tops. The deep mauve of the lone redbud tree offered a sharp contrast to the green pines along the river, but the color lay muted behind the mist. He took a deep breath, and the crisp scents of water and pine filled his lungs. The rain's patter with the river lapping against the shore added a gentle refrain.

Dayvee stood with their group at their usual fording point where the river bank wasn't as steep, and the span was wider, probably two hundred feet across. Here, the water didn't run so swiftly and wasn't as deep, so they probably only had to swim half. He didn't spot any white caps, and the water wasn't churning.

"I thought the river would be higher with all the rain." Codee threw a stick and watched it drift downstream. "We should be able to cross safely."

Franko turned and hugged Elayni. "We need to take the longer bridge route with our loads, so we'll have to part here." Then Tinay embraced her. Dayvee, Codee, and his friends clasped forearms with the traders. Their companions touched noses.

"May Kun go with you," the traders called as they moved off, pulling their loads across the valley.

"And also with you," the sub-pack replied.

The rain stopped and the sun peeked out. "I don't think we've seen the last of the rain, so let's get across." Codee wrapped a leather strip around his weapons, securing it to his belt. "Make sure your weapon pouches don't come loose." He pulled off his boots. "Stow your outer clothing and boots, then tie your rucksack to your belt so you're not encumbered as you swim."

Dayvee snugged the ties tight on his weapons. They had too much sentimental value to lose. A part of Clay, his mother's first companion, still protected him.

"Won't our rucksacks get water logged?" Geno asked.

"They'll float for a while, and we'll dry everything on the other side," Codee replied. "They probably won't hinder your swim, but we'll make sure. If they get caught, cut them loose. I prefer to lose things over Calupi."

After Dayvee finished his preparations, he scrambled down the bank. He and Jaycee waded out behind Codee and Wilee. When the water rose to Dayvee's neck, he swam. A quick glance behind him found his rucksack and his friends all trailing him. Half-way across now. He should be able to touch soon. A thundering roar pierced the air from upstream. A huge wave of churning water rocketed toward them. Dayvee gasped. *Oh, no. Kun help us.*

Codee's shout was barely heard. "Swim!"

Dayvee put his head down and stroked faster. He reached the point where his feet could touch, so he stood and ran through the water for the bank. The deluge caught him and knocked him over, tossing him as if he were a leaf. The wave poured over him, and the water rose as he tumbled in the turbulence. Then it passed, leaving the water deeper. He reached down with his feet and found purchase in the pebbly grit. It swirled between his toes as the current still pushed against his legs, aiming to sweep them out from under him.

Grit stung his eyes. A quick swipe cleared his vision enough to look for Codee, Jaycee, and his friends.

I'm okay, Jaycee paced the bank. All their companions had reached it.

Codee stood only an arms' length in front of him, and the bank was just a few feet beyond him. His uncle reached his hand back. Dayvee grabbed on and stretched his arm behind him to Brando, who already had Elayni in his grasp. Brando clutched on to Dayvee's hand, and he towed them closer. Where were Tayro, Geno, and Chayla?

Dayvee kept scanning and found Tayro, not so far away, and trudging closer to shore. There was Geno, farther downstream, but near the bank they needed to reach, using some brush to pull himself up.

Dayvee's gut wrenched when he finally located Chayla. The wave's maelstrom still claimed her in its grip downstream in the center of the river. Her arms thrashed, and she struggled to swim while the current swept her farther from them.

Dayvee needed to help her. With one frantic yank, he brought Brando close enough to put his hand in Codee's. Then Dayvee grabbed his knife, cut the line to his rucksack, and threw it on shore.

Brando's eyes widened as his gaze fixed on Chayla. His face filled with horror, and he shouted, "Take Elayni, and let me go."

"No, I swim faster." Dayvee turned and ran into the current.

Codee hollered. All Dayvee caught was Brando's name and something about a rope, but he didn't wait to learn more. No time. Chayla's head had bobbed under again. He drove his body toward Chayla with all his strength.

If he could only save Chayla, he'd never again complain that swimming fast meant nothing. The current took him swiftly. He stopped a few times to locate Chayla's bobbing head. If he didn't position himself right, the current could take him past her. Almost there. Her head bobbed down again and didn't come back up.

No! Dayvee got to the part where he saw her last. Frantic, he dove down through the churning depths and stretched his legs and arms around in the water. Something brushed his leg. His hand clamped onto the rough texture of a rope. Must be the line that tied Chayla's rucksack to her. One end seemed heavier.

He broke the surface and heaved on the rope, treading water and letting the river batter him and sweep him farther. Chayla's waist, and then her shoulders, broke the surface. Dayvee wrapped an arm under her and brought her face out of the water. She made a choking sound.

Dayvee lifted Chayla onto his chest and held her there while he struck out for shore. Clawing the water with one hand, he couldn't swim fast enough on his back to fight the seething current, so he cut a diagonal path. It would bring them to the shore eventually. He strained harder to make up for not using an arm.

Out of the corner of his eye, Dayvee spied an approaching tree trunk slicing through the river's current straight for them. It might go over the top of him onto Chayla. With no time to escape, he flipped on his side, supported Chayla's head, and put his back to the trunk, shielding her. It whacked into his shoulder so hard it threw them forward, and then bounced off to twirl around them, brushing his head. Pain knifed his shoulder. Maybe he should have grabbed onto the trunk. Too late now. Plus, who knows where they'd have ended up.

Dayvee gently lifted Chayla again and tried to swim. The agony stole his breath, and he couldn't make his shoulder or arm move right. He switched and managed to use the injured arm to hold Chayla. His left arm and feet would have to propel them to shore.

Dayvee's body dragged wearily, and his shoulder throbbed as he drew closer to the bank. A cramp ricocheted through his right leg.

Could he reach now? He sent his feet down and felt the rocks, so he stood supporting most of the weight on his left leg. Thankfully, the current didn't suck at his feet here. Chayla had only made that one choking sound in all this time. His bad arm still pressed her to his chest, so he switched arms to lay her back to see her face. Had she already met Kun?

13

Lost Refuge

"Refuge is always available if you seek it through Kun." ~ Kwutee.

Chayla's tiny body stood out against the backdrop of the muddy water—so white, lips blue. She lay limp in his arm and didn't draw a breath. Dayvee's anguish rose. Had he been too late? No. She couldn't be dead. Kwutee had shown them how to breathe for someone. Dayvee pinched her nose, put his mouth over hers, and blew in. Her chest lifted. She sputtered. Water spewed from her mouth. She coughed and then drew in another breath. Her eyes fluttered open.

Relief flooded Dayvee. "Don't worry, I have you."

She hacked a couple more times. The blue had left her lips, but even her freckles appeared pale. "Thanks." She grabbed his arm and shakily stood.

Dayvee steadied her. "You all right?"

"Yes. But I want out of this river."

Now that he had stopped swimming, the cold sank in. Water dripped from his hair, and silt had his eyes stinging again. The taste of fish clung to his lips, and the heavy damp scent seemed cloying.

Chayla took a step toward the bank and wobbled. "My rucksack's heavy."

"It's waterlogged. You'll have to help me pull it in. My shoulder's messed up."

Together they hauled it out of the water. Dayvee grabbed his knife to cut the rope. "I think I can get it over." He gestured toward the steep bank, at least twice his height.

"Go ahead," she said.

Dayvee took the rucksack with his left hand and let the water pour from it. When it slowed to a drip, he threw it. It didn't make it over, but snagged near the top on a projecting rock. Close enough. Now, for them. The bank's sharp face lifted straight up from the water. Could he and Chayla climb it? With one arm, it seemed impossible. They could walk the shallow edge of the river to where the bank wasn't as steep, but Chayla already shivered from the cold.

We're here, Jaycee sent. He, Cato, Bruno, and Wilee paced the bank's edge.

Brando's and Codee's faces peered over the top. A rope sailed toward Dayvee. Yes.

He wrapped it around him and Chayla. "Can you tie it?"

Her fingers trembled, but she made a secure knot.

Together with Brando and Codee pulling, they clambered up the bank. When they neared the top, Brando grabbed Dayvee's right arm and lifted them over.

Dayvee's scream escaped before he thought, but he managed to cut it off short and gnash his teeth. Pain ripped through his shoulder. A pop sounded.

Brando's hands flew off Dayvee, and he bit his lip. "I'm sorry. I didn't know you were hurt."

Jaycee nudged Dayvee. *Feels better now.*

He was right. Pain no longer stabbed Dayvee's arm. "I think you fixed it."

Chayla fumbled with the rope. Brando grabbed the knot and unraveled it. "Are you okay, Chayla?

Her lip trembled. "Yes, only cold and tired."

Brando embraced her and scooped her off her feet to lay her down. "You should rest." He grabbed her hands and rubbed them, oblivious to everyone else. So it *was* Chayla who held Brando's heart. Dayvee's worry over competing with Brando for Elayni evaporated.

Codee turned to Dayvee. "We need a fire. Are you able to collect wood?"

Dayvee flexed his arm. Just an ache. "Yes."

"All right, I'll go back and help the others." He strode off with the rope.

Chayla still had the shakes. When Dayvee and Elayni had survived falling through the frozen lake, the animals helped them warm up.

Call them, Jaycee sent.

"I'll ask animals to warm you until I can get a fire going, so don't worry when they come."

Chayla's eyes widened. "Thanks, I won't."

Dayvee reached out to the animals nearby. *I'd be grateful if anyone with a warm coat would come and share some warmth.*

A raccoon and squirrel scampered down from trees maybe twenty feet away. A rabbit emerged from a hole and hopped over to them, trying to avoid the coyotes flitting through the grass. A fox bounded through the brush, ignoring the mink winding through it. A groundhog popped up from an earthen mound and waddled over. All of them lay across Chayla to warm her.

Dayvee walked to the tree line and gathered the driest branches where the trees grew more dense. When he returned with his arms loaded with wood, Brando still sat with Chayla's hands in his.

"I'll need your fire kit." Dayvee dropped the wood. "Mine's back on the bank somewhere."

Brando took off his rucksack, grabbed his fire kit, and handed it to him. Dayvee lathered the kindling with the fungus, struck the stones together, and lit it. Then fed it more wood.

Brando tore his gaze from Chayla. "It seems awful to say now, but you should have let me go."

Dayvee scratched his head. "Why? I swim faster."

"But we may need a Kayndo, so you can't be the one to take risks. Let me confront the danger."

Did he want to coddle Dayvee? Jaycee sent, *Doesn't he know what he's asking?*

How could he not? But I won't give up self-respect.

"Brando, I'm not hiding while you deal with the danger. Whatever else I become, I'm Calupi." Dayvee couldn't keep his exasperation from his voice. "Don't ask me to slink."

Codee and the rest of the trainees jogged up to them. They gaped at the blanket of animals over Chayla. Tayro turned wide eyes on him as if he were seeing Kun. Codee sported a wide grin. Geno took a step back—as if Dayvee were a hyena. Elayni raised her brows.

Was it so shocking? They had discussed Dayvee's gift, and they knew about the frogs he called to prank Codee. Maybe it was because there were several different animals this time. Were they going to treat him weird now? Dayvee's spirits dropped.

"Tayro, can you check Chayla?" Codee asked.

"Sure, if the animals will move, and she'll trust me."

You can go now. Thanks for coming, Dayvee sent to the animals. They scurried away.

"I think everyone will agree we can trust Tayro," Codee said. They all nodded, and Tayro knelt beside Chayla."

Elayni held out his rucksack to Dayvee. Her hand shook. She must be cold. Surely, she wasn't afraid of him. Dayvee grabbed it. "Thanks."

"Get the wet stuff laid out by the fire," Codee ordered.

After he spread his stuff, Dayvee speared Chayla's rucksack and laid out hers.

"What caused the river to do that?" Geno asked.

"There must have been some obstruction upstream." Tayro put some raspberry and nettle leaves in a pan of water to make tea.

Codee slapped his leg. "Exactly. The pressure of more rain must have broken it free, and that huge wave came down. I should have taken the longer route. I knew the river was too shallow."

Dayvee laughed. "Are you saying you made a mistake?"

Codee eyes sparkled, and he smiled. "Doesn't happen often, but I told you leaders weren't Kun."

"Everyone should have some tea," Tayro said. "It will warm you and give you energy."

They drank the tea, and Codee checked their things. "These are dry enough. I want some distance between us and this flooding river."

Tayro took Chayla's empty cup. "She needs more time to recover."

"I don't want to hold everyone up." Chayla trembled. "I'll be okay."

You'll hold us up if you get worse," Codee's tone rang with authority. "Geno, make a travois for Chayla to ride in."

The pain in Dayvee's shoulder had receded to a twinge, but his muscles felt too tight. He rubbed them. Codee looked over at him. "Tayro, will you check Dayvee's shoulder?"

"Sure." Tayro moved toward him.

"I trust Tayro, but it's not necessary. I'm fine."

"Who asked you?" Codee snapped. "It's a leader's responsibility to make sure their Calupi can perform their duties, and no one gets to tell us differently."

Codee was acting like Leeto again. Dayvee slid his shirt off. Tayro probed his shoulder. "No numbness or loss of feeling?"

"There's just a little stiffness."

Tayro let go of his arm. "The swelling should go down tomorrow, but once you dislocate it, they go out easier." Dayvee hoped to avoid that.

"Did you hear me tell you to let Brando go?" Codee asked as they changed into dry clothes.

"No. I heard only the words *Brando* and *rope*."

Codee handed him a red fringe. "I don't want you earning more of these."

So Codee, too? Dayvee put the fringe on. "Leeto said if I ever left pack-mates in danger to slink off and hide, I'd earn his disgust."

"Things change."

Not that much. Calupi loathed cowards. As soon as they got Chayla situated on the travois, Brando took the poles, and Codee led them away from the river at an easy trot.

"Geno, pull the travois," Codee ordered. "Dayvee, take the lead. Brando, with me."

What did Codee want with Brando? Dayvee glanced back at them. Brando's hands moved wildly, and a frown dotted his face.

Codee looked up, saw Dayvee watching, and dropped back farther. *Jaycee, can you hear what they're saying?*

Yes, but Luko's ordered us companions not to reveal the leader's confidences. That doesn't mean I can't help you learn for yourself.

Dayvee smiled to himself. *Will you share your hearing?*

Of course.

Every bird call got louder. Dayvee heard the slight breeze rustling, and Brando's voice seemed right next to him. "You couldn't stop him either."

"You were supposed to talk to him," Codee said.

"I did," Brando retorted. "He refused. Blame the leaders who taught him never to turtle."

Aha. So Codee had put Brando up to that. But when did Brando become a willing pawn for Codee and Leeto to use? Dayvee's anger spiked. He'd have to be careful what he said around Brando now. He already knew too much.

"Just tell Elayni to go next," Codee said.

"No," Brando exclaimed. "I won't let you use her."

"Are you going to risk the consequence of breaking your vow?" Codee asked.

The silence grew heavy. Dayvee stole a surreptitious glance back. A red-faced Brando stalked up to Elayni.

Elayni whispered, "You okay?"

Brando's reply was hushed. "Codee was upset Dayvee risked himself."

She squeezed his arm. "Did you talk to Dayvee?"

"He said no."

"Then I'll talk to him." Elayni was going to go along too.

Dayvee's heart shattered. Apparently, some sympathy still lay with him, but they did the leader's bidding now. He could have accepted that. Leeto *was* alpha. If they had only told him their loyalties had changed. Instead, they conspired secretly with Codee. He trusted them, and they betrayed him.

Thanks, Jaycee, but I'm done now.

Dayvee's hearing returned to normal, and Codee moved up and took back the lead. All the trainees turned sympathetic faces on Brando. Was *everyone* conspiring against Dayvee?

He turned away and fought the tears. Brando and Elayni had

taught him what love was. To care about someone so much that when they suffered, you hurt worse. It had been true for Dayvee. Wasn't it for them?

Jaycee nosed him. *I love you like that.*

Thanks, I love you like that too.

Several hours later, Codee called a halt. "We'll camp here."

Although it was still early afternoon, Dayvee's body dragged. Brando put a hand on his shoulder. "What's wrong?"

Dayvee recoiled and jerked away. "I don't want to talk about it." What else could he say when everything would get to Codee? He didn't want to hear Brando repeat another's words. Dayvee crawled in his bedroll early to feign sleep, but it claimed him.

...

Dayvee sighed. Still morning. Five days after leaving home, and each day went slowly. Was it because the tension lay thick between him and the others? Their path skirted between grasslands and forests, unfamiliar to the trainees, so Codee mostly led. Dayvee's shirt clung to his back from sweat. It was so much warmer since they left their mountain range. And noisier. Had every bird burst into song?

What was Jaycee doing? He and Bruno sniffed at something in the grass. There was a rustle, then a furious flurry as pheasants burst into the sky. Dayvee threw his nails at the same time as Brando cast his. Two birds dropped to the ground.

Brando retrieved them and raced to catch up. "Here." A smile graced his face as he handed Dayvee's to him.

"Thanks." Dayvee forced a return smile.

Brando's face fell. That hadn't fooled him. Dayvee had learned to talk without saying much of consequence around Codee, but that only earned hurt looks from Brando and Elayni. Better to stay silent. Brando's shoulders sagged.

Codee slowed from their normal fast jog. Great. A walking break to gather nature's bounty.

Some tall stalks poked out above the grass at the edge of the tree line. Ferns with circular snail-like buds. Fiddles. Dayvee went over to pluck some, and Jaycee joined him. When he glanced up, the rest of the group had almost disappeared in the distance. Did he and Jaycee need their help getting to Harthome? Not really. The animals could guide him. Brando and Bruno came running back. Why? Would he get in trouble from Codee if Dayvee left his sight?

Would they follow if Dayvee left with Jaycee? If he wanted to stay ahead, he could, he ran faster. First, Dayvee wanted to see a clan meeting. Then he and Jaycee could leave. He broke into a trot to catch up to the others. Jaycee matched his steps as Brando and Bruno joined them.

Elayni found some milkweed shoots. Wild garlic, leeks, and asparagus soon joined the plants in their pouches. Dayvee spotted some small white flowers with vines running sideways between them. Jagged teeth edged the leaves and little red berries hung among them. He called out, "Strawberries."

All the trainees rushed over to pick as many as they could without losing Codee. Dayvee stuck a few of the succulent treats in his mouth. When they moved back into the forest, they found morel mushrooms popping up. Their wrinkled brown bodies blended in, so Dayvee kept a sharp eye around dead trees.

Codee put a handful in his pouch. "I think each of you trainees' have areas were you excel, but others you should work on. I'm going to share those assessments with you. It could help Dayvee or his second assign tasks better." Codee's eyes locked on Dayvee.

Did he want him to name his second? How could anyone appoint a second they couldn't trust? It wouldn't have been a problem before, but not now.

I smell a zing, Jaycee sent. *A bad storm with lightning's coming."*

"Pair up to search for shelter," Codee ordered. "Elayni and Dayvee, Brando and Chayla, Geno with me."

There was no shelter for Dayvee. His refuge, the ones who had always provided him solace, no longer cared.

Where does Kwutee say to find a refuge? Jaycee sent.

Dayvee recalled Kwutee's words. *There's no better refuge than Kun.*

Maybe you should look for His.

Jaycee was probably right, but he was too vulnerable to dwell on it more. Calupi mustn't be weak. He shoved everything aside and focused on the task given them. Lightning was coming.

As they tromped through the woods, he caught Elayni staring at him. "Can we talk?" she asked.

She couldn't love him. Not if she was willing to conspire against Dayvee. "I think we should focus on our search."

Maybe you should ask the animals, Jaycee sent.

Of course. Thanks.

Dayvee reached out to the animal nearby. *We need shelter from the storm. Is there any close?*

A small flying squirrel stood on a nearby branch. What appeared to be a skin flap opened and ran from under its arms to its legs and made its body appear almost square. *A rock overhang, Kayndo. Follow me.* Dayvee pointed toward the squirrel for Elayni. They hurried after it as it glided from tree to tree. A cliff appeared with a large stone slab projecting out. It should keep them dry.

Thanks.

You're welcome. The squirrel took another leap and soared off.

Jaycee nosed him. *I passed our location on.*

Elayni went under the overhang. She sat and patted the ground next to her. "Won't you tell me what's going on with you?"

Dayvee joined her, but stayed standing. "It's too thin."

The others reached the shelter just before the heavens opened up. Thunder boomed, lightning lit the sky, and wind bent the trees. Kun's power on display. The rain poured down in sheets. Explosions rocked them as lightning hit nearby trees. The wolves paced their shelter.

"I'll give your assessments while we wait." Codee shouted over the storm.

Was he trying to distract them? Did Dayvee even want to hear? Wouldn't Codee just tell Dayvee how terrible he'd done, like Leeto always did?

A lightning flash lit up Codee's face. "Dayvee, your weakest skill was trading. You should never let a trader know you're in a hurry. The other skills you're more than capable of handling. Hunting and leading you excelled in."

Dayvee stopped his foot tapping. Codee smiled. "One more leading tip—weigh the advice, but do what your heart tells you is right for the Vita—regardless of whether it's popular. You've never been afraid to take the difficult path. Don't start now." He motioned to the others. "Your sub-pack will support you."

Maybe if Codee told them too. That wasn't fair, not with all they'd been through. But he couldn't rely on them anymore. After Codee's evaluations, the rain stopped, but the wind gusted strongly.

Codee led them out into the mud. "In an hour, we'll be at the clan meeting. I won't be introducing you as trainees, but adults, since there isn't a job I wouldn't trust you with. Your training's over, and you have your assignment."

The goal Dayvee had been striving so hard to achieve was accomplished. He was an adult Calupi. As leader of an adult sub-pack, Dayvee was now beta. He should be thrilled, but he didn't feel like celebrating.

Brando howled. Smiles broke out on the other trainees, their first in days. Codee would say it was Dayvee's fault for acting like a lone wolf, but was that so bad? It kept people from turning on him.

"What are our ranks?" Tayro asked.

Codee's eyes twinkled. "You're all talented. Your ranks are...Dayvee-five, Brando-eleven, Elayni-twelve, Tayro-thirteen, Chayla-fourteen, and Geno-fifteen. Each of you has earned high status."

Everyone's mouth was hanging open. Dayvee closed his. It was rare to be ranked in the top-half of the pack and considered high status right after training, but more shocking was where. The first ten ranks were beta. Dayvee's sub-pack had been ranked as high as they could be without being beta.

Codee handed out the thin strip of leather with blue beads between two knots that marked their rank. No one wore them at home since they knew each other's ranks. Dayvee slipped it in his rucksack.

"Put them on," Codee ordered. "They should be worn whenever you meet new people."

Dayvee pulled it out and wrapped it above his bicep, letting the five beads show in front. Why did Leeto tell him for so long he wasn't good enough, then rank him so high? The only ones above him were Leeto, Milay, Codee, and Kwutee. He'd be fighting Calupi when he returned. They'd challenge him for his rank.

You'll win, Jaycee sent.

Maybe, but he wouldn't be the only one fighting. No one gave Brando the credit he deserved. At least the leaders finally acknowledged his talents. Is that what betraying Dayvee gained him?

"The command ranking for your sub-pack is Dayvee's to assign." Codee paused.

The silence became heavy. Dayvee wasn't ready to rank them, yet.

Codee pursed his lips. "White River Pack is closest to Harthome. Their keeper will conduct the choosing, and some clanspeople will want to attend." He picked his way over some fallen limbs. "And if needed, all the clans are preparing to answer the Kayndo's call." Codee gestured to Brando. "Take the lead. Dayvee, come with me."

Dayvee dropped back. Codee took a pouch out of his rucksack. "Sharmayn wanted you to have this money. You might need it now."

The heavy pouch clinked as Dayvee took it. The fiery red hair and laughing green eyes of Sharmayn popped into his mind.

Who? Jaycee sent.

At eight, I ran away to a town. She offered to be my mother. Sharmayn would expect him to visit since Leeto wouldn't stop Dayvee as an adult. He stowed the pouch in his rucksack. "Can you get her a message? Tell her it would take something this important to keep me away."

"I'll send it, but I wanted you to know you don't have to do this. You can relinquish Jaycee and leave. There's enough money there to do anything you want."

"Would Kun select another to be Kayndo?"

"I don't know."

Dayvee couldn't turtle. "I already made my choice. I wanted to be Calupi—even more than I wanted a mother who loved me."

Codee put a hand on his shoulder. "Then embrace it and stop trying to avoid Kun's plans for you."

Dayvee shrugged his hand off. "I know what I'm supposed to do."

"I haven't heard your command ranks."

Codee wouldn't let him wait. If something happened to a leader, their second had to get the others safe. Dayvee's trust might have changed, but their abilities didn't. "Brando's my second, Elayni's third, Tayro's fourth, Chayla's fifth, and Geno's sixth.

"I figured." Codee skirted a puddle. "What else is bothering you?"

"I don't want to add to your fun. You'll have to guess which plan to hurt me worked."

Codee's face fell. "I don't enjoy it."

"Then stop letting Leeto use you to do it." Dayvee stalked away with Jaycee to join the other trainees. A huge crack split the air. Dayvee froze.

What was that?

"Run!" Codee shouted.

14

Surprises

"Prevent being caught by surprise by planning for the worst." ~ Leeto

Tib strode into the castle. Servants turned wide eyes on him. No wonder. Soil, sweat, and torn clothing weren't expected on a prince. Too bad. He was helping Taluma. His sense of satisfaction swelled. His muscles ached, but he'd accomplished much more than listening to people bicker. The Kagard retinue surrounding him was just as dirty. It went much faster now that he had willing hands to help.

Sixty of the ancients' weapons had already been made, and he had craftsmen working on more every day. His stomach grumbled in complaint at the lateness of dinner. Tib didn't do formal dinners. Too busy for them. Varian would have a tray waiting for him with some of his favorites. After he met with him, he'd bathe and change. He came to Varian's room and knocked.

One of Varian's personal guards opened the door, "The prince is here."

"Show him in," Varian ordered.

As Tib entered, both Varian's hands flew up in one of those flashy gestures he loved. "Tib, you're working much too hard."

Tib smiled to himself at Varian's consternation over his welfare. "It needed to be done."

"We do need to be ready for Nolan when he invades, but you could have taken time to clean up," Varian said.

"I didn't want to make you wait."

"You know me too well." Varian's hand waved in a flourish toward a tray. "From the looks of you, you got a lot accomplished, but your dinner's cold."

Tib grabbed the tray and sat. Several quails, swimming in a pear sauce, lay nestled next to sides of rice, asparagus, and egg custard for his dessert. Digging through ruin piles all day was hungry work, so Tib didn't mind if it wasn't hot. He swallowed a mouthful.

"We did get a lot accomplished, but I'm not sure it's going to help. The wolf that's coming won't choose me. And a different king probably won't want to use the ancients' weapons."

"We have to stop the Calupi. Are there Kagards at the clan meeting?" Varian asked.

What was Varian thinking? Tib lost his appetite. "I won't kill the Calupi."

"All of us will be slaughtered without the ancients' weapons." Varian's hand waved as he spoke. "A few deaths could save many."

Tib's stomach lurched. He sat his tray down. "Not that. We need to figure out another way."

"Relax. I'll think of something." Varian rubbed a finger across his chin. "Blake and the Pericards that escaped are camping outside the city. Their supporters are gathering there."

Figures. Tib didn't trust Blake after he let Father take something to hasten his death. "Maybe we should arrest them."

"It might be better to infiltrate their camp to learn who our enemies are, and what they're going to do."

Varian really had great advice. Tib was thankful for it. He picked back up his tray. "That's a great plan if we can find someone to do it."

"I keep telling you not to worry and trust me to take care of this stuff while you get the weapons made."

Varian kept proving he was more than capable of handling everything.

Tib swallowed another bite. "Okay, I will."

#

Dayvee leapt forward on Elayni's heels at Codee's order to run. His heart pounded. He scanned for the danger.

A tree was falling. Coming too fast. They'd be crushed.

Dayvee flung himself over Elayni, tackling her to the ground. Elayni cried out as branches crashed into his back. The weight pressed

Dayvee against Elayni, pushing her into the ground. But he wasn't in pain. He breathed in the fresh scent of rain as Elayni's damp hair filled his face.

"Are you okay?" he asked.

She turned her head, and his lips brushed her soft cheek. "Yes, are you?"

His breath caught. Normal around Elayni. Only now, Dayvee felt torn. His arms wanted to keep Elayni enfolded in them, but his feet were already scrambling for a purchase to get away. His body was as conflicted as he was. He had to remember she didn't love him. "I'm fine. I'll try to get some of this weight off us."

He lifted himself to his knees and hands while he pushed back against the weight above him. Sticks cracked as they broke, scraping him. He and Elayni only got caught by the top of the tree where the branches were thin. He poked his head out and gave Elayni a hand to help her up.

They scrambled over the limbs to get free. The others were emerging too. Codee hadn't gotten entangled. None of the wolves had. Four feet were faster than two.

"Is everyone okay?" Codee asked.

Everyone nodded. Codee's eyes traveled over them. Dayvee only saw scrapes. Thank Kun. Codee signaled with a wave, then hiked up his rucksack and walked forward. Their sub-pack fell in behind him.

Less than a half-hour later, Dayvee picked up a faint rumbling. As they pressed on, it grew louder. Like the roar of a stampeding herd of buffalo. Must be the clan meeting. After only hearing forest creatures and birds, Dayvee's ears didn't like it. Just how many did it take to make such a din?

They topped a rise and below them, where the trees opened to meet the grasslands, a huge tent city stretched as far as he could see. Tents in all shapes, sizes, and colors, as different as the clans that inhabited them.

In between the tents, people and animals roamed. Bears, buffalo, mountain lions, wolves, hyenas, elk, deer, zebras, horses, donkeys all mingled together—grazers and predators. Dayvee made out raccoons, rabbits, squirrels, and tons of others. So many birds, they seemed everywhere.

Codee stopped. "Look for the Calupi."

Dayvee didn't see them. He didn't want to use his gift and sort through all the mind voices. They assaulted him in a chaotic jumble, too difficult to understand. Sharp pain stabbed his head. He rubbed his forehead.

"I see them." Codee took a few steps.

Dayvee's stomach roiled under the onslaught of pain. He fought to hold the nausea at bay and faltered.

Codee glanced back, "Are you okay?"

"Yes." Dayvee stopped rubbing his head. "It's just all of those animals are trying to talk to me at once."

Brando and Elayni moved up beside him. Elayni glanced down the hill, then shook her head. "That would drive me crazy."

Codee turned around. "Remember what I told you."

"Yes, but it doesn't work. I can't shut them up. Maybe I can get the voices to soften. Just give me a second." Dayvee tried to send to all of them. *You can't all speak to me at once. Please, I'll call you when I need you.* The shouts receded to whispers. "Okay. I think I can go now."

Codee pivoted and took them down the other side of the rise. People must be cooking. The aromas drifted of roasting meat, baked bread, and maybe fruit pies? The scents all mingled together. Many Dayvee didn't recognize. Never had he seen so many people and animals. The pack meetings didn't have near this many.

"Everyone isn't at the meeting yet. Later there will be more." Codee's voice rose above the din. "Delegations will come and go all summer, but the merchants stay."

More? Dayvee couldn't even imagine it. Some merchants yelled out, hawking their goods. So many, he spun his head every which way trying to take it all in. People stood at wagons and tables to sell clay pots, dishware, utensils, rugs, oil lamps, candles, carvings, hides, assorted clothing, and all kinds of weapons. He goggled as much as his friends.

As Codee led them through the throngs, the trainees and their companions all bunched close behind him. Dayvee didn't want to lose Codee. This was beyond his experience, and it made him apprehensive. Every time he took note of the animals, his head buzzed again, and his steps faltered.

Jaycee pressed against his leg, Elayni linked her arm in Dayvee's, and Brando reached over Jaycee to take his other arm as they gently guided him. When Dayvee started to pull away, he received a raised eyebrow from Elayni. Brando's sharp gaze studied him. Dayvee gave in and let them lead him.

As they moved through the clan meeting, a group of familiar small earth-toned tents came into view. Just a couple of hides slung over a rope, with several Calupi standing in front of them. Sure could tell wolf clan spent very little time in tents and preferred caves. Codee stopped. "Does anyone know where we can find the Kwin?"

A big man with black hair and a large nose stepped forward— Brodee. "That's easy. They're on the north-west edge. As usual, they claimed all the grasslands north of them for the grazers."

They'd come in from the south-west, but they'd been heading east. The wrong direction. Good thing they stopped.

"Thanks, Brodee." Codee clasped his arm, then he glanced toward Dayvee and his friends. "You probably recognize the alpha of Big Pine pack from pack meetings."

His friends released Dayvee's arms, and they all straightened to give Brodee a nod.

Brodee's gaze traveled over their arm bands with their ranks, then locked onto Dayvee's face. "Are you the one?"

Codee answered for him. "It's uncertain if he'll be needed, but yes." He gestured to Brando. "He's the other."

Brodee crooked a finger at his second. Luegee went over to Brando. "Come with me."

Chayla clutched the neck of her shirt. Geno and Tayro shuffled their feet. Elayni formed a circle with her fingers, asking through signal if Brando would be okay. He gave her a nod. She chewed her bottom lip as Brando and Bruno moved off with Luegee.

What did he want with Brando? And why was everyone worried? "Where's he taking Brando?" Dayvee asked.

"It's not your concern." Codee made a flat chopping motion, and then closed his hand. Those signals meant Dayvee was to leave it alone and be silent. "He'll rejoin us soon."

Unease filled Dayvee. Even if he was beta now, Codee was second. To defy Codee in front of another alpha would hurt his respect and force a confrontation he might regret. *Jaycee, do you know?*

Yes, but I can't reveal the leader's confidences. Bruno's not worried, so you shouldn't be.

The sub-pack sure is.

Codee turned back to Brodee. "You'll have to excuse me for not introducing them properly to you, but we don't have the time. They need to get the prince's companion to him before the king dies."

"You haven't heard then." Brodee's tone held remorse. "Our king's dead. We received word less than an hour ago."

Dayvee sucked in his breath. They didn't make it in time. Taluma was bereft a king.

"I never met him, but he followed the Vita." Codee frowned. "I'm sorry he's gone."

"They say the prince assumed the role of king without being chosen." Brodee's eyes flitted to Dayvee. "It might mean trouble for you."

Did things ever go right for him? Dayvee stopped his foot tapping.

Codee's face set in a grim line. "Thanks for the information, but it makes speed even more essential. The choosing must be held." His fingers brushed Graydee's head. "Then the companions will decide who will be king."

"The hyena delegation is here demanding action. They still want to extend into your territory, and they want sanctions from you for killing that hyena pack. The Clan council waited, so they can deal with the trespassing sanctions against them as well. But it sounds as if the hyenas want your necks regardless of their decision."

Gasps escaped the sub-pack. Would they be fighting hyenas again so soon? Even with the crisis going on with the king.

Codee patted his weapon's pouch. "They'll meet our teeth before they get to our necks. Is the Calupi council here yet?"

"Yes, and anxious to get it over, but Dugee said he'd rather you speak for your pack."

To be assigned Wolf Mountain's representative on the Calupi council wasn't a duty anyone wanted and it lasted a year.

Codee nodded once. "He must be worried that if the ruling isn't in our favor, he'll face Leeto's wrath, but I need to see our Calupi off first."

"You have our support, but the news we might need a Kayndo has most clans concerned about fights between us now." He gestured at Dayvee. "The clan council wants to meet him. That might help you, but otherwise they might let the hyenas move to keep the peace."

"We don't have time for council meetings. They needed to be at Harthome yesterday."

Many complained both the Calupi and Clan councils wasted time in endless discussions. Dayvee didn't want to meet with either, but he'd endure it to keep from sharing their territory with hyenas. He released a heavy breath. It was Codee's decision.

"May Kun go with you." Brodee clasped Codee's forearm.

Codee returned the clasp. "And also with you."

Brodee's gaze turned to Dayvee again. "If you call, we'll answer."

Codee opened his hand to release Dayvee from silence. "I'd be honored," Dayvee replied.

They hurried through the meeting, passing different groups. A group of people and zebras stood in front of square-shaped tents with black stripes and poles in each corner. Those must sleep at least a dozen people. Were they playing some game? Was it dice they tossed? One man hollered over at them. "Codee, introduce us."

Codee waved, but kept moving. Coyote clan's tents looked similar to Calupi, small and earth-toned. They preferred stone dens too. A group of them arm wrestled over a log. A watcher shouted, "Codee, come arm wrestle with us."

Codee kept moving, then a deer brought him up short as it ran in front of them and over to some clanspeople who stirred pots on a fire ring. Smelled like garlic, wild cabbage, maybe chicory cooking. So many scents wafted through the meeting Dayvee couldn't be sure. The tents were earth tones and conical with poles that met in the center. They could hold at least six people. Deer clan spent much of their time in tents too.

"Codee, come taste the soup," A man called. Their faces all held smiles.

"Can't." Codee plunged forward again.

"You're sure popular." Elayni ducked under some brightly dyed cloths strung on a line that waved in the breeze.

"Not me. They want to meet Dayvee. Just ignore them."

Dayvee found it impossible to ignore the animals. Just too many. His skull pounded, and his stomach churned. His steps faltered again. "Maybe we shouldn't."

Codee weaved around a slow moving badger family. "We don't have time for everyone to pledge to you."

"I know, but maybe we should take a few minutes to talk to everyone like we did with the pack." Dayvee rubbed both temples. "They don't like being ignored, and it's impossible with the animals."

"It might be dangerous." Codee pointed to a man dressed in flaxen-spun clothing standing at a table that displayed beads. "There's more than clan here, and some city people hate the Vita and the clans." He whispered, "They'd love to prevent us from having a Kayndo."

A sense of foreboding rose in Dayvee. "Why do they hate us?"

"Different reasons." A donkey almost bowled into Codee as it trotted past. "Maybe we terminated a lease of an animal they abused. Maybe a family member hurt a clan member and received a judgment. Some don't like paying for meat and want to hunt. Others blame us if they believe they're paying too much for a land lease."

"We don't set the land leases. The king does." A skylark flew by only a few inches in front of Dayvee's nose.

"Yes, but the clans are exempt since we don't build permanent structures, and our territories are set aside to remain wild. That doesn't sit right with some of them. I don't believe their complaints are justified. But they do, and they'd kill you without a second thought."

Dayvee pointed to where some clanspeople beckoned. "If I expect them to answer my call, I should at least acknowledge them."

"Humph. All right. Tell the animals to let everyone know that you'll speak on the North end in an hour. That should give us time to meet with the Kwin, and if you leave immediately afterwards, it will be safer."

Dayvee reached out to all the animals and sent the message. It seemed to work. His headache relented as the animals quieted. People stopped trying to speak to them, too, now that they knew he'd meet with everyone. Several Kagards moved among the crowds. The flat pieces of bone sewed to the padded leather uniforms made them easily distinguished from the rest.

The soldiers looked grim like the ones Dayvee had seen before in that town he visited. Maybe the king's death weighed heavily on them. Or else the burden of enforcing Taluma's laws.

As Codee wound through a flock of geese, two Calupi stepped in front of them, blocking their way—Petee and Chancee. Codee's response was instant. He pulled his nails, leaving his thumb extended out as his fingers clamped around the rawhide grip.

The signal.

Danger. Get ready to meet it.

Dayvee and his sub-pack pulled their weapons.

15

The Meeting of the Clans

"When the pack's threatened, ensure the future's safety first." ~
Leeto to Dayvee.

Brando and Bruno followed Luegee and his wolf companion behind
tents, away from from the crowds, until they came to an open area. A
dozen strangers stood there in assorted clothing of buckskin and furs.
Each wore a headband with an animal painted on it to announce their
clan, and most had companions with them. His judges. A boundary of
stones marked a ring on the ground.

Brando didn't recognize the two Calupi who walked toward them
leading a bound man. Their captive didn't wear a headband, and his
clothing was lighter and finer. He must be from the city. Brown hair
topped a small head and face—like a turkey's, it didn't fit his body. He
had a long neck too.

Luegee addressed their prisoner. "You've been judged and
received a death sentence for your crimes of murdering two Calupi and
planning to kill the Kayndo. Normally, you'd die in a ring of death, but
we're giving you an opportunity to live. If you kill your opponent in
the ring before he kills you, we'll only take off the fingers that killed
our pack members. We'll even bandage them and allow you to leave.
Do you wish to fight?"

So that would be the test. Brando had suspected it might not be
easy, but this? The man certainly deserved to die. But could Brando do
it? He had never killed a man. When he threw his nails at Nero in the
ring of death, he knew where they landed—the right hand that had
tortured Dayvee. Not Nero's jugular.

The man's brown eyes locked onto Brando, and a smile crossed his face. "I'll fight the kid."

"Don't try to leave the ring. You wouldn't get too far." Luegee cut the man's bonds. "Go on in." The man walked into the ring, then Luegee waved a hand toward Brando. "Do you understand? It won't be a normal fight. Once you step foot in that ring, one of you walks out. The other dies."

The city man was bigger than Brando and muscle bound. That long neck might make a good target, but could he kill someone?

Remember he's received judgment, Bruno sent. *If not you, it will be another. And if he goes free, he might succeed next time in killing Dayvee.*

Brando braced himself. "Yes. I understand."

"And you still want to take this test?" Luegee asked.

Dayvee was already upset with Brando, and he probably wouldn't approve. Regardless, Brando had to do what he could to eliminate a threat to his family. He really wished their sub-pack was here to support him. Chayla's adorable face popped into his mind, then each of the others. The pack might call him a tiger, but he didn't want to face this alone. Would this be the last time he saw them? He made his voice firm. "Yes."

"Give me your pouches." Brando undid them and handed his weapons over. "You must use your hands. Do it quickly and without hesitation. Even if you succeed, but take too long, you'll fail." Luegee gestured to the ring. "Take your place."

Brando made himself stride confidently into the ring to take the side opposite the stranger. Bruno sat near the perimeter to watch. *Let out your howl.*

For his family. Brando howled. It might be weak, but it was heard.

Luegee's arm dropped. Brando had no time to measure the man's skill. He charged forward. The man swung his fist, and Brando dodged. He slammed his arm into the man's neck as he ran past. The man flew back and crumpled to the ground. Brando pounced. With all his force he drove his left fist into the man's throat.

The man choked and gasped for breath. Brando threw both hands around the man's neck, pressing his fingers into his larynx. Harder.

The man's eyes bulged as his hands grabbed for Brando's arms, trying to pull them away. He bucked beneath Brando, arms, hands, and knees flailing. The veins in his eyes turned red and bloody. Then finally, those eyes rolled back, and he lay still.

Brando had taken a life.

His stomach churned. Bile rose to the back of his throat. He forced it down. They were testing him.

Two people came in and carried the body out. Brando forced his shaky legs over to where Luegee beckoned him outside the ring. Luegee handed Brando his knife pouch. "There were two men caught together. Both received the same sentence. The other also agreed to fight and will get to use a knife. You can too."

Brando had to do it again? Not trusting his voice, he just gave a nod. They led a lanky man into the ring. Brando secured his pouch and went back to his place. He studied the new opponent as they cut his bindings. Black hair, ferret face. They handed the man a knife. Brando made himself howl again. It sounded strangled.

He pulled his tooth and watched Luegee for the signal. A tingle at the base of Brando's neck warned him as he caught a blur in the corner of his eye. His body moved without conscious thought to avoid the danger. The man's knife clattered to the ground.

The reflex training Brando and Dayvee did kept him alive.

The man ran toward him. Luegee dropped his arm to signal. Should Brando risk a tooth throw being fatal on a running man? He had no time for errors. With his right arm leading and left held back with his knife, he ran forward to meet him.

The man grabbed for Brando's knife hand. Brando knocked his arm aside. The man's other hand swung out in a hook toward his temple. Brando jumped and took the punch on his left shoulder, driving forward to stab his knife under the man's chin and up to his brain. When he released his grip on his tooth, the man crumpled to the ground, lifeless.

He'd drawn his last breath.

Brando leaned over him. It took a hard pull and the man's head coming off the ground before it would give Brando's knife up. He swallowed hard and wiped both sides of his knife on the man's sleeve to clean the blood off. Tears threatened. He widened his eyes to stop them.

Brando took two deep breaths and forced his chin up. His hands shook as he slid his tooth back in the pouch and moved from the ring. Stomach cramps assaulted him.

Bruno came to him and nosed him. *I never doubted you for a second.* Brando sure did. He wanted to crawl in a corner and cry, but he couldn't.

Luegee handed Brando his nail pouch. Did Luegee notice his shaking hands? Brando secured his pouch to his belt as a giant of a man wearing a hide like a cape approached them. The wrinkles that creased his face and his short gray hair betrayed his age. A grizzled bear with a silver face ambled at the man's side. An Ursan. Could it be Bunjee's great uncle? He led the council.

"Do you know why we almost lost the war with the false king?" the Ursan asked.

Brando had years of practice of not letting it show when he hurt. He could do this. "Because the Kayndo was killed early, and most of the animals scattered. The battles became chaotic after that." Did the Ursan catch the tremble in his voice?

"That's right. Many more lives were lost, and almost the Vita, because someone failed to take the Kayndo's safety seriously. Your hands were clean, so we needed to be sure. The first kill is difficult."

They needed to understand.

He made sure his voice didn't crack. "The second was just as hard." Brando lifted his hand that still held a bloodstain. "But even if I have to bathe in his enemies' blood every day, I won't stop spilling it because he's my family."

"All right, we'll support your leader's choice." The Ursan clapped Brando's shoulder. "You'll be in charge of the Kayndo's defense."

Relief filled Brando. He had passed their test. Even if how he did it repulsed him. Could Chayla stomach the sight of Brando if she knew? Could Dayvee or any of the others? He sighed inwardly. None of his misgivings could change it. It was done and could not be undone.

"Did you give Codee your vow to follow our orders?"

"Yes. We all did."

He handed Brando a rolled up piece of hide. "They're written there, but the most important thing we want you to remember is not to hesitate. We'll deal with any repercussions. Is that clear?"

"Yes." But could they fix the pain in his heart from causing those deaths?

"As of now, nothing's off limits. You pull your weapons and use them at the first sign of danger. Our definition of threat is loose, so don't wait to be certain." He clasped Brando's forearm. "May Kun go with you."

#

Dayvee's hand clamped firmly down on his nails. Codee's danger signal meant he believed Petee and Chancee to be a serious threat. Codee and Wilee jumped back to join Jaycee in front of Dayvee. It pulled him up short. Elayni and Evee ran to the front too. Chayla, Cato, Tayro, and Topay pressed against his sides while Geno and Graydee took his back.

Dayvee was ringed and trapped. To even see past Codee, he had to stand on his toes. He had pulled his nails, but couldn't use them without hitting the others. What were they doing? Calupi protected young children by ringing them since they weren't able to defend themselves, but they shouldn't be doing it to Dayvee.

Codee glanced at the others and gave them an approving chin lift. Dayvee stood in a cage formed from the bodies of his friends and their companions. He fumed. Calupi, like their companions, hated being caged.

Petee and Chancee's attempt to waylay them had Codee speaking with menace. "Stand aside now. I'm warning you."

Were Petee and Chancee carrying on Nero's plans to kill Dayvee? He needed out of this ring. He couldn't even see.

I'll share my body with you, Jaycee sent.

Dayvee looked out from Jaycee's eyes and felt the rumble as Jaycee growled. Every one of the wolves displayed their teeth, and their hair stood erect. Surely Petee and Chancee knew to attack their sub-pack was suicide. That didn't mean they couldn't do harm before they were killed.

Dayvee wasn't defenseless, even if he was cut off. There was a whole meeting of animals around him. He reached out to the deadliest he could find nearby. Others were being drawn to the confrontation. Some Kagards approached. Before they arrived, a bear and mountain lion reached the front of their Calupi ring. The bear rose up on two feet and roared. The mountain lion screamed.

There, now *that* was better.

Petee and Chancee's eyes widened, and they backed a few steps. Their companions had their tails and ears down. Submission.

Petee put his hands up, palms out. "We don't want any trouble. Please, we only want to ask Dayvee to forgive us."

Dayvee reached out to Petee and Chancee's companions. *Are they serious? Is this a ploy?*

They really want to be forgiven and don't want to hurt you.

Dayvee popped back into his body and sheathed his tooth. He raised his voice. "Let me through. They don't want to harm me. I've spoken to their companions."

Codee and Elayni moved to the side, creating a space, but they didn't put their weapons away. Dayvee slid between them. When he took another step forward, Codee and Elayni did too.

Thanks for your help, Dayvee sent to the bear and mountain lion.

You only need to call, Kayndo. They moved away.

Two more steps brought Dayvee to Petee and Chancee. "Why should I forgive you? Your actions harmed us and our pack."

Chancee hung his head. "We've turned back to Kun. If you'll just give us a chance, we won't disappoint you."

"Leeto has exiled you. I can't reverse that." Dayvee shrugged. "You'll have to try to get another pack to accept you."

"The exile was bad enough." Chancee spread his hand in the air displaying the white X over his pack mark. "But now everyone knows we tried to harm a Kayndo in waiting. They won't even speak to us. The council might decide to mark us as Lobo's. But our companions are tired of being alone. So please, let us fight with you so we can redeem ourselves."

How could Dayvee be sure they wouldn't change loyalties again?

If you let them join us, make them give you vows, Jaycee sent. *And ask their companions to inform you if they intend to break them.*

Dayvee's focus returned to Petee and Chancee. "How much farther before we get to where the Kwin are?"

"Just a few minutes' walk from here," Petee answered.

A group of Kagards approached—Dayvee counted ten. One asked, "Is there a problem?"

"Not anymore," Codee answered curtly.

The Kagards studied them as if memorizing their features. They finally marched away.

Dayvee gestured to Petee. "If you meet us at the Kwin encampment, I'll give you an answer." They nodded and walked off. *Kun, help me discern what you want me to do.* Dayvee turned to the others. "What does everyone think?"

Codee's wrinkled nose showed his contempt. "They shouldn't have held us up. Leeto wouldn't want you to give them another chance."

Tayro's mouth pursed. "They were desperate and worried about their companion's happiness. Kun teaches us to forgive."

"How many times should I forgive those that betray my trust?" Dayvee asked.

Tayro's large eyes widened more. He was no fool and probably suspected the question was also meant for him. "Kwutee says as many times as they repent."

Elayni chewed her bottom lip. "I doubt I could trust Petee after he tied me and Brando up."

She had a point. And Dayvee had his own terrifying experience trapped by Chancee.

Geno shrugged. "Dayvee, I'll support any decision *you* make." Geno had changed since Dayvee had called the animals to aid Chayla. Maybe Dayvee should speak to him, but he'd be leaving soon.

Chayla's quiet voice could barely be heard over the noise around them. "I don't see how you can refuse. If they turned back to Kun, someone needs to let them prove themselves, and no one else will."

Her answer tugged at Dayvee's heart. "All your advice was good, but my heart says Chayla's is right for the Vita."

They nodded. Maybe after hearing it, they thought so too.

Codee moved them slowly on as they discussed it. Dayvee glimpsed a wolf weaving in and out of the crowd, coming at a fast trot toward them. It was Bruno with Brando following. Brando's face appeared ashen, and his hands shook.

What had they done to him? He wore a strange grimace as if he were going to be sick. Codee met him, gave him a chin lift, and handed him something. A red fringe. To earn that, Brando must have put himself in danger. Dayvee's heart skipped.

Codee took the lead again, and Elayni beckoned Brando over to her. When he joined her, she put a hand on his arm and squeezed it. Brando put his fringe on, but his feet dragged. Why did he look so depressed? Dayvee doubted anyone would tell him anything.

He should have sent a bird after Brando, so he could use their eyes. But to spy on his friends? If they were his friends, why did they keep things from Dayvee? A slow burn moved up his neck to his cheeks. He was tired of it—their secrets, their betrayal, and them treating him like he was incapable.

Dayvee was a beta. A leader worthy of respect took on the danger first. What leader hid behind their packmates? Up ahead, herds of horses grazed around large, dome-shaped, brightly colored tents that must hold twenty people. The Kwin couldn't be missed.

Dayvee stopped.

He couldn't wait any longer

He must confront his friends.

16

Recognition

"No matter who's at fault, leaders are held responsible when things don't go well." ~ Leeto

I *am beta. I am a leader. I am Calupi.*

The rest of the sub-pack stopped behind Dayvee. Codee glanced back, then came to them. Dayvee lifted his chin. "You put a child's ring around a Calupi leader?"

Codee released a heavy breath. "Even Calupi need help against multiple foes, so the council mandated guards. You are a leader, but too valuable to risk." Codee gaze was level, not abashed at all. "Your sub-pack wanted to do it, so I trained them."

That's why Codee had him out each evening to set snares or hunt. To hide it. If his friends were focused on protecting Dayvee, instead of threats to themselves, it put them in more danger. He didn't want that. Jaycee's growl sounded. "No one should have kept that from me!" The sub-pack had moved up to bunch around Dayvee. "So how long have you been my *pretend* friends, doing Codee and Leeto's bidding?"

"We *are* your friends," Elayni protested. "We were asked the day we left if we wanted to guard you or let another go. We agreed not to inform you because we didn't want to be replaced."

Dayvee recalled when his friends left the ceremony room. She went with Franko. Had Leeto used their families to convince them? "Before, we chose our own pack with our friends, over theirs. I'd have done it again if you had." He glanced at each one ending on Brando.

Brando's brown eyes were soft and sad. "I encouraged them to do it, since I've been doing Leeto's bidding since then. Much of what I said wasn't my words, and I repeated yours."

Elayni's hand fluttered to her throat. "What?" The others fixed scowls on Brando.

His beseeching eyes fell on Dayvee. "My vow lasted only until you learned, so I'm speaking my own words now. I never wanted to hurt you."

Mist formed in Dayvee's eyes. "It hurts when the ones I love betray me." He turned to Codee. "What's the lesson this time? Don't trust anyone?"

"No. Who does Kwutee say you can always trust?"

"Kun and my companion," Dayvee answered.

"Yes." Codee frowned. "But Leeto doesn't want you relying on anyone else too much. That leads to disappointment, if not worse."

Dayvee snorted. "I'm completely convinced you and him will disappoint me."

Elayni reached for him. "I'm really sorry."

Dayvee stepped back. "Don't." His voice broke. "I loved all of you, but you didn't return it."

Brando's face resembled a caught deer—eyes wide and frozen.

"We *do* love you," Elayni cried out. "It was an awful mistake. Don't be like Leeto. He's only disappointed because he demands perfection." Sobs turned her voice ragged. "Remember our friendship."

"You didn't."

Codee gestured to Brando. "They proved they're capable. But it's them or someone else. Which do you prefer?"

"I think I'd prefer it if Jaycee and I go alone from here."

"Please, don't leave me," Elayni pleaded. Tears fell down her cheeks.

The tears broke Dayvee's resolve. What wouldn't he do to stop them? His confusion cleared about his feelings for her. His body might not be certain, but his heart was. She held it captive, and those chains couldn't be undone easily. There wasn't any way he could go through with leaving her. His heart screamed at him to wrap his arms around her, and tell her 'never.' But he couldn't let Codee know that. He looked away from her face.

Codee's lowered voice filled with threat. "I'll bind you before I allow that."

"Pfft. If you can catch me, you'd have to fight me. No matter who wins, it will take time we don't have."

Jaycee's growl split the air. Wilee didn't challenge it.

"They have to let me see the threats, and fight too, or I won't take them." Dayvee snapped, "I will *not* be cordoned off."

Nice growl, Jaycee sent.

Codee put his hands up palm out. "Agreed."

"Are there more secrets they're ordered to keep from me?"

"No."

Dayvee couldn't let Leeto take his friends. He bottled his anger at them. "I haven't forgotten our friendship. But if someone wants you to deceive me again, will you come to me?"

"Yes." Five friends nodded fervently.

Dayvee let his anger at Codee out. "I don't believe making a sub-pack betray their leader protected the pack. Tell Leeto if he does it again, I *will* challenge him or leave."

"All right." Codee looked around them. "Everyone must know who you are, now. So can we go? We *are* in a hurry."

Codee was deferring to him? Dayvee couldn't resist a wicked grin. "Yes."

They approached the group of Kwin clustered at the front of their tents.

One stepped forward at their approach. "I'm Serano, the Kwin leader of Grassy Knoll Herd."

"I'm Codee, Wolf Mountain Pack's second. We thank you for helping us with our need."

"We all follow the Vita. Your need is ours." Serano waved a Kwin forward. "This is Reko. He'll accompany you and bring the horses back afterward."

Reko's hair shade matched his soft eyes, russet brown like a coyote. His youthful face was long and thin, but it fit his tall, lanky body. A splashy headband with frolicking horses announced him as Kwin.

Codee appraised him. "He's young."

"Yes, sixteen, but he knows that route better than any other here, and you'll find him capable."

"Ours are capable as well." Codee's words swelled Dayvee's chest.

"We were told you'd need six horses?" Serano said.

"Yes. I'm not going," Codee's answer sent apprehension through Dayvee. Was he ready to take on the challenges without Codee? No, but he wasn't going to admit it.

"I'll get them." Reko strode into the grass behind them to their herds.

Codee put his arm on Dayvee's shoulder and squeezed it. "You're in charge now. I stuck twenty red fringes in your rucksack this morning since you'll be awarding them. If you run out, you know how to make more."

"Thanks." Dayvee motioned to Petee and Chancee, who stood to one side waiting. They slouched forward, heads lowered. Their companions slinked after them.

"I will forgive you," Dayvee said. Both heads came up.

"If they join us, they need to accept my challenge," Brando declared. "Chancee, for trapping you in a cave, and Petee, for putting a bare blade to Elayni's throat."

Codee spat out, "You pulled a weapon on a pack member?"

Jaycee's hair bristled, a low growl rumbled in his throat. A red haze surrounded Dayvee's vision as rage welled in him. The wolf side wanted out.

Yes, Jaycee sent. *Let it out.*

Dayvee moved to Elayni and put his finger under her chin to raise it. No visible scars on her neck. "Did his tooth so much as scratch you?"

She blinked. "No."

He brushed his finger softly under her chin before letting go. Then he rounded on Petee. "You should consider carefully before answering my call. You'd have to meet Brando's challenge and give me a vow of loyalty."

"We'll answer, and you won't regret it. We won't be far behind if you need us." Chancee and Petee left. Their companions trailed them, but their heads and tails were up now.

Several horses followed Reko to Dayvee's side. "Have you ridden before?"

"No, but we're willing to learn." The backs of those horses appeared awfully tall to Dayvee. He couldn't show his trepidation. "I need to talk to everyone in about thirty minutes. Then we'll be ready to go."

"Okay, I'll show you what to do."

A yellow-gold horse with a white mane and tail pushed its nose against Dayvee and snorted. Its breath steamed through his clothes to warm his skin as it spoke. *Hello, Kayndo. I'm Sunray.*

Hi, Sunray.

Reko tapped Sunray on the side. "This is how we signal to make it easier for a rider to mount. Some kneel, some stretch out." Sunray's front legs folded back, and she kneeled. "Get on and sit there." Reko pointed to a hide across Sunray's back. Dayvee climbed up and settled himself as the other Kwin helped Dayvee's friends.

Reko touched the horse's knee again, and Sunray rose to her feet. The motion made Dayvee lurch back, but he righted himself. The ground sure appeared a long way off. He gripped the horse harder as his apprehension rose.

Sunray flicked her ear. *I'll take care of you.*

Thanks.

Jaycee sent, *I'd prefer you used your own feet.* Dayvee, too, but he couldn't let his fear win.

A larger black horse with patches of white moved toward Sunray and Dayvee. *I'm Shilo, Reko's companion.* He tossed his sculptured head, and his black and white mane flew up as his parti-colored tail swished against his rear legs. *You're in for a treat.*

Reko handed Dayvee two leather pieces that attached to another wrapped around Sunray's nose and neck. "Pull one to turn or both to stop or back up." He made a clucking sound. "At that signal, your horse will move forward. To go faster, just do it again." Reko put a hand on Shilo's neck and vaulted onto him. "Everyone cluck once."

Dayvee did and Sunray moved at a walk to follow Shilo. His friends trailed him. "I'll have my companion direct your horses," Reko said. "Just concentrate on staying on."

Every step jostled Dayvee. He clamped tighter.

"Relax your grip," Reko called out. "Move with the horse." He led them out into the grasslands toward the west where the woods bordered it, away from their herds.

Dayvee would have to be jogging to keep up on foot. Reko asked, "Are you ready to go faster?"

His heart lurched, but Dayvee answered, "Yes," along with his friends. He clucked. Sunray's hooves hitting the ground threw Dayvee up and down, flopping him around. He teetered, but Sunray shifted under him.

"Set back some," Reko hollered.

Dayvee adjusted. It made it a little better.

"We'll try the third speed now. If the horses come to a stop quickly, you could be thrown over their head, so sit back."

This gait was more a back and forth motion and much smoother than the up, down trot, but the ground raced by so fast it gave Dayvee a queasy sensation in the pit of his stomach. Jaycee ran alongside Sunray. When Reko brought them back to a walk, Dayvee lurched a little forward, but not too far. Good thing Reko had warned him.

They turned and came to a stop. "There's one more gait, the gallop, and we'll use it if we're in danger. Wrap your hands with the thongs in your horse's mane and hold tight."

Reko yelled out, and the horses raced over the grass. Dayvee clung to the horse. The mane whipped in his face and stung his eyes. He could barely see.

This is fun, Jaycee sent.

The ground rushed by in a blur. Wow, this was flying. Dayvee raised himself a little and clutched Sunray's mane less. Then Reko slowed them, and they were back in the third gait.

Dayvee breathed a sigh of relief. Then the horse trotted again. The transition threw him. He slid. He was going to fall.

His grip on Sunray's mane helped to slow his slide as she moved to right him. Between them, Dayvee stayed on as she slowed to a walk. He sat up and let go of her mane.

Dayvee's fingers held strands of white hair. *Sorry for pulling your hair out.* Sunray tossed her head.

"Normally, I'd start with a few hours and gradually increase your riding time," Reko said. "Otherwise, you're going to be really sore."

Didn't he know any Calupi? Dayvee and his sub-pack weren't weak. "We'll survive. We have to get Jaycee to the capital quickly."

"Okay, but remember I warned you." Reko glanced at the people and animals flowing north into the grass plain. "Looks like they're ready for you."

Had the whole meeting come? "I'd like to change into our ceremony clothes first."

"You can change there," Reko gestured to one of the colorful Kwin tents. "It's empty. Help yourself."

"Thanks."

They dismounted and ducked inside. More splashes of vibrant colors adorned rugs on the floor and blankets that divided the tent. Dayvee changed behind a blanket then returned to the opening.

When they left the tent, Reko pointed to an area that hadn't filled up. "The horses and I will wait there."

"All right." Dayvee's heart fluttered and stomach knotted as he grappled with what he should say. What would Leeto tell them? He'd demand they answer his call to prove themselves and uphold the Vita, but Dayvee didn't want to use guilt. He drew a blank. *Kun, please give me the words you'd have me say.*

His friends ringed him, but left a small opening in front. He strode forward and stopped a few steps from the crowd. Let them see the Kayndo. No slouching. He drew himself up.

All those eyes trained on him, most of them older, many of them leaders. He was certain they'd find him inadequate. His mouth dried, and the silence grew heavy. To calm his nerves he picked out the young faces, forced his tongue to unglue, and spoke to them.

"I am Dayvee, son of Leeto, Wolf Mountain pack's alpha, and chosen to be Kayndo if necessary." Applause swelled up. Animal noises joined in.

He raised his hand, and they quieted. "Thank you for coming since I don't have time to see you individually. Now that King Layton's with Kun, we need to get to Harthome quickly." He drew a breath and continued. "If the prince isn't chosen and doesn't follow our laws, I become Kayndo—then it falls to us to make him step down, or we lose the Vita. I'm not willing to lose the Vita. Are you?"

"No!" Their response exploded around him and in his mind.

"I can't do it alone, and I'd be honored to have your help." He raised his fist in the air. "Will any of you answer my call and fight alongside me?"

A sea of clenched fists stabbed the air, and a thundering roar answered, "I will."

"Thank you. With *your* support I'm certain we'll succeed. We go now to Harthome. May Kun go with us and you. And may we *always* keep the Vita!"

"May we always keep the Vita! May we always keep the Vita!" The chant sounded through the crowd. Then another filled the meeting. "Kayndo, Kayndo, Kayndo."

He wasn't the Kayndo yet. Didn't anyone understand that? He moved toward Reko, but the crowd surged forward and surrounded him. The press of bodies brought him to a halt. His friends drew close to shield him as the crowd jostled them. Hands grabbed for him.

One pulled a bead from his clothes and in awe exclaimed, "I have one of the Kayndo's beads." More hands pushed around his friends and their companions to grasp his beads. His sub-pack pushed back. Dayvee wanted to flee, but they were hemmed in. The shock left his mind reeling, and he felt violated. What could he do?

Jaycee's growl pierced the air. The other wolves joined in, but it didn't bother anyone. They were clan and knew the wolves wouldn't attack.

Brando drew his nails. The sub-pack did too. "I won't risk the Kayndo's safety. The next person that gets too close will lose their fingers."

A space opened around them. Brando winked at Dayvee. The

jockeying stopped, but people stood on tiptoes to see him. Anxiety filled Dayvee. His friends' faces were set in grim lines. Had they expected this?

Codee waited by Reko. He squeezed Dayvee's shoulder. "Well met. Leeto would be proud." Then he slapped Brando's back and gave a chin lift to the rest. "Looks like we made the right choice in guards."

Dayvee snorted. His friends could have been hurt. "Why didn't you warn me?"

"I never guessed it would be that bad. I only knew Leeto's received several requests to see you." Codee clasped Dayvee's forearm. "You better go."

Were Codee's eyes tearing? He acted as if the parting might be permanent, like Leeto had. Maybe they were right. Not many Calupi lived to old age. Codee had given Dayvee some of his most special memories like his first hunt and visit to a town. He didn't agree with everything Codee had done, but it had been at Leeto's command.

Dayvee took a breath. "I forgive you and I understand why, but I can't forget. Maybe one day, but not yet."

Codee nodded once. "Thanks."

Dayvee returned his arm clasp. "Thank you for everything you did for me." Each of his friends clasped Codee's forearm. Dayvee mounted Sunray. "I'd rather change after we get away from all this." Reko led them deeper into the meadow.

Codee yelled out to them, "May Kun go with you."

"And with you." Dayvee and his friends waved.

#

Codee watched his nephew and friends ride off North. His gut told him they headed for trouble, but Leeto ordered him to let them go alone. Dayvee had to take the lead now, without looking to him. Pride surged in him. Dayvee had proved himself a leader. That speech was the Kayndo speaking, and the clans knew it. He won them all over. They couldn't wait to answer his call.

Wilee, can you pass Dayvee's speech on to Wolf Mountain? Leeto might even bust his shirt.

The companions are already passing it to all the clans, Wilee sent. *Dayvee will have much more support than here.*

Brando's shout pierced the air. "Dayvee, watch out!"

Codee's gaze shot to the grassy plain where the horses had broken into a run. The wolves streaked toward the western side, and the woods that bordered it. *Wilee what's happening?*

Someone's shooting arrows at them.

Codee ran toward them assessing the situation. No cover. Dayvee's horse came to a stop. The other horses were still fleeing.

"We need to help the companions!" Dayvee raised a fist in the air, spread his fingers, then flung them down.

The signal to make themselves small targets and spread out to confront their attackers. Dayvee threw himself off the horse and ran bent over toward the woods. The sub-pack sawed on their reigns to follow. Codee had failed to teach them how to fight from a horse, so Dayvee chose the Calupi response to hidden foes. But for the Kayndo it was too dangerous.

Codee yelled. "No. Get out of there. We'll handle it." Dayvee stopped and turned back, but he wasn't running. Codee knew why. *Wilee, ask their companions to return. And tell Dayvee that's not a defensible position.*

More arrows streaked toward the sub-pack. Geno screamed. An arrow stuck out of his thigh. Their wolf companions raced out from the woods, back toward them.

That got Dayvee running back east toward his horse, but arrows still rained. They had plenty of help here. Codee needed to use it. "Someone's shooting arrows at the Kayndo!"

Clanspeople and companions ran toward the western tree line. A bear led the charge, but could they stop those shooting in time? Too many strides still separated Codee from Dayvee.

"Reko, help us direct our horses to get between Dayvee and those woods," Brando yelled out.

As the sub-pack's horses galloped to shield Dayvee, Codee took back every bad thing he had ever thought about Brando. A horse screamed. An arrow protruded from Elayni's horse's rump. Another sailed towards Dayvee. Codee wasn't close enough to stop it.

17

The Last Option

"Fleeing invites a chase so use it as the last option. Defending your back is difficult." ~ *Codee*

As arrows came toward them, Sunray dodged and put forth a burst of speed. The jostling made Dayvee's balance waver. His seat precarious, he clung to her mane, pressing his legs tighter against her sides. All of his friends' horses and their companions raced around him. Reko led the way, escaping north. No more arrows flew. The shooters were probably fleeing too.

A hill didn't break Sunray's speed. She galloped up it, then flew down the other side. Reko veered, leading them west into the tree line. Why? The shooters had come from the trees. Maybe since the forest offered more cover. The horses wove between the trees and jumped over obstacles without ever slowing. Dayvee desperately hung on.

The crashing as the horses plowed through the brush was too loud for Dayvee to speak to Reko. *Shilo, tell Reko as soon as he thinks it's safe to stop so Elayni's horse and Geno can be treated.*

Reko halted in a small clearing. Dayvee slid down, and his sub-pack did too. Holding on so tight made Dayvee's legs wobbly and numb. When Jaycee nudged him to greet him, it almost knocked Dayvee over.

Tayro wrapped a hand around the arrow in Geno's leg. "This will hurt, but it didn't hit your artery." Tayro snapped off the shaft and then worked the rest from Geno's leg carefully. He poured some medicine on and bandaged it. "You'll limp for a week or two, but you'll be fine."

Tayro did the same for Elayni's horse. "I don't think this will restrict her movement."

We lost your attackers. Wilee's mind voice got Dayvee's attention. *The scent of the Kagards' who spoke to us earlier was in those trees. We're not sure if they're responsible or chasing the culprits. But they left on horses.*

Should I ask their horses to stop?

No. We don't know if they're helping you, but the Kwin are pursuing them to find out. Codee says he can't see the prince being behind this attack. It would be easier for him to harm you after you arrive. So continue to the capital, but be careful. He says give each of your friends a red fringe. They earned it.

I shouldn't have gotten off Sunray.

Codee says now you'll know a horse's best defense is speed. When riding, fleeing is not the last option, but the first.

Okay. Thanks for the report.

Reko led them away in a canter. After a while, Reko switched to a fast trot. They alternated between those two gaits and rode due west for hours with their companions running alongside.

Cramps attacked leg muscles Dayvee never knew existed. His thighs were rubbed raw, and he couldn't feel his feet. Loaded with a full rucksack, he could jog for miles, but this horseback-riding sorely tested him. He'd rather go on foot and face their pursuers, but he couldn't risk his sub-pack's safety to spare himself.

The sun almost set before they came to a grassy area with flowers blooming in a profusion of colors. Reko motioned to the meadow. "We could camp here. I don't think our enemies will try to follow at night since they can't see our trail."

"Sounds good." Dayvee stopped Sunray. He should have asked a bird to scout. Probably too late now with it getting dark. He reached out. Great, an owl was nearby. *Can you scout behind us?*

Yes, Kayndo.

Dayvee slid off Sunray. His numb legs collapsed and sat him on the ground. He managed to rise, but his thighs and buttocks screamed to him that riding hurt.

His friends' awkward stances made their discomfort clear, but none complained. Not even a groan from Geno. Only his limp betrayed his injury. Dayvee's pride surged for the group he led. He turned to Reko, "Is there anything we need to do with the horses?"

"Just rub the sweat off, remove the hide and halter, and release them." When they finished, the horses went to the stream to drink.

The owl's whisper filled Dayvee's mind. *Kagards are camped maybe an hour's ride behind you. I didn't locate anyone between them and you. But I can't see underneath where the trees are thick.*

Thanks.

Jaycee nosed him. *We wolves are going to scout our back trail. We'll investigate those wooded areas.*

Concern sent a chill through Dayvee. *I hope you won't confront anyone without us. Those arrows travel far.*

We won't even be seen. Jaycee glided into the woods with the other wolves.

"Everyone should change out of their ceremony clothes. Brando and I will gather wood. Chayla, you fill the water bags. Tayro and Elayni will fix dinner. Geno, I'm ordering you to stay off your leg." Dayvee ran a hand through his hair. "I'm really sorry you were hurt. I should have made cover our first priority."

Geno's face crinkled into a frown. "It's not your fault. I wanted to go after them too."

Dayvee's guilt lightened a little, but his accountability as leader wouldn't let him excuse his actions.

Geno spread his ground hide and sat down. "When you finish changing, bring me your rucksack."

"Why do you want it?" Dayvee asked.

"The bottom corner's frayed. While I'm doing nothing, I'm going to fix it."

Somehow Dayvee always managed to end up with tangles when he sewed, but he didn't want Geno to take up his slack. "I can do it."

"You're using your gifts to help us. Fixing is all I can offer, but sometimes I can make things better, so I'd really like you to let me."

"Okay, thanks."

When Dayvee switched out of his ceremony clothes, the gaps in their beads and fringes showed several torn off. He folded them back in his rucksack and took it to Geno.

Brando went over to the tree line to gather wood. Dayvee joined him and let out a chuckle.

"What?" Brando asked.

"I was just thinking you might need to throw some of your snakes and frogs if we deal with more crowds. Otherwise, I might not have any clothes left."

Brando snorted. "No sense wasting frogs and snakes then. You naked will petrify them." His arm brushed Dayvee's when he grabbed a branch. Dayvee jumped back.

Brando's breath blew out. "You can't stand our touch, can you?"

"It's not intentional. I think my body's trying to avoid more hurt, like when a porcupine gets close. I'm going to pray about it."

Brando's face twisted. "I can't take this guilt. Put me in the ring. I won't fight back."

How could Leeto get to Brando? "You should tell me what happened with Jonesee."

Brando kicked the ground. "A quincee."

Rage at Leeto shot through Dayvee. "Cackles. You said you tripped."

"I did. After Jonesee stuck his foot out when I tried to escape."

"Did they hit you?"

"No, I was dazed from the fall. Before I could get up, they bound me. Then Andee was going to take me to Northern Platte Pack." Brando hung his head. "Leeto would only free me if I submitted and vowed to do his bidding."

Dayvee stepped on a branch and pulled the end to break it in two. "I'd have come after you."

"I didn't want to be responsible for you leaving Jaycee, but I shouldn't have hurt my *real* family. I wish I could take it back."

"So what did they make you do at the meeting?"

"You'll think even less of me, but I won't keep it from you." Brando mumbled. "I killed two people."

Dayvee's jaw dropped open. Brando broke down in tears after he killed his first deer. He hid his sensitive side anymore, but it must be tearing him up, like it would Dayvee. If he had just sent a bird after him, maybe he could have stopped it. "I'm sorry."

"Me, too." Brando drew a ragged breath. "But they wanted to kill you, and I'd do it again to protect my family. Am I still in yours?"

"Yes. If Leeto tears us apart, he wins, and the hurt won't stop." A movement drew Dayvee's attention. Only a garter snake twisting away.

Brando broke branches off a dead tree. "I'm not sure I want to go home."

Dayvee had to blink to keep tears back. "I don't think I ever will."

"You love Wolf Mountain."

"Four out of four Kayndo's never went home. They're already coming for me, and they don't care that I'm not Kayndo yet."

Brando held a huge bundle of wood. "I'll do everything I can to make sure you get to go home."

"Just make sure our sub-pack gets home, whether I do or not." Dayvee waved toward the camp. "Go on back. I need to pray."

"Can you stay in sight of camp to do it? My orders include not leaving you unguarded."

Dayvee sighed to himself, then nodded. Maybe the prince would be chosen. He wouldn't be needed as Kayndo or be hunted. And all this would be like a bad dream.

He hung back when they reached the camp. Dayvee had made plenty of mistakes himself. He wasn't even angry at his friends now, but he couldn't convince his body. *Please Kun, mend all of the pain and hurt each of us suffered. Bring us back together again and safely home.*

The sub-pack was working at making a fire ring. They quit talking and stared when Dayvee came and put his wood down. "What? Do I have something on my face?"

Elayni wrapped her arms around him. His body didn't flinch. His breath caught and his heart sped up. He put his arms around her and pulled her closer. Her hair tickled his nose, and he breathed in deeply of her scent, sweet like a strawberry. *Thank you, Kun.* "I'll go get some more wood if this is your reaction."

Elayni laughed. All his friends embraced him in a group hug.

Their arms didn't repulse him. It felt great. Afterward, he handed them each a red fringe. "Codee says well met, and you earned these."

They soon had the fire lit. Tayro and Elayni put dried meat, beans, carrots, onions, and herbs in a pot over it. Nothing fresh. They couldn't gather Kun's bounty on horses, especially while fleeing from pursuers. Reko joined them and took his food rations out.

"You don't have to fix anything." Dayvee pointed to the pot. "We have enough to share."

"I'll prepare some too," Reko said. "You can try Kwin rations, and I'll try Calupi."

When it was ready, Dayvee took a spoonful of Reko's dish with some type of meat, grains, berries, and maybe honey? It held a sweet taste that his tongue welcomed after their all too familiar rations.

Elayni swallowed a mouthful. "This is good."

"I agree." Tayro looked in his bowl. "What's in it?"

"We use ground corn, oats or barley, and then add nuts, seeds and berries, some dried meat, honey, and the fat from animal organs."

The wolves came back into camp as Dayvee finished eating. He breathed a sigh of relief, then filled Jaycee's bowl with food. *Find any people?*

Just the Kagards.

Reko handed Dayvee a flask with a salve in it. "All of you should apply this to any aching muscles. It smells and you'll feel some heat, but it will relieve some soreness."

What muscles of Dayvee's *didn't* ache? "Thanks."

"Eventually, your muscles will toughen, but the tighter you grip, the sorer you'll be."

Dayvee's better toughen up fast. They'd ridden only a half-day.

After Elayni and Chayla came back from applying it, Chayla handed the salve back to Reko. "It did help."

Reko's hand lingered on Chayla's longer than necessary to take the salve. His smile flashed at Chayla and Elayni. "I'm glad I could aid two beautiful women. Are all the women in your pack as attractive as you two?"

Chayla's cheeks turned crimson. Dayvee shot Reko a glare. He needed to leave the Calupi women alone.

Elayni giggled. "Most of our pack thinks Jolay is the most beautiful."

"I don't believe it." Reko ogled them. "Maybe as beautiful, not more." He turned to Dayvee. "You wolf mountain men are very fortunate."

"We don't think appearance is as important as ability." Dayvee threw a stick in the fire a little too hard, and sparks flew. "It won't put food in the pot."

"You sound like you're immune to your women's beauty." Reko shrugged. "I'm not."

Elayni gave Reko her full smile, the one that stole Dayvee's breath. Heat rose to Dayvee's neck. She shouldn't encourage Reko. When she glanced at Dayvee, he shook his head.

Elayni frowned and gave Dayvee a glare. It was her place, as a Calupi adult, to tell Reko if his attention was unwanted. If Reko didn't listen to her, pack law would unleash Dayvee's hands, but otherwise they were tied.

He wasn't the only one unhappy. Brando had stiffened, and Bruno's low rumble meant trouble.

Can you tell Brando we need Reko? Dayvee asked Bruno.

Yes.

Brando gave Dayvee a nod, but his eyes still scrunched. Reko might find a surprise in his bedroll tonight.

"What's in this salve?" Tayro asked. "I'd like to know how to make more."

Dayvee gave Tayro a chin lift. Nice subject change.

"It has witch hazel, mallow, great burdock, and comfrey," Reko answered.

Dayvee caught Geno staring at him, like the people at the clan meeting did. Unease filled him. Leeto spent many evenings talking to packmates to sort things out. Maybe Dayvee needed to do the same. He went over to where Geno sat with Graydee and spoke quietly, "You don't share your opinions with me anymore. Is it because I might become Kayndo?"

Geno's thick eyebrows almost met. "No, it's because I trust you to come up with the best answer."

"I'm not always right." Dayvee exhaled heavily. "You know I've made mistakes. I need everyone's honest advice. Yours too."

Geno slid a hand through his dark black hair. "My advice is you do the thinking, and I'll support you and protect you."

Geno's square jaw had set. Dayvee must not be good at working things out. "I'm not going to change your mind, am I?"

Graydee's ears went up, and Geno's smile almost covered the width of his face. "No, but don't worry. I might not give advice, but I've got your back." His face and tone turned serious. "You have my word on that." He handed Dayvee his rucksack.

Dayvee took it and tested the patch over the frayed area. It didn't give at all. "Why is my rucksack shiny?"

"I rubbed oil and pine sap over it to keep the water out," Geno replied. "It might make it better."

"Thanks."

Reko left them to give grain to the horses. Brando rose. "I think we should train."

"You want to do it in front of everyone?" Dayvee asked.

"I don't care if Reko learns how good we are. And I'm already teaching our sub-pack. They can train, too, but I'll excuse Geno since he's injured."

What? Brando had Elayni and Dayvee hide their training for years, and now he was teaching others. "Did Codee and Leeto make you share?"

"No. They still don't know. But our sub-pack is guarding you now, so I want them as skilled as I can get them."

Tayro took off his rucksack. "He made us vow not to challenge you before he'd teach us."

"I don't want anyone using our own methods against you when you're alpha." Brando put his rucksack in their pile.

"Can they challenge you?" Dayvee asked.

"Yes." Brando grinned. "But I love a good fight. Now, come on. Show them how well you can do it."

Dayvee rose, but he grumbled. "I'm too sore to be anything but pitiful tonight."

Jaycee and the other companions joined Geno and Graydee to watch. As Dayvee moved through the routines with the sub-pack, the brisk exercise did help loosen his muscles, but they still complained. Sweat streamed between Dayvee's shoulder blades.

Reko came back into the light of the fire. "What are you doing?"

"Fighting exercises." Brando snapped out a side kick.

"Would you like to wrestle?" Reko popped both sides of his neck, then flexed his biceps.

Bruno's tail thumped the ground. Brando's wide grin couldn't be missed even by firelight. "I'd love to."

"Do men look for opportunities to best one another?" Elayni stopped mid-punch. "Reko, you should know Brando's considered really good by the Calupi at wrestling."

"Don't let her scare you, Reko." Brando wiped sweat from his forehead with the back of his hand. "After riding on horses all day, how good do you think I'll be?"

Reko's teeth flashed as he laughed. "I'm not considered bad by the Kwin, and I'm used to riding on horses." He winked at Elayni. "And I don't look for opportunities to best men, but I sure look for ones to impress women."

Brando chuckled. "I won't make it easy."

"Do you want to wrestle in the dark or wait?" Geno asked.

"I don't like waiting," Brando picked up two sticks.

"With the light from the fire and moon, it's not really that dark." Reko motioned to one side of the fire. "The ground is pretty soft there, and I don't see any rocks."

"Looks good." Brando drew his tooth, and with two strokes, sharpened one end of both sticks, then tied a rope to the other. He stuck the sharpened point of one into the ground until it stood firm. Then he walked until the rope was tight and dragged the other stick through the soft ground until he had a perimeter line in the shape of a ring. Everyone helped place rocks around to mark it.

Dayvee placed the last stone down. "Try not to injure each other and don't end up in the fire. We have to ride tomorrow."

Reko looked over at Brando. "Does he always try to take the fun out?"

"No." Brando snorted. "He usually adds to it. He might ask some animals to wake you tomorrow."

"Opposite sides," Dayvee called. They took their places. "Reko, we consider a wrestling match over when an opponent puts a hand to the others throat. Ready?"

They both assumed fighting stances, their heels lifted and their heads lowered to make their necks harder to reach. "Yes."

"Go."

The two circled each other, grappling, each trying different holds. Reko stuck a foot behind Brando's leg and pushed. Brando allowed the match to go to the ground, but pulled Reko with him and flung him to the side. He rolled on top of the Kwin.

Reko tossed Brando off and sprang over on top. One would be on top, then the other, but not long enough for either to put a hand to the throat. Brando jumped to his feet. So did Reko, and they grappled again. Dayvee thought Brando had Reko, but the Kwin was dexterous and slipped from Brando's hold. Then Reko maneuvered Brando into an awkward position, but couldn't topple him.

Brando had the greater strength, Reko had the greater flexibility, and both had balance. Brando stalked with a fluid grace while Reko danced. Brando slammed Reko to the ground, and mid-roll, he pounced, placing one arm on the Kwin's legs to stop his roll and the other on his neck. Brando's hand recoiled as if Reko's neck was on fire. He scrambled away, but he had won.

Dayvee reached out to Bruno. What's going on with Brando?

He killed one of those men by throttling him.

Reko stood. Brando drew a breath, straightened his shoulders to resume his bravado act, and winked at Chayla and Elayni. "Impressed?"

Elayni shook her head, while Chayla laughed and answered, "Yes."

I am, Jaycee sent. Brando's wrestling always impressed Dayvee.

"It was fun." Reko smiled.

Dayvee's eyelids grew heavy. "We should get some rest. We'll need to leave early to stay ahead." If only his aching muscles let him sleep.

"What about posting a watch?" Elayni undid her braids, and golden tresses cascaded to frame her face.

Reko goggled at her. "You can if you want, but it's not necessary. The horses will alert us of danger." It wasn't necessary for Reko to keep his eyes glued on Elayni.

The wolves will guard. Jaycee and the wolves rose to pace a circle around their camp.

Dayvee's owl sent, *I'll hoot if anything approaches your camp.*

They had plenty of watchers. Dayvee crawled in his bedroll and closed his eyes. He woke from sleep at a snuffling sound near him. Hot breath steamed over the back of his neck. Dayvee yelled and grabbed for his nails.

18

Alarms

"If your body sends a warning, but you can't see the danger, don't doubt it's there." ~ Codee.

Dayvee sprang from his bedroll, nails ready to take on the threat. Sunray backed up at his yell. It was only the horse?

Jaycee's ruff stood as he raced from the tree line toward Dayvee. *I'm fine, Jaycee.*

The sub-pack had jumped from their bedrolls and pulled their nails.

Embarrassment sent warmth to Dayvee's cheeks. "Sorry. False alarm. But I didn't know who or what was breathing down my neck."

Reko's laughter rang out. He was already awake and stood at the side of their camp brushing the horses. The sub-pack cracked up too. Dayvee joined in with a sheepish chuckle. He had overreacted.

Brando's crooked smile creased his face. "Reko had a friend wake you, Dayvee."

"I didn't put her up to it." Reko came closer, and the other horses followed him. "But it's good you're quick to respond if we're threatened."

Brando fired a punch at Dayvee's shoulder that he blocked. "Yeah, we'll sleep much better knowing we don't have to worry about sniffing horses."

Shilo, Reko's companion, approached Dayvee. *Sunray's young and curious, but she should have better manners.*

Sunray shoved her head into Reko. He scratched her. "She likes attention, so she can be pushy, but she'll work her heart out for you. She won't let you come to harm."

Dayvee sent to her. *I didn't mind you smelling me. I just didn't know it was you. Thanks for helping me yesterday.*

She sniffed at him. *You're welcome, Kayndo.*

"Before we ride, we need to check and clean hooves on the horses. To examine them, I press here." Reko's fingers splayed across the hump above Sunray's hoof. She lifted her front leg up and curled it back. "She has a rock that needs to be removed." He dug it out with his knife. "You should try now."

Dayvee inspected Sunray's other hooves as his friends did the same with their horses. Then Reko fed them more grain from his rucksack. The Calupi took care of their own companions, and they all ate a quick breakfast.

The sky had turned a shade of gray, so sunrise wasn't far off. The curve of a brilliant golden arc peeked up on the horizon and lit up the sky with bands of pastel shades—turquoise-blue, lilac-purple, plum-red, goldish-orange, and buttercup yellow.

Dayvee sorted through the whispers calling to him. *I'm Spiro,* an eagle sent.

Can you scout the Kagards' camp for me?

Sure, Kayndo.

Dayvee mounted Sunray. Reko led them away at a canter as the sun rose. Dayvee envied their companions running alongside. His legs already protested riding on horses, but he had to bear it. Calupi aren't weak.

Spiro sent to Dayvee, *The Kagards are just stirring. I can keep flying above them if you want?*

Do you have a mate or young in your nest to care for?

Not yet.

Then yes, I'd appreciate you watching them.

Reko set a fast pace, but not a reckless one. Dayvee couldn't blame him. Their life wasn't in peril at the moment. They switched from the canter to a trot. Then Shilo slowed to a walk, and Reko came alongside Dayvee. "The horses need to rest some, so if we need to flee, they can."

A worry kept niggling at Dayvee. They followed no trail and often seemed to zigzag. "Our path isn't very direct. Couldn't our pursuers get ahead of us?"

"No, they don't know where we'll end up, and even if they did, it wouldn't work." Reko pointed to a thicket the horses picked their way around. "These brambles have slowed us some, but they'd be much worse if I took a direct path."

Jaycee left to investigate something with the other companions. What if the companions ranged too far and weren't able to catch up?

Don't worry. We're faster than horses, Jaycee sent.

When the wolves returned, they flushed a pheasant. Dayvee reached for his nails, then hesitated. What if Sunray jumped, or he lost his balance? Would he hit a friend? A stick rose in the sky, slammed into the pheasant, and returned to Reko, who caught it in his hand. The bird plummeted to the ground. Reko drew a pole slung in a sheath across his back. He speared the pheasant with it and put it in his pouch without ever breaking gait. Everyone stared at him.

"Are those a Kwin's weapons?" Dayvee asked.

"Two of them," Reko answered. "I used the cumback stick to knock the bird from the sky. And this is the cujo." He lifted the pole further up. Sharp points protruded from it. "One side has spikes, the other side is stone. I can sweep an animal's legs when I get close or spear things, but mostly I use it to knock brambles away from Shilo's legs." He slid the pole back in its sheath.

Hmmm. A weapon and tool in one. "Those would be useful for someone on horseback." Dayvee shifted on Sunray. Maybe the new spot would ease his soreness. "I wouldn't mind if my nails came back to me. Do you have more weapons?"

"Yes. This is my Bola." Reko pointed to the rope around his waist. "When I throw it, the balls on the end wrap around an animal's legs, and it falls. Last is my knife, but I usually use it to clean hooves."

"You seem skilled. Is the cumback difficult to master?" Elayni asked.

Reko puffed at her praise. "It takes practice. You shouldn't try and hunt, just focus on riding. I carry plenty of rations, and I'll keep adding birds and rabbits we scare up."

Dayvee glanced at the sun. Only mid-afternoon. Why did the sun move so slowly? He was so tired of the misery. Reko had set the pace at a fast trot again. Dayvee's least favorite gait, and the one Reko used the most. The jostling sent new cramps and stabs into his muscles.

"We need to detour around." Reko flicked a hand toward the east. "Otherwise, we'd be in one of the ancients' large ruins."

A giant arch cut off part of the sky ahead, broken and rusted with vines hanging on it. Dayvee shivered. Surprising, the arch hadn't toppled, but it threw an ominous shadow on the piles below.

Reko took a wide path to skirt the ruins. "They are too dangerous to ride through. The horses would get their feet shredded, and the piles could shift and swallow us."

Dayvee nodded. "They can hurt people on foot too. And our keeper teaches that the ancients' things can contaminate your spirit and take you from Kun."

Yes. This is close enough. Jaycee sent.

"Our keeper teaches the same," Reko said.

At least an hour passed before the ruins' scarred terrain finally disappeared. Sharp aches clamored again for Dayvee's attention. The meadow they rode through might make a nice place to camp. If only it wasn't too early. Jaycee and the other companions loped toward them, coming back from one of their side trips. A warning rattle pierced the air. A chill raced up Dayvee's spine like a fast moving spider.

Sunray jumped away from the rattle and broke into a gallop. Dayvee tried to clamp his legs around her. He was sliding. *Stop, Sunray.*

Her back legs lowered as she jerked to a sudden stop. Dayvee flew forward and caught himself on her neck. The mare's legs shook, her sides heaved. She tossed her head. *We need to flee.*

Jaycee reached their side. Dayvee's heart was in his throat as the other horses thundered past them, with his friends clinging to them. *Jaycee, is there any danger now?*

No, we're clear.

We're safe. Dayvee sent the message to all the horses so they'd stop fleeing.

Brando isn't clear. Bruno's voice resounded in Dayvee's mind.

He's back there. And he's been hurt.

#

Codee dismounted to examine the horse prints of those they followed. Something seemed peculiar. The cliff rose on one side here, so the trail narrowed, and the tracks went to single file. The prints muddled together, some over the top of others, but the ground was soft. It didn't take much for him to distinguish the tracks of Dayvee's group from the fresher Kagard prints.

Fewer now, Wilee sent. That's what had bothered Codee. There weren't as many. He and Wilee walked back and found two sets of tracks that split off in a different direction from the others. Ten still pursued Dayvee. They still outnumbered the sub-pack.

Codee sighed. The desire rose again to be with Dayvee. But Leeto had given different orders, so he followed Dayvee's pursuers instead. The Kwin had offered him a horse to ride and waved the lease fee due to Codee's reputation as one of the best trackers in the clan. Serano's anger with those who put an arrow in their lease horse assured Codee of their aid.

Serano chose twenty Kwin to go with them after the attackers. Wilee passed on to Dugee, Codee's order for him to represent Wolf Mountain on the hyena situation. Dayvee's safety had to come first. With King Layton dead, few doubted that Dayvee might need to become the Kayndo.

Serano rode over to where they examined the tracks. Codee straightened to report to him, "Two turned off here and left the main group. The others still follow Dayvee. If we ride hard, we should catch them within the hour."

Serano pointed at four Kwin. "Follow the two that separated. We'll continue after the others."

Codee hurried to remount as the other Kwin surged forward. Once in the saddle, he clucked his horse into a gallop to catch up. A tingling rose at the nape of his neck, warning him of danger. He reined his horse in and scanned the area. A shadow darted behind a rock on top of the cliff. "Watch out!"

A crashing rent the air as rocks tumbled down the cliff side.

19

Reward

"Don't fear death, to be with Kun is the greatest reward." ~ Kwutee

Codee's horse shied away from the cliff and the cascading rocks. He urged it to flee after Wilee, who streaked away from the cliff. Screams pierced the air as rocks plunged into horses' legs. Kwin and horses fell under the assault. The slide of rocks stopped, but arrows streaked down from above.

Codee guided his horse to take cover behind the thick trunk of a tree, like Wilee already did. Kwin raced to do the same. The arrows came from the top of the cliff. Not within good range of Codee's weapons, but if he had a shot, he'd try. He drew his nails.

A Kwin crawled out from beneath one of the horses and limped toward the trees. Serano galloped his companion out of cover toward him and, without slowing, extended an arm. The Kwin grabbed on, and Serano flung him behind him. An arrow flew toward them. Codee barely caught the quick motion of Serano throwing his cumback.

It knocked the arrow away and then returned to Serano. His companion circled. They galloped into the tree line near Codee and pulled up. The screams of the horses under the rocks reverberated around them. Those weren't just horses, but companions. Under the weight of those screams the Kwin's faces contorted to show grim mouths, gritted teeth, and anguished eyes.

Movement drew his attention at the top of the cliff. Codee brought his arm back to throw his nails, then stopped his release. They wore Kwin clothing. A cujo swung in the air, but he could see little else of the struggle since brush blocked his view.

"It's safe now," Serano shouted. "See to the companions."

Kwin surged toward their fallen, some riding double. Codee kept his horse at a slow walk to hang back and not get in the way. Wilee stayed at his side.

All but one of the Kwin's injured companions had quieted. The Kwin that Serano had rescued cradled the head of the last one screaming. The other Kwin rode back toward Codee.

Serano's face twisted as he came up to Codee. "We need to give him space to end the suffering."

Codee couldn't believe what he was hearing. "He'll kill his own companion?"

"Three legs are broken. His companion can't stand, and his lungs will fill so he'll suffocate. Slowly. In pain. No Kwin would allow that."

Wilee sent to Codee. *We both know Kwutee has used enough drugs to keep a companion pain free until the end, and those hasten its death. Kwutee's not here.*

I understand, but his own companion? That would be like killing Jolay. I don't think I could do it.

That's too bad since I'd prefer a quick death, Wilee sent.

The screams stopped and quiet reigned, broken only by muffled sobs. Serano choked out, "His companion is free of pain, but now he has to endure his own."

The Kwin faces were awash in tears. Codee fought to hold his own back. The four Kwin, who had ridden after the attackers, returned leading two extra horses with Kagard bodies slung over them.

Serano rode over to them. "You should have used the bola. I wanted to question them."

"They were behind too much cover," one explained. "And with the companions screaming…" His voice broke. "We killed them before they took more of us."

The Kwin returned to their fallen. They dismounted, spoke quietly for a few minutes, embraced each other, then rode back to Codee.

Serano's horse came to a stop. "Five companions are dead. Two Kwin are injured, but not seriously. They'll ride the Kagards' horses, and those that wish to return to the meeting will.

Codee took a deep breath. They might never want another

companion. The one that killed his probably wouldn't.

Serano's face darkened like a storm cloud. "They need to feel the wrath of the Kwin."

"Remember we can't ask questions if they're dead."

"A quick death would be too merciful. They'll face Kwin justice. I assured those with dead companions that we'll serve it."

"The races?"

"Yes."

"Pain or death?"

"It will depend on whether they repent. I hope they don't."

Codee had never seen a Kwin judgment race, but the stories he heard painted a vivid picture. A man with legs free, but his hands bound and tied to a horse, running behind it as it galloped. He'd falter and be dragged on the ground since no man could run as fast as a horse.

The first obstacle would be mud. If he hadn't fallen already, he would then. Next, he'd be dragged over hot coals to receive burns on his flesh while the horse jumped over them. He'd feel some relief as he got dragged through water, probably a creek. The relief would turn to agony as his lungs burned with the desire for air.

Then he'd leave the water and be dragged through thorn bushes, even sharp rocks, until his body ran with blood. Those who received the race of pain lived, but they'd suffer.

If the judgment was the race of death, the man would finally come to a line of Kwin with cujos, and everyone would bludgeon him as he went by. No one had ever survived the race of death, like the ring of death. Codee shuddered. He wouldn't want to run those races, but he wouldn't want to face a Calupi ring sentence, either. Five companions dead and Dayvee in peril kept his sympathy in check.

"We better catch them before they kill any of our sub-pack, or Leeto will want them to face Calupi justice."

"Let's ride." Serano's companion galloped away, and Codee urged his horse to follow. Kwin fell in around them with their jaws set.

#

Dayvee pulled Sunray's rein and turned her around. Bruno loped toward Brando, who lay where Dayvee had heard the rattle. His heart pounded. Did Brando break something during his fall? Did a snake get him?

He reached out with his mind and found an entire nest of snakes. *Please don't bite my friend, or the wolf that's coming.*

Sorry, Kayndo, a snake answered. *He's already been bitten twice, but he'll not be harmed more. Or the wolf as long as he doesn't attack us. We were just protecting our families from being trampled.*

Don't attack the snakes, Bruno. Then Dayvee asked the snake, *if I come up, will you bite me?*

No, but don't tread on us or let the horses.

Dayvee sent to all the companions. *No one else should approach.*

You may need me, Jaycee sent.

I'll be okay. Trust me.

Dayvee slid down from Sunray and hurried to Brando. Coiled bodies of rattle snakes lay thick among the grass near him. Brando's deep blue eyes were soft, and his face held a sheepish grin. "I knew you'd come."

Dayvee lifted him, staggering away under the weight. Brando probably weighed what Dayvee did. Was he clear? He didn't see more coils. He lay Brando down. Bruno sniffed at Brando's arm. His tail and ears went down. Bruno sank down by Brando's feet, resting his head over his ankles.

The snake's urgent thought shot through Dayvee's mind. *We won't bite your group if they stay on that side of you, so they don't step on us.*

Come now, but don't go beyond me, Dayvee sent to all the companions.

The horses trotted closer with his friends. "Brando's been bit by rattlesnakes," Dayvee hollered.

Brando's face parted in his crooked smile. "I should have picked a better place to nap."

Was Brando putting on a brave front? He must know Calupi had died from rattlesnake bites. Since Brando received two, what chance did he have? Jaycee ran up to nuzzle Dayvee, then he slunk over to

Bruno and lay beside him. Jaycee's sorrow came through their bond. It made it even harder for Dayvee to push down his emotions and be strong for Brando. Their friends arrived and swung down from their horses.

Reko leapt off his. "You can turn the horses loose. Shilo will keep them back."

Tayro hurried to Brando and knelt at his side. "Where are you bitten?"

"My right arm." Brando pointed to the holes in his sleeve.

"I'll need your shirt off." Brando sat up and slid out of his rucksack. Tayro grabbed it. "You shouldn't move, or you'll spread the venom. Let me help." Tayro unfastened his shirt ties. "Your arm is probably going to swell." He pulled his shirt off.

"I have a short sleeve in my rucksack," Brando said.

"It will be easier to monitor your heart without it. Just rest now." Tayro helped him lay back.

Dayvee's panic turned his voice sharp. "Do you have any purple cone flower, Tayro? Should we look for some? How can we help?"

Tayro sorted through his rucksack and took out some flasks. "I already have it and some other stuff mixed. But he'll get cold. He could use a fire and his bedroll."

Geno and Reko went to find wood. Elayni grabbed Brando's bedroll from his rucksack and covered him with it. Chayla handed Elayni hers, and she threw that around him too.

Tayro put his palm up. "That's enough." He poured some liquid into a cup and held it to Brando's mouth. "Take a drink."

As Brando did, his face puckered. Then Tayro poured something over the back side of Brando's right arm. There were two sets of punctures above the elbow only a few fingers width apart. Black mottling rose around them.

Tayro drew a head-band out of his rucksack. "Within an hour, you're probably going to be real sick. I need to know your symptoms to help. Do you have pain in your arm?"

Brando grimaced. "Like hot pokers."

Tayro tied the head band around Brando's arm above the bites.

"I'm not cutting your circulation, but it may slow the venom some. How is your vision?"

"I'm seeing spots."

"Your vision will probably get worse. Anything else?" Tayro asked.

"I'm sick to my stomach."

Tayro poured something else in the cup and had Brando drink it. Geno and Reko came back with the wood and got a fire going.

"Am I going to see Kun today?" Brando asked Tayro.

"Not if I can help it." Tayro glanced at Dayvee. "Ask the snakes whether they dry bit or used venom."

Dayvee latched onto the hope. Maybe they only dry bit to warn Brando. Didn't snakes try to save their venom for their prey? He reached out to the snake. *How much venom did my friend get?*

The other snake that bit him was younger. His venom is potent, but he didn't use much. I'm older and my sac wasn't completely empty when you called. A rabbit would die. A man probably will too. And even if he survives, his arm will be damaged. I'm sorry, Kayndo.

A huge lump rose in Dayvee's throat. *Not your fault. Mine. I should have called sooner.*

Why hadn't he checked what animals were around? Codee wasn't here pressing Dayvee to speak to them, so he'd stopped listening and pushed back the whispers. He'd reached out only when he wanted something.

Deep down, he knew why he hid from it—he didn't want to be Kayndo. Didn't want people treating him different, didn't want the responsibility, so he kept his weapon sheathed while Brando had been bitten by snakes. Well, no more. *Please Kun. I'll embrace your gift, just don't let Brando die.*

Dayvee's heart quaked. Should he tell Tayro in front of Brando? Brando would want to know the truth. Dayvee dropped beside Brando and clasped his other arm. "You got venom. Not all the sac. The snake isn't certain you'll die, but says your arm will be messed up."

Brando blanched. Then his mouth set in a determined line.

Tayro's eyes widened. "I had hoped I was wrong." He took

something from his pack, some type of bladder maybe. "I'll do what I can." He placed it over Brando's bites and squeezed it. A sucking sound filled the air.

Brando stiffened, and his teeth gritted. "I want to let Tayro, Geno, and Chayla join our family. Is that okay, Dayvee and Elayni?"

"They've earned it," Dayvee replied. "As long as you're still okay with it when you recover."

"I will be."

"I think all the sub-pack should be family." Elayni sniffed. "But we agreed to let you decide that, Brando."

"Now we should ask them. First, you should know there's just one rule in our family, a vow to do our very best to care for each other. So do you want to make that promise?"

"Yes," three solemn voices answered.

"All right. You're now family, and I'm counting on you to take care of Dayvee. He's no good at avoiding trouble."

"I'm not five years old," Dayvee groused. "If you think I need a babysitter, then you better be the one doing it."

Brando grinned. "Don't expect his thanks. Take care of each other too. And remember to laugh sometimes, you'll need that."

Elayni chewed on the corner of her lip. She put her hand on her hips. "Just because our family's bigger, doesn't mean we won't need you. Don't you leave us." Her voice cracked. "You fight this."

"Just think…you won't have to put up with my pranks."

"I'll put up with them," she whispered.

"Everyone's my witness." Brando's crooked smile flashed again. "You heard her."

Dayvee couldn't hold back his tears. "I can't do this without you."

"Even if I survive, my arm's going to be messed up." Brando's mouth pursed. "I can't protect you with one arm."

The snakebite wounds Dayvee had seen flashed through his mind. The flesh was eaten away by the venom. Some people had to have arms or legs removed from the damage done to them. Anguish ripped through his heart. "I'll take you with one arm over anyone else with two."

"I'm not giving up on Brando or his arm." The snap in Tayro's tone was rare. "We all know what Kun can do, so everyone should pray for him."

His friends bowed their heads. Dayvee did too. *Please Kun, heal Brando.*

"You have to leave, Dayvee." Brando's face scrunched. "You need to go to the castle and get away from our enemies."

Dayvee's chest tightened. "Don't even ask."

"I won't ask you to leave me alone, but let Tayro stay, and the rest of you go. We can catch up later, or if I meet Kun, Tayro can."

"He's right," Tayro said. "I'll stay and take care of him."

Dayvee gave them a shake of his head. "I'm not going. Any enemies can meet our nails, and we'll make up the time when Brando can travel."

They'll meet my teeth, Jaycee sent.

Lines creased Brando's face. "We vowed to protect you. They have to take you from here."

"That's impossible." Dayvee set his jaw. "Even if they bind me, no horse will carry me until I okay it, and I'm *not* abandoning you."

Jaycee's head lifted. *Nice flash of teeth.*

Dayvee wiped his eyes. "I'm really sorry. It's my fault you were bitten."

Brando shivered. "Why would you say that?"

"If I had just called the snakes sooner," Dayvee exhaled heavily.

"You didn't fall or put your hand down in a snake's nest."

"But I could have stopped it!" Dayvee wailed.

"If you're laying blame, it goes to me. I was lost in thought and didn't react fast enough."

Tayro squeezed Dayvee's shoulder. "Accidents happen, and only Kun can predict them."

Dayvee ran a hand through his hair. "None of you would even be here, but for me."

"You couldn't stop me." Brando moaned, but cut it off. "I won't regret coming if I meet Kun. I had a great family that gave me a good life, and I'll see you when you join me."

Elayni broke down and sobbed. Dayvee stood and reached for her. She fell into his arms, and they clung to each other. Chayla came to them, then Geno, and Tayro. They all hugged and cried, but they were missing someone.

Dayvee pulled back. He sank down by Brando and grasped his left forearm again. He could still touch him, but maybe not for long. Elayni grabbed Brando's hand. Chayla and Geno came, and each found a place on his arm to hold. Then Tayro washed his bites again. The swelling and black mottling had grown larger. The two sets of punctures had split open, almost as big as a thumb. If they continued to widen, they'd merge into one.

Brando's eyes locked onto Geno. "I should tell you what I was thinking about." His nose crinkled. "Maybe you can make it work. You know how Reko uses his cumback?"

"Yes." Geno blubbered.

"I was thinking about how to make Calupi weapons easier to retrieve on horses. The tooth would be easy." He sucked in a breath. "A light line to pull it back. Strong enough to remove it, but not so heavy it messes up the throw."

Geno's brow furrowed. "The line wouldn't need to be long if we get close with the horses first."

Brando winced, his voice more ragged. "Right. The nails will be harder, but maybe a line around the center hole running underneath..."

Tayro gave Brando another drink of something in a flask. "How are you feeling?"

"Not good." Brando's body shook and he gasped for breath.

Tayro's eyes filled with sorrow. "Don't try to talk more."

Those eyes confirmed it. Tayro didn't think Brando would live.

20

Peril

"The enemy within can be harder to defeat than the one outside."
~Kwutee

Brando didn't try to speak. Too hard for him to get any air in. But he listened and tried not to cry out. Tendrils of pain crept through his body from the snakebites.

Dayvee glanced at Tayro. "How long until he recovers?"

Tayro swiped his forehead with the back of his hand. "If he lives, in two days the venom should be gone."

Brando's jaw fell open. Two days. Their enemies would be here long before then, and Taluma needed Dayvee. But Dayvee wouldn't leave. *Kun please take me or heal me quickly, and if I live, let me use both my arms to protect the Vita.*

Dayvee's face and posture stiffened. "No more ifs. From now on, it's when Brando recovers." Authority infused his voice. "We all want to be here until then. Since we have things to attend to, we'll take turns."

The sub-pack's attention had riveted to Dayvee at his crisp tone. "First, everyone take care of your companions. Then, Geno and Elayni will help Reko tend the horses. When you return, Chayla and I will prepare dinner. After its ready, everyone will eat and drink something."

Elayni shook her head. "I couldn't eat."

"I don't want to either, but we will," Dayvee declared. "We'll all need our strength when Brando's better."

She nodded. Brando was proud of Dayvee. He had sounded like the alpha he was meant to be. He wouldn't be able to be Dayvee's second now. But an alpha needed a second.

Dayvee's gaze fell on him. "Brando won't be alone tonight, but each of us needs to sleep, so we'll take shifts. When he recovers, everyone will have to ride, and I won't have you falling off your horses from exhaustion." He filled Bruno's and Jaycee's bowls with meat. "Brando, can you ask Bruno to eat this?"

Please eat.

Bruno nosed the bowl, took one morsel out, then dropped it. His head plopped on Brando again. *I feel too sick and sad.*

He forgot the wolf felt what he did. *I'm sorry for putting you through this.* Brando moaned at another sharp stab of pain.

A whimper escaped Bruno. *I'll never be sorry I chose you.*

Brando closed his eyes. He must have slept awhile, but the waves of agony that crashed through his body one on top of another woke him. Night had fallen and stars winked at him. His moans turned to sobs, then into a scream, and back to a sob. Spasms sent his body writhing, and he couldn't control it. Bruno's body jerked beside him as well.

Arms wrapped around him. Dayvee held him from thrashing against the ground. Tears ran down Dayvee's face. His whispered prayers filled the night. "It's my fault, Kun. Please spare Brando's life and release him from this pain. I'll take his pain. Give it to me."

Brando let his heavy eyes close again. *Kun, don't do it. Dayvee can't have my pain.*

The next time he woke, Elayni held him, and she too prayed to Kun to spare him. Her touch didn't set his blood racing. He'd always love Elayni, but he wasn't in love with her. Now he understood the difference.

Tiny Chayla took her place. Her little pixie face twisted with sadness, her nose red under the scattering of freckles. Those soft almond eyes brimmed over with tears. Please don't cry. Those tears wrenched his heart and begged him to stop them. She prayed to Kun too. And she pleaded with Brando to fight to live. He had no more fight left, but she'd find someone better than him.

Spasms racked his body again. A giant white wolf stood before him. Was he dreaming? Dayvee had told him about JoKayndo's visit to him. The wolf cocked his head, turned, then took a few steps, and glanced back. It wanted him to follow. How could he? Wait, he wasn't in his body. He was looking down on it. Free from his body and pain, he trailed JoKayndo.

A bright light appeared ahead. Peace washed through Brando. Then came love and acceptance. So cherished. All the empty spots in his heart filled. Joy swelled in him. His smile couldn't be stopped. In the light, his mother beckoned him. He took a step toward her.

JoKayndo blocked his way. *Look behind you. Then you must choose. Go back or stay.*

Brando looked. There lay his body with its arm swelled as big as his leg. The flesh around the punctures torn open, and a large chunk eaten away. His friends surrounded him, and Bruno lay across his feet. Brando's gaze found his mother. Her face beamed with joy. Then his friends' faces, sad, tear stained. Bruno nuzzling his leg. *They need me, don't they?*

Yes, the Kayndo needs you, and so do the others. If you go back, you'll have to take care of them and the Vita. Your duties will be heavy. Which do you choose?

I'd rather stay with you, but I'll go help them so the Vita isn't lost. I can't abandon Dayvee to do it alone.

He was back in his flopping body. The pain burned like a fire, consuming him. He screamed. Then the light came. A cool liquid washed through him and quenched the raging fires. *Kun is pleased with your faithfulness.* JoKayndo's voice rang in his head. *He has answered your friends' prayers and granted healing.*

Brando woke. Bruno bounded up to lick his forehead. *Hi, Bruno.*

I missed you, the wolf sent.

Tayro lay close to his injured arm, then Chayla, and Geno beside her. A little beyond them was Reko. Brando turned his head to see Dayvee on his right, and Elayni squeezed next to him. Could a Calupi ask for better friends? He remembered only a little. Waves of agony and his body's contortions. Tayro treating him and everyone praying for him. JoKayndo. Was it real?

Dayvee jerked up to a sitting position. "Tayro, he's awake."

Tayro eyes flew open and widened. "How are you feeling?"

"Better."

"Does it still hurt?"

"Only a dull ache around the bites." Brando stood, shakily. His friend's faces were spinning, then stopped.

Tayro grabbed his forearm. "Take it easy."

"I'm okay." Elayni and Chayla ran to him and hugged him. Maybe there was something to be said for this experience. Brando never had a serious injury or illness. The attention was nice, although he didn't miss the pain. The others came to wrap arms around him. He smiled to himself.

His family refused to abandon him. Dayvee stayed even when everyone counted on him to get to Harthome. His mother needed to wait. Brando wouldn't desert them either. He stepped back from their embrace. "Need my shirt." He found it and slid his left arm in.

Tayro spoke with a healer's authority. "Let me see your injury before you cover it."

Brando held out his right arm. The swelling and angry black lines from last night had vanished, but a big chunk of his flesh was missing. His arm would sport scars, but hopefully it wouldn't affect its use too much. For once Brando was glad he was left-handed. "How long have I been out for?"

"It happened yesterday afternoon," Dayvee answered. "You were pretty bad last night."

Tayro examined his wound. "I'll bandage it." He poured more of the coneflower mixture on it and wrapped a cloth around it. He let go of Brando's arm. "I'm really glad I was wrong."

Brando finished putting on his shirt. "Your eyes told me you didn't think I'd survive."

"If someone goes into convulsions, they received enough venom to stop their heart. Yours did stop, but it started again." Tayro scratched his head. "And your arm should be much worse."

"I was needed so Kun answered my family's prayers." Brando gave them a crooked smile. "Who else would keep you laughing?" He turned to Dayvee. "We better go. The Vita needs us to hold a choosing, and I've held you up long enough."

Dayvee's eyes twinkled. "That's a good idea, but I think we'd better take care of the companions and eat first."

After he fed Bruno, and grabbed his own quick breakfast, Brando climbed on the horse. His friends mounted too while the companions milled around them. He wasn't sorry to be leaving this meadow even though his arm wasn't nearly as sore as his thighs and buttocks. He sent a heartfelt prayer to Kun for healing him. A shadow above drew Brando's attention. An eagle flew nearby.

What was wrong with Dayvee? He had slumped forward over Sunray's neck.

"Dayvee, what's wrong?" Brando hollered.

Dayvee straightened and his eyes lost their glaze. "Sorry." He pointed to the eagle. "Spiro warned me our pursuers are close, so I was body hopping with him."

"Could you see them?" Elayni asked.

"Through Spiro's eyes I could even see a fly on one of their horse's ears. There're ten of them. They're crossing the creek we drew water at, so they're only a few minutes behind us and beating their horses to go faster."

Reko's face contorted. "Shilo's in contact with Serano's companion. The Kwin are close behind them. Tears came to Reko's eyes and then a plea. "Oh Kun. No." He choked out, "Serano wants us to flee and let them serve the judgment of the Kwin."

"Agreed," Dayvee said.

Hold on." Reko yelled, "Yup!" The horses jumped into a gallop. The wolves raced forward too.

Brando wrapped his legs tight around his horse. Why had Reko been so upset?

They killed five of their herd's companions, Bruno sent.

Anger flooded Brando. *We should fight to defend the Vita,* he sent to Bruno.

It's not our judgment to serve unless we have no choice.

Could they stay ahead? Brando placed his hand on his weapon's pouch. They might need to fight anyway.

21

Sin against the Vita

Take more than you need and everyone suffers. Greed starves your packmates. ~ Jaycee

The trees thinned to reveal to Codee the backs of Kagards as their horses galloped across a large field.

Serano pulled up. "Reko warned us about rattlesnakes here. We'll skirt this field."

The Kagards' horses jerked to a stop, then fled bucking and crow hopping from the meadow. Kagards hauled on their horses reins, but couldn't stop them.

They heard the rattles, Wilee sent.

The horse's white eyes and foam-flecked bodies showed their terror. Kagards fell off. The Kwin threw their bolas at those unhorsed before they could draw weapons. Codee counted six on the ground. Kwin dismounted and picked their way carefully over to them.

Four Kagards kept their seats as their horses escaped the meadow. Kwin raced after them. The Kagards' horses' knees buckled. They collapsed and rolled. Two Kagards lay pinned, but the other two leapt off and ran. Kwin cast their bolas around them, and they crashed to the ground.

The Kwin bound the Kagards' hands, but left their legs free. They tied a line around their necks with a slip knot. If the Kagards fled, they'd choke. They brought them in front of Serano, who was mounted on his companion.

Serano's hard face revealed his anger. "I'm going to ask you some questions. My companion will know if you lie, so don't."

"Why should we talk?" a Kagard asked. "They already told us we received judgment."

"Yes," Serano said. "We will watch the finish of a race when we meet with our herd in a few days. When it starts depends on you.

Refuse to answer, and it begins now."

#

By their ninth day of horseback riding, Dayvee's muscles had finally quit complaining. None of the Calupi rode like Reko— in complete sync with his companion—but they were able to keep their seats. Reko said they'd reach Harthome today. What might await them there? No matter what, Dayvee was tired of waking to rush somewhere else. It was time to arrive.

The grass here brushed Dayvee's calves as Sunray trotted through it. At least this area was level, but it was only a matter of time before Sunray splashed through one of the low swampy patches or climbed another of the wooded hills with thick brush that dotted the landscape. Their path switched often between them.

Jaycee and the other companions loped up to them, coming back from one of their side excursions. Jaycee's tongue lolled as he joined Dayvee running beside Sunray. Spring was much warmer here than in the mountains.

Having fun? Dayvee asked.

Always, Jaycee sent.

Dayvee should learn to appreciate every moment the way Jaycee did. Reko's sigh drifted back. The Kwin's cheery disposition had turned somber. He couldn't even mourn with his herd since he accompanied the Calupi.

Elayni moved her horse up to ride beside Reko. "Can you tell us more about the Kwin and how they live?" she asked.

Reko flashed her a weak smile. "Sure. But try not to be too jealous. Remember, if you life-mate with a Kwin, you could live like we do."

Dayvee swatted at a biting fly. The Kwin life couldn't be better than Calupi.

It's not, Jaycee sent. *Wolves are the best companions.*

Reko slowed them to a walk. "Horses travel in small bands. They're always on the move to find fresh grazing so Kwin are too. We're never stuck long in one place."

"I wouldn't like not having a home to return to," Chayla said.

"Our tents are home, and they go with us."

"Do the Kwin have many leases?" Brando's hair appeared darker—almost black—when damp from sweat.

"Hundreds. Farmers, merchants, Kagards, traders, and travelers all need horses. Short leases have a Kwin assigned to accompany them. Long leases get checked once a year, so we can't stay in one place long."

Dayvee adjusted his seat on Sunray. "Are that many horses driven out of the wild herds?"

"The stallion drives out both the colts and fillies either as yearlings or two year olds. That's when we offer them the choice to be lease horses. Some choose to, others remain wild."

Geno called over, "Most wolves don't leave the pack. We offer the few that do a choice to be guard wolves. Lone wolves die quickly otherwise, but it's their choice."

Reko flicked a fly off his companion's neck. "Injured or pregnant horses that feel vulnerable often join with us too. And when grazing becomes scarce, we get more. Grassy Knoll herd actually consists of several herds. Three companion herds, eight lease herds, and we monitor a dozen wild herds."

"Wow. That's a lot of herds."

"Some only have a few horses. Just like in the wild, there're bachelor herds, filly herds, and those with a stallion and mares."

Parts of the Kwin life were the same as Calupi. Reko's care for the horses showed he followed the Vita. If only Reko didn't flirt so much. Dayvee had heard once that Kwin had multiple wives, but hadn't believed it. Could it be true? "Calupi life mate with one woman for life. Do the Kwin?"

"It depends. We'd all like several. The more wives a Kwin can provide for, the more his status rises, but we have to convince them and our herd we can afford them. We mate for life, too, and we don't steal wives. But all single women can expect the attention of Kwin men."

Dayvee closed his open mouth. All his friends looked wide-eyed at Reko. How he treated Elayni and Chayla must be normal for Kwin.

Still, Dayvee didn't like it.

Dayvee sent to Evee, *Can you ask Elayni for me if she wants to share a life-mate?*

Elayni glared at Dayvee, then gave Reko one of her huge smiles that showed her dimples. "It sounds like women are valued."

Reko's smile was much warmer. "Yes, and our women know it. But our wives don't need to be Kwin. They can be from the city or other clans. Our leases provide for them, and they can live as they wish."

He seemed to be working awfully hard to convince Elayni she should life-mate him, and she was hanging on his every word. Dayvee let out a heavy breath.

Elayni frowned at Dayvee, then asked Reko. "So how do your wives contribute to your herd?"

"Those who live with the Kwin gather as we travel. Some enjoy transforming the long grasses of the plains into baskets and rugs. You've probably seen some."

Chayla rode up to ride on Reko's other side. "Yes, they're stunning. I'd like to know what dyes you use to get those vivid colors."

"They bring good prices, so our dyes and techniques are kept secret." Reko shifted and Shilo moved closer to Chayla. "If you life-mated a Kwin, you'd learn them."

Elayni pushed a golden lock of hair from her face. "What about wives with other companions? Do they live with the Kwin or their own clans?"

"That's up to them. It's nice when we travel to have a wife on the other end, so we don't mind as long as any children stay summers with the Kwin. Then they can experience our life and be given the option to choose it."

Chayla frowned. "Aren't your wives and children lonely if what little time you have is shared between several?"

"They have their own interests, so they aren't available much either. When we do have time together, we make it special so the memories last."

All clans had different customs that worked well for them and their companions. Bunjee said bear clan children only saw their fathers in the winter. But Elayni and Chayla should figure out Calupi customs were best. Dayvee reined Sunray closer to Elayni. "Can we talk?"

"Okay."

Dayvee stopped their horses. Brando turned his horse and trotted back to them.

"I want to talk to Elayni alone." Dayvee waved him off.

Brando gave him a wink. "I'll leave you then." He made a signal to Elayni by laying one finger on top of another.

"Are you still keeping secrets?" Dayvee snapped. "What's that mean?"

Elayni blushed. Brando's grin was sheepish. "Sorry. It's Codee's." Brando ran a hand through his hair. "It means to keep you shielded."

"Is Elayni more capable than I am?" Dayvee demanded.

"As capable," she asserted. "I passed the tests too."

"It's not about abilities." Brando mumbled, "Elayni and I gave vows you didn't."

"You should fill me in."

"Cackles," Brando exclaimed. "You won't like it." He blew out an exasperated breath. "One was if it came to it, you'd be the last of us to die."

The heat rose in Dayvee, and his anger exploded. "You shouldn't have, and you *really* shouldn't have let her."

"I couldn't stop her."

Dayvee reached out to Brando's horse. *Take Brando for a run.*

Brando's horse wheeled around and galloped back toward the others. Brando's holler drifted back, "Dayvee!"

Dayvee shouted, "Work on your stopping while you enjoy the ride."

Elayni chewed on her lip. "Let him stop."

Dayvee fought to get his anger under control. If Leeto were here, he'd have Dayvee swimming laps again to cool it. "I will in a while, but I'm not very happy with either of you right now."

"Didn't you want to talk to me?" She batted those long eyelashes at him.

Dayvee took a breath. "Yes. Why are you encouraging Reko?"

Twin spots fired her cheeks. "You haven't asked me to life-mate. Did you think I'd just wait when others are interested?"

"What if I have to be Kayndo?" Dayvee groaned. "Have you ever heard of a Kayndo being life-mated? I haven't. I don't even know if they can."

Her eyes flashed. "Well, maybe you better find out. You can't win a race if you crawl, and the pack wouldn't expect me to wait forever."

She clucked to her horse and trotted back toward the others. Dayvee watched her go with a lump in his throat. The pack did encourage them to find suitable life mates soon after they became adult Calupi, but that didn't mean they had to. Codee waited sixteen years after his first life mate died. Dayvee would wait for Elayni. Apparently she wouldn't for him.

She stopped her horse and called back. "Come on, catch me if you can."

He put Sunray in a canter, and they raced back. Elayni went up to ride beside Reko. Dayvee directed Sunray in behind them. Her laughter drifted back.

Brando returned with Bruno. He guided his horse beside Dayvee, riding so close they almost brushed legs. "Elayni's not as easily influenced as when we were kids. She knows she's a high-status Calupi who's desirable, and she finally understands her parents absences weren't her fault."

"If you'd have refused to give vows that could force you into harm's way, the others might have followed your example."

"I'd try to protect my family regardless." Brando took his headband off and wiped sweat from his forehead. "The vows just let them know it so they didn't replace me with someone who wouldn't."

Bruno glanced at Dayvee from where he trotted stiffly beside Brando. The wolf averted his eyes, but his ears drooped to show his disappointment in Dayvee. Bruno was right. They had almost lost Brando a week ago. What if he fell from his horse again? Was that protecting the pack? "I'm sorry Brando. I shouldn't have gotten so angry, and I acted stupid sending your horse running."

"Do you want me to agree with you?"

"Someone needs to. Codee tells Leeto when he's behaving like an idiot. I know Leeto doesn't listen much, but Codee does it. Can you tell me, and I'll try to listen?"

Brando laughed. "Sure, that's one duty I'll enjoy."

Reko led them out of the marshy mess onto a dirt road. Maybe the biting flies would be less. The terrain grew less marshy and gave way to woods, then fields on one side of the road. Earthen homes dotted the fields, and people worked in them planting. A horse pulling a wagon came down the road, so Reko led them over to the side. The driver passed them with a wave.

More people traveled down the road. The Calupi attracted a few curious or wary glances, but they cut wide, away from the wolves, and no one said anything to them. Some people pulled carts with long poles behind them. Between the poles sat a box, and underneath two wheels turned, one on each side. Dayvee called to Reko, "How do they make those carts?"

"They peel and soak willow twigs, weave them tightly together with dried rushes and grasses to form whatever shapes they want them, and then bind them together."

A few Calupi owned chairs made like that. The sod and clay homes gave way to houses built out of brick, or rock, even a few wooden ones. Anyone could collect dead trees and limbs from Taluma's forests, but only Botanees were allowed to cut a living tree down. Now that Taluma's forest had grown back, they did harvest some, but the demand for wood was always high, so it was expensive.

Reko motioned Dayvee forward. He clucked to Sunray and they trotted up to ride alongside Reko.

"Before we get to Harthome, I need to tell you something," Reko said.

Dayvee heart skidded. Had Elayni agreed to life-mate with him?

"I want to pledge to you I'll answer your call and aid you however I can." Reko smiled. "If I have travelers, they may not like it when I strand them, but I'll come."

Whew. Relief flooded Dayvee. "I'm honored. I thought you'd tell me one of our Calupi women agreed to life-mate you."

Reko laughed. "No, not yet. But I'm working hard on it."

A harpy eagle is flying toward you, Spiro sent.

Dayvee had never seen a harpy eagle. They lived in the far southern part of their continent, except one. Must be Seemo.

Jaycee nudged Dayvee. *Gojo, the companion of White River Pack's keeper is in mind reach. Seemo is coming to take you to them.*

A huge bird appeared in the sky with a white head on a light gray body, black rings around his throat, black stripes on his wings and tail, and black markings on his legs. The eagle's magnificence stole his breath. Brando whistled his appreciation.

I greet you, Kayndo.

Dayvee stopped Sunray. *I welcome you, Seemo. Your service to King Layton and the Vita is well known.*

Seemo flew down and perched on the branch of a large oak tree on the side of the road. He bobbed his head. *I wanted to guard the king's body, but I promised him I'd stay to make sure Taluma followed the Vita.*

I'm sorry for your loss, but I'm glad you're still here. Will the prince be happy to see us?

Probably not. The queen hasn't left her rooms since the king's death. Varian, from the other continent, advises the prince, and they banned animals from Harthome. Seemo's head lowered. *When the prince was young, he yanked my feather. I bit him, and he never got over it.*

Dayvee clenched his teeth. Didn't the Prince have any respect for companions? *Many Calupi were nipped when we used a wolf as a play thing, but we learned better.*

He learned too well. The only animals still there are those who remain hidden, but they keep us informed.

How does he expect to be chosen if he doesn't let Jaycee in?

Seemo ruffled his feathers. *He's given orders to allow you in, but the animals are afraid it's a trap. They're trying to learn more.*

Dayvee relayed his conversation with Seemo to his friends.

Chayla shook her head. "We can't go then."

"We have to." Tayro's horse stamped a hoof impatiently. "Our laws say we can replace him if he fails or refuses the test, but the companions can't tell us if we don't go."

Dayvee turned back to Seemo. *Thanks for the warning.*

Seemo's talons bit into the branch he perched on. *The clanspeople who came for the choosing have set up camp outside the wall since they weren't allowed in. Others loyal to the Vita have joined them.*

I just got a glimpse of Kagards moving in the woods ahead, Spiro sent.

Jaycee's urgent thought rushed in. *We'll investigate.*

Be careful, Dayvee sent.

The companions padded into the woods.

A few minutes later a loud bang almost like thunder reverberated in the air. Dayvee's heart leapt. *Jaycee, are you okay?*

Yes. They are leaving. Give it a few minutes, and then come see.

When they rode up, a different scent wrinkled Dayvee's nose, similar to smoke, but tangier. The companions had ringed something. Dayvee and his sub-pack dismounted. The wolves parted for them. The antlers had been cut off a buck's carcass, and it had a round hole in its side smaller than a spear or knife wound. A pool of blood congealed around it, and bloody boot prints led away. The Kagards must have killed it, but with what and why? They didn't even take the meat.

Jaycee's confusion slammed into Dayvee too.

Others at camp have seen this before, Seemo sent. *The Kagards are testing the ancients' weapons on animals.*

The ancients' weapons. *Could the deer be contaminated?* Dayvee's heart raced, and he took a couple of steps back. His sub-pack did too. *Did they get too close?*

The camp has eaten the meat with no ill effects, Seemo sent. *The Kagards are well-fed, so the meat's not valued. Maybe they take the antlers as evidence.*

How could the prince do this? *How long has this been going on?* Dayvee asked Seemo.

Since the king's death.

"This is sin against the Vita," Tayro exclaimed.

Chayla touched the deer's body. "We need to stop it."

"I hate to waste the meat, even though we're in a hurry." Dayvee blew out his breath. "Those camped can surely use it."

"We can take it without losing much time." Reko pulled his knife and field-dressed the deer. Then, he retrieved a folded hide, rope, and a long piece of leather from his rucksack. He unfolded the large hide, maybe a buffalo's. Several leg bones of some animal were sewn to the edges framing it, and more bones were attached underneath in vertical rows. In between the bones lay gaps for folding.

"Can you grab his back legs and help me?" Reko asked Geno, who stood closest. They lifted the deer onto the hide. "Shilo can pull the deer behind us easily." Reko slid the leather circle over Shilo's head, and it came to rest on his chest. He attached one end of the ropes to the collar, and then slid it through rings along the bone frame of each side of the hide. Finished, he mounted.

As Shilo dragged the hide, the edges pulled up so the deer wouldn't fall out, and the bones on the bottom kept it from being torn to shreds. With that type of travois, the Kwin didn't need to find poles. Dayvee and his friends left the scene of carnage with the companions and returned to the road. A few minutes more of riding brought them to a large wall.

Reko pointed. "The wall surrounds Harthome."

It sure obscured Dayvee's view of the city. Only roofs, and in the distance the stone turrets of a castle rose above the wall.

A line of people headed for an opening with huge wooden gates. Seemo led them away from the gate, but along the wall until they came to a river channel. Reko gestured. "That supplies the water for Harthome. It goes through a tunnel under the wall." Seemo turned from Harthome, following the river upstream into a wooded copse.

Pines weren't thick here like at Wolf Mountain. Oaks reigned predominant, but maples, pecans, hickory, elms, and cedar were sprinkled in too. The din of voices rose. Wood smoke from campfires covered the forest scents.

The woods opened onto a large meadow where a large number of tents fluttered in the breeze. People and animals filled the gaps in between them. Probably not half as many as at the clan meeting, but it was the second largest group Dayvee had ever seen assembled. This close to the city walls, Harthome's residents and Kagards must know the camp was there. It'd be impossible for it to be missed.

The clamor subsided, and the camp fell silent as everyone watched them approach. The animal whispers turned into shouts in Dayvee's head. He rubbed his temple. *I can't talk to you all. You'll have to wait.*

Brando and Elayni looked at him with faces creased in concern. Could he hide anything from either of them? He tried to smile. People rushed forward to greet them. Their companions' ruffs rose.

"Stop, Dayvee." Brando pulled his nails.

22

Contamination

"Guard your soul so you don't lose your connection to Kun." ~ Kwutee.

Dayvee reined in Sunray as Brando yelled at everyone approaching from the camp, "A few at a time! I won't allow us to be mobbed."

"We'll greet them first." the shout came from a gray-headed stranger. A wolf stood at his side. "Everyone else should return to your duties. You can meet them later."

Must be the keeper assigned to do the choosing.

It is, Jaycee sent.

Dayvee slid off Sunray. His sub-pack dismounted, too, as Reko vaulted from Shilo.

The group with the keeper still moving toward them held several Calupi and a few city people. Must be Pericards since they were dressed like Kagards, but in black. Dayvee expected all strangers. Wait. Only dark-brown hair and a strong forehead were visible on someone who stood behind the keeper, but they looked familiar. Could it be?

"Let Juno and I speak to them. Then I'll introduce you."

A voice he knew. Yes! A packmate. Wolf Mountain's messenger Drako was here. Even though he and Leeto were the same age, thirty-four, they were nothing alike. When Drako came home, it was always a celebration with exciting stories of his travels.

The others hung back as Juno and Drako jogged toward them.

The sub-pack wolves stiffened, and their ruffs bristled. *Drako's a packmate, and Juno's his companion,* Dayvee sent to them all. *They don't get home much so you haven't met.*

Juno's tail wagged exuberantly as he touched noses with the

wolves. Drako clasped Dayvee's forearm with one hand and slapped his shoulder with the other. "Well met."

Dayvee returned the clasp. "I'm *really* glad you're here."

Drako's soft brown eyes sparkled, and he wore a broad smile. "We came for the king's funeral, but stayed to help you."

We'll fight to defend the Vita, Juno sent.

Dayvee smiled back. "I'm honored."

As Drako clasped arms with each of the sub-pack, Dayvee motioned to Reko. "This is our Kwin friend, Reko. He helped us get here safely."

Drako clasped Reko's arm. "Well met."

Reko pointed to the travois. "We brought a deer killed by the ancients' weapons for the camp."

"Thanks. At least the meat won't be wasted." Drako gestured toward Juno. "He sent the message. Clanspeople will come for it." He turned back to Dayvee. "The Pericard captain, Blake, has taken charge here. Most are clan and don't like it, but he has the keeper's support."

"For a city person, Blake's not too bad," Reko said. "He's fair. Everyone's treated strictly."

Dayvee gave the camp in the glade another look. All the clanspeople camped with animals on one side, city people on the other. "I might need them all."

"That's what Gaylo said, but he doesn't trust everyone here." Drako flipped his hand toward those waiting. "I'll introduce you if you're ready."

"Just a minute and we will be." Dayvee removed Sunray's leather hide and reins. *Thank you, Sunray, for your aid.*

You're welcome. She head-butted his stomach. Dayvee handed Reko the reins and hide. "Will you be returning to your herd now?"

"I have a place I'll rest the horses and then start back."

"We'll miss your friendship, but we understand duty." Dayvee clasped his arm. "May Kun go with you." He turned back to Drako. "Okay, take us to them."

"Wait a second for the ring," Brando snapped. His friends finished handing their horses gear to Reko.

"Leave the front open." Dayvee sighed. "See what I put up with, Drako? They treat me like I'm five."

"I know it's against what you've been taught, but they're right. Will you let me close the ring?"

"You can join us, but I won't be sealed off."

"You'll never convince him differently," Brando said. "You can take Elayni's place, and she can help Geno protect his back. If anyone reaches for Dayvee, remove their fingers. They pull a weapon, go for the throat. Act first and ask questions later."

"Brando!" Dayvee hollered.

"You need to let me follow my orders."

"I know you have orders, but don't get too carried away." Dayvee couldn't suppress his grin. "You won't like my prank when I call a bear to give you a hug."

Brando laughed and lobbed a fist at him that he dodged. "Now I get to tell you you're acting like an idiot. That wouldn't be a very friendly prank."

Dayvee returned the punch, but Brando blocked it. "It'll be friendly. I'll call a female bear."

Brando snorted. "See what we put up with, Drako? If you're ready, we are."

"I'm ready." Drako joined the ring. "But I'd like to see a bear hug you, especially after I found the frogs you packed me last time."

"I bet it gave you a laugh." Brando chuckled and signaled with a slash of his thumb. The sub-pack undid the flaps on their weapons pouches as they walked forward. When they neared the others, they stopped.

Drako pointed to the gray haired Calupi. His pecan-toned face only held a few wrinkle lines. "This is Gaylo, keeper of White River pack and his pack members; the Pericard captain, Blake, and his Pericards; Theron and Chase. Everyone, this is the beta, Dayvee, his sub-pack, and their companions."

The Calupi lowered their heads and studied him surreptitiously while the Pericards inspected Dayvee. Did they expect to see a Kayndo? Dayvee felt like a pretender. He wasn't the stuff of legends.

Leeto had never considered him good enough, but his sub-pack believed in him and elected him their leader. He couldn't let them down.

Dayvee pulled his shoulders back and lifted his chin. "Greetings."

White River Pack's companions sank to the ground and exposed their throats to Dayvee, just like Wolf Mountain wolves did at his choosing. Their voices resounded in his mind. *I'm yours to lead.*

Blake, the Pericard captain, took a step closer. Early to mid-thirties maybe? He had dark brown hair cropped short, and steely gray eyes that traveled over Dayvee's entire length. Did his frown mean he found Dayvee lacking?

Brando's hand moved to grip his nails. They weren't pulled, but the action screamed readiness.

Blake lifted one eyebrow and crossed his arms. One of Leeto's intimidating moves, but Dayvee wasn't going to let himself be cowed. He met those flint eyes and didn't look away.

Blake dropped his gaze first. "Pericards protect the heart of the kingdom—a Kayndo or king—but we have neither. If you'll trust me, I'd like to help you so we have a purpose again."

Brando drew himself up. "Dayvee trusts everyone, but I don't. Kagards already attacked us once."

Dayvee gave Brando a small head shake. "Captain Blake—"

Blake interrupted, "Just Blake. I'm not the captain now."

"Okay Blake, I was going to say until you show me I can't, I'll assume you're worthy of trust."

"Varian threw anyone who wouldn't swear their loyalty to him in the dungeon. Every Pericard and a few of the Kagards still refused." Blake frowned. "Only a few of us escaped."

Dayvee wasn't sure yet whether to be glad they'd evaded capture, but he'd give them the benefit of the doubt.

"We have food and drink ready." Gaylo motioned to the camp. "We would have held a feast, but we didn't want anyone other than Pericards and clanspeople learning your identity. I'm afraid the others will figure it out, anyway, with how everyone's acting."

"We ate recently and need to get Jaycee to the prince."

Their faces fell. "We should talk first," Gaylo said.

Dayvee relented. "Maybe we could eat a little while we discuss things."

"Great. Come with us." Gaylo turned and walked toward the camp.

"Have the Kagards tried to bother you?" Dayvee trailed after them with his sub-pack and their companions around him.

"Not yet," Gaylo answered.

Greetings, Kayndo.

Hello Kayndo!

Kayndo, I'm here to help!

Animals shouted at him until Dayvee's head stabbed him. He stumbled and caught himself.

Gaylo weaved around the tents and animals. Excited people pressed close to them. "Give them time to eat, and we'll introduce you."

Butterflies flew in the pit of Dayvee's stomach. Gaylo led them to White River Pack's fire and tents. His packmates sat on hides among the grass there. As Gaylo named them, they stood and greeted them with exuberant handclasps.

"Help yourself." Gaylo pointed to baskets of food lined atop a log close to the fire. Sticky balls filled one. A wave of homesickness hit Dayvee with the memories of Milay pounding grain, mixing it with honey or maple syrup, then pressing it into balls to fry in oil. They were still warm to the touch. He put a few in his bowl.

"Sit here." Gaylo gestured to a hide that lay spread out closest to the food and fire—the spot with the most honor. Dayvee, Drako, and his friends sat, and their companions plopped down around them.

Gaylo seated himself and Blake nearby. Lines of concern wrinkled Blake's face as he glanced at Dayvee. "Varian probably ordered the attack against you. If you go to the castle, the Kagards won't let you carry in weapons, and they use the ancients'."

Dayvee swallowed a sweet mouthful. "Can their weapons be defeated?"

"Not easily. We do know they'll clog if not kept clean." He waved his hand. "We'd like to hold the choosing out here so we can minimize the risk."

"Will the prince agree?" Elayni asked.

"I don't know. His father's choosing was held outside so the crowds could watch, but they don't honor our traditions." Blake frowned. "The prince believes Varian's people will invade us."

"Is the threat real?" Dayvee popped his last sticky ball into his mouth.

"Juno judged him." Drako let out a heavy breath. "Varian believes it's real."

"I'll go there now, tell Prince Tibalt you've arrived, and ask him to come for the choosing." Blake's tone rang with authority.

Was he making the decisions that should be Dayvee's? Faces trained on them. Was everyone waiting for his reaction?

Show them who Kun chose to be Kayndo, Jaycee sent.

Should Dayvee risk losing the city people? Either that or lose respect from the clanspeople. "Are you asking to carry *my* message or telling me?"

A corner of Blake's mouth turned up a little. Maybe he respected strength. "I'm asking."

Dayvee crossed his arms. "Won't they try to throw you in the dungeon again?"

"Carrying a message should be safe enough."

Jaycee nudged Dayvee. *He's being deceitful.*

"My companion sensed your deceit. It *is* risky for you to go, so the answer's no. I need what you can tell me about Harthome."

"I'll take your message if you want," Drako volunteered. "Prince Tibalt's not happy with me, but he knows I'm the pack's messenger."

"All right, but be careful." Dayvee uncrossed his arms. "Tell the prince that his companion is here, and he should meet us today or tomorrow for the choosing."

After Drako and Juno left, Gaylo introduced Dayvee and his sub-pack to everyone in the camp. Hours passed and still Drako hadn't come. Dayvee reached out for Juno. *What's going on?*

They wouldn't let me in. Drako's in the castle, but they're making him wait to see the prince.

A drum beat began, and a haunting flute trilled a melody. Someone joined in with a lute—a hollowed out gourd with strings attached. Dayvee enjoyed the music, but couldn't relax. His nerves kept his foot tapping.

Clanspeople got up and danced. A group of Calupi close to their age approached. A young woman asked Brando, "Would any of you like to dance with us?"

Brando grinned. "We're on duty."

"Even if I weren't capable, it wouldn't take all of you." Dayvee waved a hand toward the dancers. "Go enjoy yourselves."

Chayla rose. "I will." She went with them.

Brando scowled. Elayni joined them, and young Calupi men jostled each other to dance with her. Cackles.

"Why don't you go dance?" Brando asked.

"With all of you surrounding me?" Dayvee sighed. "We'd end up falling over each other's feet."

Drako's coming, Jaycee sent.

Finally.

Chayla and Elayni came back as Juno loped up with Drako behind him. Dayvee rose and clasped Drako's forearm. "We were getting worried."

"Sorry. They wanted to get back to us in a week." Drako huffed. "I told them unless we received their answer today, we'd consider it a refusal. They still made me wait until now."

Gaylo gestured to the food. "See to your needs."

Drako filled Juno's bowl, then his. Gaylo passed Drako the Razi. He took a drink. "The prince said that Jaycee and his sub-pack should come to the castle so he can get to know him before the choosing. He claimed it was a reasonable request since we train ahead." Drako handed the Razi to Dayvee and sat next to them. "With Juno not allowed in, I couldn't be sure whether he was lying."

Dayvee tried not to make a face when the Razi burned his throat. "What does everyone think?"

Brando frowned. "It's foolish to go to a predator's den and leave your weapons behind."

"I don't like it." Elayni passed the Razi to Tayro without drinking.

Tayro sipped it. "Me either, but most will say it *is* a reasonable request." He handed the Razi to Blake.

Blake swigged a drink. Tears came to his eyes, and he coughed out, "We'll all go."

Brando snickered. "Would they let everyone in?"

"No," Blake passed the Razi to Gaylo. "But we can try to force our way in."

"With all the people here, surely we'd outnumber them," Chayla said softly.

Drako cut a chunk of venison steak. "When the Kagards at the gate believe they face a threat, a bell is rung and people from Harthome rush to defend the walls." He narrowed his eyes at Blake. "Tell them how many."

"They'd have at least four times what we do."

"And the ancients' weapons too," Drako said.

"I'm not leading everyone to slaughter." Dayvee put a hand on Jaycee's head. "Jaycee and I will go tomorrow. Everyone else can stay here."

I have to go to the prince to judge him, Jaycee sent. *But I can go alone.*

Who would speak for you? We go together.

Brando pushed his bowl back. "If you go, I'm going."

"So am I," the rest of his sub-pack announced while their companions' same thoughts echoed in Dayvee's head.

"The Pericards need to go to protect you," Blake claimed.

They couldn't protect Dayvee when they'd be so outnumbered. They'd just share the risk. "This is ridiculous. You'd just be adding more people to a possible slaughter."

"You're not getting rid of us. We'd follow." Elayni's eyes met his. "We swore oaths."

Brando's jaw set. Yes, they'd follow regardless of what Dayvee said. He released a heavy breath. "The sub-pack can go with me." He glanced at Blake. "But I'm not taking anyone else."

Blake sighed. "I really think it's a trap."

"My duty to take Jaycee to the prince cannot be shirked." Dayvee ran a hand through his hair. "But I'd be stupid not to consider the risk and plan for it. I've spoken to some animals there. They can help us if we run into trouble, but it might aid us to have a distraction."

"What were you thinking?" Gaylo asked.

"A false attack. I don't want anyone hurt. Just give them something to think about other than us."

Blake rubbed his chin. "The Pericards can do that."

"The clanspeople will help," Gaylo said.

And their companions, Juno sent.

"Great, I'll let you know if we need it, but if the soldiers come after you, flee."

A Pericard came over and carried a bundle to Blake. "You wanted this?"

"Yes Jerrod. Take it to him." Blake tilted his head toward Dayvee.

Jerrod handed it over. What was it? Dayvee undid the hide covering. Probably four feet in total length. Inside lay a shaped stick— one end wooden with a black rod extending from the wood. The rod glinted. He ran his fingers across it—smooth to his touch.

"Jerrod took that weapon from a Kagard," Blake said. "He can demonstrate it for you."

An ancients' weapon? Dayvee's heart lurched. He dropped it and jumped up with his sub-pack. Brando kicked it away from them. Dayvee grabbed Elayni and twisted his hand to give the signal Calupi seldom used—retreat. The sub-pack and Drako backed further from it. Gaylo sidled away from it too.

Brando drew his nails and shouted, "Are you trying to contaminate his soul?"

Gaylo's packmates pulled their weapons too.

"It won't hurt you." Blake put his hands up, palm out. "That isn't one of the ancients' weapons. They made it in Harthome. Jerrod and I both used it without harm."

Gaylo held his arm out straight as if to hold everyone away from the weapon. "It looks like the ancients' metal."

"Yes," Blake admitted. "The metal was collected from the ruins and melted down."

"After the wars, the ancients' things made people so nauseous it killed them." Gaylo's voice shook. "Even now some are dangerous, and copies can still contaminate your soul."

Jerrod gritted his teeth. "Our souls aren't contaminated."

"Did either of you have a hard time stopping when you used the weapon?" Gaylo signaled with his thumb. Everyone put their weapons away—except Brando.

"I wanted to use it again, but I didn't," Blake answered.

Gaylo rubbed his chin. "Would you be willing to destroy it?"

Blake's shoulders fell. "I won't enjoy it, but I'd do it if you believe it's harmful."

"No." Jerrod threw up his hands. "It can help us, and if you don't want to use it, I do." He lunged for the gun.

Jaycee and Bruno got there first and stood over it, growling. Jerrod hesitated, but didn't retreat.

"Don't try it," Brando snapped. "The wolves and I consider that weapon a threat, so I suggest you back up."

Jerrod took a few steps away.

Gaylo's face became stern. "You both are contaminated. Blake, your exposure must not have been as long since you can fight the compulsion."

"You're wrong," Jerrod exclaimed. "I'm not contaminated."

"I'm not wrong, but I don't know what stage of contamination you're in." Gaylo's brow knitted. "First comes telling yourself that you used one of the ancients' things without harm, and you can use more. Second, you'll convince yourself their things are better than ours. Third, you'll amass more, but lie about it and keep them hidden. You won't be able to get enough. Greed will corrupt you, and you'll collect more of our things too. Then comes the fourth stage where you'd harm your own brother if he tried to take them from you."

Tears sprang to Jerrod's eyes. "Third. I have one of their knives in my pocket, and I wanted to get more. I *am* contaminated."

"I know. Take it out and drop it, then back away," Gaylo ordered.

Jerrod's hand shook as he pulled it out. He clasped it so hard his knuckles turned white.

Blake barked, "Now!"

Jerrod let it fall, and he backed away. Gaylo glanced at Blake. "Some get better after they understand." He pointed toward the weapons. "They should be buried, but I don't want to risk anyone."

Jaycee's thoughts buffeted Dayvee. *We'll bury them. The contamination doesn't affect us.* Jaycee picked up the gun in his mouth, and Bruno took the knife. The companions left.

"Blake had the Pericards set up a large tent across from theirs for your use tonight." Gaylo held out the Razi to Brando. "It's away from everyone else, so you'll be safer."

"I'd rather have rock walls." Brando sheathed his nails and took another drink.

"Me too, but there aren't any caves for miles," Gaylo said.

Brando handed the Razi to Blake. Blake passed it to Drako without drinking. "My Pericards can take guard shifts so you can sleep."

"That's not needed," Brando's tone was crisp. "We'll rotate. And we have orders to kill anyone who approaches Dayvee while he's sleeping. I won't think twice, so warn your men."

Just how many orders had Dayvee's friends received? The council shouldn't have taken their ability to judge danger away. "What if a child does?"

Brando blanched. "We'll just make certain that doesn't happen."

When they hadn't allowed others to get too close to them before, it just made enemies. How could Dayvee prevent that from happening again?

23

The Castle

"Conquering your fear doesn't mean your legs won't tremble, it means you move forward in spite of them." ~Codee

Dayvee's apprehension increased as Harthome's wall came in view. The massive wooden gates stood open, but Kagards blocked the entrance. And more patrolled above on the thick, stone wall. Although the sun was barely up, a line of people already waited to go through. Dayvee and his sub-pack joined the line. The strangers drew back to give the Calupi and their wolves space.

When their turn came, a Kagard hailed them. "No animals are allowed in Harthome."

"This is the prince's companion." Dayvee touched Jaycee's head. "And we're the castle sub-pack."

"Oh." The Kagard smirked. "Prince Tibalt's expecting you. Hand over your weapons and rucksacks."

What choice did they have? Dayvee slid off his rucksack, removed his pouches, then held them out.

The Kagard took them. "When you leave, you can pick them up." His tone held mirth. Was he mocking them?

"Everything better be there when we return," Brando threw his rucksack down on the ground.

"They'll be safe enough in the barracks," The Kagard replied. "I need to search you for hidden weapons."

Dayvee didn't want him handling the Calupi women. "We don't have other weapons. Calupi don't lie."

"You won't get in unless I check."

"Go ahead." Elayni held her arms out.

Jaycee's low growl rumbled. Dayvee clenched his fists. "Don't grope."

The Kagard just slid his hands over Elayni quickly. He did the same with each of them. "Follow me."

They trailed him through the city's narrow and winding cobbled streets. Dayvee had visited a town, but never a city. The people here were more numerous than those at the clan meeting. They all raced around like mice or squirrels, going in different directions, but somehow they missed running each other over. The city people parted like water going around a rock in a stream for their group—maybe because of the wolves.

Don't we look friendly? Jaycee cocked his ear in a wolf laugh.

The buildings, made mostly from brick, butted up next to each other. Some even shared the same outer walls. Only small patches of the sky peeked between the roofs. And too many of these streets and houses looked the same. The loss of the sun and familiar landmarks confused Dayvee. He wasn't sure if he could find his way back.

Don't worry I can, Jaycee sent.

If the prince was chosen, Jaycee wouldn't be at his side. The lump rose in his throat. How would he bear the huge void? He pushed his anguish aside. This wasn't the time.

They climbed a rise and came to another wall of stone around the castle grounds with more Kagards walking along the top. The heavy wooden gate stood closed.

"They have the prince's companion," their Kagard hollered out.

The gate swung open. Ten more Kagards joined their group. They escorted the Calupi up to the huge castle. Large gray blocks of stone formed the outer walls. Four towers rose on each corner, maybe as tall as twenty people standing on each other's shoulders. Between each tower ran a rectangular structure that stretched at least that far. The Kagards opened a massive door. They entered a foyer. Some small arched windows far above their heads let in light. Several tapestries with faces adorned the stone walls. Tayro whispered to them, "All of Taluma's kings."

A long line to see the Prince had already formed. Dayvee's boots thudded against the hard stone floor as he and his sub-pack joined the line.

Tib scanned the room from his perch on the uncomfortable, ornate throne. Father's face stared back on the tapestry across from him. Would his father approve of Tib's actions? The empty seats along the wall where Father's advisors had sat mocked him. The huge map of Taluma displayed on the other wall reminded him why it was necessary.

A Kagard came into the audience hall. "They're here."

Thirty more Kagards waited. Everything was in place. "Bring them in."

Six Calupi entered with their Kagard escort. Five of them bunched around one in the center. He must be the one who'd become the Kayndo. They had young faces like Tib's own. Their colorful beads swung on the fringes of their ornamental rawhide clothing as they drew closer. Huge wolves stalked alongside them. They strode to the rope and bowed. Someone must have filled them in on etiquette.

Tib raised his hand. "You may speak."

The tall blond in the middle pointed to himself. "I'm Dayvee, Your Royal Highness." He waved toward the others. "This is the rest of the castle sub-pack." He named them each, then touched the wolf at his side. "And this is your companion, Jaycee. Would you like to come meet him now?"

Tib couldn't stop his reaction. He scooted back on the throne.

"You don't have to. Jaycee can tell that you fear him." Dayvee's face scrunched. "He won't choose you, so you've lost the title of prince. You can't qualify to be king. Will you abide by our laws and step aside?"

If Tib stepped aside, Taluma's soldiers would meet the invaders' guns with swords and arrows. They'd be slaughtered. He had to do this for Taluma. His hand rose to signal the Kagards. They grabbed nets from the satchels they carried and ran forward, throwing them over the Calupi and wolves.

The Calupi howled, and the wolves growled. The menace couldn't be mistaken. Even hampered by nets, the Calupi and wolves fought and

Kagards fell as they tried to keep them contained. Two of the Calupi escaped the nets—Dayvee and Brando. They fought back to back, sweeping out at the Kagards' legs and driving fists into their throats. Kagards fell and gasped for air around them. Brando and Dayvee blocked and fought together, and where they went, mayhem followed.

"We need to get the others out," Dayvee called. They backed toward them.

"Don't let them free the wolves!" Tib didn't want those beasts attacking him. Kagards tackled the two and brought them to the floor.

A Kagard grunted as Dayvee threw his head into his nose. More than one Kagard yelled out as wolf teeth found their marks even through the nets. Tib needed to stop that. He signaled for the Kagards who waited with the guns. They aimed them at the wolves.

"Don't!" Dayvee made it to his feet and dragged several Kagards with him in front of the wolves, blocking the Kagards' shots. Kagards toppled him to the ground again. He fell on his stomach. Kagards held his arms and legs, pinning him against the floor.

The guns fired. Elayni screamed, "They're killing them!"

Darts hung from the wolves. "They're only drugged to make them sleep," Tib explained.

"But why?" Dayvee's shocked voice asked.

"We didn't want them sending for help," Varian said. "Stop resisting now, or they die."

The Calupi froze. The Kagards dragged the Calupi to their feet and bound their arms behind their backs.

Tib didn't particularly care for the clanspeoples' animals, but he didn't want to kill anything. That's why he had the Kagards use the darts.

Varian rose and walked toward the Calupi. "The Kayndo better order them not to attack Harthome, or your companions will die."

"Do you think the clans would risk sending a Kayndo to you?" Elayni asked.

"Our informants told us one of you is the Kayndo," Tib said.

Tayro grimaced. "Maybe your informants were fed the wrong information."

"I'll kill a companion if someone doesn't tell me who the Kayndo is." Varian's hard tone almost convinced Tib. But that wasn't the plan.

Brando glared at Varian. "Maybe you'd be happy if I told you I'm the Kayndo."

Elayni's lips pursed. "I could tell you I'm the Kayndo."

"Would it please you if I was the Kayndo?" Dayvee asked.

"We go from no Kayndo to several Kayndos." Varian circled around them. "It should be easy for you to let them know you don't need help." Then he stopped at Dayvee. "Next time, if you don't answer right, you could die." He motioned to the Kagards. "Take them to the dungeon."

Why was Varian threatening their lives? Tib shook his head. "I told you I don't want them killed."

Varian sighed. "You should let me handle this, Tib, if you want to prevent a war."

#

Dayvee and his friends were prodded through the castle's halls and down several steps. He wrinkled his nose. The smell of urine and vomit pervaded. Stone walls separated small cells. The only things not stone were thick wooden doors with small rectangular slots near the top. The Kagards led them to one and removed a stout wooden beam across the door. They shoved them inside and slammed it shut. A thump announced the beam back in place.

The cell was maybe six feet by eight. Two buckets were the only comforts. One held water and a ladle. The other must be used as a latrine. At least the sub-pack was together except for their companions. Dayvee reached out for Jaycee again. Their link wasn't as strong. Jaycee must still be unconscious, but at least the bond told him he was alive.

Maybe their bond was doing more than that. Dayvee's body felt sluggish. The fight didn't last that long. He shouldn't be this sapped after the adrenaline wore off. It must be the drugs they fed the companions affecting them too. He ignored his waning strength and reached out to the animals whispering to him to ask for their aid. As soon as night fell, they'd come.

He scrutinized his friends in the dim light. Brando's eye appeared swollen. Elayni's hair was loose from her braid and mussed, but she seemed okay. Geno and Chayla showed no visible injuries, but they all sagged as if exhausted. "Is anyone hurt seriously?"

"No." They shook their heads.

"Let's see if we can remove each other's bindings," Dayvee suggested.

"Small wrists made sliding out easy." Chayla waved her loose hands. "I'll untie you."

After she freed him, Dayvee shook his wrists to bring back the circulation. "I'm sorry. I didn't expect so brazen an attack."

"Varian and Tibalt are to blame, not you." Brando scuffed his feet. "You fought hard, but without our weapons, and with us so outnumbered, it was hopeless."

It hit Dayvee. He'd gone for the neck and crushed windpipes. His stomach clenched and bile rose to burn his throat. Life was sacred. Because of Dayvee, some of those Kagards would never see another sunrise. He moved to the latrine bucket, fell to his knees, and threw up everything in his stomach.

Brando put a hand on his shoulder. "It hurts me too. We did what was needed to protect our family."

Tears clouded Dayvee's vision. He wiped them and then flipped his hand over. His loathing rose. "This hand disgusts me. Calupi don't take life without a judgment or theirs being threatened. I was wrong. They only put the companions to sleep and locked us up."

Brando grabbed his hand. "We didn't know that. Wolves don't make good pets, so why cage them? Varian *will* kill us if we don't escape."

Brando was right. They needed out of this mess. Brando let go of him. "Do they know what happened outside?"

Dayvee rose and whispered in case the Kagards' listened. "I've kept them informed. Gaylo said since Tibalt ignored our laws and refused to step aside, the Vita is in peril. He and Gojo say I have to assume the role of a Kayndo now and fix it."

"Then you should send out the call." Brando slapped his fist in his palm.

Was Dayvee good enough to be Kayndo? No, but it didn't matter. To do nothing wasn't an option. "I agree." He reached out. *I need every animal to pass on my call for aid to everyone not already here. Those that can respond should join the keeper, Gaylo, outside of Harthome.*

I'm sending it, blasted into his mind as so many answered.

Dayvee rubbed his temple. "It's done." The confinement in this cage was already getting to him—as if worms crawled below the surface of his skin. "I told Gojo they shouldn't do the distraction we planned since Varian threatened to kill our companions if they're attacked."

Geno tested the door to their cell. "This is too solid to give. If I had my tools in my rucksack, I could remove the hinges, but I'm sure Kagards are posted out there."

Brando growled. "I wish we had our weapons."

Tayro grabbed Dayvee's arm. "I might be able to counter what they used on the wolves if I can get to them and my medicines."

Elayni sighed. "If we only had our rucksacks."

"The animals can't get to them yet," Dayvee whispered. "They'd be discovered and shot during the day, but they'll try tonight."

Spiro sent to Dayvee, *A large group of Kagards with guns are leaving Harthome and moving toward the camp.*

Dayvee reached out for Gojo. *Tell Gaylo to flee. Kagards are headed your way.*

They're going. Gojo sent. *Companions will take turns hiding nearby if you need us.*

A scuffling alerted them. The slot slid open in the door. Only Tibalt's eyes and nose were visible peering through it. "I'm sorry. I didn't want Varian to throw you in the dungeon."

"Then why didn't you stop him?" Elayni asked. "Aren't you in charge here?"

"It was necessary," Tibalt proclaimed. "Varian's trying to help us."

Dayvee sighed. Did Tibalt really believe that?

Brando snorted. "Hard to believe anyone who cages us wants to help us."

"You don't understand," Tibalt declared. "If we don't use the ancients' weapons, we won't be able to win when King Nolan invades."

Geno scratched his head. "What does that have to do with holding us prisoner?"

"If I'm replaced, the ancients' weapons will be banned again."

"Weapons can be defeated." Elayni propped a shoulder against the cell wall and leaned against it.

"Not these." Tibalt sounded certain. "We'll just hold you until we make enough, and then we'll be too strong to be attacked."

"If you don't step aside, those who follow the Vita will try to stop you." Dayvee had to make him understand. "There *will* be war, regardless."

"Not if you convince them to help us. Then we can let you out and prepare for the invaders together."

"Why would we do that?" Chayla asked.

"You surely can't want Taluma invaded by King Nolan. He isn't a good person. He assassinated Varian's father, who was a king there. And you like animals, but they don't treat them well."

"And how is that different than what's already happening here?" Tayro asked. "Our king was assassinated, animals are banned, and you're killing them with the ancients' weapons."

Brando leaned to place his back against the wall. "If you want to learn who was behind your father's death, just look at who benefitted. Varian gained your trust and became your advisor."

"Varian isn't harming us." Tibalt exclaimed. "He warned us and killed Maydlan."

Something plopped on Dayvee's boot. He choked back a scream. Probably one of Brando's frogs. Through the dim light, he made out the little gray body of a mouse. It carried a slip of paper in its mouth. *Tell Tibalt this came from Maydlan.*

Dayvee took the paper and held it to the slot. "This belonged to Maydlan."

Tibalt's eyes moved away as his fingers reached in to take it. "How did you get it?"

"A mouse left it. Look, we're trying to help you. My father taught me there can be only one leader at the top. A title can't decide it, the followers do. I don't think you lead here."

"You're wrong," Tibalt snapped.

The weariness in Dayvee's body was getting harder to ignore. He joined his friends in leaning back against the wall. "You didn't want us in the dungeon, but here we are. If the Kagards are following Varian, we could be in a lot of danger."

"You won't be harmed." Tibalt spoke with conviction. "When we have enough weapons, I'll free you. I hoped we could be friends. My friends call me Tib."

Dayvee was too exhausted to be gentle with the deluded prince. "Friends don't cage their friends, Tibalt."

"I wish I didn't have to." Tibalt left.

Dayvee let himself slide down the wall to sit on the stone floor. "Everyone get comfortable. Try to conserve your energy and rest."

Chayla's breaths turned loud and fast. "Are the walls moving in?"

"They must be." Geno exclaimed. Everyone's breathing quickened.

The cell did appear smaller. Dayvee's skin crawled, and his senses screamed they were in danger. "The walls aren't moving. Your mind plays that trick so you work hard to get free. It's happened to me before when I was trapped. To stop it we have to escape this cell even though we're still here. Everyone close your eyes. Chayla, tell us a story and take us away from here."

"Thick ash from a world on fire rained down and coated everything. Herrick and his few remaining soldiers sought shelter in a cave." The sub-pack's breathing relaxed as Chayla launched into their pack founder's story. "A giant white wolf and several gray surrounded them, there. A voice penetrated Herrick's mind. 'Kun has heard your prayers and sent us to help you, to teach you a better way to live.' Was Herrick going crazy? Who was in his head? The white wolf stepped closer. 'My name is JoKayndo—'"

A clomping sound interrupted Chayla's story. Must be several people's footsteps, and they were coming nearer. They scrambled to their feet.

"These prisoners should be in separate cells," Varian's voice rang out. "Separate them."

"We don't have that many empty cells," someone complained.

"You can put them in with other prisoners, but not each other." A strange laugh rumbled almost like a cough. It sent chills through Dayvee. "I'll do some house cleaning soon, and you'll have empty cells."

"Back to back. Me, Brando, and Tayro, front line," Dayvee ordered in a whisper.

A scraping alerted them. The door opened. Several Kagards came rushing in, but there wasn't enough room to force in more.

Brando waved at Dayvee to drop back. Not happening. No time like the present to prove he should be in front. Dayvee drove his fist in a Kagard's face. The Kagard staggered.

Varian grabbed a Kagard's arm. "If they don't stop fighting, run to the wolves' cell and kill them all."

Dayvee raised his hands, palm out. His friends did the same. Kagards grabbed him and bound his hands again. The one he hit threw a punch at Dayvee. He ducked and it hit a Kagard behind him. They both slammed Dayvee against the wall.

"Stop it," Varian commanded. "I need him conscious. Separate the others, but bring him to the… *play* room."

24

Tortured

An attack on one hurts us all. Each injury weakens our pack. ~Jaycee

As Kagards dragged Dayvee to a room in the dungeon, Varian ordered, "Some of you go get the wolf that was with him."

Ropes dangled inside from the ceiling and floor. A table stood nearby with several things on it. Was that a whip? Cackles. He had to get away before they tortured him.

Dayvee yanked against the bindings on his hands, but they held. He kicked out at the Kagards. Six dragged him to the floor as he drove his knees and feet into them.

"Look." Varian held a knife to Jaycee's throat.

Jaycee's legs and muzzle were bound, but he opened his eyes to slits. *If you can get away, do it. The Kayndo's safety is most important.*

There were too many. Dayvee couldn't let them kill Jaycee over a futile struggle. He stopped resisting.

The Kagards took his boots off and hauled him to his feet. They secured Dayvee's wrists to the ropes, pulling them to raise his arms and suspend his body from the ceiling. They tied his ankles to the floor to stretch his body taut, then laid Jaycee on the floor next to him.

Varian gestured to the table. "This equipment and room were apparently used by your false king to get answers. I've found it helpful too. So who is the Kayndo?"

Dayvee's shoulder's ached as he hung from the ropes. "If you learn who the Kayndo is, would you kill him?"

Varian made that strange evil laugh that sounded like a cough. "I'm not going to kill him. Now, who's the Kayndo?"

Don't answer. He was deceitful. Jaycee sent. *He'll kill you.*

Dayvee kept silent. Varian stared into his eyes. Was Varian trying to read him? Dayvee dropped his gaze to the floor. The gray stones held rust colored stains. Blood. Icy fear enveloped him like a cold mist on the mountain and sent chills racing through him.

"I'm curious if you and the wolf actually feel each other's pain." Varian picked up a knife and put it at his neck. He dropped it down, slashing through Dayvee's shirt. The cold knife scratched a thin line down his chest. It didn't sink deep, just enough to sting and make him bleed. The knife turned warm as his blood coated it.

Varian moved around to his back. The knife pricked him again and traveled from the nape of his neck down his back to tear his shirt, then along each sleeve. The knife traced lines in his skin, and blood dripped as his shirt fell off him in pieces. "That's better. I didn't want your shirt to get in the way. What's the C scar on your back stand for?"

"Courage."

"You'll need it."

Dayvee steeled himself. Calupi couldn't be weak.

Varian put the knife down on the table and picked up the whip with long leather cords knotted around small shells and rocks. "Who is the Kayndo?"

Dayvee didn't answer. Varian swung the whip across Dayvee's back.

He jumped against the ropes as the sharp points penetrated his skin. A moan escaped. Jaycee's muted growl behind the muzzle turned to a whimper.

"Who is the Kayndo?"

Varian flung the whip over Jaycee's side. A muffled yelp came from Jaycee. Dayvee groaned. *Kun, please end the torture.*

"It's true. Double the hurt. How wonderful. Now, who is the Kayndo?" Varian asked.

Dayvee kept silent.

Varian put down the whip and grabbed something else. "This is supposed to be a mummified bear's leg." A corner of Varian's lip turned up.

"I've learned the back side tickles." He ran it under Dayvee's arm gently. Dayvee snorted and tried to pull away, but he couldn't get far.

"I hate to be laughed at." Varian flipped it and raked the claws down Dayvee's side, opening grooves. Dayvee screamed. Pieces of his flesh hung from the claws.

Varian held the torture instrument above Jaycee. "Who is the Kayndo?"

If I tell him, he'll have no further reason to torture you, Dayvee sent.

No. Jaycee's head lifted a little. *He'll kill us both.*

I think he will anyway.

Gojo is willing to share his body with us.

Varian drew the claw down Jaycee's side. Dayvee left his body for Gojo's. He smelled the woodsy scent and looked out from brush to see Harthome's wall. But what was Varian doing to Jaycee back in that room? Could he use his own body's eyes and ears like he did with Jaycee, but keep his awareness in Gojo's?

Let's try, Jaycee sent.

Dayvee let the desire fill his mind. He looked on as four deep gashes opened in Jaycee's side. Blood soaked the wolf's fur, but Jaycee didn't react. Dayvee felt no pain, just the soft grass beneath him as he shared Gojo's body.

Varian grabbed the whip again and flailed Dayvee's back over and over. He'd pause and ask Dayvee who the Kayndo was. Then resume. At least he concentrated on Dayvee and left Jaycee alone.

"This will get an answer." Varian signaled to the Kagards. A couple of them lowered the ropes on his arms. Dayvee's feet touched the floor now, but they snugged the ropes on his ankles, so he was held fast.

Varian picked up a long handled instrument with a block of stone on one end. He swung it. The stone slammed into Dayvee's foot with a crunch that reverberated through the room.

Dayvee prayed again for Kun to rescue them. To make the torture stop. A loud crack sounded as Varian smashed Dayvee's other foot.

"Even if I untied you, you couldn't escape now." Varian's voice grated like a donkey braying. He picked up the knife again. "If you don't answer me, I'll carve until you die. Then I'll play with your friends. If I need to kill you all, I will."

Dayvee's mind reeled as he grasped for a solution. His plan to distract their captors with a false attack hadn't considered drugged companions. Now he was out of time. He sent to all the animals whispering in his mind. *When I die, please aid my friends' escape.*

#

Tibalt drew out the rumpled scrap of paper Dayvee had given him. A corner was torn. He carefully unfolded it.

My darling Maydlan,

If you're bold enough to act, you hold the key to my freedom. How do you get to the bird if you can't fly? Attack the chick, and the bird will come to you. Or others will come to its rescue and leave the bird defenseless. Distract and attack. I'll help you make your escape. With the bird gone, the chick will set me free. Then we'll be together, and I can hold you in my arms.

Varian

Could the note be a fake? No. Tib was certain that flowery writing was Varian's. Varian *had* planned the attack on Tib's father and duped both Maydlan and Tib. Heat flooded Tib's face. What a fool he'd been, considering Varian a good friend. He hadn't cared about Tib. The betrayal hurt Tib to the core. Could he have been more wrong? Tib's trust had killed his father.

He waved the note at his Kagards. "Varian killed my father. I want him arrested, and the clanspeople freed."

The only one he knew well, Dirk, let out a snort. "The four of us in this room are probably the only ones who'd believe Varian killed your father. Not near enough to arrest him. Don't you know what's been going on around here?"

"I've been kind of busy preparing for the invaders, but how could Varian have gained so much support?"

"If Pericards and Kagards don't swear loyalty to your regent, they're thrown in the dungeon, supposedly on your orders. Varian filled their positions with people who share his views and don't like the clanspeople."

How could Tib have been so stupid to give those orders? "Did you swear loyalty to him?"

"Yes, but they don't have a companion judging, so we lied. We can't stand Varian. The only reason we stayed and went in those ruins with you was because Blake asked us to protect you."

Tib paced the room. "Why didn't you tell me, Dirk?"

"It sure seemed as if you shared his views. Varian tortures those in the dungeons, so we didn't want to risk ending up there."

Torture? Tib's heart sank. He didn't want anyone harmed, and he told the Calupi they'd be safe. "I need to free them."

"He only uses the ones he hired himself to guard the dungeons. No one gets released without Varian's permission, and he doesn't give it."

"What about the other garrisons? If the Kagards here are loyal to him, I'll ask them to come."

"They keep the pigeons guarded, but knowing Blake, he's already warned them, and they're on the way to join the Kayndo."

"The Kayndo is probably in our dungeon."

"Yes, and Varian wants to learn his identity. He's probably already torturing them."

"I have to try to stop it."

"For some reason Varian still wants you thinking well of him. Maybe because of the other garrisons. He might stop the torture if you act as if you believe he misunderstood you. Tonight they won't have as many on duty, and you have the key to the bolt hole. We can try to free them then."

Tib grabbed some paper. "Okay. I'll do that, but I have another job for you four."

"What?"

"I don't want Varian to use the ancients' weapons against our own people." Tib wrote two orders. "You need to go to the barracks with a wagon and get those weapons. Give them my order for you to take the weapons to the city so the craftsmen can fix a firing problem. My other order goes to the craftsmen. They're to stop making the weapons and release all three wagons of them that were to be delivered. You need to hide or destroy them all."

"That would leave you without any protection. After I give them your orders, Varian will know you had a part in it."

"I won't be chosen, so you're protecting the wrong person. Hopefully by the time Varian learns, I'll have escaped with the queen and the other prisoners. Either way, this could protect a lot of lives."

The other Kagards gave Dirk a nod. He sighed. "All right. We'll do it."

Tib handed Dirk the notes. "Afterwards, don't come back. I don't want you to face Varian when he learns you took them. Good luck."

"You too."

Tib left his room. When he got to the dungeons, those posted at the door turned to him. "Prince Tibalt. What do you need?"

Tib donned the arrogant attitude that Varian usually displayed. "I want to see the Calupi, Dayvee."

"Varian won't like it. He's playing with him, and he won't like being disturbed."

"He's what?" Tib demanded.

The Kagard exhaled heavily. "Torture."

"Show me where," Tib commanded.

They hesitated, then led Tib to a room in the dungeon. Dayvee stood stretched between ropes. His eyes were open, but he didn't seem to be aware of Tib. His chin lay on his chest. Blood painted his body, and a pool lay on the floor. Varian stood nearby holding a knife.

Tib stomach turned. "What are you doing?"

Varian shot Tib a sneer. "You didn't say I couldn't hurt them to learn what we need to know, Your Royal Highness. Taluma's welfare is at stake."

"I know you were only trying to help. I should have made it clear I didn't want to use torture, but now you know, so let's return him to his cell."

"Of course, Your Royal Highness." Varian's tone was condescending. "But he can't walk."

Beneath the blood, Dayvee's feet appeared flattened. A lump choked Tib's throat. He forced it down. "The Kagards can carry him, and they can return the wolf too."

Dayvee's eyes lost their gazed look. He let out a sob. Tib hated what had been done to him. "I'm sorry. I told you that you wouldn't be harmed."

The Kagards removed Dayvee's ropes. They grabbed his arms and dragged his feet across the stone. Dayvee's screams echoed through the dungeon.

"I said carry him," Tib yelled. More Kagards grabbed Dayvee's legs and picked him up. "I'll get our healer to treat you."

"Ja—cee—fust," Dayvee pleaded.

The wolf lay in the corner. Blood soaked lines on his coat marked the grooves in his flesh. He shuddered at the injuries. Tib was torn. If he left Dayvee, would Varian hurt him more? Probably not since he knew Tib was returning. And could he trust Varian's Kagards to fetch the healer quickly or have him treat the wolf? "I'll be back in a minute." Tib ran for the healer himself.

#

Jaycee and Gojo insisted Dayvee return to his body before it shut down. They wouldn't let him escape the agony longer. He shouldn't be so weak. His friends needed him.

Varian opened a cell door. "Throw him in."

The Kagards swung him, then let go. Dayvee soared through the air, then crashed into the floor. The pain exploded in his feet and back. "Owww."

"My efforts are finally being rewarded." Varian came in and drove his boot into Dayvee's foot.

Dayvee's wail rolled through the dungeon.

"So who is the Kayndo?" Varian asked.

Dayvee couldn't have answered if he wanted. He'd have to stop sobbing first.

"Stop hurting him." Chayla cried out.

"Then tell me who the Kayndo is," Varian demanded as he kicked Dayvee's other foot. Dayvee shrieked and tried to pull his feet away from Varian.

"Come fight me, Varian," Brando yelled.

"Leave him alone." The voice came from a clump in the back of the dim cell. A man stood and emerged as he moved forward. Dressed in a tattered Pericard uniform, he had a thin haggard face with sunken eyes and dark hair.

"I told you you'd be next, but don't be jealous, Latham. I'll make time for you when Tibalt leaves. And we will talk again, Dayvee." Varian strode out and bolted the cell door.

Dayvee fought to stifle his sobs as wave after wave of pain assaulted him. Everyone would hear. Calupi aren't supposed to be so weak.

"How badly are you hurt?" Tayro shouted.

Dayvee couldn't open his mouth if he wanted to keep his sobs from turning to screams.

"Answer him, Dayvee." Elayni's voice sounded frantic.

Latham leaned over him. "I take it you're Dayvee?"

Dayvee gave him a small bob of his head.

"Varian hurt him pretty badly," Latham yelled.

The door to the cell opened to show Tibalt. "I have the healer." A short man with blonde hair and a grim face stepped inside.

Through his clenched teeth and ragged draws of air, Dayvee forced it out. "Ja—cee."

"He's treated. He'll be fine," Tibalt answered.

"You said we wouldn't be hurt," Chayla cried.

Latham snorted. "Varian's hurt several, but no one else has received treatment."

"I didn't know." Tibalt's face fell. "The healer can see them next."

"If any still live." Latham moved to the back of the cell and slumped back down.

Tibalt turned even paler. Dayvee sucked air through his gritted teeth. Could Tibalt really have known so little?

"Please, Tibalt, let me help," Tayro pleaded. "Dayvee trusts me."

"Bring him." Tibalt waved a hand at a guard.

The guard shook his head. "We can't release prisoners."

That confirmed Dayvee's suspicions. Tibalt didn't rule here.

"I didn't tell you to release him, just to bring him," Tibalt replied arrogantly. "He can share this cell." Tibalt snapped, "Now go."

When they brought Tayro in, he fell to his knees beside Dayvee, and the color drained from his face. "Oh Kun, what have they done to your servant?"

Dayvee had tried to serve the Vita, but why had Kun let this happen?

Tayro untied Dayvee's hands and asked the healer, "Do you have anything for pain?"

As they discussed what to use, Dayvee quit listening to focus on not screaming or writhing in agony.

"Drink this." Tayro held a cup out.

Dayvee choked it down. Tayro's voice grew distant as if it came from far away, but he was right there. "I have comfrey if someone will bring the medicines in my rucksack."

Pain forked as Tayro and the healer prodded the twisted lumps that no longer resembled feet. Dayvee didn't need to scream. Only a few moans still escaped. Much better than before.

Deep creases lined the healer's face. "I can't feel any bones in his feet. They must be in pieces." He sighed. "He won't be able to walk again."

Tayro's voice sharpened. "Anything's possible with Kun. He can fix what we can't."

Kun had healed Brando, and others the keepers couldn't. Would he help Dayvee? A cripple couldn't be a wolf's companion. Tobee flashed across his mind with his deformed legs. Dayvee would rather Varian had killed him than that. *No Kun, No. I beg you to heal me. Please. Don't let me lose being Calupi.* He drifted away from consciousness.

25

Abandoned

"Hardships aren't reasons to quit, they're challenges to beat." ~Leeto

Someone was pounding at Tib's door. He opened it to find four Kagards and Varian, who said, "You should see something in the courtyard."

Tib needed to get rid of them, so he could get his mother and those in the dungeons out of the castle. He forced a yawn. "I was going to sleep early. Can't whatever it is wait until morning?"

"No, but it won't take long. Where are your guards?" Varian asked.

"I was tired of not having any privacy, so I released them."

"You won't be able to release the ones I've assigned to you." Varian motioned toward the burly Kagards that made two of Tib. "Now come."

Varian turned and strode away. One of the Kagards grabbed Tib's arm and yanked him out. "Go."

Tib stumbled and caught himself. His heart raced. They weren't pretending Tib had any choice anymore. But why? Did Varian discover Tib's plans? Had someone talked? Tib's hands itched for a weapon. He should have grabbed the ancients' dagger from his room before opening the door. A dagger wasn't enough against four Kagards and Varian anyway.

Tib traipsed after Varian through the castle halls to the grand foyer, with the Kagards breathing down his neck. Then out to the courtyard where his boots clicked against the paving stones. The sun had almost set. The gates in the wall around the grounds stood closed.

Several more Kagards stood around a wagon with a few feet of planks running up three sides. Could it be? Varian circled to the back where it was open, and they could see inside. The weapons were loaded in it. Tib's heart plummeted. One of the Kagards Varian assigned to him grabbed Tib's arm and held him.

Some of the Kagards parted. Even in the shadows of the wagon, Tib made out Dirk and the rest of his former guards sitting on the ground with ropes wrapped around them. Upon seeing him, Dirk's shoulders sagged.

Varian waved a hand at the weapons. "Where were you taking these Tib?"

Tib stuck to his story. "To the craftsmen. Some of them aren't firing right."

Varian grabbed some guns and handed them out to the Kagards around the wagon. Keeping one for himself, he loaded it and put the barrel to Dirk's head. "You don't mind *us* testing them, Tib, do you?"

The other Kagards pointed their loaded weapons toward Dirk's group. Tib's mouth dried and his tongue didn't want to unstick, but he forced it. "Yes, I mind. I never said they all didn't fire right, just some. Release my guards. They just followed my orders."

Explosions split the air and holes riddled his guards. They slumped over. The Kagard let go of Tib. He ran toward Dirk, collapsing to his knees beside him. Oh, no. He had gotten them all killed.

Tib choked and tears flooded his eyes. He gagged, wanting to vomit.

"I think these are working fine." Varian's tone was condescending. "Your guards swore an oath to me. That's what happens to those that break it."

Rage filled Tib. He blinked back his tears. "I can't believe I ever thought you were a friend. Are you helping the invaders?"

"No, I wouldn't help King Nolan, and I *was* fond of you until you crossed me."

"So fond you killed my father."

"He stood in the way of what I wanted, and you should thank me. You weren't happy with his plans for you."

Varian must want Taluma's throne, but he was crazy if he thought

Tib would thank him. "Talumans won't accept you as king. Our other garrisons and the clans will stop you."

"I don't care about the title, just the power. If you do as I say and make sure the garrisons do, you can keep the title."

Varian would probably shoot Tib too, but he wasn't helping the man who murdered his father. Tib crossed his arms. "I'm not going to order anyone to aid you."

"Take a good look at your guards. Do you see the bruises they received before I killed them? Now ask yourself if you want the Queen to suffer next. Your choice Tib."

His mother was all Tib had left. He couldn't stand the thought of her hurt. He had to play along for now and hope Blake had already contacted the garrisons. "I'll do what you say."

"How do the garrison's commanders know the orders come from you?" Varian demanded.

To discover that, Varian must have tried sending orders in Tib's name. A small group of Kagards might be fooled, but not the garrison commanders. "If I told you, you wouldn't need me, and you'd have no reason to treat my mother well."

"All right, but I better not get a pigeon saying they can't comply. Write the order that every garrison's Kagards are to report to Midtown. Tell them Captain Hubert will take charge there to flank those against us so we can destroy them between our forces."

Tib wrote the messages with a heavy heart. After he finished, the Kagards Varian had assigned him escorted Tib to his room and stayed with him. He fell into bed and tossed awhile trying to figure out a solution before sleep finally claimed him.

#

Dayvee woke in pain. Kun must have abandoned him.

A couple of torches lit the cell. In the dim light Dayvee picked out Tayro lying beside him, and the Pericard curled in the far corner. Their regular breathing signaled they slept. Dayvee forced himself to a sitting position. A moan escaped.

Tayro's eyes shot open. "I'll give you something for pain."

Dayvee gritted his teeth to keep his cries in. "Not if it puts me out or deadens my mind. I have things to do."

"All right, just a little willow to take the edge off."

Dayvee drank the liquid and reached out to Gojo. *Can you inform Gaylo I'm unable to perform my duties? Another will need to be chosen to be Kayndo.*

I already relayed what Varian did, but I'll give him your message.

Only a few seconds passed before Gojo's thoughts resounded in Dayvee's mind, *Gaylo says until Kun appoints another, you're the Kayndo. Don't shame the Calupi name. Do your duty, even if you need to crawl.*

Gaylo sounded just like Leeto. He had no sympathy for Dayvee's plight. Were all Calupi leaders the same? Would Dayvee ever ask his friends to crawl? He wouldn't have to. They'd willingly do it to aid him. Was he the only weak one?

Gaylo says everyone is praying for your healing and escape.

Didn't they think he prayed to Kun when he was being tortured? What good did it do him? If he didn't get his sub-pack out, they'd share his fate.

"Tayro," Dayvee whispered.

"I'm here."

"Do you have what you need to try to bring the wolves around?"

"Yes, they left my medicine pouches and flasks."

"Set to work on that." Dayvee sent his thoughts out to the animals. *We need the tool and weapon pouches from our rucksacks in the barracks, medicine delivered to our companions, and your aid around the walls.*

We can climb down the barracks chimney and retrieve your rucksacks, a raccoon's reply filled his mind. *Only I don't know how we'd get them into the dungeon.*

There's a crack in the castle's outer wall, a rat sent. *But we couldn't force anything large through.* Other animals barraged Dayvee with ideas to help.

Do what you can, Dayvee returned.

It wasn't long before the rat reached out to Dayvee, *Some tools are delivered.*

May I use your eyes?

Yes, Kayndo.

Everything appeared huge and blurry from the rat's perspective. It was really hard to tell much, but it was better than nothing. A giant dark shadow shaped like Geno worked on the door. Another shadow must be a Pericard lying nearby. Dayvee could make out a broken water bucket when the rat got close enough to nudge it. After the rat got under Geno's feet, he figured it out. A shape like a knife was under Geno's belt. He must have made a wooden knife from the bucket.

Can you get in the other cells to check on my friends? The floor stretched forever as the rat scampered over it. Two giant blurs must be the Kagards. Probably fewer were posted at night.

The rat squeezed under a cell door. A tall hazy figure next to a short one revealed them as Elayni and Chayla. No Pericards with them.

The rat scurried out to slide under another cell. A fuzzy form moved back and forth. It had to be Brando, pacing. Another dark shape nearby. A Pericard must share his cell too.

Dayvee returned to his body. Tayro handed him a small pouch and whispered, "A little needs to go in each wolf's mouth."

"How long will it take?" Dayvee handed the pouch to the rat.

"About twenty minutes." Tayro's shoulders fell. "Without knowing what they used, I can't be sure it will work."

Dayvee shifted his weight and pain stabbed him. The sudden intake and exhale through his pursed lips sounded like a whistle.

Latham's eyelids fluttered. He'd risked Varian's wrath for Dayvee, but how better to gain his trust? Could Dayvee be sure Latham wasn't one of Varian's informers?

Tayro grabbed a flask. "Let me give you some more pain medicine."

Dayvee had to stay alert. "Not now." A rodent procession came into the cell. They worked together to push and pull the weapons pouches to where Dayvee sat on the floor. *Thank you.* Dayvee handed Tayro his weapons.

Are you okay? Even through his grogginess, Jaycee's thought came in strong.

Yes, Dayvee sent. According to the rat, the companions were held in a cell in another corridor and guarded. *You'll be free soon.* He sent to all the companions, *Pass on to your chosen that mice will bring their weapons. But I don't want to kill anyone unless we need to.*

Jaycee's confusion cleared. *If you stay, so do I.*

How could Dayvee hide anything when they shared thoughts? *No, you're able to escape.*

I understand not risking your packmates, but why stay caged? If Varian kills me, I won't go down easy.

Shame rose in Dayvee. If he had something to support his feet, could he walk? His boots lay in the torture room, but they wouldn't fit his misshapen feet. "Tayro, can you put something on the bottom of these bandages to make them hard?"

"Yes, I have pine resin, but I don't think your feet would hold you. To stand would be excruciating, and your feet are still swelling."

"Do it anyway."

Tayro took one of the torches off the wall. "Tibalt left these so I could see to treat you. I'll try not to get it so hot it burns you.

"Do you really think you can hurt my feet more?"

"Yes." Tayro heated the pitch. He poured resin from his flask over Dayvee's bandages. They grew hard and inflexible and rubbed against his swollen and broken flesh. Tears rimmed his eyes. *Can any companion hear me from Gaylo's camp?*

I'm just outside the wall, Juno answered. *But all the companions at the new camp are within your mind reach.*

How long to sunrise?

Stars are bright. At least two hours, maybe three.

Good, Dayvee sent back. *Some of us might escape the dungeons tonight.*

I'll pass your message on and meet you once you get past the wall.

Dayvee pulled his tooth. "Pssst." Latham opened his eyes. "Can you come closer?"

"You have a knife."

"I won't use it unless you threaten us." *Graydee and Gruno, ask your chosen to tell their Pericards what I'm telling Latham.* When Latham leaned over him, Dayvee said softly, "We plan to escape tonight."

Latham eyes lit up. "Will you let us come with you?"

"After my sub pack gets a head start, I'll help you. And you can free the others."

"Varian plays at night." Latham shook his head. "I'd rather not wait."

"It won't be long. I'll risk my escape, but not my sub-pack's freedom. Anyone who does anything to prevent it will die. Do you have assistance in Harthome?"

"Some of us Pericards have families in the city, but we'd hate to take any pursuit to them."

"If you can climb, look for a squirrel at the eastern corner of Harthome's front wall. He'll lead you across, but go between Kagard rounds."

"You must be the Kayndo."

"I'm Calupi. If you join Blake and let a companion judge your truthfulness, you can learn the Kayndo's identity." Dayvee sent to Graydee, *Has Geno opened his door?*

It's only propped now, Graydee answered. *He says as soon as you're ready, he is.*

Do what you can to help Geno, Dayvee reached out to all the companions and animals.

We'll fly into the Kagard's faces, a bat sent.

"You Kagards, come here to the end of the hall so I can talk to you." Wasn't that Tibalt? Dayvee's heart leapt to his throat.

Elayni's mimicking Tibalt, Evee sent.

Dayvee sure loved Elayni's voices. *Now.*

A scuffling sounded and a shout rang out, but was cut short. A few minutes later a thumping announced the bar on his door was being removed. Dayvee's spine tingled. Would it be Kagards or his friends?

The door screeched open, and Brando's face peered in.

"Are the Kagards bound?" Dayvee managed to keep his voice even.

"Yes, and we locked them in the girl's cell."

Geno, Chayla, and Elayni followed Brando in. Now if Dayvee could just convince them. Elayni charged over to him.

Tayro held a hand up. "Don't jostle him."

She stopped and sucked in a breath. "How bad is it?"

Tayro didn't answer, so Dayvee did. "Bad enough not to risk our sub-pack. Their healer said I won't walk again."

"No." She whispered. "We vowed."

Since the Pericard shared his cell, Dayvee reached out to the companions. Please pass this on to your chosen. *I'm not even able to be Calupi. Kun will have to appoint another Kayndo, but until he does, my authority exceeds all other. I'm releasing you from your vows, except those given to me, and ordering you to get our sub-pack safe.* Then he spoke to his friends aloud. "If you truly love me, do this. Brando, I'm giving you the honor."

"No, we can carry you," Brando proclaimed.

"You can't fight or flee very well carrying me. Varian wants to do this to each of you. Do you think I want to bear that guilt? If you get the rest safe, I'll be happy regardless."

Elayni wiped her eyes. "I'll stay and help you."

"No. Everyone's going. That's an order."

A tear escaped Brando. "I can't abandon you. Please. I'm begging," Brando cried out. "Don't make me do it."

"You're not abandoning me. You're just going first. Our companion's need you, so don't waste more time, or we'll be discovered. Just follow the animals and they'll get you out, but you'll have to swim. Go. Protect the Pack."

They were Calupi. Surely they wouldn't defy a Kayndo's order, but Brando wasn't always predictable. Dayvee sighed. "Can't I count on you, Brando?"

26

Escape

Wolves value freedom more than life. We bite off a leg that's trapped.
~ Jaycee

Brando had a duty to perform, even if his heart was heavy because he left Dayvee. The thick bar he carried from the cell door was reassuring, and the torch he had removed from a wall shed a little light on the gray stone in the dungeon's dank corridors. They all looked too similar to Brando, but the bats he followed appeared to know the way.

A quick glance back revealed his friends' downcast faces, lit by their torches. The bats turned into another passage and then flew back, sweeping low at his head. Must be a warning. *"Put out your torches."*

After allowing enough time for their eyes to adjust to the darkness, he crept forward. Two more Kagards stood in front of a cell near more wall torches.

The bats dove at the Kagards. Brando raced to close the distance. He swung the bar at one's head. The thunk and recoil up his arm as the Kagard slumped to the ground gave him pause. Regret washed in. Did he kill him? Geno held his knife at the other's throat as Elayni tied and gagged him.

She went to the one Brando felled. "He's breathing." She bound him.

Brando removed the bar to the companion's cell and dragged the unconscious Kagard in while his friends led the other. Chewed pieces of rope lay on the floor. The wolves stood free of bonds. Bruno staggered over to him. *Let's get out of here.*

The floor swayed under Brando. The dizziness must be coming through his bond with Bruno. An effect of the drugs? Hopefully it wore off soon. Compassion for the wolves and anger for the Kagards that did this to them warred in Brando. He touched Bruno's head. *I missed you.*

After his friends and their companions came out of the cell, Brando bolted the door. The gashes on Jaycee and his mincing gait sent Brando's anger soaring. Jaycee turned the other way and broke into a lope. His gait wobbled, but he kept his feet.

"He must be going to Dayvee," Geno said.

Dayvee would prefer it if Jaycee left the castle, but Brando couldn't order a wolf. They answered to the highest-status wolf present, and that was Jaycee. "I'm going back too," Brando declared.

Tayro's eyes widened. "You're going to defy the Kayndo's order?"

"He wanted us and the wolves safe. Everyone can still get to safety if you go on without me from here."

"I'm either coming with you or following." Elayni's bottom lip was in her mouth.

"Me too," the others announced.

"He won't like it, but I guess we're all going then because I'm not leaving him here, orders or not."

The bats flew off the other way. But when Brando turned toward their old cells, they circled around and came back. They'd made it half way when Bruno stopped. *Jaycee's at Dayvee's cell. He's not there, but Jaycee's tracking him.*

Shouts rang out, "The prisoners have escaped!"

"Find them!"

Dayvee says to flee. There are too many guards between him and us. He says the animals are aiding him, so he doesn't need ours.

Brando's heart sank. Even with the animals' help, how could Dayvee get away? Racing footsteps echoed. A group of guards ran around the corner. "Some are over here!"

Cackles. Brando hoped the wolves could keep up. He pivoted. "Run!"

As Brando raced back the way they came, the bats overtook him. They flew around a corner, and Brando followed with the sub-pack on his heels. The clunking footsteps behind them didn't make the turn and kept going. More shouts resonated as the guards chased someone else. Was it Dayvee? They trailed the bats through several more twists and turns, up some steps, and out a side door into the garden. Once they hit the night air, the wolves lope' became less ragged, and the grogginess Brando felt from Bruno subsided a little.

Brando hugged the darkest areas in the garden, out of the light of the moon. The bats led them to a hole underneath the castle wall. The ground had been washed away and eroded by tree roots. A groundhog was in the hole, throwing dirt up to enlarge it.

There aren't any Kagards on the wall directly above us, Bruno sent.

Brando tapped Geno on the shoulder and whispered, "Go first, quickly."

The groundhog backed out, and Geno wormed his way through, followed by Graydee.

Graydee says it's clear, Bruno sent.

Brando crawled through last. His shoulders stuck in one tight spot, but he pushed with his boots and propelled his body through. He rose to find himself in a side street. Large shadows loomed to mark homes along it. They jogged down the deserted street. The bats dove to warn Brando, and then flew around behind a home. They darted to cover.

Bruno brushed against him. *Some Kagards are close. They're searching the city for you.*

Maybe they should fight? But the wolves were dizzy and exhausted, and their Calupi were feeling it too. *How many?*

Six in this group, but there are more within shouting distance.

Footsteps clomped against stone. Brando peered around the corner. The sky had turned a dark gray—maybe an hour before sunrise. He picked out the group of Kagards marching hurriedly down the street. They stopped several times and scanned the area. Brando moved back. His heart raced.

If the Kagards discovered them, they'd have to kill them, or he and his friends could end up in the dungeon again. He'd die fighting before he let them get back in Varian's hands.

Me too, Bruno sent.

The footsteps faded. Brando peeked out. The Kagards had disappeared from his sight, so he hurried the group forward through several more streets. A splash alerted Brando that they had reached the river channel that supplied Harthome's water. He just barely made out two otters swimming—a mother and her pup. Must be more of Dayvee's help. He had said they'd have to swim.

The otters' webbed feet, long nails, and tail let them race through the water like a horse might gallop over land. The sub-pack couldn't hope to keep up. And the channel appeared narrow. Would it be swift? Regardless, Brando had to try. How much longer before Kagards discovered them? He squashed the desire to dive in since there might be rocks. He waded out into the inky river until the ground gave way. The cool water washed over his head. He bobbed up and swam.

If he stayed still, the current took him backwards, but slowly. The bats flew off, but the otter's silhouettes glided in front of him. They rolled on their backs to look back at him as he followed them to the stone wall. The tunnel that allowed the water to flow through the wall into Harthome revealed a gap with a few inches above the water's surface. Good. Wolves didn't like their noses submerged.

Once he swam in, the tunnel's darkness swallowed the otters and Brando's friends, but the sound of water splashing assured him he wasn't alone. The black gave way to gray when he left the tunnel. Bruno and the others weren't far behind. The otters led him to the bank, and then swam away.

Brando grabbed the scruff of Bruno's neck to help him onto the steep incline. After he aided his friends and their companions, he hauled himself out.

Dayvee says the raccoons climbed the wall with your rucksacks and left them under a willow tree, Bruno's thought rang in his head. Only one willow grew nearby.

Brando and his friends scrambled under the tree and grabbed their rucksacks. One remained, Dayvee's. Brando hated the reminder. He took them deeper into the tree line.

Company coming, Bruno sent. Brando pulled his nails.

#

Tib startled awake. Shouts and racing footsteps reverberated in the castle. He sprang from bed. "What's going on?"

The Kagards Varian had assigned Tib didn't answer, but one rushed out the door. It still left three with him, and Tib had no weapons. They'd searched and confiscated anything in the room he could possibly use for one.

Only a minute must have passed before the Kagard returned and addressed the others, "The Calupi killed the Queen and escaped. They're hunting them now, but we're to stay with the prince."

Tib's legs weakened. The floor swayed. Almost as if he stood in a dense bog and was sinking. Air so thick, he couldn't breathe. He tried to pull himself out of the dark sludge that wanted to swallow him. "Are you saying my mother's dead?"

"Yes," the Kagard answered. "I heard you helped the Calupi. They just paid you back."

Tib sank back on his bed before he fell. He stuffed his face into a pillow. It turned wet with his tears. He'd hoped his mother would pull out of the despair that had enveloped her since Father's death. No chance of that now. He was all alone. Why? Why would the Calupi kill her?

"Did they kill any Kagards?" One of them asked the other who'd come back.

"No, some were knocked out in the dungeon and tied up, but we don't have any dead."

Why would the Calupi spare the Kagards and murder his mother? Maybe Varian was blaming her death on the Calupi. Varian was responsible for Father's death. And he'd already threatened Tib's mother. He probably killed her. If so, he just lost his leverage. Tib wasn't going to do anything else for Varian.

27

Distractions

"Don't let distractions lead you away from Kun's path, or you could get lost." ~Kwutee

Brando searched the gloom, trying to see around the darker areas of tree trunks and brush to discern any movement. Bruno sent, *It's friends.*

Juno bounded up to touch noses with their companions. He trotted over to Brando and smelled him, licked his hand, then moved to his friends.

Behind Juno, Brando picked out Gaylo, Drako, Reko, Blake, and a few of Gaylo's pack members weaving through the trees on horses. Some of the horses dragged a travois behind them. Relief surged through Brando. They'd escaped and others were here now to help.

Gojo ran up to them with his tail wagging. Drako, Reko, and Gaylo dismounted to greet them. Reko clasped Brando's arm. "We brought travois for the wolves since they've been drugged."

"Thanks." Brando returned the clasp. "They're exhausted, but I didn't think you'd still be here."

"I left, then turned back when I heard the Kayndo's call. Where is he?" Reko asked.

Brando hated to admit it. "I don't know."

"Are the Pericards bringing him?" Blake demanded.

"No." Brando shuffled his feet. "He said he'd help them escape, too, but they don't know he's the Kayndo."

Blake's jaw dropped open. "How could you leave him? Couldn't you put the Kayndo's life before your own?"

Elayni spoke softly, but with heat. "Dayvee ordered Brando to protect our sub-pack and us to leave him. It killed us to go—" Her voice broke. She wiped her eyes. "But we're Calupi."

Drako turned to Blake. "Calupi value the friend at their backs, but to be chosen to keep the pack safe is the highest honor our leaders give. That order's never refused. Our pack's needs come before our own."

Brando had almost refused, but he didn't think Dayvee could forgive him if he didn't free their companions. And his plan to go back had gone awry.

"Don't you people understand?" Blake glared at them. "We can afford to lose others if we have to, but not the Kayndo. We only have one, unless Kun's appointed another?"

Gaylo shook his head.

"I didn't think so. We need Dayvee to keep Varian from destroying Taluma." Blake's tone sharpened. "If he gets out of this, I'll assign Pericards to guard him."

Brando wanted to challenge Blake, but he was right. Brando could have just hurt Taluma. He drew himself up. "Now that they're safe, I'm going back in to find Dayvee."

"Don't be a fool." Blake pointed to the sky. "The sun's coming up. None of us could get far without being spotted."

Brando clenched his jaw. "Then I'll go as far as I can."

Drako grabbed Brando's arm. "Dayvee's speaking to Juno. He crawled out of the castle, but can't make it to the river before sunrise, so he and Jaycee are hiding. He'll try to get out of Harthome tonight." He clapped Brando's shoulder. "Dayvee wants to tell you thank you. Well met."

Tears filled Brando's eyes. Dayvee had escaped. Elayni flew the few feet to him, then hugged him. Tayro, Chayla and Geno joined them.

Gaylo signaled his packmates. They trotted off with their wolf companions. Gaylo turned to them. "Get your companions situated so we can leave."

"Where are your pack-mates going?" Brando asked.

"They'll lead any followers that come beyond the wall in the wrong direction."

"Won't that put them at risk?"

"No. They're Calupi. They'll meet us later," Gaylo stated with conviction.

"I don't think we should go to your camp without Dayvee." The betrayal had Brando gritting his teeth. "I don't want their informers learning he's not with us."

"You'd be in more danger alone." Gaylo gestured to their wolves. "If one of your companions will allow us to cover them, you can tell everyone the Kayndo's injured and will talk to them later."

That wouldn't be a lie. Bruno clambered on the travois. *You can cover me. Dayvee says to go and do it quickly. He doesn't want us this close.*

"Is the camp far?" Chayla asked.

Brando took in his friends' sagging bodies. None of them had slept any that night.

Blake turned his disdain on Chayla. "Not too far."

Brando had to force his anger down. As Dayvee's second, he should have authority over Blake. But now wasn't the time. Rabbit in the hole. Brando couldn't pretend he didn't want to tear Blake apart. The Pericards weren't even clan, much less Calupi.

Their companions claimed those that weren't pack had dung that stunk. Calupi called outsiders dung among themselves. Brando definitely agreed when it came to Blake. But Dayvee would say they needed him. Cackles. Dayvee dealt with dung so much better than he did.

They rode away, following Reko. The sunrise turned the sky aglow. The faint shouts of the searchers had grown distant. With their head start, the Kagards didn't have much chance of catching them, especially with Calupi decoys. But would they find Jaycee and Dayvee? A black dot in the sky drew closer—Spiro. Dayvee watched over them, but who was watching over Dayvee and Jaycee?

Kun, please protect them, Brando prayed.

. . .

Brando slept until midday and then woke with Bruno's hunger pains. Must be a good sign. The hide sides of the large tent ruffled in the breeze around the support poles they were tied to. The tent was larger than Brando was used to, but it was what the Pericards set up for the Kayndo, and most of the camp believed he slept here. The guilt he felt for leaving Dayvee squeezed at his heart. *Bruno, is Dayvee still free?*

Yes, Jaycee says he just dozed off. The first he's slept.

The fist clamped around Brando's heart squeezed him a little less with the news Dayvee hadn't been caught. Bruno padded behind him as Brando tiptoed around the others still sleeping and went outside. The field they were in was huge, much bigger than the previous clearing Gaylo had used to camp at. More people and animals had answered Dayvee's call and were beginning to fill it. Tents crowded the grassy landscape. The Pericard tents and the Kwin's large colorful ones dwarfed the small earth tone ones the Calupi used to blend into the landscape. People bustled around the camp working on assorted tasks.

Another field lay beyond theirs, but it was planted, so it would be left alone. Their field was bordered on the opposite side by woods. The faint sounds of the river's babble came to Brando where it ran behind them. The front of the field was marked by a dirt lane that wasn't much more than a path with more fields beyond it.

Brando filled Bruno's bowl with meat. The wolf scarfed it down.

The sun's warmth embraced Brando, and bird songs filled the air. It seemed wrong to enjoy the beauty around him without Dayvee.

Blake approached them from the camp. "Did you rest well?"

Blake couldn't know Dayvee hadn't, so maybe it wasn't meant to be a reminder. "Yes," Brando answered curtly.

"I'll go to Harthome tonight with some Pericards." Blake's voice became hushed. "Just tell Dayvee we're coming and ask him where he's hiding."

Bruno's low growl sounded. Heat crept up Brando's neck. He hated waiting to go get Dayvee, and his patience was already being tested without this. "I may let one of you come with me since you know the city, but I'll go. You can't even speak to him without a companion."

"We don't need a companion if you tell us where he is. If you care about him, let the Pericards take over protecting him. We're more capable."

Brando had enough of his insults. Maybe a distraction would be a good thing to get his mind off Dayvee, and Blake needed put in his place. Bruno bared his teeth and let out a growl. *Let him see yours.*

Brando clenched his fists. "I challenge you. Meet me in the ring, and I'll show you how capable I am."

"One sparring match doesn't make a Pericard," Blake asserted. "The best of all the volunteers are chosen and trained as Kagards. The best Kagards train and test to become Pericards. Maybe I can convince you if you'll follow me."

Oh why not? Brando couldn't get Dayvee until night fell anyway. He and Bruno followed Blake to another of the Pericard tents across from theirs. Theron stood in front of it.

"How's Tucker doing?" Blake asked.

"We didn't catch him sleeping." Theron fiddled with the hilt of his sword. "I was getting ready to do the last assault since he only has a few minutes left."

"I was going to ask Brando to do it."

"Good." Theron's gaze traveled up and down Brando. "This late, we shouldn't make it too difficult."

Blake gave an amused snort and turned to Brando. "Tucker's a Kagard taking his last Pericard test. If you can get by him to attack a straw dummy, you'd be one step closer to proving to me you can guard the Kayndo."

They made it sound as if this were a challenge. Maybe it was for a Pericard. Brando didn't have to do it, but he had never yet turned down a *challenge*. "One? What else do you want?"

"I want you to take Tucker's place." A glint sparked in Blake's eyes. "I won't ask you to do it for two days without sleep. Just prevent me from getting through once."

"I've proven myself to our pack, our clan council, and most importantly, Dayvee. You can't change my assignment, and I'll still be guarding him regardless of the outcome. But it sounds like fun, so I'm willing to do it under one condition." Brando drew himself up. "I win, and you accept *my* challenge to meet me in the ring."

Blake nodded. "All right. Go around the back of the tent, and you'll see Tucker. Your best chance is to surprise him. I'll follow."

"Can I use my weapons?"

"Yes, but not your companion." Blake answered. "It has to be done without aid."

I'll still be watching, Bruno sent.

Blake pointed to his pouches. "Give your weapons to Theron to wrap so no one dies."

Brando pulled his tooth. He handed it to Theron, hilt first.

Theron wrapped leather strips around his blade. "Tucker's not the target, it's the dummy. But if you have to use your weapon on Tucker to reach the dummy, you'll still win."

They must consider that weak. Theron handed him back his tooth, and Brando gave him his nails to wrap.

Tucker's weapons are also padded," Blake explained. "If they hit you, and we think you'd be dead or unable to pose a threat if they weren't wrapped, he wins. If you hit the dummy anywhere, you win."

"I'll get through, and he'll lose."

Blake's face turned hard. "Then he deserves to lose."

Theron handed him his nails, so Brando ran behind the tent. Tucker stood in front of a chair with the dummy on it. He held a bow and drew the bowstring back. "Halt, state your business with the king."

Calupi didn't lie. "To kill your king." Brando raced forward. Arrows flew toward him.

28

Challenged

"Life is sweeter after you meet a good challenge." ~ Leeto

Brando dodged the arrows. One of the padded missiles caught his shirt sleeve, but it didn't tear his clothing and bounced off. The arrows flew much faster than the balls they trained with.

Tucker and the straw dummy stood behind a rope tied to two poles that stretched over Brando's path. Just a little higher than his knees, so easily jumped, but Tucker would expect that. As Brando came closer, Tucker dropped his bow to take up a sword in one hand and a club in the other.

Brando dove under the rope. Tucker plunged the club down at Brando's head and stabbed the sword toward his chest. Brando rolled into his legs. Tucker staggered back, and his weapons missed Brando.

Brando sprang up. Tucker flicked his sword at Brando's neck, and swung his club toward his side. Brando leapt back. The sword missed, but the club hit Brando's left wrist, and the sting made him drop his nails.

"You can't use that hand now," Blake called.

Tucker lunged toward him. Brando darted to the side. When Tucker's sword followed, Brando dropped to the ground and used his legs to sweep Tucker's. Tucker fell releasing his club. Brando dove past him for the dummy. Tucker's fingers wrapped around his ankle, but Brando's momentum and height let him reach. He plunged his right hand with his tooth into the straw dummy. Tucker's sword hit his back. Too late.

Tucker's face fell. He'd worked hard to pass the Pericard test. Remorse rose in Brando as he stood and picked up his nails from the ground.

"I wish you took it that easy on us, Brando," Geno called out. "You didn't even use your fists." When had the sub-pack come?

Brando and Tucker stepped over the rope and went to their watchers. Theron slapped Tucker's shoulder. "Welcome to the Pericards. Your time was up before he made it through."

Blake slapped his shoulder too. "Yes, but next time be ready for someone on the ground."

Tucker's face lifted, and he smiled. "Yes, Captain."

"I thought you said you weren't the captain now?" Tayro asked.

"I'm just filling in until the contests elect our new captain."

Theron flipped out his thumb toward Blake. "He knows the same as us—he'll win and be captain again."

"Nothing's ever certain. Everyone but Brando needs to wait by the tent," Blake ordered. "Brando, you can take Tucker's place. That dummy's the Kayndo, so don't go easy on me."

Brando clicked his tongue and gave them a wink. "I won't."

Blake, Theron, and Tucker walked around the tent as Brando moved back to the dummy. A shadow alerted Brando to Spiro flying above. Was Dayvee watching too?

Yes. He wants to know what you won't do to get a fight, Bruno sent.

Brando chuckled. *Ask him whether he's safe.*

Dayvee says no one's come close.

The patter of running feet warned Brando. He glanced over his shoulder. Blake had snuck around to the other side. He ran toward him with his sword drawn. Brando pivoted and threw his nails. The wrapping kept them from penetrating, and they bounced off Blake's forehead, leaving a red mark.

Blake's jaw clenched. "You never asked the question."

"You had a weapon drawn and ran toward the Kayndo." Brando couldn't suppress his grin. "According to our leaders, I don't ask questions, I act."

Theron walked toward them with another Pericard. It was the one who shared Dayvee's cell last night.

"I'm glad you escaped, Latham." Blake clapped his shoulder.

"Thad dropped our stuff over the wall, so we have your weapons."

"Thad's dead." Anger infused Latham's voice. "Along with several of our brothers."

Blake grimaced. "I heard."

Latham turned to Brando. "Did Dayvee get out?"

"From the dungeon, not Harthome." Brando unwrapped his tooth and slid it in his pouch.

A deep frown creased Latham's face. "Dayvee said I needed to be judged. I'm loyal to the Kayndo, so will you tell me his identity?"

He's sincere, Bruno sent.

"Dayvee's the Kayndo." Brando took the leather padding off his nails, then sheathed them.

"I'm sorry, Blake." Latham's shoulders sagged. "I told him I'd be back after I freed the others, but he left."

"Dayvee's good at escaping aid." Brando handed the leather pieces to Theron.

Blake huffed. "If you had any hint, you shouldn't have left him."

"I know I failed. Tell him I freed everyone like he wanted." Latham slid Dayvee's tooth pouch off his belt and held it out to Brando. "Can you thank him for loaning this to me?"

"He must have really liked you." Brando took Dayvee's pouch and put it on his belt, behind his own. "This holds a piece of his mother, and it's irreplaceable to him."

"Then I'm glad I wasn't caught." Latham unclasped his Pericard shirt. "I won't resist, Blake. Go ahead and kill me."

What were they doing? Blake grabbed his sword, pulled it out part way, then slammed it back down into its sheath. "I won't take your heart, but you'll be dead to your brothers."

"What's that mean?" Brando demanded.

"A Pericard's purpose is to protect Taluma's heart—a chosen king or Kayndo. If the heart dies, so does the body." Blake crossed his arms. "So we can't fail. Any Pericards who do, risk the same outcome, but I only killed him symbolically. He'll need to leave us since no Pericard will acknowledge him now."

Brando sympathized. Pack law wouldn't excuse Brando in

Leeto's and Codee's eyes. Not when Dayvee's life meant more than all of theirs. Leeto might strip Brando's status, but he wouldn't exile him. And Latham didn't even know.

"You can't fail a duty you're not given, or protect someone you don't know exists." Maybe Brando could make Blake reconsider. "You wanted Pericards to go to Harthome for Dayvee. I won't tell you where he's hidden, and I'll only take Latham."

"All right, Latham." Blake blew out a heavy breath. "I'll make an exception, but next time your blood better spill before his, or your death won't be symbolic."

"I'd be dead anyway if he didn't get us out. My blood will spill before his."

And city people thought Calupi were crazy? If Brando made a mistake, the animals they hunted might kill him, but Leeto wouldn't. "Dayvee won't like that."

"The Pericards don't answer to Dayvee," Blake said.

Didn't the Pericards recognize a Kayndo's authority? Brando gave him a head shake. "You tell him that."

Drako and Gaylo, with some of Gaylo's pack members, came over to the sub-pack. "What are your plans for getting Dayvee?" Gaylo asked.

Brando had allowed himself to be distracted long enough. He found Blake's flinty eyes. "We'll need to meet in the ring later. There are more important things to attend to." He walked toward the Calupi. Bruno sprang forward to meet him.

One of Gaylo's packmates was staring at Chayla with a goofy smile on his face. She smiled back. Brando's stomach knotted. He needed to ask Chayla to life-mate before someone else did. But what if she turned him down? Why would she take the pack's tiger when she could have anyone?

Tayro paled and his eyes misted. Brando closed the distance between them. "What's wrong?"

"Topay asked Jaycee about Dayvee's feet for me. Jaycee says they're worse and he's in agony." He wiped a hand over his face and huffed, "He needs to be treated."

Brando's stomach churned. "Go ahead and fix something up. We know some animals can get in."

Tayro ran to the tent with their belongings and ducked inside. Brando and their sub-pack entered and found Tayro digging flasks out of his rucksack. Blake, Gaylo, and Drako trailed after them.

Brando rifled in his own rucksack and took out a pouch with nuts and berries. "We should also send him water and food, small things the animals can carry."

"Dayvee likes plenty of small things." Elayni brought her pouches out.

"Maybe Seemo will know animals that can get them to him," Brando said.

Gaylo's face creased in consternation. "You've been acting as if you're Dayvee's second."

Homesickness washed over Brando. No one expected anything of him at Wolf Mountain. He'd like another to take charge, even Leeto, so he didn't bear the responsibility. Gaylo must not think Brando was capable, but Dayvee was relying on him. Brando raised his chin. "That's because I am."

"He didn't introduce you as his second." Gaylo glanced at the others. "Did anyone know Dayvee appointed Brando?"

Tayro, Geno, and Chayla shook their heads no. "Yes," Elayni declared. "Dayvee told Brando years ago the only way he'd be alpha was if Brando would be his second. Dayvee depends on him."

Brando squared his shoulders. "The bond that binds us is as strong as the one between twins. It wasn't formed in a womb, but years of relying on each other forged it in our souls. I know how Dayvee thinks, and I don't intend to fail him."

"You did last night," Blake said.

Brando gave him a glare. "He doesn't think so."

Tayro came to stand beside him. "If Brando says he was Dayvee's choice for second, then he is, and I'll follow him."

Geno gave him a smile. "Me too."

He sought out Chayla's pixie face. Would she trust him? "Brando will lead us well." Her soft voice spoke with assurance.

Warmth filled Brando. They were the ones who mattered to him, and they thought he was capable.

"Brando wouldn't claim it if he weren't certain." Drako gave Brando a chin lift.

"A childhood remark isn't enough." Gaylo frowned. "It's not just a sub-pack, but the Kayndo, and the appointment needs to be known." His eyes glazed. "Wait. Dayvee's talking to Gojo. He says he appointed Brando second, Elayni third, Tayro fourth, Chayla fifth, Geno sixth. He apologizes for assuming Codee informed you."

Brando repressed his chuckle. Who'd have thought Codee would keep anything Dayvee said to himself?

All the Calupi lowered their heads to Brando to recognize his authority. Gaylo's head sank lowest, even though he had doubted him. "Dayvee's sending some birds and wants to thank you for your help."

A cooing sounded. Brando ran out. A flock of pigeons littered the ground in front of the tent. Pigeons shouldn't raise suspicions in the city. They split the medicine and food between them. The birds flew away, and everyone followed Brando back in the tent.

"I don't think Dayvee will be able to swim the river tonight," Tayro said.

Why would Tayro doubt it? Brando didn't. "Dayvee swims like a fish. Without feet, Dayvee can do it."

"Jaycee told Topay Dayvee's doubled over with pain and shaking. He's probably feverish. By tonight he could be unconscious or delirious."

"What about your medicine?" Desperation made Brando's voice sharp.

"It will help, but I can't treat him effectively from here." Tayro wiped his forehead.

Brando groaned. "Okay, we need ideas for getting him out now, not tonight."

"You know Harthome." Tayro turned to Blake. "Are there things coming out of the city—carts, baskets, wagons—that Dayvee and Jaycee could be hidden in?"

"Yes, but horses aren't allowed in, so the wagons are loaded outside the gates. Maybe for a price you could smuggle him through."

A glimmer of hope rose in Brando. Each of them carried a little money Codee had sent with them. Brando didn't have to ask. His friends took the coins out and handed them over.

"Do you think this will be enough?" With bated breath, Brando opened his hand to show Blake.

"I don't know." Blake shrugged. "The Kwin deal with the merchants. They're the ones to ask."

"Geno, go get Reko and explain," Brando ordered.

Geno ran out. Not five minutes later, Reko slid inside the tent. "I should have thought of it last night. I know just the person to help us."

Blake gave him a hard look. "If you're referring to our mutual friend, he'll know I can't back my threat now."

"But we know he can be bought."

Brando handed the money to Reko. "Will it be enough?"

Reko looked at the coins. "Depends on how much of a reward Varian offers for Dayvee. Don't worry. If we're short the Kwin will contribute."

Relief filled Brando as Reko put the coins in a pouch. "I know you all want to go," Reko said. "But they'll be looking for Calupi. I have some city clothes that should fit Brando." He glanced at Elayni. "The rest of you will have to stay here. Even taking Brando adds risk."

Elayni's eyes brimmed with tears. "Bring him back."

Brando clasped Elayni's forearm. "You're in charge until we return." He turned back to Reko. "I agreed to let Latham go with me."

"The Pericards are too well known, but he can hide in the woods outside the wall with the horses." Reko gestured to Tayro. "You can, too, so you can treat Dayvee sooner."

Blake's frown deepened. Brando didn't trust Blake not to follow them. *Bruno, pass on to the others not to let him.*

Juno says don't worry, Drako will keep Blake here.

As Brando and Bruno left the tent, his friends called out, "May Kun go with you."

Reko flipped his hand toward the wolves. "Bruno would stick out like a fish flying with birds. He can wait with the horses."

At least Brando didn't need to worry about Bruno getting back in Varian's clutches.

If you're hurt, I'll feel everything through the bond.

Brando sent to the wolf. *If I'm caught, hurry and bond with another. Varian will kill me anyway.*

...

After leaving Latham and Bruno hiding in the woods with the horses, Brando and Reko approached Harthome's wall on foot. Several people loaded wagons to the side of the gates.

"Chandler's not here, and I don't trust these others," Reko said in a hushed voice. "Two escaped Calupi could bring them a lot of profit."

Brando's hope sank. Maybe they could convince them. "Dayvee has money. Not just what Codee gave us. His almost-mom gave him more."

"The Kwin will match the reward, but I don't know where their sympathies lie, or if they'll double cross us and collect twice."

"I'm willing to take risks to get Dayvee out."

"Then let's try going in the gate. Chandler's enough of a risk, but he's good at what he does. Let me do the talking."

Two lines had formed on each side of the gate. The one trying to come out was even longer than the one going in. There were twelve Kagards at the gate, double the amount they had last time, and they were searching every cart. Reko whispered to Brando, "They're being really thorough. Chandler is the only one who can get Dayvee past that."

They joined the line going in. The smells from Harthome and the people around them assaulted Brando's nose—sweat, sewer, and smoke all blended together in a repugnant mix. His apprehension spiked as they moved closer to the Kagards. Brando wiped his damp forehead. If the Kagards tried to apprehend him, could he win free against that many?

"State your business in Harthome." At least the Kagard asking wasn't one Brando had seen before, but would he search them? They both had hidden weapons on them.

"We work for Chandler." Reko rubbed his back and griped. "It's killing us."

The Kagard's nose twitched as if he smelled something rotten. He motioned them in. Brando followed Reko up the street. He grabbed Reko's arm and tilted his head at the pigeons along the wall. Reko gave him a small head shake, no.

He led Brando around the people through a maze of narrow streets with rows of buildings crowding each other to block the sun. They approached a large brick building, square in shape. A burly man with fiery red hair stood in front of it shouting orders at some other men loading carts.

"Chandler," Reko called out as they approached.

The red-headed man turned, and his shifty eyes scanned them. "What do you need, Reko?"

"Can we talk business privately?" Reko asked.

"Certainly." Chandler waved his hand for them to follow and entered the building.

Even with several lamps lit, it took time for Brando to adjust to the loss of the sun. He struggled to navigate without falling into anything as Chandler weaved between towering piles of boxes, casks, and crates. Some open crates lay on the floor with straw packaging hanging out. Chandler motioned them inside a smaller room absent the clutter. It held only a desk and a few chairs. He shut the door. "What's the business?"

"We have to get a Calupi and wolf out of Harthome."

"I was hoping that wasn't what you wanted. The Kagards are offering a huge reward for the Calupi who murdered the queen while she lay in bed." Chandler's face wrinkled in disgust. "Do you think I won't turn you in?"

Brando pulled his knife from his boot.

29

Rescue Attempt

"Don't tell me you tried to do something, tell me you did it." ~ Leeto.

If Brando let Chandler turn them in, they'd be dead. Brando steeled himself. He might have to kill him. Reko opened his hand. The signal everyone in the clans knew, *friend*. Brando reluctantly put his tooth back in his boot. "We didn't kill the queen."

Reko turned back to Chandler. "Our missing Calupi is the Kayndo. Do you really think he'd have killed a queen who supported the Vita? And if the Kayndo succeeds, the ban on animals in Harthome will be lifted. You'll be loading wagons here again instead of at the gates. Plus, you'll have my gratitude and some money to sweeten the deal."

Brando sucked in his breath. Why did Reko reveal who Dayvee was?

Chandler crossed his arms. "And if they catch you, I could be in the dungeon."

"No, you'll tell them we stole your cart. But I don't intend to get caught."

Chandler's beady eyes locked on Brando. "Can I trust you and the Kayndo not to reveal my aid?"

"As the Kayndo's second, I can speak for him." Brando drew himself up. "You have my word we won't disclose it, and a Calupi's word isn't broken."

"I *am* tired of loading at the gates." Chandler uncrossed his arms. "How much money?"

Reko and Chandler swapped numbers back and forth until they settled on an amount. "I expect my next lease to be very reasonable," Chandler said.

Reko handed him all their money. "It will be."

"Follow me." Chandler led them from the room. "Take one of the hand carts and those special ones." He pointed to two long boxes. "And don't make me wait too long for them to return."

"I'll pull the diseased bit, and you'll have them back today," Reko said. Chandler nodded and left them. His shouts drifted back as he directed his workers.

Brando helped Reko load the boxes onto a hand cart. Both the boxes and cart were made from some type of stiff cane lashed together. "What are these boxes?"

"Coffins. Chandler trades in a lot of things, but no one else wants to do this or get near them. That's important when you smuggle." Reko picked up the long handles of the cart and pulled it out onto the street. Brando walked beside him. People drew back and opened a space for the death cart.

Brando whispered, "I'll keep my word and I'm grateful, but do you deal with smugglers much?"

"It's complicated. You can't share this, but the council prefers clanspeople who break laws to face clan justice. King Layton and Blake preferred it, too, as long as their clans don't allow them back. But city people didn't want them just turned over and freed, so we have an arrangement with Chandler. The clansperson being held 'dies' in the dungeon, and the death cart picks them up."

"So how come you didn't get any of the Pericards or us out like that?"

"Blake made sure he was the only one to ever discover the 'deaths', so no one at the castle except the king knew. And Blake said everyone left in Harthome he trusts is in the dungeon. We both know Chandlers not there."

"I don't trust him either," Brando huffed. "Why did you reveal Dayvee's identity?"

"He needed to know why it was in his interest to help us. That's what he cares about. And I trust he won't want to bring more attention from the Kagards to his business. Blake caught him smuggling something of the ancients', and he agreed to help us rather than go to the dungeon."

When they went to the wall, the pigeons cooed at Brando and flew to the ground. They must have recognized him from when he sent the stuff to Dayvee earlier. The birds took a few steps, hopped some, flew a short distance, and then alighted to walk again. The people in the streets put Brando on edge. He scanned their faces. Most didn't return his gaze, but looked away. When so many people lived in a city together, did they stop looking at each other? Maybe no one would notice him and Reko pursuing the birds.

The pigeons led them through the maze of streets toward the castle. Brando's stomach twisted at the sight of the Kagards at the castle gates. They went past it and up a hill. The scent of flowers was as heady as in the queen's garden. But now the queen was dead. Sympathy surged up for Tibalt. Brando lost a mother too.

He topped the rise to see a large open area devoid of buildings. Trees and bushes appeared widely scattered—some full of blooms. A few benches rested under the trees. Wood signs and stones with writing peeked out from the grass. Grave markers. A cemetery.

Reko snorted. "How appropriate Dayvee would hide here, but it's risky."

It appeared deserted. "Why?"

"They claim it's for the hero's of Taluma. Mostly Kagards and Pericards are buried here, but there's a section for Kayndos, kings, and queens. Hopefully, they'll wait a few days for the queen's funeral, like they did with the king, to allow people from farther away to come. The pigeons stopped at a hawthorn tree full of clusters of white flowers.

Hidden by the trunk, tall grass, and petals, Jaycee lay pressed against Dayvee. Brando couldn't see Dayvee's face for Jaycee's fur, but his arm lying over the wolf appeared so pale. Neither lifted their head. *Oh, Kun.* Were they too late? "Dayvee?"

Jaycee's chest rose so he was breathing. Dayvee turned his face to reveal a sickly pale pallor, except for the twin patches of red on his cheeks. "I knew you'd come. Thanks. You too, Reko."

Reko scanned Dayvee, and his mouth formed a grim line. "You're welcome."

Brando squatted and clasped Dayvee's forearm. Much too hot. "I gave Reko's friend my word and yours that we wouldn't reveal his aid."

He returned the clasp. "I'd have done the same."

Reko took a bar on the cart and pried the coffin lids off. "Let's get you two out of here."

"Jaycee's sleeping. I gave him the medicine Tayro sent so he'd be out of pain."

"You should take some." Reko frowned. "You won't be discovered unless you or Jaycee cries out."

"I've taken all he sent, but I won't cry out, and I think Jaycee is beyond making noise. I'll caution him if he wakes."

"Okay." Reko lifted a body out of one of the coffins. Brando had thought they were empty.

"I was hoping I could wait a little bit longer before meeting Kun." Dayvee's smile was wan.

Brando's heart pinged. Dayvee's joke might become a reality if he didn't receive treatment soon.

Reko waved at the coffins. "These have air holes so you won't suffocate. And the bodies are fake. They're just there to convince the Kagards if they look."

Reko removed a false bottom. "Help me lift Jaycee." Brando helped Reko place the heavy wolf into the coffin. "Now Dayvee."

Brando was careful to grab an arm and leg and not Dayvee's feet. Reko did the same. His feet brushed the ground when they lifted him up. Dayvee didn't make a sound, but his bottom lip was in his mouth, and fresh blood dribbled down it.

They put the false bottom over them and fake bodies on top. Brando picked up one of the handles, and Reko grabbed the other. They hurried down the hill and meandering city streets toward the gate. People scurried out of the way. "Diseased bodies are buried outside Harthome in the woods," Reko whispered to Brando.

The people lined up at the gate, and the Kagards eyed them as they approached it. Brando's stomach churned as if a toad jumped inside. Reko extended his hand, palm out. "These two might have been diseased." The watchers all took steps back.

"Go on out." The Kagards waved them around the line.

Brando tried to control his nerves as they pulled the cart past the gate. Every time the coffins bumped or the wheels creaked, Brando wanted to leap away. His neck prickled. Any second he expected the Kagards to shout stop. Or to shoot an arrow in his back. He'd like to run, but Reko kept the same agonizing slow pace.

They finally reached the woods. The coffins bounced on the cart as they pulled it into the rough terrain.

Reko stopped. "I'll pull. You try to steady the boxes."

Brando walked at the back of the cart, holding the coffins, as Reko made a circle to come out of the woods above the gate at the river. Past floods had made the area next to the river bare of trees with not much brush, so the cart rolled easier.

"We need to go back in the woods to escape any prying eyes before we bring them out," Reko said.

As soon as the woods were deep enough to obscure them, Reko stopped and whistled the signal agreed upon, a warbler call. He grabbed the bar and pried the caskets open. Brando helped Reko take out the fake bodies and open Dayvee's.

Dayvee's breath was labored. "Get Jaycee. He woke and his panic's rising from being trapped."

Brando lifted the false lid, and Jaycee lunged out. Bruno came loping up. He nosed Brando, then Jaycee and Dayvee. Bruno darted off. Where was his companion going?

Hoof beats pierced the quiet as Latham and Tayro rode up. Tayro leapt off his horse and ran to Dayvee before the horse could slide to a stop. Latham's mouth dropped open. It impressed Brando too. They'd all seen Reko perform that trick, but Brando wouldn't attempt it. Latham rushed over once the horses stopped.

Tayro threw his bedroll on the travois, then motioned to Dayvee. "Let's lift him onto it."

Brando took Dayvee's arms while Tayro picked up his legs. As soon as they situated him on the travois, Tayro grabbed a flask, and with a healer's authority, barked orders. "Reko, pour this over Jaycee's wounds. Brando, cut Dayvee's leg bandages off, but be careful not to stab him. Latham, help him." After Reko took the flask, Tayro held another to Dayvee's lips. "Drink." Dayvee swallowed.

Brando drew his knife. "You know I'm not supposed to let anyone near Dayvee with a weapon but us."

"Dayvee released our vows." Tayro's tone was short and didn't invite debate. "Latham was judged sincere, and I need every one's help to treat him faster."

"I won't harm him." Latham pulled his own knife. "You know Blake will take my heart if I do."

"All right. Go ahead." Brando slid his knife under the bandage and worked it back and forth until he cut a piece out and could slide his knife in further.

A moan escaped Dayvee when Brando jostled his leg. "Sorry."

Latham worked on the other leg. He slid his hand in between Dayvee's leg and the knife. There wasn't enough room for a hand. He'd get cut to keep Dayvee from being scratched. Would Blake kill Latham for a scratch? Apparently Latham thought so.

Tayro moved to treat Dayvee's grooves on his chest. "Can you sit up?" Dayvee struggled with Tayro's help to a sitting position. "Lean forward so I can wash it better."

When he did, it revealed his back. Brando sucked in his breath. The grooves and whip marks riddled Dayvee's flesh. The old C burn and strap scars Nero inflicted had faded, but these new grooves and cuts painted angry red slashes next to them and ranged all over his back. In some places, ragged pieces of flesh just hung.

Tayro treated Dayvee's back and bandaged it. "You can lay back now."

Brando finally forced his knife the entire length and tore the bandage open to reveal Dayvee's foot. He choked his bile back. A foul stench assaulted his nostrils. But the sight of the mutilation was even worse—a red, rounded, tangled mass, unrecognizable as a foot, with toes pointed to the side instead of forward. The top of the red mass bore a rough imprint of a stone, and the deformed bottom of the blob widened and bent where it had been smashed.

Brando averted his eyes. Tears welled up. The Kwin's and Latham's eyes were wet too. How could anyone with any compassion see the mangled foot and not shed tears? Nero had been terrible, but he couldn't compare to Varian. Like comparing an ant to a bear. *Oh why Kun, must Dayvee always suffer?*

Tayro worked swiftly. He cleaned Dayvee's foot and poured medicines over it. Latham removed the right foot's bandages. It had fared no better— a broken horrendous mess—a twin to the left foot. Latham's hand dripped blood, and Tayro handed him some clean bandaging before moving over to treat the other foot.

Bruno loped up to the travois with Dayvee's rucksack in his mouth. *Dayvee asked me to retrieve his rucksack from the willow tree.* He dropped it on Dayvee.

"Thanks, Bruno," Dayvee's words were faint.

Tayro slid the rucksack to his side and finished his treatment, then put another blanket over Dayvee, and fastened a rope around him. Dayvee's eyes had closed, and his breathing was ragged.

Jaycee got on the other travois. Tayro had checked Jaycee's wounds too, but they weren't infected. They probably bothered him some, but his limp had to be a result of sharing Dayvee's pain.

Reko waved them off. "I'll meet you back at camp. Shilo will wait here while I return the cart and caskets."

Brando hung back a second. He needed to speak to Reko alone. "I owe you more than gratitude for your aid today. If you need anything, just ask, and I'll do everything I can to honor the debt."

Reko gave him a nod, his face just as solemn. It was a serious vow. An unconditional debt.

Brando put his horse into a gallop to catch up with Dayvee. Bruno loped at the side with his tongue lolling. When he closed the distance between them, Brando directed his horse alongside the travois. Dayvee's eyes snapped open, widened, and he muttered, "Kagards."

Dayvee says Kagards ahead, Bruno sent.

Brando reined his horse in. Latham and Tayro did the same. Dayvee thrashed against his bindings. Tayro slid off his horse and went to Dayvee to feel his head. "He's burning up so it could be the fever speaking. There weren't any Kagards earlier."

Brando could just make out Spiro circling ahead. "They could have come while we were in the city."

Topay and I will check. Bruno and Topay loped forward.

"Topay says there's a large group," Tayro said. "At least two dozen on foot, and a couple horses are pulling wagons carrying the ancients' guns."

Not enough to take on the camp, but plenty to put Dayvee at risk.

Latham waved toward the trees. "Going through the woods will be harder with the travois, and it will take longer. We could go back to the road or cut through the fields, but we'd be easy to spot."

"Leave me," Dayvee mumbled.

Brando snapped, "We're not doing that again."

Tayro remounted. "He's not doing well. I'd rather not delay."

Bruno and Topay loped back to them. "I'll try to draw them off," Latham said. "But I'm not sure all of them will leave those wagons."

What if Brando gave them what they wanted?

Let's do it, Bruno sent.

"Bruno and I will help you, Latham." Brando dismounted and handed his reins to Tayro. "Take the horses with you. Wait to take Dayvee through until Bruno tells Topay it's clear." Brando jogged behind Bruno. Latham trailed them.

They circled to get in front of the Kagard group, hiding in the tree line. The Kagards came to a stop. A downed tree blocked their way.

One of them shouted, "Drag it out of there."

Some of the Kagards hauled it from their path. One grumbled, "Captain Hubert, can't we just take the road so this doesn't keep happening?"

"No," the one that had shouted replied. "According to the scouts, several large groups are traveling it to join with the Kayndo. We can't risk encountering trouble if we're to get these guns to Midland and flank them."

"Think we can prevent that?" Brando whispered to Latham.

"I don't carry this bow for nothing." Latham jumped to grab the branch above them, then scrambled into the tree.

Brando moved in front of the Kagards to give himself a head start and stepped out of the tree line.

Latham hollered, "Run, Kayndo! There's Kagards."

Brando looked over as if surprised and darted into the tree line as shouts sounded behind him. Huge cracks rented the air as the ancients' weapons fired. Thuds and screeches broke the quiet of the woods as bullets hit trees. Cackles. They weren't very good with their weapons. With all the errant shots, they might hit Latham, even if they couldn't see him.

Crashes split the air as they moved through the brush like a herd of buffalo. Good. There were quite a few following him, and he could easily tell where they were.

Brando slowed and waited until they saw him again, then ducked behind a tree.

"Over here," one shouted.

He zig-zagged, letting them get occasional glimpses of him, leading them farther away.

Bruno loped up. *They left only a few Kagards behind. Latham shot them, but he's injured. Tayro took Dayvee safely past and left your horses there for you. I'll take over now.*

Okay. Brando and Bruno let another Kagard get a glimpse of them together. Then Brando climbed a tree. *Be careful,* Brando sent to Bruno as he darted off.

The Kagards tromped through the woods under him. Brando's breath caught. Would they look up? He pulled his tooth. They outnumbered him by far. To throw his weapon wouldn't be the smartest thing he ever did but that didn't mean he didn't want to.

He held back his laugh as Bruno set a thicket to shaking. They finally caught the wolf's signal and ran up there only to get scratched by briars. Bruno was long gone, but he let them catch sight of him again to lead them further away. Brando slid down from his tree perch and raced back.

As he drew close, a crashing rent the air. One of the carts sailed down into the river.

They heard that. They're returning, Bruno sent.

"Help me with the other," Latham called. He had a bloody bandage wrapped around his arm. "How badly are you hurt?"

"Not very badly." The wagon was already on the bank, and Latham had set the horse free who hauled it. He was pushing on the back of it.

Brando ran to help. He grabbed onto the rough wood. His biceps tightened and stood rigid as he strained. He gritted his teeth as he forced his body to push harder. The wagon inched over the bank. The guns spilled out as it hit the water with a crash.

"Let's go." Brando ran to the horse and jumped on.

Shouts rang out as the Kagards saw them and the wagons.

Brando's heart pounded as he clucked his horse to a gallop. The crack of gunshots and whistle of bullets filled the air.

30

Hopeless

"Kun doesn't say He won't ever let us fall, just that He'll help us up."
~ *Kwutee*

The Kagards aren't chasing you, Bruno sent to Brando. *They're busy trying to retrieve the weapons from the river. I'll catch up.*

Bruno joined him when they arrived at camp. Brando and Latham slowed the horses to a trot to ride right up to the tent. The sub-pack was carrying Dayvee in. Jaycee limped behind them. Brando leapt off his horse, and Latham grabbed his reins. "I'll take them to the Kwin and come back."

"Thanks." Brando hurried in with Bruno. A pallet now stood on the other side of the tent. His friends placed Dayvee on it. Jaycee plopped down on the floor, and Bruno and the other companions joined him. Brando would bet the pallet was made by Geno. He accomplished that quickly.

"This will make it easier to treat him," Tayro said.

Dayvee's eyes were still closed, and his breathing labored. Occasional moans escaped him. Elayni clutched his hand. Her eyes kept darting to Dayvee's feet, and tears dripped off her chin. Brando clasped Dayvee's forearm and put an arm around Elayni to shore her up.

Geno and Chayla were sniffling. No one seemed to be able to bear it. They had sworn to protect the Kayndo with their lives, but they let this happen. Dayvee somehow attracted the attention of evil and let it go on a rampage against him to keep it from those he loved.

"Should we put another cover on him?" Elayni asked as Dayvee's body shook.

"No, too many aren't good for his fever." Tayro sank to the floor

---

beside Topay and buried his head in his hands. "Leave his feet uncovered so I can treat them."

Gaylo and Blake burst in. "How is he?"

Tayro lifted his head. "Not good. Go ahead and examine him. Then tell us it doesn't matter if the Kayndo's feet are messed up."

They walked toward the pallet. Brando extended his palm. "That's far enough. He's unconscious. Any closer and I'll have to kill you."

Tayro sighed. Brando shot him a glare. "Yes, Dayvee released us, but he also said he trusted our judgment. Mine is that, with or without vows, we should follow our orders."

"It's all right." Gaylo's voice cracked. "I can see from here." Both men's faces had turned white.

The flap of the tent opened, and Latham came in.

"Gaylo, will you check Latham's arm?" Blake asked.

Gaylo unwrapped his bandage, probed around, then cleaned it. "Just a flesh wound. See me in the morning, and I'll clean it again." He gave Latham a hard look. "When did you sleep last?"

Brando took in the red eyes. Apparently not recently.

"I don't know. Varian played at night, so our brothers…screamed during it." Latham choked out, "You can't sleep through that." A tear fell.

"Your brothers who escaped are sleeping in the tent across from this one." Blake's voice was ragged. He waved a hand toward the flap. "Go join them."

Latham shook his head. "It was my turn with Varian. I should be the one hurt, not him."

"You can't do anymore. And your shift's over. That's an order."

Latham slumped and plodded out of the tent. Gaylo went to Tayro and put a hand on his shoulder. "Can I ask what you're giving Dayvee for the infection?"

"I'd welcome any aid." Tayro rattled off a litany. "Do you know of something else to try?"

"No, you've done it all." Gaylo's mouth pursed. "There's only one thing left. If the infection in his feet keeps spreading up his legs, you'll have to do it soon or bury him."

Tayro wiped his eyes. He shuddered. "I was going to give it until tomorrow morning to see if there's any improvement."

"I know it's difficult."

"Difficult?" Tayro's voice filled with panic. "It's horrific."

Alarm coursed through Brando. He tensed and locked eyes with Tayro. "What?"

"He'll need to cut the infected part of his legs off to try to contain it before it's too late," Gaylo gravely said. "If not, he'll die."

"No." Brando rushed to them. They had to understand. "He'd rather die."

"I don't want to lose him," Elayni wailed.

"His feet are useless, so there won't be much difference." Sorrow infused Gaylo's matter of fact tone. "Since the infection hasn't spread above his knees, Tayro can cut them off there if he does it soon."

"There's a huge difference. He won't have any hope he'll recover." A lump rose in Brando's throat to choke him. "I won't make him live like that."

Blake looked at Tayro and snapped. "We need a Kayndo. Cut off his entire legs if you need to."

#

Dayvee woke, his mind fuzzy. "Where am I?"

"We're back at camp." Brando hurried to his side. "This is Blake's tent."

Elayni ran her fingers through Dayvee's cowlick, smoothing it. "I'm here, and Tayro's taking care of you."

The shouts that woke Dayvee sank in. His desperation built. "They don't cut me up. You hear me, Tayro? Listen to Brando." He grabbed Brando's forearm. "Don't let them."

Brando returned his clasp. "They'll have to kill me first."

"No, Dayvee. Live." Drops wet his face from Elayni's tears.

He couldn't let her tears sway his resolve this time. "Not like that." He met Brando's gaze. "I'm absolutely certain you won't fail me. You never do." Dayvee's own eyes teared when he turned back to Elayni's flooded ones. "I've been blessed to have my sub-pack family share my life, and I love you all. We'll meet again when you join me and Clay."

Blake and Gaylo came over to him. Blake's face turned hard. "Quit the good-bye's. I'll call every Pericard in here and cut your legs off myself if I need to. Do you want Taluma to be without Kun and as dark as Varian's continent?"

Dayvee was already visiting that dark place. *Oh, why did you leave me, Kun? I trusted. I believed. JoKayndo, where are you? If you can blow the rocks from a cave, you can heal my feet.*

Brando crooked his thumb across his bent index finger. Elayni's eyes widened at the signal asking Dayvee for permission to kill Blake.

Maybe Gaylo saw it too. His voice was sharp. "The Kayndo can't do what he wants."

Did Gaylo expect Dayvee to flop on his belly to do his duty? He'd be a burden to Jaycee and those he loved. Unable to hold his head up. "No Calupi—you included—could bear it, but you ask me to do this?"

"Your pack needs you. Don't shame them." Gaylo's voice cracked. "Tell Brando to let us."

"What good would he be to the pack? He wouldn't be able to hunt or fight to defend them or the Vita. Surely Kun would appoint another, better Kayndo. But Keepers didn't lie. Could he refuse? Bring shame to his pack?

What about Dayvee's own shame at what he'd be reduced to? Could he live with it? Always slinking. No status. Seeing Leeto and others look at him with eyes full of disgust. The need of the pack was supposed to come over his own. He cut off the anguished moan that escaped him. "I'm ordering you, Brando. Let them."

Brando shot Tayro an icy stare. "I doubt I'll be able to forgive you."

"Me either." Tayro shuddered. "But they're right. The Vita comes first."

Dayvee couldn't break down further, or he'd end up sobbing. A ragged breath helped him get control. "After you do it, Tayro, stay away a while. Give me some time to remember that I love you."

A tear leaked out of the corner of Tayro's eye. He brought a cup to Dayvee's lips. "Drink this medicine. Maybe it will work so I won't need to." Dayvee obediently drank. Then got trapped in Elayni's gaze. He got lost in those light blue pools and swam like a fish, away from those who wanted to cut him in pieces and take every shred of dignity from him.

Cool liquid splashed over his feet waking him. Tayro poured a flask over them. It eased the raging fire burning inside a little. Dayvee slept again, then woke. Tayro stood over him with his tooth out.

Dayvee mumbled, "Slice my neck. It will be more merciful."

Tayro blanched. "I'm only cutting slits in the tops of your feet. They're swelling too much and cutting off your circulation. Maybe it will allow some of the infection to drain."

The knife going into Dayvee's dead feet didn't hurt. But after Tayro sheathed his tooth, the agony slowly grew, relentless like fifty nails being pounded into his feet at the same time. A whimper escaped him.

"I know it doesn't seem like a good thing, but it is. If your circulation dies, I'd need to cut them off too." Tayro held a cup to his mouth. "It's pain medicine."

Dayvee guzzled it and slept again. Crazy dreams haunted him. Tayro, Gaylo, and Blake had their knives out. "Take them off," Blake ordered. Their blades sawed into his legs.

Dayvee screamed and woke. His friends' faces were wrapped in a haze, but they looked so concerned. Brando and Elayni's hands held his arms tight. He returned the clasp and closed his eyes. Then another dream. He was in the castle's torture room. Elayni hung from the ropes. Varian grabbed his whip. Dayvee flopped on his belly on the floor, unable to stop him. Varian's evil laugh rang out. "I told you, you wouldn't walk again."

"No!" Dayvee woke with cool water on his face. He tried to talk, but gibberish came out. He closed his eyes. Another dream, this time JoKayndo. The great white wolf wanted him to follow him. Dayvee struggled to pull his body after JoKayndo with his arms, but he couldn't keep up. The wolf receded in the distance. *Come back, JoKayndo.*

His eyes cracked open. It was dark. He felt for and found his legs.

They were still there, but only until Tayro removed them in the morning. Tears stung the back of his eyes.

Sweat poured off him. He was so hot. He needed air. He needed water.

Elayni slept on one side of his pallet, Brando the other. No Calupi could have better friends.

Dayvee scooted up so he'd miss hitting Brando, and then slid off and onto his knees. Ouch. He had to get used to using his knees. Jaycee padded behind Dayvee as he crawled out of the tent. A nicker greeted him.

Thanks for coming Sunray. Can you kneel? Dayvee crawled on, and she carefully stood. *Take me to the river where the water is clean and cool.*

Sunray walked to the bank's edge as he clung to her mane. She lowered her front legs. Dayvee rolled off her, down the bank, and into the cool water. Ahh. That was better. The water lapped against his body as he floated. He let the small current carry him downstream. He'd always loved the water. It wouldn't be a bad way to die. No slinking. No hurting anymore. He should just let himself sink. The cool water washed over his face. He let his breath out, and the bubbles rose.

No matter how many times a wolf's legs are knocked out from under him, he gets back up to fight, Jaycee sent. *You have to get up.*

I'm tired of fighting. I'm not strong enough to bear the burden, the shame, or this agony. I really can't stand putting you through this pain too. Kun won't even help me. Will you please bond with another?

No.

Then don't ask me to live with the guilt of hurting you.

If you go, I will too, Jaycee sent. *I'll guard your body until I die.*

31

Shadows

"The sun brings both the light and the shadows. Both serve a purpose." ~ Kwutee

Brando woke with a start. What had woken him? He scanned the tent. No intruders. But Dayvee's pallet was empty. His heart fluttered. Could Dayvee have been kidnapped? Wouldn't the companions have alerted them?

He left with Jaycee, Bruno sent. *And he didn't want us to wake anyone.*

Ugh. Brando dashed to the opening. Not quite sunrise, but close. Gray had replaced the blackness of night. Enough light to discern hand prints and knee impressions in front of the tent. How far could Dayvee have crawled? He did have stamina. He'd escaped the dungeon by himself and went up that hill to the cemetery. Then Brando spied hoof prints. They could be from yesterday. He knelt and touched them. Damp, and too crisp to be yesterday's. *Bruno, will you call to Dayvee? I need to find him.*

I'm not getting any response.

Can you track him?

Yes. Bruno dashed off, muzzle high, sniffing the air. Brando ran to keep up. A horse's scream pierced the morning's quiet. Sunray pranced up ahead. Bruno raced toward her. Dayvee must have ridden Sunray, but he wasn't on her now.

Reko came running up. "Shilo told me Sunray wants us to follow her." Sunray nickered at them and then trotted toward the back of the field with Bruno. Brando and Reko ran after the animals to the river's bank. The wolf and horse turned and headed downstream. Brando's chest squeezed him as he struggled to keep their pace, but he didn't slow. Bruno bounded down the bank. Jaycee lay on shore. He raised his head as Bruno licked his face. Where was Dayvee?

There. In the river. A body.

Lifeless.

Dayvee's head rested against a log, but the rest of him was immersed. Brando and Reko jumped in and lifted the limp Dayvee out beside Jaycee. Was he breathing? "Dayvee, do you hear me?"

Dayvee's eyes fluttered open. "Yes. I can always count on you." Jaycee nosed him, and Dayvee touched the wolf's head with a shaking hand. Shivers racked his body, and his teeth chattered.

The water wasn't even cold, but Brando hadn't been in long. "What happened?"

"I was too hot. I rode Sunray and got in, but couldn't get out. Sunray tried, but couldn't help me. So I told her to get you or Reko in the morning." Dayvee gave them a sheepish grin. "I must have fallen asleep."

Dayvee wasn't looking Brando in the eye. Could he be hiding something? He'd wait to press him until they were alone. "You didn't have to wait."

"I didn't want to wake you. Thanks for coming too, Reko."

Reko gestured to Sunray. "She can carry two. You better get him back and covered."

Brando and Reko lifted Dayvee on Sunray's back. Brando slid on behind him and "yup'd" to Sunray. She rocketed up the bank and broke into a canter. Jaycee's lope was rough, but he kept up with Bruno and Sunray. The rest of the sub-pack raced down the river path toward them. Brando didn't slow, just guided Sunray around them.

Dayvee still shivered, and Brando needed to warm him. "You have to start thinking about preserving your life rather than how fast you can sacrifice it. You're killing me."

Sunray trotted around the tents in the camp until they came to theirs. Several Pericards stood in front of it. They weren't there last night, but Blake had said he'd assign Dayvee new guards. Brando might as well get something useful from them. He jumped off Sunray. "Help me carry the Kayndo into the tent." When they got inside, they laid Dayvee on the pallet.

The Pericards' faces held lines of concern. "Leave us now," Brando ordered. When Blake learned Dayvee got to the river unguarded, he would fly into an uproar, but Brando deserved it. He helped Dayvee change his clothes, then covered him with blankets. "This is getting to be a habit."

His friend—now Kayndo—smiled at him. His teeth stopped chattering. "My feet don't hurt as badly."

"Next time you decide to do something like that, you call me first. Agreed?" Silence answered him. Brando's exasperation sharpened his tone. "Dayvee."

"I put you through a lot by making you leave me in the dungeon, so I'll give you this one." Dayvee's sheepish smile returned. "I won't go swimming at night without you."

Brando needed to make it plain. "Not just swimming."

"I can't agree to that, even though you deserve it." Dayvee tensed. "I feel as if I'm in a cave and the roof's collapsing. I need to get out."

"We just want to be your ceiling platform."

"I love the platform, but it's keeping me pinned, and I can't breathe."

"It's no different for us. We can't get up and let the rocks crush you."

"I know, and the weight of being Kayndo is impossible to bear." Dayvee ran a hand through his hair over his cowlick. "I wanted to sink last night and free us all."

Brando sucked in his breath. "Are you able to face it now?"

"Yes, because I had the freedom to go back. My whole life I wanted to be Calupi, and I got through it with the memory of when we weren't. Remember when we were younger and went plunging, how we'd float on our backs and admire the stars and then the sunrise over the mountain?"

Brando let the memory fill his mind. He heard the frogs croaking, watched the stars twinkle, and smelled the crisp scent of pine while he drifted weightless with Elayni's and Dayvee's hands entwined in his. He clasped Dayvee's arm. "That's a really good memory."

Dayvee returned the clasp. "Yes, and when the sun rose, we'd climb down the mountain and race back to the cave. The only things I had to worry about was letting Elayni win, so we didn't hurt her feelings, and facing Leeto's criticism. That gave me the strength to care if we keep the Vita, and the pack can keep making memories like that."

Dayvee's reverie was broken at the drumming sound of racing feet.

Brando reached for his weapon. Elayni flew into the tent and flung herself over Dayvee's chest. He winced, but hugged her back. She sobbed. "Don't scare us like that again."

Dayvee patted her back. "Shhh. I'm okay."

Tayro came rushing in. "How is he, Brando?"

"He says his feet don't hurt as much."

Elayni straightened. The corners of Dayvee's lips turned down. "Don't you think you should ask *me* how I feel?"

"Sorry, you weren't making sense last night. I need to look at your feet." Tayro uncovered the hide. "I think the infection's on the run."

Relief hit Brando. Dayvee would survive this.

"Maybe my swim was a good thing," Dayvee declared.

"Probably the medicine worked in spite of your swim." Tayro put the hide back.

Dayvee grabbed Tayro's arm. "Thanks for everything. I'm really sorry about yesterday. I do love you, and I won't let myself forget it again."

"It's okay. I wouldn't even have a pack if it weren't for you."

Dayvee sat up and grabbed his rucksack from behind the pallet. "All of you have my gratitude." He drew out the red fringes. "You risked yourself in Harthome to keep your packmates and the companions safe." He handed them each a fringe. To Brando, he gave two. "And you risked your safety again to come back for me." He lay back and yawned. "All night swimming is tiring, so if no one minds, I'm going to sleep a little."

"We don't mind." Brando tilted his head toward the door. The sub-pack left the tent with their companions. The Pericards backed up to let them out.

Brando tied his red fringes on his weapon's pouch. "I won't deny his right to award these, so I'll wear them, but I don't think we earned them. Somehow we've *got* to do a better job." His friends' heads bobbed in agreement.

Gaylo and Blake ran up to them. "How is he?"

"He's better—almost himself—but tired," Tayro answered. "He's resting now."

"Then I'll come back later." Gaylo strode away.

Brando glanced at Blake. "Do you have suggestions to protect him, besides assigning different guards?"

"Yes, walk with me." Blake motioned to the Pericards. "No one in or out but us."

Brando wouldn't trust them alone. "Geno and Tayro stay with Dayvee."

Chayla and Elayni followed after him and Blake. Their companions' gaits held a spring as they accompanied them. A light breeze played among the tents and ruffled Brando's hair. The sun's rays chased the night's chill away. Going to be another warm day. With the sun up, the camp had come alive.

The city people in their flax or wool-spun clothing stood out among all the clanspeople in buckskin. Gruels and teas bubbled on lit fires. Scents wafted—oats, honey, maple, raspberry, and chicory. The clanspeople shot admiring glances at Brando and his friends. After they learned his guards left the Kayndo, would those looks turn scornful?

When they reached the dirt lane that fronted the field they camped in, Blake finally stopped and turned to Brando. "Not many know the Kayndo's identity. If we put some bandages on you, we could tell everyone you're the Kayndo." Blake gestured to Bruno. "Dayvee could talk to your companion to give you his instructions." His nose wrinkled. "But I'm not sure if *you'd* be willing to suffer when his enemies target you instead of him."

Bruno and Evee's growls sounded. *Time for the ring?* Bruno sent. *Soon.*

Elayni glowered at Blake. "Do you still doubt Brando's love for

Dayvee after he just risked his life for him?"

"I didn't mean to offend you," Blake said.

"Yes, you did, and your plan has three flaws." Brando held up one finger. "Anyone with a companion will know Dayvee's the Kayndo. They don't lie, and neither do Calupi." He raised a second finger, "I already told most everyone I wasn't the Kayndo, but he'd speak to them later." He put his third finger up. "And Dayvee will *never* agree. You figure out how to fix those, and I'll be your target."

Bruno sprang away, streaking toward camp with Evee and Cato. *Dayvee's in danger.*

"Cackles!" Brando raced toward the tent.

#

Varian stood over Dayvee with his knife. He snapped awake. It was just a dream. His breathing calmed. Shadows played along the tent side. Were those people? Did they hold knives? Maybe he was still feverish? Maybe he wasn't. His heart sped up, and he grabbed for his weapons. They weren't on his belt. Brando had his tooth, and Elayni had taken his nail pouch to dry it.

He hated being helpless. Should he call his friends? If the shadows weren't real, they'd think he was crazy. His mind screamed at him to do something. But what? He rolled off the pallet. Ouch.

Jaycee's growl pierced the air. Graydee and Topay joined in, and the wolves charged out of the tent. Geno and Tayro sprang forward to get in between Dayvee and the shadows. A blade pierced the tent's hide.

"What are you doing?" Was that Latham's voice? "Pericards, help!" A grunt came as the shadows merged.

Wolf shadows leapt among them, mouths snapping. Growls pierced the air, followed by screams and then thuds as shadows collapsed to look like lumps. More shadows joined them.

"Is everyone in the tent okay?" Brando shouted.

"We're fine," Tayro answered.

"I want Pericards on every side of this tent," Blake hollered.

Elayni burst in. "Latham needs your help, Tayro."

Brando and Blake came behind her, carrying Latham. Chayla had squeezed next to them and held a bloody hand over his throat.

While Tayro grabbed bandages, Dayvee motioned to the pallet. "Lay him there."

They placed him on it. "Lift your hand, Chayla." Tayro pressed the bandages down on Latham's throat, but blood spurted, soaking them. Tayro's sorrowful eyes revealed there wasn't any hope.

Oh no. Sorrow infused Dayvee. If only he wasn't so helpless, he could have aided Latham, maybe even kept him alive.

"Did I stop the threat?" Latham gurgled out.

Latham killed two. We wolves killed the third, Jaycee sent.

Blake clasped Latham's hand. "You didn't fail, brother. I'm proud of you."

"Thanks." Latham mouthed. He drew one last breath, and then his eyes rolled back.

Tayro slumped. Anguish rose along with guilt in Dayvee. They surely were after him, not Latham. Bandages were still wrapped around Latham's arm. Dayvee snapped, "Who assigns an injured guard?"

"I didn't assign him. His bedroll is out there." Blake rubbed his hands over his face. "He took it upon himself to sleep near you."

Jaycee growled and so did Dayvee. "After you threatened to kill him."

"There are reasons for our traditions." Blake's voice was torn. "Latham thought you deserved his life, so don't let it be in vain." He scooped up Latham's body and carried him out.

Gaylo ran into their tent. His eyes darted to Dayvee on the floor and the blood on the pallet. "Are you okay?"

"Yes. It was Latham who went to Kun." Dayvee wiped at the mist in his eyes. "He and the wolves killed my attackers. I didn't even have my weapons."

"Sorry." Brando took off Dayvee's pouch and handed it to him. Elayni brought his nails.

Varian must have been behind this attack too. Dayvee needed to stop him. "How many people have responded to my call?"

"Almost as many as a clan meeting, with more streaming in."

Brando's eyebrows shot up. "Bruno says everyone from all four meetings are coming. The closest are three days away."

"I'm not waiting for them all, but I'll give it three days to make certain we have enough."

"Let us in." Drako demanded from the entrance of the tent.

Reko yelled, "The Kayndo's in danger!"

"I'm okay," Dayvee called out. "Let them in."

"Not without Blake's permission," a Pericard said.

What? Dayvee crawled toward the entrance. "Then I'll go to them."

"We can't permit that, but we sent for the captain."

"They can go in," Blake said.

"Come in too, Blake." When they entered, Dayvee rose to his knees and glared at Blake. "I'm the Kayndo. Why aren't your men following my orders?"

"Pericards answer only to me."

As Leeto's son, Dayvee knew all about leadership challenges. His position on the floor wasn't the best place to meet one, but he raised his head. "Gaylo, is there any person who has more authority than a Kayndo?"

Gaylo's eyes trained on Jaycee. The wolf's hair stood on end. "No. Even a king has to answer to you."

"Can anybody replace me?"

"Only Kun can assign a new Kayndo."

Dayvee put menace in his voice. "Then I don't understand, Blake, why they don't answer to me. I didn't escape the castle dungeons so you could cage me. Are you loyal to the Kayndo or not?" He gave the signal, putting his thumb out as he pulled his nails.

32

Brothers

"Siblings grow beside each other. Pericard brothers die beside each other." ~ Blake

Dayvee's sub-pack and Drako crowded around him, pulling their weapons too. The companions sprang forward at Blake, growling. Dayvee kept a lid on his anger. He'd only use his weapon if Blake forced him to.

Blake's eyes widened. "You don't think I'm loyal after all I've done for you?"

"You said you wanted to aid us." Dayvee let his voice heat. "If the return you expected was to usurp the Kayndo, I won't pay that price. I'm *not* Tib."

Blake's face scrunched in puzzlement. "Several kings and Kayndos died when they didn't make good decisions about their own defense. That's why Pericards answer to their captain."

"There's no reason I'd accept for you to undermine my leadership." Dayvee pointed a finger upward. "My authority comes from Kun. If you *think* you have a higher authority than Him, you're listening to the deceiver."

Yes. Blake hasn't put any stars in the sky. Bare your teeth, Jaycee sent.

"I only need to send one thought"—Dayvee tapped his finger against his temple—"and every clansperson in this camp will respond to throw you Pericards out and kill any who resist."

Blake held up his hand, palm out. "Please don't. We only want to aid you."

"Your aid looks like control. I won't accept your orders and you and your men don't take mine. If neither will submit, one leader has to go. And the Kayndo can't be replaced."

"All right. I'll do it. I'll submit to your authority. If you'll allow it, I'll give you my oath, and I'll tell my men I believe you're worthy to hold theirs too.

Dayvee didn't let his face soften. "They'd have to be freely given. I don't want coerced ones. But if vows affect me, I want them sworn to me. What're your oaths?"

"The Kagards swear the *K*'s—to be the knuckles to protect the kingdom and either the Kayndo or a chosen king—with the help of Kun. The Pericards vow in blood that, with the help of Kun, they'll give their whole heart to hold the wall of fists that protects Taluma's heart.

"A blood oath means their life is the price for breaking it," Drako explained.

Dayvee put his nails away and signaled the others to do the same. "If I accept your oaths, am I stuck with Pericards for life?"

"No," Blake answered. "Once the threat's eliminated, and we have a chosen king, the Pericards will protect him."

"I plan on that being shortly. But until then, would I have to put up with you hovering over me too?" Dayvee shifted and pain stabbed his feet. He couldn't let it show. There's no way he'd reveal weakness in front of Blake.

"I don't intend to fail." Blake's gray eyes bore into him.

Dayvee met his gaze. "This is the vow I'd want; you'll be loyal and follow the Kayndo's orders to defend Taluma and the Vita with the help of Kun. I don't want any blood oaths. And if they aren't sincere, my companion will know."

Blake's shoulders drooped. "Pericards want to give blood oaths. It makes them brothers, and they wouldn't trust a captain who didn't do the same."

"I'll allow them in blood with one condition—you can't kill any Pericards who fail. Find another consequence." Dayvee waved his hand toward the tent entrance. "Go think it over while I speak to Reko. Any who want to give their vows should meet me in front of the tent. But know this. I'm Calupi. I *won't* be caged."

Blake gave him a nod and ducked out. Gaylo clasped Dayvee's arm. "And you thought you needed feet. Well met."

Drako gave Dayvee a grin with his arm clasp. "If you need us, call."

"Thanks," Dayvee said. The two Calupi left together.

"You wanted to talk to me?" Reko asked.

"Yes. Sunray pledged to be my feet." Dayvee sighed. "I really should have checked with you before taking her up on it."

"I don't own Sunray. I'm sure there're several horses that will volunteer to serve the Kayndo. No Kwin would refuse them."

"There are others, but she insisted it be her," Dayvee admitted.

Reko chuckled. "I told you she can be pushy."

"And that she'd take care of me, which she has." Dayvee's knees were going dead. "Jaycee told me this field we're using is yours. I'm confused, since you're Kwin,… are we delaying the planting?"

"No. This will remain fallow this year. It's actually my grandfather's." Reko tugged his headband down a little. "But I *am* Kwin, and I won't give that up, so I hire help for him."

"You've been a huge help to *us*. If there's anything you need, ask for it, except for one thing."

"What's that?"

"Our women. They're not mine or Brando's to give, and I kind of like them around."

Elayni's eyes locked on Dayvee. His heart plummeted. He had dreamed of life-mating with her, but now he wouldn't. Not when it meant he'd be a burden.

Reko chuckled. "Aww, you took the fun out of me asking Brando for them." He clasped Dayvee's arm and left.

"I thought these might help you." Geno handed a set of crutches to Dayvee, but they were different. Geno had padded the tops, and they had a handle that jutted out half way down. The bottom had four spindles that curved to touch the ground. When Dayvee fingered them, Geno said, "I think those will make them better. They should add stability to support you if you're standing in one place."

Geno could improve anything. With the help of the crutches,

Dayvee stood. Yes, this gave him a much better view than the one from his knees. "Thanks. I *really* appreciate it."

As he left the tent with his sub-pack, a cheer sounded. A Pericard crowd minus their helmets had gathered. People from the camp milled behind them. Curious, maybe?

Blake waved at his men. "They're thrilled you'll take their vows."

"I'm glad some Pericards respect me." Dayvee gave them a smile.

"Latham told them you risked yourself for our brother's sake," Blake said. "And I respect you; I just think you're going to make our job difficult."

Dayvee laughed. "My father says the more difficulty the better. It keeps us sharp."

"I'm not sure I'd like your father." Blake's brow knitted.

Brando snorted. "You wouldn't be the only one."

Blake turned his steely gaze on the Pericards. "At the Kayndo's request, a Pericard's failure won't mean his death. But they'll feel my fists." He glanced at Dayvee. "That should be acceptable to a Calupi. Can I come through now?"

"Yes." Dayvee's friends made room.

Blake knelt in front of Dayvee and sliced his palm with his knife. Dayvee scooted his crutches out far enough to lower himself to his knees so he wouldn't lose his balance, then cut a line down his own palm. Blake clasped Dayvee's hand. The blood felt warm and sticky as it mixed. Blake gave him his oath while blood dripped.

"I'm honored, Blake, to hold your oath." Dayvee didn't let go. "Brando, will you ask Bruno to judge my words?" Brando nodded once, so Dayvee continued. "This is my oath to the Pericards. I vow that I'm willing to sacrifice everything, including my life, to appoint a new king, restore the Vita, and be worthy of your fealty."

Brando touched Bruno's head. "He says Dayvee's vow was sincere."

Dayvee released Blake's hand, but Blake didn't back away. "You don't answer to us."

"Any Calupi would lose credibility among the clan for breaking a vow. A Kayndo needs credibility, so I'd answer for it."

"Then I'm honored to hold it. I've never done the bath with the heart, but you gave us your vow, so may I touch your head?" Blake asked.

Dayvee didn't understand, but it probably wouldn't hurt to play along. "Yes."

"We give our vows and willingly shed our blood for one another and our heart." Blake held up his bloody palm. "The blood mingling unites us with each other, and our purpose making us brothers." He wiped the blood on Dayvee's hair. "Now, you do the same."

So that's why they weren't wearing their helmets. Dayvee smeared his bloody hand in Blake's hair.

"This blood bath unites us with all our brothers who came before us and willingly shed their blood to keep Taluma strong. Latham was the latest in a long line, so wear it with pride." Blake stood. "Are you ready to receive their vows?"

Dayvee let his gaze travel over the Pericards. "Only if they wish to give them." He raised his voice. "And if you do, the oath you already gave to your captain isn't released. But if our orders contradict, I'm the Kayndo, so you need to follow mine."

They lined up to grasp Dayvee's hand, give their vows, and wipe blood in his hair. "Brother," each said. The blood dripped down Dayvee's scalp. The sharp scent filled his nostrils as he rubbed his hand on fifty-six heads. Then the Pericards smeared their blood in each other's hair.

Dayvee didn't let his relief show when they switched to Kagards, and the blood bath was over. The Kagards came forward in small groups to give their vows. After the last of them, Blake lowered his head. "Thank you for that part about following my orders."

A leader needed to have respect. Dayvee should tell them his opinion. "I think you're a great leader, so I never wanted to take your men from you. But I don't want anyone confused about who has the final say."

Blake straightened. His chin lifted.

"Just one other thing." Dayvee hardened his voice like flint. "Don't make the mistake of reaming my sub-pack again. You *don't* have *that* authority."

"I understand. All of us have given you our vow now." Blake waved at the crowd amassed behind them. "But other people in camp have asked to give you theirs. With your permission, I'll have everyone give you a vow of loyalty with a companion judging their truthfulness. It should weed out any more attackers or informants."

"That's a good idea." Dayvee glanced at Chayla and Geno. "Go judge them. All vows should be sworn to the Kayndo."

"Will you agree to no exceptions?" Blake asked.

"All but my sub-pack. And the only penalty for not giving one is to be escorted from camp."

"Everyone else will trust your sub-pack if they give their vow too," Blake mumbled.

Elayni chewed her bottom lip. "We'll give our oath."

"Do you think I'd ask my right or left arm to give me a vow? It's already one with me."

He looked at Blake. "Everyone else needs to trust my judgment."

Blake shifted his weight. "With your agreement, I'll ask for volunteers to form a perimeter around the camp. No one will get by without giving their vow and a companion testing them."

"Agreed."

Dayvee ran a hand through his hair. The dried blood made it rough and clumpy. "When do you wash it off?"

"Tonight." A corner of Blake's lip turned up. "You're the first to be claimed as a brother who didn't take our tests. But we know you could have passed them."

Maybe before he was crippled. They obviously considered their brotherhood an honor, so Dayvee couldn't act like it didn't matter. He'd have to wait to wash. Blake walked away with Chayla and Geno. Most of the Pericards went with Blake, but five stayed to form a second ring around his sub-pack. Like he needed a second. He might not have feet, but he had his weapons.

He whispered, "You should have done it, Brando. You like having family."

"I like mine small," Brando replied softly. "Besides, I remember you wearing Nero's blood once. Who needs brothers like that?"

Dayvee groaned at the thought of more Neros. Tayro held a bandage out. "I want to treat your hand."

"I didn't cut it that deep."

Tayro tone was as hard as Kwutee's. "It still can get infected."

"Let him." Elayni grabbed his arm. "We don't want to hear your ramblings again."

Dayvee's heart raced at her touch. He pulled away and used Brando's expression. "Yes, mother Elayni."

Her face fell at the brush off. Remorse rose, but Dayvee had to treat her like that now. She needed to forget about him and find someone with feet to life mate.

...

The borders of the field could barely be seen beyond the sea of tents. Dayvee had made this same ride to the river last night, but with the amount of people and animals streaming in today, it was much harder for Sunray to pick her way through. The bank was one of the few clear areas left, so he urged her up it and turned to face the huge crowd.

They were wedged between tents in every available space. People pushed forward against his sub-pack and Pericard rings, pressing them tighter against Sunray. His sub-pack and the Pericards pulled their weapons.

"Not too close. We don't take chances with the Kayndo's safety," Brando shouted.

Everyone here had given him their vows. Surely they didn't want to hurt Dayvee. A man reached for his leg. The man's pinky fell to the ground as his horrendous scream split the air. Blood spurted. The crowd drew back.

"Well met, Chase." Brando gave the Pericard a chin lift. "No one touches the Kayndo without his consent."

It didn't take long for Brando to have the Pericards doing what he wanted. As Gaylo bandaged the injured man's hand, Dayvee shot Brando a glare. Brando's cocky grin showed no remorse.

The babble of voices from the crowd rose. Sunray shook her head and her mane flew. She trumpeted out a horse scream. Everyone fell silent.

Dayvee lifted his head and squared his shoulders. They needed to see him as a leader, not a cripple. "I'm Dayvee, son of Leeto, alpha of Wolf Mountain Pack, who was selected by Kun to be *Kayndo* and restore the Vita."

A cacophony of animal sounds—shrieks, howls, neighs, barks, yips, honks, bellows, stomps, snorts, and chirps—all echoed in his ears.

"I want to thank everyone for responding to my call." Dayvee went on to reveal his plans, and then asked if anyone had suggestions. After considering each, he made his decisions and explained what they were. No one argued with him.

"All right. Since plans could change during the battle, you'll receive any new instructions from your companions. If too many animals speak at once, I can't understand. So if you have questions, send them through your leaders' companions. If you're not from a clan, form groups and select a leader. I'll appoint someone with a companion to each. As always, leaders are held accountable for those under them. So if there're problems come see me."

The noise level reached a crescendo.

Can you scream again? Sunrise's blast quieted them.

"If anyone doesn't want to risk injury or death, I won't hold it against you if you decide to leave now." No one moved. "Thank you for your suggestions and support. In three nights we attack. May Kun grant us success."

A huge roar of applause and animal sounds followed Dayvee as they left. "Brando, the companions tell me the clans have held fighting competitions every evening. I think we should go."

"Really?"

"Why not? I can't compete, but if anyone else wants to, I'll watch and support you."

"What about guarding you?" Brando asked.

"It doesn't take all of you." Dayvee gave him a smile. "Just try not to get hurt too badly."

"You're beginning to sound like Mother Elayni." Brando chuckled. "It's a good idea. People should know they can't defeat me and get to you."

Elayni rolled her eyes. Dayvee laughed. "Sounds like a good excuse to me." He reached out to Bruno. *Tell Brando, after he impresses Chayla, to pull her aside and talk to her before it's too late.*

Brando winked. "Yes, Kayndo."

\#

Brando woke and looked for Dayvee. Good, he hadn't left again, but his eyes were open. Did he sleep at all? Jaycee's whimpers had revealed a difficult night for them. Everyone was stirring. Tayro checked Dayvee's feet.

"I want to try boots today," Dayvee declared.

"Give us an hour to fix some up." Tayro took a deer hide out of his rucksack. He and Geno discussed what to do and measured Dayvee's distorted feet.

Tayro and Geno didn't need Brando's help. He pulled his knife and whittled on his latest wood carving while Tayro and Geno cut a pattern out of the hide, sewed it, and stuffed it.

Concentration lines creased Tayro's forehead. "These are going to be large so you can get them on and off easily, but we can pad them." He prepared a mixture of melted pine sap, hooves, and beeswax to the outside to waterproof and harden them.

After the mixture dried, Tayro took out some of the stuffing and brought the boots to Dayvee, who pulled them on. Brando put down his carving. Would they work?

With the help of his crutches, Dayvee brought himself off his pallet and sat his feet down. He winced, but they took his weight. His face split in a huge smile. "Thank you."

Company coming, Bruno warned. Drako, Juno, and Blake came in with food baskets. Dayvee frowned and glanced at Brando. He got the message. They needed to hunt and not be so reliant.

Drako set the food next to Dayvee. "Gaylo wanted us to bring this. He says not to worry about hunting. There's plenty."

"Will you join us for breakfast?" Dayvee asked.

"We already ate with Gaylo," Blake replied. "I'm going to hold the captain contests tomorrow."

"Good." Brando chuckled. "I didn't want to hurt your chances by meeting you in the ring first."

"Maybe I should thank you." A glint lit Blake's eyes. "But I don't think you'll do as well against me as you did last night."

Ha. Brando gave him a smile. "Want to wager on it?"

Drako ran a hand through his hair. "All the clans want to hold contests too. It might relieve the stress of waiting. We can include a swimming and climbing competition to select who goes into Harthome first."

Might be fun. Even if Brando didn't compete, he could place bets.

Dayvee opened the baskets and filled Jaycee's bowl. He only chose a piece of dried fruit for himself. "I think that's a good idea. You two should judge since you'll be leading them."

Brando and the rest of the sub-pack filled their bowls. Blake wiped a hand over his forehead. "I still think I should go with you."

Dayvee swallowed his mouthful of fruit. "You know the city. This will help me."

Blake gave him a small nod, then thumped his fist over his heart in a salute. Drako raised a brow. "I thought that salute was for a king."

"It's for the heart of Taluma—a Kayndo or chosen king. When we give the salute to Dayvee, it acknowledges him as Taluma's heart and says he's worth protecting with our fists. If he returns it, he acknowledges our fists as worthy to protect him." Dayvee brought his fist up and returned the salute.

Drako clasped Dayvee's arm and glanced at Blake. "Our arm clasp is a statement too. It says 'friend.'" Drako and Juno left the tent with Blake.

"Wilee says Codee's almost here." Dayvee smiled. "We should go meet them."

Brando groaned inwardly. Unlike Dayvee, Brando never had any expectations on him until recently. Elayni had given him heck over his pranks, but it was never serious. No wonder Dayvee worried so much. What would Codee do?

33

Deserted by Kun

"No one but you can separate you from Kun." ~ Kwutee.

After leaving the Kwin, Codee and Wilee made good time. But when the call came, they pushed harder. Wilee was in mind reach of Jaycee for the last few hours. Wilee filled Codee in on what had happened to Dayvee.

Codee's spirits sank in a downward spiral at the grim news. He must have gone too easy on the young Calupi he'd trained to guard Dayvee. Would they have done better if he had acted more like Leeto? If Codee had been there, maybe he could have drawn Varian's attention to himself.

He sighed. It was done and could not be undone. At least the Kayndo still lived. As he approached what looked like a former wheat field, animals and people came in view. The number that had answered Dayvee's call in only a few days amazed him. A group splintered off from the others and headed toward him. A wolf trotted alongside them.

A Calupi with Pericards, Wilee sent.

When they reached them, the strange wolf nosed Wilee as the Calupi came forward to extend his arm to Codee. "Greetings, you have come in response to the Kayndo's call?"

Codee clasped his forearm. "Yes, I'm Codee, second in Wolf Mountain, and my companion's Wilee. The Kayndo's my nephew.

"I'm Solo. My companion is Sago, and we're from White River. To join us, you must give an oath to the Kayndo with Sago judging you. Otherwise, you're free to go wherever you want, just not around the Kayndo."

Codee needed to remain civil. He'd gone without sleep to get here sooner, and now they delayed him? But the oath was a good idea. "I'll give it."

He vowed to be loyal to the Kayndo, to follow his orders, and to uphold the Vita. They let him pass. Another group approached him. Dayvee rode a horse inside his sub-pack ring, with a second ring of Pericards around them. But if Dayvee was riding, his guards should too.

"Let him through," Dayvee ordered when the Pericards reached Codee.

Codee's former trainees wore frowns and, all but one, lowered their gazes. Dayvee held his head high. Dark circles ringed his eyes, and he sat stiffly. Wolves hid pain, but all the years monitoring packs let Codee read a wolf's condition. Jaycee's ears drooped. His coat was dull. Eyes once bright appeared glazed. The wolf revealed his chosen's distress.

Dayvee reached down to clasp Codee's hand. "I'm glad you're here. You made it quickly." His warmth appeared genuine.

"I didn't have as far to go."

Dayvee nodded. "We have food ready, and you look like you need rest."

"We ate, but we could rest."

"Then come." Dayvee turned his horse, and Codee took up a position beside him. The sub-pack made room. When they entered the camp, the crowd looked at Dayvee with awe, but they sent prickles of unease through Codee. Too easy for a knife to be thrown. He drew his nails.

"Everyone here's given the vow." Dayvee waved his arm at the crowd. "You can relax."

"Someone could still sneak by a sentry," Codee retorted.

Dayvee stopped in front of a large square tent of hides sewn together, and poles in each corner. Crutches leaned against it. A Pericard grabbed them and brought them to Dayvee. "Thanks." He slid down from his horse, propping himself between them. Then, one at a time, he moved the crutches and swung his feet forward.

When they entered the tent, Dayvee went over to a pallet and sat.

Codee asked, "Do you mind if I see what Varian did?"

"I need to treat you anyway." Tayro grabbed a couple of flasks from his rucksack.

"You *should* see so you'll know that I can no longer be Calupi," Dayvee declared.

Codee better fix that attitude. "You'll *always* be Calupi."

"I can't fulfill a Calupi's duties." Dayvee dropped his head. "And I won't be a burden or another Tobee."

Tayro signaled with a tug to Dayvee's shirt. Dayvee removed it, and Tayro unwrapped his bandages. The grooves and slashes weren't easy to miss. Codee walked around Dayvee. The amount of skin missing revealed how raw and painful his injuries must be. Codee couldn't show sympathy. His nephew didn't need his pity, but his strength.

Tayro washed each, then rubbed a paste on them. Dayvee flinched occasionally, but didn't cry out. Tayro bandaged him again.

Normally, Codee didn't tear into a beta in front of the Calupi they led. And Dayvee was Kayndo now. But they should learn too.

Codee turned his voice hard and said what Leeto would, "Tobee's deformed legs aren't holding him back. He let others tell him he couldn't do it and never tried to prove them wrong, so no one respects him." Dayvee cringed but Codee didn't soften his tone. "You *will* continue to fulfill your duties. And you *won't* tell me you can't or let *anyone* tell you differently."

Dayvee's eyes grew wide. "But how can I?"

"By whatever means are necessary. Do you think Leeto or I haven't endured pain? Look at our scars. We never let difficulty stop us and neither should you."

"This is more than a little difficulty. I never stopped after Nero beat me." Dayvee reached down, pulled a strange boot off his foot, and threw it to the side. "But how can you expect me to claim I can do a Calupi's duty now?"

One look at the mangled mess and Codee's hope for Dayvee to recover died. He gritted his teeth to keep from ripping into the sub-pack. They shrank from him, all except Tayro, who took Dayvee's other boot off and poured his flask's liquid contents over the distorted feet.

"Your duties are those of the Kayndo." Codee glanced at the sub-pack. "Unlike others, you can't be replaced. But Jaycee said you crawled to do them. So what's the problem?"

"When I'm done being Kayndo, what then?" Dayvee's eyebrow's lifted.

He'd only been Kayndo a few days. At this rate, he wouldn't survive the role. Codee blew out his breath. "You'll return to the pack or castle and have new duties assigned."

Dayvee rubbed his temple. Maybe his head ached again from the animals speaking to him. He caught Codee's gaze and quickly dropped his hand. Good. He hadn't forgotten Leeto's training. To succeed now, he'd have to climb a really steep cliff. Far easier to slide down. But if Codee threw him a little hope, he might grab on and fight to pull himself up.

"Can you see me going on patrol or checking a wolf pack?" Dayvee demanded.

"Why not? You can ride a horse. A lease could be arranged, or you can do duties that don't require much walking."

"Like Miko's?"

Codee shot him a glare and crossed his arms. "I was thinking about teaching the young children, but don't you slight what Miko does so diligently." He stole another glance at the sub-pack who wouldn't meet his gaze. "Have you ever known the lamps to go out? No. Miko won't let us flounder in the dark."

"I know people won't treat me special forever. I never wanted to be the Kayndo anyway." Dayvee drew a ragged breath. "All I ever wanted was to be Calupi." Tears rimmed his eyes. "Thanks."

Codee gave him a nod and turned to the sub-pack. "Leave us now. In thirty minutes you can come back."

None of them moved. Codee let out a little of his frustration. "What are you waiting for?"

They turned questioning eyes to Dayvee. "I told them they answer only to me. And it's not their fault Varian chose me, or that I released their vows and ordered them to leave."

"You cannot release their vows to me. Could you release mine to Jolay? No, those vows weren't given to you. You could order me to do it, but I *wouldn't* follow that order without new guards and vows."

Dayvee's eyebrows shot up. A frown marred his face.

Wouldn't? Codee had already pushed Dayvee once. Now he'd done it again. Codee and Leeto had both taught Dayvee better. A Calupi questioning a leader was okay, but not defying one. Dayvee was drawing himself up. Jaycee growled.

Codee lowered his head. "Sorry, Dayvee. I didn't mean *wouldn't*. But I'd ask you to reconsider."

"I know this isn't going to be easy for you as Leeto's second, but *my* interests come first now. If I give you an order that contradicts what Leeto wants, I expect you to follow it. If you can't do that, go back to the pack. Leeto is not the Kayndo."

Codee let his shoulders drop. "I'll follow *your* orders."

"Good. I don't accept coerced vows. It wasn't right for you to gain theirs with threats, so release them." Dayvee's eyes glinted. He meant it.

Codee didn't really want to release the sub-pack from their oaths, but he'd have to. "If they're not coerced, can I ask for new ones?"

"If I want vows, they're sworn to me, but I don't want theirs. Protecting me is dangerous." He glanced at Brando. "And difficult. If they want to stop, they should be able to. Release them."

Codee turned to the sub-pack. "I'm releasing you from your vows to protect the Kayndo." He focused again on Dayvee. "You're right about your sub-pack not answering to outsiders, but they belong to Wolf Mountain. Yes, you have more authority than a packleader, but so does the council. They still recognize our right to rule our pack, and work through us to avoid conflicts between us and those we lead. Do you want to cause more trouble for your friends?"

"No. I was wrong." Dayvee waved at his sub-pack. "*You* still answer to our pack, so you should take Codee and Leeto's orders unless they contradict mine, just as Blake's Pericards still answer to their captain." Dayvee cocked his head toward the door, and they filed out.

The Kayndo didn't answer to Codee, and he let him know it. He was proud of him, but he still needed to address the other issues. Better do it carefully. He softened his tone. "You hurt them when you had them desert their duty."

"Didn't you teach me to protect the pack over an individual?" Dayvee asked.

"The Kayndo's an exception. That's why you have guards—and they left you."

"On my order." Dayvee shook his head. "They can't defy me. I'd call the animals."

"Since when has Leeto allowed us to use the too difficult excuse? The most important job outside of being a Kayndo is protecting one."

"I don't want them blamed for my actions." Dayvee's shoulders fell. "And I don't need guards. I'd like my friends to be friends."

"Kayndo or not, the council mandated guards, so you'll have them, and your friends will have to answer for this." Dayvee's spine became rigid again. Would Dayvee allow it? Codee hated to remind him he wouldn't be able to assume the alpha role now. "They'll have to face us eventually, and Calupi have long memories."

A grimace revealed Dayvee's concern. "Are you going to replace them?"

"Not yet, but Leeto might. And if they abandon their duty again, I'll send them home and strip them of all status. They'd never live it down."

Dayvee blew out a heavy breath. "I'm sure glad you came to let me know what I've done wrong."

Now there was the nephew he loved. Codee chuckled. "Sure, Leeto's not here, so I had to fill in, but you did some things right."

"Humph. It seems like you and Leeto like to leave that part out."

Codee laughed. "Seems to me you have plenty of people willing to swell your head."

Dayvee waved his hand at the tent flap. "That's not for me. It's for the Kayndo in the stories."

"You're not going to get blind admiration from me."

"I know that." Dayvee smiled. "Thanks."

"You're welcome. Now, no more limiting yourself. Don't forget all things are possible with Kun."

"I know they're possible. I've seen the evidence of what Kun can do. But why has He deserted me and left me and Jaycee to suffer?"

Kun hadn't deserted him. He lived. But was he ready to hear that? Codee's exhaustion tore at his focus. What could he do? If only Kwutee were here.

Gaylo is, Wilee sent.

Codee wiped at his gritty eyes. Maybe White River's keeper could help Dayvee.

He's coming.

The sub-pack came back in. Codee gestured to their companions. "The wolves and Gaylo are going to stay with Dayvee and call Wilee if they need us. All of you can come with me." The sub-pack trailed him out.

#

Gaylo left the tent as Brando and his friends arrived. When Brando ducked inside, Bruno came over to greet him.

"Where's Codee?" Dayvee asked.

"He said he needed to talk to some others in the camp," Brando answered.

"Good. All of you should do the same. Go enjoy yourselves. Jaycee will stay with me."

Codee just reamed them. Didn't Dayvee understand? Brando couldn't give Dayvee time alone, now, no matter how much he resented it. He crossed his arms. "Everyone else can go, but I'll stay."

A frustrated sigh came from Dayvee. "All right," he finally said. As soon as the others vacated the tent, Dayvee put his weight on his feet. Then he picked up his legs and forced them a step. He collapsed on the floor moaning.

Brando ran to him. Dayvee growled. "No. You may watch, nothing else."

Brando would rather experience the pain than watch. Why didn't Kun heal Dayvee? Kun had healed him, and the Kayndo was more important.

Dayvee rose with his crutches. He took one step, two. A scream escaped him. The Pericards rushed in.

"Sorry. I'm not being hurt." The Pericards withdrew. "Come on," Dayvee moved toward the tent opening. "We'll go elsewhere for this."

Sunray and Stormee waited outside. Brando didn't want to see Dayvee torture himself, but he climbed on Stormee and rode with him. Jaycee and Bruno trotted at their sides.

Brando glanced down at Bruno. *Can you tell Wilee what Dayvee's doing to himself? He needs to talk sense into him, or he'll never heal.*

Wilee says Codee will come when he can, Bruno sent.

Dayvee wouldn't like him telling Codee. They reached the woods. Sunray and Stormee weaved in between trees and tents until they were clear of any watchers. Dayvee stopped Sunray at a small clearing.

Sunlight dappled the area, and a flash of purple showed Brando violets blooming along the other edge. Leaf rot, acorns, and sticks littered the ground and plants poked up through them. Wouldn't Dayvee fall more on this terrain?

Brando needed to stall. "Can we talk?"

Dayvee slid from Sunray to stand upright on his crutches. "Sure."

Brando jumped off Stormee. "You said I should speak to Chayla."

"Yes. She's attracting interest, but so are you." His forehead furrowed. "Was I wrong about you liking her?"

"No." Chayla was high status, beautiful, and caring. Many had desired her. Still hard to believe. He felt ten feet tall. "She's agreed to life mate me."

"Congratulations." Dayvee smiled. "I'm happy for you both."

"Thanks." Brando's grin couldn't be stopped. "We're going to ask Gaylo to hold the ceremony after the battle. I wanted to tell you first."

"I wish you a safe and dry den, pups with full bellies, and a mate that hunts well."

Jaycee and Bruno's tails wagged. *Our expressions are best,* Bruno sent.

Dayvee put his weight on his feet, took a hand off his crutches, and slapped Brando's shoulder. "I think you've chosen well. You'll make a formidable pair."

Dayvee didn't act in love with Elayni anymore. "Were you interested in Chayla?"

"No. Chayla's great, but you know another holds my heart."

Brando wanted Dayvee and Elayni to find some happiness too. "Talk to her. Several also desire her."

"I won't ask Elayni to life-mate." Dayvee dropped his head. "She deserves someone with feet and status."

"Elayni loves you. Not your feet or status. But if you refuse to ask her, then tell her so she isn't waiting."

"Agreed. I'll talk to her." Dayvee lifted his head to glance up as Spiro flew overhead. "When will you let the others know about life-mating Chayla?"

"When we get back."

"Why don't you see if Gaylo will hold the ceremony tomorrow?" Dayvee asked. "Then we can celebrate instead of worry."

"What if something were to happen to me?"

"If Calupi waited until no danger existed, we'd never life mate. Like the companions say, seize the moment."

Yes, Bruno sent.

Brando's heart leapt. "I better ask Chayla first."

"Maybe. But if she's life mating you, she should get used to surprises. Doesn't she mind frogs?"

Brando chuckled. "Frogs are a small sacrifice to net such a fine catch."

Dayvee laughed. He took a step, then moaned, and another. Codee's eyes held a twinkle when he rode up on a horse. When he caught Brando's gaze, he hardened his face. He leapt down.

Dayvee's brow shot up as he looked at Brando. "You told him?"

"Our whole family will suffer if I fail to protect you again. And I don't want to watch you hurt your feet more."

Codee drew himself up. "I'll be with him. You can go."

Dayvee pointed his finger toward the camp. "You can leave too. I don't want to do this in front of anyone."

"Why are you hiding?" Codee demanded.

"I don't want people thinking less of me if I scream," Dayvee mumbled.

Codee stiffened. "There's a solution."

"What? Don't try to make these worthless feet walk?"

"No. You should be trying to walk, and if you're not trying hard enough, I'll tell you. But you *can* stop yourself from screaming."

Dayvee clenched his teeth and took another step. No moan escaped him, but a small whimper came from Jaycee.

Heat flushed Brando's neck. "His feet will be worse."

Codee narrowed his eyes at Brando. "Go."

With misty eyes, Dayvee spit out. "Go."

Brando mounted Stormee and rode back. They were both crazy.

34

Caged

Cages kill us. Our body may live, but our spirit dies. ~Jaycee

Brando reached for his weapon as the tent flap rustled and drew back. His friend's did too. Dayvee swung into the tent on his crutches with Codee following. Brando released his tooth. Sweat soaked Dayvee's clothes, and his lip was bloody. Codee's eyes didn't hold their normal twinkle, and he dragged as if he'd just lost a fight. Maybe it hadn't been so easy for Codee to watch Dayvee hurt himself in his attempt to walk.

Codee slapped Dayvee's back. "Well met. You should do that every day in front of the tent, so everyone can see how Calupi face injuries."

Oh great. Was this a punishment? *Bruno, tell Dayvee it would put Elayni and Chayla in tears to watch that.*

Dayvee's eyes widened. He received the message.

Brando had to steel himself. "I'll go away with you when you want."

"All right. Thanks." Dayvee sat on the edge of the pallet.

Codee smiled. What? Dayvee rolled his eyes and then tilted his head toward Wilee. The wolf's tail wagged. Codee had played him.

Brando never liked being outsmarted, but it gained his grudging respect. "I'm going hunting with Geno and Tayro. Elayni and Chayla will stay with you, Dayvee, and repair our ceremony clothes."

Chayla pulled her sewing kit from her rucksack. "But you can't help us sew."

Brando smiled to himself. Dayvee's sewing always ended disastrously.

"If you want, I'll go hunting with you." Red lines marked Codee's eyes.

Codee was the best hunter in the pack, but his exhaustion was plain to Brando. "No, you taught us well. You should rest."

A wistful look crossed Dayvee's face, but his mouth quickly firmed into a resigned line. Before he was hurt, Dayvee's hunting skills came close to rivaling Codee's. But if Brando took him now, it could be dangerous for him.

Dayvee shot him a smile that didn't touch his eyes. "So Gaylo and Chayla agreed?"

"Yes," Brando grinned. "But I haven't asked Codee yet."

Codee's twinkle returned to his eyes. "Ask me what?"

Had he guessed? "Chayla has agreed to life-mate with me." Brando draped an arm around Chayla's waist and pulled her close. She looked up at him and gave him her shy smile. It felt so right—her head didn't quite reach his chin, but covered his heart. Perfect fit since she owned it. "Gaylo will hold the ceremony tomorrow if our pack's in agreement?"

Codee's face hardened. "What about Rashee?"

Brando wanted it intensely. Rashee—the designated time when a newly mated couple left with their companions to depend only on each other until they knew each other's thoughts and could finish the other's sentences. If they didn't twine their souls, arguments could spread to family members and beyond to the entire pack. To have the Rashee experience with Chayla would be incredible. But neither of them wanted to leave their friends in peril.

"We'd like to wait until after the battle." Brando held his breath. Would Codee permit it?

"It might take more than one battle to restore the Vita. I'll allow thirty days before you go. Dayvee needs to agree to release you, and both you and Chayla have to agree to leave for Rashee regardless."

"I agree," Dayvee said.

Chayla's pixie nose scrunched. "I agree."

Brando blew out his breath pursing his lips. What if the Vita wasn't restored by then? Rashee could take weeks. If they were at Wolf Mountain, he wouldn't be in any hurry to share Chayla's time.

But they weren't. Could he abandon the others with the fight unfinished? What else could he do? Wait longer to life-mate? No way. He wasn't about to let Chayla change her mind. "I agree."

"Then you have mine and Leeto's blessing." Codee smiled and extended his arm. "Congratulations."

"Thank you." Brando released Chayla to clasp Codee's arm.

Chayla looked up at Codee. "Will you speak for my parents since you've been like a father to me while you trained us?" Chayla thought her parents would be thrilled she life-mated a pack-mate. They might not be so happy once they learned it was Brando.

"I'd be honored." Codee hugged her. He must believe her parents would be pleased. "What about you, Brando? Do you want me to speak for Jonesee?"

Didn't he get it? "No." Brando glanced at his friends. "My family's here."

His friends nodded. Codee shook his head. "You have a father who should be acknowledged, even if he wasn't around much."

Bruno stiffened as Brando tensed. "Jonesee made a choice not to be my father when he refused to help my mother or me."

Codee blew out a heavy breath. "You're wrong about Jonesee. Believe it or not, he tried to help you and Keeli."

"I heard her beg him to leave the pack."

"You were really young. Maybe she did in the beginning, but Jonesee met with me and Leeto to tell us he was leaving. He hated to break his vows, but he was willing to do it to help Keeli. Then she came and begged Jonesee to stay. That's why he can't face the memories or you. He blames himself for giving in."

Brando couldn't let tears fall. "Whatever Jonesee's reasons, he made his choices. So have I. When he took part in the quincee, I told *you* and *him* I don't have a father. Not that I ever did, but I no longer want to change it. All my family is here, and they chose to care for me."

...

The sun was setting when Brando and his friends each pulled a travois into camp, laden with two deer and a wild boar. When Brando entered the tent with Bruno, he found Chayla and Elayni putting the last beads on their ceremony clothes. Codee slept in his bedroll. Dayvee's pallet lay empty. "Where's Dayvee?"

"He's talking to people." Elayni's tone was exasperated. "We argued over his order to stay here. The Pericards volunteered to go, and he finally agreed to take Theron with him and Jaycee."

"What did Codee say?"

Codee opened his eyes. "Nothing. I slept through it."

Brando sighed. "I'll find him."

"I'll go with you." Codee rose.

"Now you know what we deal with." Brando pulled the tent flap open. "Get used to arguments, and if you sleep, Dayvee escapes."

Codee followed him out. "I just talked to him about allowing you to protect him."

"That doesn't work. He hates being trapped too much."

Codee's face darkened. "Humph."

"Don't start thinking it's a fear to be faced. It's not like that. He just gets tense and wound up if he can't get out. I get that way too, along with the rest of the sub-pack."

"All clanspeople do. Our companions can't stand entrapment, and we've picked it up." Codee let out a deep breath. "It's why the clans punish with loss of status, exile, or in extreme cases pain, or death, but not imprisonment." He grimaced. "That's too cruel. We'll only use that for rabies, to protect the pack."

Brando nodded. "We used to relieve the tension by escaping together. But now he leaves me and Elayni too."

The crowd made it easy to find Dayvee. He stood in the center, propped between his crutches, with Theron and Jaycee next to him. Dayvee's body sagged. Probably tired. He acknowledged Brando and Codee with a glance. Then Dayvee clenched his teeth, put his weight on his feet, and grasped a man's forearm. "I'm sorry, did you say your name was Reed?"

"Yes," the willowy stranger answered. "I was King Layton's Botanee advisor."

"I want to thank you for coming," Dayvee said. "With your help, we might be able to put things right. Is there anything I can give you?"

"No, Kayndo. I'm proud to defend the Vita with you."

Codee raised his voice. "Sorry, but the Kayndo can't meet everyone tonight. He needs to sleep, as do you."

Brando met Dayvee's eyes and tried to read his soulful face. Relieved maybe, but determined. Dayvee turned back to the crowd. "I do want to meet each of you, so I'll be available tomorrow evening again."

The crowd dispersed. Sunray picked her way through to Dayvee and kneeled. "I'm tired, Brando. I'll ride back. I didn't call the other horses since it's so crowded here."

"I'll ride on Sunray with you." Brando climbed on behind him. Dayvee turned to Theron. "Thanks for coming. I'm sorry about the argument, but I won't be roped off."

Codee drew himself up. "You should be roped off. Don't you remember what happened at the Clan meeting?"

"I think we caused that by not allowing people near me. Now they can come up. If they want a bead or anything else, I'll give it to them."

Codee shook his head. "You're making it too easy for someone to stab you. If you see Kun, you'll fail your duty."

"I know that I can't even permit myself to die. My sub-pack and Pericard brothers do a great job, so I won't be stabbed."

Theron stood straighter at the praise. Dayvee flicked his hand. "You can go now, brother." Theron saluted Dayvee, and he returned it. Dayvee called back over his shoulder as Sunray moved away at a walk. "We'll meet you at the tent, Codee." Sunray strode the opposite way toward the river. "Let's go swimming, Brando."

"You're exhausted. You need to sleep."

"I don't think I can." Dayvee slumped. "But I can't swim very well, either, and you're tired." Sunray circled back toward the tent. "I'll get back in my cage. It just makes me despair like when Chancee trapped me."

"That tent has hide sides."

"The tent is not the cage."

Brando's fatigue was making it hard to follow. "What are you trying to tell me? That *I'm* your cage?"

Every time you and the sub-pack put me in that ring, it shows me you think I'm incapable. You don't believe I can defend myself, hunt, or even ride through camp alone. You're not just a cage. You're my ring of despair."

#

Nero held a burning stick to Dayvee's feet, and the red, hot agony seared into him. Dayvee groaned and opened his eyes. Another dream, except for the pain. Brando was looking at him. Did his second sleep anymore? Dayvee didn't sleep that much, but whenever he opened his eyes, Brando's met his.

The boy who never showed concern turned into a man who worried more than Dayvee. Another intense gaze—Codee's. Did they really think he needed more watchers?

The torment slammed into him again and begged him to give it some release. To scream. No one would give him a minute alone so he could. He was so tired of acting brave.

Dayvee stiffened and tried to ride the waves of agony. A stifled whimper came from Jaycee. Codee's hard face showed no sympathy. Why was Dayvee so weak? He shamed the Calupi name. Could he blame Kun for not wanting to heal him?

He glanced over at Elayni. She still slept. He admired the perfect features of her face, relaxed for a change. All his friends' faces had been too pinched lately. What was he doing to them? Another day to get through. He set his teeth, grabbed his crutches, and rose.

Brando waved a hand at the entrance. "I've got to cut up and prepare meat for the feast tonight."

Dayvee forced himself to smile. "I can still sit down and use my tooth. I'll help you once I take care of Jaycee's needs."

"Me too." The voices blended together as their friends rose.

As they skinned the game and cut up the meat, Blake came over carrying a couple of baskets. "I have good news. The pigeons came in, and the garrison's have agreed not to aid Tibalt unless he's chosen." He jiggled the baskets. "Oh, and Gaylo asked me to bring these to you."

"I appreciate the news and breakfast." Dayvee met Blake's steely gaze. "Tell me about yourself. Do you have a life mate or children?"

"Never had the time," Blake sat the baskets down.

Dayvee finished separating a haunch of meat. "That's too bad. Do you have parents or siblings?"

Blake's mask cracked into a frown. "I have parents and a sister living in Harthome, along with a couple of nephews I'm ashamed to say I don't really know."

"We're not far from Harthome. After the contests today, take time off to spend with them. See if Reko can get them a message to meet you outside the walls. They shouldn't be in the city during the attack. And not just you. If any Pericards have loved ones in the castle or Harthome, let's get them out."

Blake fingered his sword hilt. "What if they aren't loyal to the Kayndo?"

"If they can't give the vow, they shouldn't come here, but surely your men can think of an excuse to get them somewhere else safe, even if they need to stay with them."

Blake let go of his sword. "I shouldn't leave when I'm needed."

"I can't promise you another visit with your loved ones. If you don't have a second, appoint one. Both are orders, Blake."

A corner of Blake's mouth turned up. "All right, and I have a second, but we call him a sergeant."

"Theron seemed quite capable. Does he have family there?"

"No, his is in the country."

"Perfect then." After an exchange of salutes, Blake left him.

When they finished cutting the meat into sections, Brando and Geno dug a pit, burying the meat under hot coals to cook all day. Afterwards, the sub-pack tore into their breakfast, but Dayvee had no appetite and only picked at his. If he'd just quit biting his lip, things might not taste like blood. His lip held so many cuts; it must reveal his weakness to everyone.

People kept coming up, offering smiles and dishes to contribute to the feast. Faces in the camp had been tight with worry when Dayvee rode through yesterday. Maybe this diversion had helped.

He would like to set his worries aside. Leeto said to get good advice and pray. But Kun didn't answer Dayvee's prayers. Gaylo had told Dayvee that he should accept Kun's path and thank Kun for allowing him to be an inspiration to others. He might be able to thank Kun for his own suffering, but he couldn't thank Him for Jaycee's.

Dayvee reached out to his mice friends at the castle. *Were you able to keep the Kagards awake?*

Yes, between us and the raccoons climbing in their beds, they couldn't rest. We keep stuffing their guns with twigs, but they clean them often. And the animals making charges at the wall have them on edge.

Good. Maybe they'd think the real attack was another false alarm.

Dayvee turned to his friends. "Brando and Chayla, go spend some time together. After your life-mating ceremony, plan on leaving for one day of Rashee. The attack isn't until tomorrow night, so don't come back until dusk."

Brando glanced at Codee. "We better come back in the morning since you need us."

"No, Dayvee's right."

"Don't even try to argue with the Kayndo and your pack leader." Dayvee chuckled. "Have you forgotten how to enjoy yourself?"

Brando grinned. "No."

"Good. And from now on I'll allow only one guard at a time in camp. I don't care what you do, as long as you rest and enjoy yourselves. This is a lot like a clan meeting. Brando, Chayla, Tayro, Geno, and Codee are off duty now. Elayni can guard first."

They were all shaking their heads no. Why was his sub-pack always the hardest to get to accept his orders?

Codee sighed. "Are you determined to make guarding you more difficult for your friends?"

"No." Dayvee waved his hand at them. "Look at their pinched faces and red eyes and tell me they can fight well. Do you think they need to kill themselves with exhaustion when not much can get by a companion?"

Codee gave him a short nod. "Your sub-pack *should* be at their best when we fight."

Everyone left but Elayni. As soon as they cleared the area, Dayvee turned to her. "I think it's time we get even and prank Brando."

35

Seize the Moment

"In an hour we could be dead. Embrace this moment." Jaycee.

The trodden field had turned muddy during last night's rain, but the sun had mostly dried it and burned away the earlier fog. The hide Dayvee sat on kept most of the dampness away as he and his friends watched the Pericard contests. The crowd stood thick around him, but Dayvee's position in front gave him an unobstructed view. Brando and Chayla strolled up to them.

Elayni stood and linked arms with Chayla. "We'll go get ready now." The girls moved away.

Brando plopped down in Elayni's spot. "What did I miss?"

Dayvee filled him in. "All the Pericards competed in archery. Thirty-two advanced to duel with staffs. The winners crossed swords. Only eight are left for the sparring match. Apparently, anyone who hits the ground will be out."

Brando grinned. "That's the one I wanted to see."

"Do you have a big wager on this?" Tayro's tone was disapproving.

"I never place bets big enough to hurt anyone. I didn't wager at all on this." Brando snorted. "No one wanted to against Blake, but I did make some other bets." He chuckled. "Part of my winnings is a bowl of nut crisps. Nayti from White River will bring them to you later, Dayvee."

"I appreciate it, but you should win things for Chayla, not me."

"Chayla suggested it," Brando said. "She's worried since you're barely eating."

Dayvee blew out his breath. When he thought Codee might send his friends home, it wrenched his heart. But they shouldn't scrutinize him all the time. It made him feel smothered and set his skin to crawling.

Movement drew his attention. The eight Pericards competing in the sparring match split up around the square they had made by stringing ropes between poles sunk in the ground. Two Pericards on each side.

"Go," Blake called. They ran under the ropes and met one another in a flurry of fists. Four went down. Three were left against Blake, and they came at him together. Might be a good strategy. Blake kicked one in the stomach, ducked a fist, then grabbed the thrower and slammed him to the ground. He swept the legs of another who fell. Only two left standing. Blake and Theron.

Blake sidestepped Theron's fist and drove his own into Theron's gut. Theron grunted and bent over. Blake flung him to the ground. Dayvee clapped with the crowd.

The Pericards swarmed Blake to slap him on the back. "We knew you'd be captain."

The crowd moved away to finish watching the other contests. Only the Pericards, the sub-pack, Drako, and Codee remained.

"Blake and Leeto would be pretty evenly matched," Codee said.

"He's good," Brando admitted.

Dayvee chuckled. "Are you worried he might win against you?"

"No." Brando flashed his crooked grin. "I'll win, but he'll be a good challenge."

Drako elbowed Brando. "I wouldn't be too sure you'll win. He's gotten better since I defeated him."

Blake came over to them. "I wouldn't call that a defeat. The king needed me, so I left."

"We would." Drako smiled. "You leave the ring, you lose. But did you try?"

"The Pericards needed to learn if we should work harder to compete with the Calupi coming." Blake's nose twitched. "I couldn't win too easily."

Brando laughed. "Don't go easy on me." He turned a wistful look on Dayvee and raised a brow.

"No. There're three days left to meet your challenge, and I need you uninjured tomorrow. Besides, if you're limping, it might be difficult to catch Chayla."

Brando's face fell. "What happened to your confidence in me?"

"I still have it. I need Blake too."

Gaylo walked up to them. "All the contests are finishing. As soon as you're ready, meet me in the lane. I'm going to make a ceremony ring there."

Dayvee picked up his crutches. "We'll come as soon as we get dressed in our ceremony clothes."

…

One of Dayvee's crutches hit a hole in the field, and it sent him sprawling. Pain slammed into his feet and stole his breath. A shake of his head kept his friends' hands away. He didn't need their help, and he'd fight to keep what little dignity he had left. Codee gave him a chin lift. He got his crutches under him again and continued. They squeezed around more tents and moved toward the front of the encampment.

"Brando," Elayni giggled. "I hope you're better at catching Chayla than you are me."

"Dayvee made me let you win all those times." Brando's blue eyes sparkled. "I'll bet we come back together. You want to wager against it?"

"No, but I'll wager that Chayla has you running for an hour or better."

"What do you want to bet?"

"A carving of Evee against making you another shirt."

Brando's crooked grin lit his face. "Okay. You should know better than to bet against me, and I could use another shirt. Listen for the howls."

"Maybe you should know better. I'll listen, but I doubt Chayla allows you to catch her in less than thirty minutes."

Chayla laughed. "Calupi women don't make it easy."

The crowd around the lane was thick. Had everyone in the camp gathered to see the ceremony? The people parted to let them through.

Brando was frowning.

Dayvee stopped at the ring, "Quit letting Elayni worry you, Brando. You can do it."

"You think so?"

"Yes. You're almost as fast as me. I mean, as I was." He gave Chayla a smile. "Sorry, but you can't win that race for an hour."

Tayro put a hide down, and they sat. Brando's brow furrowed. "What?"

"This life-mating has sure changed you. You missed a bet's details. Elanyi bet you'd be running for over an hour, not thirty minutes. She's just teasing you."

Brando's mouth fell open. Dayvee laughed with his friends.

Gaylo strode into the center of the ring with a few of his packmates, who carried a drum, a flute, and the gourd lute. They began to play the Calupi life-mate song.

Dayvee joined in with all the Calupi to sing of how Kun made Calupi companion to a wolf. But the Calupi and wolf were lonely and had so much to do defending the Vita, so Kun provided them worthy mates to help. They had children judged worthy of companions and became a pack.

When the song stopped, Gaylo beckoned to Brando and Chayla with his hand. "You can come forward."

They entered the ring and went to Gaylo's side. At a flip of Gaylo's finger, Brando and Chayla turned to face everyone. "These two Calupi want to life-mate. First, we need to learn if they're worthy of a mate." The drummer began to beat his drum loudly.

Dayvee called out with the others, "Run, Chayla, run. Prove your worth. Run, Chayla, run."

She raced away, and then Gaylo led them in another song praising Kun for saving them from the ancients' destruction and making them Calupi. As soon as it finished, the drum beat again. Brando howled and Chayla answered. She didn't sound close. So they started the call. "Run, Brando, Run. Chayla's proved her worth, now prove yours. Catch her if you can."

Brando ran after her. Another song began, and some got up to dance. When the song stopped, the howls from Brando and Chayla had become more distant. The Kwin started a song. The dancers switched too. Brando and Chayla's howls merged and became one. It hadn't been an hour. Not even a half-hour had passed. "Looks like you'll be sewing, Elayni."

She adjusted her armband. "Brando has holes in his shirt from the snake bites. He could use another."

"Brando sews well."

"I know, but he'd rather be carving."

"You didn't win. Oh, wait." Dayvee chuckled. "Your birthday's only a few weeks away."

Elayni laughed. The Ursans sang next. Their dance was a mix of shuffles, stomps, and circles. Brando and Chayla loped up, holding hands.

Dayvee clapped and whistled like everyone else. The musicians left the ring, and Gaylo beckoned Brando and Chayla in with a wave of his arm.

"Join me in prayer." Gaylo and the others bowed their heads.

Dayvee didn't. Codee glowered at him and tilted his head toward some people who watched him surreptitiously. They expected the Kayndo to act appropriately. Fine. Dayvee lowered his head, but he wasn't praying. There was no point. Kun didn't answer his.

"We pray Kun would look with favor on this union and bless this couple as they join together to honor Kun, his Vita, their pack, and clan." Gaylo raised his head and turned his gaze on the couple. "At your choosing, you agreed to put Kun and his Vita first, then to put your companion and your pack before yourself. Now you choose to life-mate. So do you agree to put your life mate's needs before your own as well?"

Brando and Chayla answered in unison, "We do."

"Do you agree to help each other follow pack law?"

"We do."

"Do you agree to raise any children from your union together, teaching them to love Kun, to follow the law, and separate from them if they're not chosen?"

"We do."

"Does their pack and family support the life-mating of these two Calupi?" Gaylo asked.

"I'm second of Wolf Mountain pack." Codee stood. "I speak as their pack leader and for Chayla's parents, Sunee and Tovay. They will welcome the joining."

With the help of his crutches, Dayvee rose with Elayni, Geno, and Tayro to say together, "We are Brando and Chayla's sub-pack and chosen family. We welcome this union." He sat again.

"Does anyone object?" Silence answered Gaylo. "You may make your marks."

Brando lifted his right hand. Chayla took it and bit him slightly above his wrist on his arm. It wasn't deep and didn't break the skin, but it left teeth impressions. Gaylo washed the area with soapy water. He dipped his needle in the bowl of ink and tattooed the imprints of Chayla's teeth into Brando's skin. Chayla gave Brando her right hand, and he put his love bite on her. Gaylo cleaned it and tattooed the circle of front and bottom teeth above her wrist.

Then Gaylo took their hands and raised them to display the marks. "Brando and Chayla proved themselves worthy of a Calupi life-mate and pledged themselves to each other before Kun and all these witnesses. Their love bites show they're each other's right arm and now life-mated."

When Gaylo let go, Brando kissed Chayla. Dayvee clapped with the others. Seemo flew above the couple with a blanket in his talons and dropped one side. Flower petals rained from the sky.

Chayla and Brando startled as petals dropped on them. Chayla's shy smile peeked out, and she held out her hands to catch some.

Brando laughed. "Good one, Dayvee. Thanks for the flowers."

"The flowers were Elayni's idea. I wanted to do snakes or frogs."

Brando brushed some petals from his hair. "For once, I'm glad for your restraint, Elayni."

The flowers quit falling, and Gaylo held up a hand for quiet. "Brando and Chayla invite everyone to celebrate with them by enjoying the feast provided. We thank Kun for providing us this bounty."

They uncovered the food and the scents wafted. Roasted meat, onions, garlic, sage, rosemary, sugar, honey, and cinnamon were a few that Dayvee recognized. The newly mated couple went first. They filled a bowl for their companions, then for each other, and switched bowls to eat the things the other chose. Then it was Jaycee and the Kayndo's turn.

Dayvee selected a spoonful from some dishes he'd never tasted before. Everyone fixed their favorites, but he couldn't try them all. There were too many. His appetite quickly deserted him. Too tense to eat. Nayti walked over to them and held out a bowl of nut crisps to Dayvee.

Dayvee didn't take them. "Thanks, but could you just put them with the rest of the food for others to enjoy."

Elayni pursed her lips. After the meal, Brando and Chayla led a dance.

"Go have fun," Dayvee ordered his friends. Elayni stayed with him since it was her shift. When the dance ended, Brando and Chayla joined hands and loped off, like any newly mated couple did for Rashee, only they'd be back tomorrow.

Elayni tucked a loose strand of golden hair behind her ear. "I thought we'd be first."

He sighed. "I can't catch you now."

"Don't you think I'd let you?"

"That part is there for a reason. I won't life-mate."

"Didn't you hear Codee?" Her cheeks fired red. "You're still Calupi."

"Yes, but status is awarded by what you offer the pack. Whatever duty I'm assigned, another could do better, so I can't offer you or the pack anything."

She chewed her bottom lip. "Do you remember what Leeto says about excuses?"

Leeto viewed them as an admission a Calupi was unwilling to do whatever it took. "I remember."

"This is the third time you've given me one about why you can't life mate me." A tear rolled down her cheek. "I don't think you really love me."

"You're wrong." Dayvee wiped the tear from her face with a finger. The impulse sprang up to feel more of that soft skin. He snatched back his hand. "I love you enough to do what's best for you."

Geno walked over to them. "My shift, Elayni, if you're ready?"

She stood. Thank Kun the conversation was over. But who would Elayni dance with? Dayvee's breath caught. Did he want to know? Not really, but he might as well get used to it. He was crippled and she wasn't.

She turned back to Dayvee. "I should be the judge of what's best for me." She stomped off with Evee.

She has a lot of spirit, Jaycee sent.

High compliment from a wolf. *I know*. Dayvee's heart ached. It refused to get over her.

The crowd broke into smaller groups, dancing, singing, and drinking at several fires. They had picked clean the nearby woods of dead firewood, but they had plenty of dried animal dung to burn. Dayvee hobbled between them to try to speak a few words to each. Jaycee, Geno, and Graydee stayed at his side.

Codee came and relieved Geno. Dayvee couldn't hide how tired he was. Codee raised an eyebrow and gave him a head shake. Everyone here answered Dayvee's call to put their lives at risk tomorrow, but there were just too many to meet them all. He surrendered to his fatigue and returned to the tent. Geno had already climbed in his bedroll next to Tayro and Elayni. Dayvee pulled his bedroll off the pallet and joined them. He woke only twice when the pain got too much. Surrounded by his packmates, he slept much better than on the pallet alone.

#

Dayvee sat outside with Codee and rolled up bedrolls while his friends took down the poles for the tent. Donkeys and horses would carry their supplies to first camp where they'd leave them. No one should go into battle weighted down.

The amount of animals and people astounded him. Even with the tents coming down, the field barely held room for them all. Blake and some Pericards strode toward them.

Dayvee gave them a smile. "Did you visit with your family?"

"Yes," Blake answered. "And the Pericard families that were in Harthome are now with Theron's in the country. We only told them we didn't want Varian to target them. And your brothers want to say something to you."

One of them stepped forward. What was his name again? Victor?

"We just want you to know we appreciate your concern for our families."

Dayvee pointed to Codee. "Tell them what Calupi do to protect the pack when we face a threat."

"We send the children, pregnant women, and the injured to safety. It doesn't matter if those remaining have family who are sent. If they value their pack, they'll fight to their last breath to ensure the pack's future is safe. We won't let the threat get beyond us."

Dayvee let his gaze travel to each. "You name me your brother, and I care about all of you. I'll fight to my last breath so our enemies don't get beyond us to your families."

Victor's chest puffed. "And we'd give our last breath to defend the brother we love, even if he wasn't the Kayndo."

Theron took a step closer. "Captain Blake and a few Pericards who climb fast are going over the wall. Ten Pericards are assigned to ride horses and lead groups through Harthome. That still leaves over forty brothers who want the honor of fighting next to your sub-pack. Will you let us do that?"

"You know being close to me is a dangerous place, but Latham's actions and yours have earned my gratitude. Shilo says there are nine horses that haven't been assigned riders. Choose who will use them. If my other brothers can keep up on foot, they may fight beside us too."

"Thank you." They saluted Dayvee. When he returned their salute, they strode away.

"Brando was right." Codee's eyes twinkled.

Dayvee chuckled. "My second usually is. What was he right about this time?"

"He said everyone who gets to know you loves you. How do you do it?"

"I follow the advice you gave me for Geno and Chayla. I make sure they know they're important to me and treat them how I like to be. Maybe you and Leeto should try it."

"I doubt I could convince Leeto. But I'm glad someone benefitted from my advice."

"I've always found your advice valuable."

"Thanks, but I already love you."

Dayvee laughed. "I still need to keep in practice."

At dusk, Brando and Chayla rejoined them, and Gaylo and Tayro passed around cups of tea.

"What's in this, Tayro?" Chayla asked.

"Several things. Salad Burnet to help with bleeding if you're wounded. There's bee pollen, barley grass, Purple Cone flower, and St John's Wort to fight fatigue and increase our endurance, along with huckleberries to help our night vision." Dayvee swigged it down.

Gaylo cleared his throat. "Let's pray."

Dayvee lowered his head to pray for the first time since the dungeon. Kun hadn't healed him, but maybe He would answer a different prayer.

Gaylo's voice rang out. "Kun, we ask you to grant us success tonight as we battle to restore the Vita."

Dayvee added his own prayer. *All right, Kun. If you want me to be an example, I'll be that. And I'll accept the pain willingly if you just keep my loved ones safe and help me pull this off without losing many lives.* Would Kun agree? Dayvee raised his head.

Gaylo gave Dayvee a nod. Time for the Kayndo to talk to them.

Dayvee squared his shoulders and raised his voice. "Varian doesn't know us. He thought that by torturing me and Jaycee he could get answers. He didn't. Then he smashed my feet and told me I couldn't escape, but I crawled away. Now he thinks he can take Taluma, our companions, and the Vita from us. Will we let him?"

The roar was deafening. "No!"

"Varian's a slow learner, so we'll give him another lesson. He will not defeat us!"

"He will not defeat us! He will not defeat us!" The chant roared through the crowd.

Dayvee smiled. "May Kun go with us!"

"May Kun go with us!" They shouted back.

36

The Attack

Loved ones aren't gone at death. When we share their stories, we see their faces in the stars. ~ Jaycee

Sunray's hooves hardly made a sound as she picked her way in the soft ground through the tree line. Dayvee stopped her. With the full moon, they probably hadn't needed the huckleberries to increase their night vision. Any closer to Harthome's gates, they'd surely be detected. His feet didn't tap anymore, or they'd be knocking against Sunray's side.

Scents wrinkled Dayvee's nose. Wood smoke and the putrid stink of the city's sewer overlaid the crisp smell of forest greenery, animal musk, and sweat. The odors from so many living in close proximity were less of a shock now, but just as unpleasant. He ground his teeth as he waited to hear from the first groups going in. How were they making out?

They must have upped the patrols, his owl scout sent. *They have Kagards everywhere.*

Be careful, Dayvee sent to Juno. *They've increased the patrols.*

We know. We've been discovered. We're fighting, but outnumbered and trying to fall back to the wall.

A ringing bell pierced the air. Harthome was alerting its citizens of an attack. Dayvee's stomach clenched. So much for careful planning. Earlier, he had broken the large herd of buffalo at his disposal into ten smaller groups. He reached out to the closest. *Can you ram the gates and get us in?*

Yes, Kayndo.

Do it.

The buffalo charged.

Now, Dayvee sent to all the animals. Sunray and his sub-pack's horses galloped after the buffalo, flinging churned up soil. Wood splintered as the buffalo rammed into the thick oaken gates with an ear-splitting crash, sending them flying off their hinges. Explosions rent the air as Kagards shot at them from the walls. High-pitched whistles sounded as bullets shrieked by. Animals bellowed, and people cried out as the missiles found their mark. The acrid scent of the gun's powder billowed.

Bats, can you fly in those Kagards' faces?

Yes, Kayndo.

Now, mountain lion and goat clans, knock them off the walls!

The sounds of scrabbling and then more screams filled the night. Dayvee raced Sunray past the gates. The gunshots stopped, so he circled her. *Bear clan, hold the opening where the gates were. Elk and Deer clan, go through the city and locate any Kagard patrols. Badger and Wolverine clans, go with them and secure Harthome's streets. Horse clan, aid Drako. Everyone else meet at the barracks.*

As his army of supporters poured through the battered gates, they split in different directions. Each group followed a small herd of buffalo and a Pericard familiar with Harthome.

Dayvee signaled to Victor, and he led off at a canter. The buffalo went next. *Let's go, Sunray.* She neighed and put him on the heels of the buffalo. Jaycee kept up. His sub-pack, their wolves, and the Pericards fell in around him. The animals' hooves echoed across the cobblestones as the beasts crowded together to navigate the narrow streets, jostling and bumping one another.

Form a line and go a few at a time, Dayvee sent to the buffalo. People emerged from their homes, armed with knives or tools, but one look at the stampeding buffalo sent them scurrying back inside.

The soldiers in the barracks are awake and fighting us with the ancients' weapons, Juno sent. *We're being cut down.*

Faster, Dayvee sent to the lead buffalo. As they drew closer, gunfire revealed the Kagards amassed in front of the barracks. Drako limped as he retreated amidst a whirl of bullets. A Kagard pointed a gun at Dayvee's lead buffalo. It misfired. The buffalo lowered its head and tossed the man forward with his horns, then trampled him beneath his feet.

Dayvee's voice was drowned out. *Sunray, can you scream?*

At her trumpet, a hush fell over the area. Dayvee lifted his shoulders and head. "I'm the Kayndo! Tibalt won't be chosen as king, so he can't succeed his father. There are many more of us coming. You can't defeat us all. Lay down your weapons and surrender."

Only a few Kagards put down their weapons. One, who didn't, pointed his gun at Dayvee and fired. Sunray reared on her hind legs. Dayvee slid off and hit the stony ground with a thud. Sunray screamed. Blood poured from her front leg.

Jaycee attacked the Kagard holding the gun, biting his arm until he dropped it. Elayni's nails landed in the Kagard's throat. He slumped to the ground, clutching his neck in order to staunch the flow of blood.

Shilo, tell Reko Sunray needs help, Dayvee sent.

Bullets pinged off the cobblestones around him as more Kagards aimed weapons at Dayvee. His heart thudded a furious rhythm. The acrid gun smoke choked him. Brando and Codee slid off their horses. Two other Calupi ran in front of Dayvee—Petee and Chokree. They flung their nails at the attackers. Bullets riddled the air around them. The death howl sounded as Petee's lifeless body fell to the ground.

Brando and Codee took his place, and then Theron and all the Pericards surrounded Dayvee. A bullet tore into Theron, and he crumpled. Another spun Chase around.

More of his army arrived, and they were fighting back. A white horse galloped up. *Sunray won't be able to be your feet, Kayndo. I will now.*

Dayvee pulled himself up. He hadn't known another horse was available. *I didn't call you.*

No, but Sunray did. I'm Ghostee and I'll take care of you. Pain racked his feet, but fear propelled him to stagger the three steps to the horse. His sub-pack's horses and the Pericards milled around him.

Dayvee grabbed Ghostee's thick mane and pulled himself on. *Thank you, Ghostee and Sunray.* "Everyone on foot, do what you can to get those injured to safety!"

Codee and Brando ran to their horses and remounted. The enemy soldiers who hadn't surrendered had formed a tight group and were retreating toward the castle with so many of Dayvee's supporters now arriving.

Guard the ones who surrendered, Dayvee sent to fox clan. The Kagards wouldn't escape the foxes. They knew every wily trick. *Ghostee, get me closer to those retreating.* Dayvee flipped his tooth at a Kagard, who aimed his weapon at Elayni. The tooth sank into his eye. The man howled, dropped his gun, and reached for his face.

Thank Kun, Geno had installed lines on their weapons. Dayvee jerked. His tooth came free, and he pulled it back to him.

Then, he slung his nails to hit another in the neck. The Kagard staggered back, then dropped to the ground. Blood poured down his front.

Bile rose to the back of Dayvee's throat, but he forced it down, wrenched his weapon free, and looked for another Kagard. His whole body shook, but stopping was out of the question.

Bullets rained down from above. *Cat and goat clans, take those walls!* Buffalo continued to trample any Kagards they could reach, but their losses were mounting. The Kagards reached the doors of the castle and were let inside.

Guns barked from the castle towers, and more bullets shrieked by, slamming into flesh. The wretched smoke from gunfire grew thick and combined with the scent of blood, sweat, and death to turn Dayvee's stomach. Cries of the wounded pierced the air as well as his heart. The stones of the castle courtyard turned bright red from the blood soaking into them. The wounded wouldn't survive if they weren't treated soon.

Dayvee called in his mind and aloud, "Fall back and take our wounded!"

Blake came running up. "Why aren't we attacking?"

"I'm not willing to waste lives." He surveyed the Kagards peering from behind the castle's battlements. "They aren't going anywhere."

"If you plan on a siege, the castle is well provisioned."

"I don't, but we have other things to attend to. Are the ancients' weapons kept at the barracks?"

"Yes."

We can bury them, Jaycee sent.

"Have a Pericard lead our companions to them." Dayvee pointed to some wounded and yelled. "Everyone help the injured to the barracks. Those with any healing knowledge, go there to assist them."

Elayni's pale face turned to him. "We know how to splint and bandage."

"Yes, so we'll aid the healers." He glanced back at Blake. "The Pericards can watch the castle. Have them stay out of range of those guns and let me know if anyone comes out." As he and his friends rode up to the barracks, he called to Shilo. *How is Sunray?*

She may recover. She's inside the barracks.

Good.

"Brando, can you retrieve my crutches from Sunray so I can walk?" Brando raced in and brought them quickly. Dayvee slid down from Ghostee.

Jaycee trotted up to him. *There are no weapons in the barracks. They must have them all.*

Figured. Dayvee hurried into the bedlam. The cries met him of wounded animals and people. Theron lay in one of the many filled bunks. Gaylo had Dayvee hold pressure on a bandage to quench his blood flow. Was it hopeless? Theron already wore the gray death mask.

"I'm so sorry I let you fight next to me." Dayvee's tears obscured his vision. "Kun, please heal Theron and let me go to you instead."

"No. Don't ask that." Theron coughed up blood. "I'm proud that Kun let me be the Kayndo's shield. I'll see you when you join me." He drew in one more breath, coughed again, and fell silent.

Dayvee held his hand until it grew cold, then Gaylo took him to another dying man who asked to speak to the Kayndo. Dayvee could only thank him.

Everyone had been treated, but they lost so many. Dayvee found a corner and slid to the floor. "Why, Kun? Must I always be responsible for people dying?"

He wiped his his face with his sleeve. He knew Leeto would tell him not to show such weakness. His tears didn't portray confidence, but he couldn't help it. People and animals had given their lives for him.

Brando and Elayni found him and wrapped their arms around him, then Tayro, Geno and Chayla. They all leaned in, hugged one another, and cried.

"Dayvee, you aren't responsible. They chose to come." Did Brando always know what he was thinking?

"If I had done a better job, we wouldn't have this many injured or dead."

Elayni shook her head. "You did everything you could to prevent it. This is Varian's fault."

"I better go try to get Tibalt to come out." Dayvee stood. "Maybe I can prevent more."

His sub-pack ringed him as he left the barracks and moved to where the Pericards watched the castle. "If we go closer," Geno said. "They may shoot us."

"We'll try to avoid that." Dayvee stopped and yelled. "Tibalt, this is Dayvee. Come out and surrender now, or I'll have the door knocked down."

"You should surrender to us!" Varian shouted back. Gunshots rang out.

They were beyond the weapon's reach. Dayvee asked the buffalo, *Do you think you can knock down the castle doors?*

Yes.

"All right, we'll split up into three groups. I'll send buffalo with each. The Kwin and Calupi can go with me through the front door since it's large enough to ride through. Blake, take your men and the city people through the side door."

Blake saluted him. Dayvee returned it and turned to Drako. "You'll take the rest of the clanspeople through the back door." He blew out his breath. "May Kun go with you."

"And also with you," Drako said as he and Blake moved down the castle's perimeter wall with their groups and disappeared from

Dayvee's sight. His stomach fluttered as if tadpoles swam inside while he waited to let everyone get in position.

We're ready, Juno and Gojo sent.

Now. Knock the doors down. The buffalo charged. "For Kun and the Vita!" Dayvee screamed as he sent Ghostee after the buffalo.

"For Kun and The Vita," echoed with a roar as everyone picked up the cry and rushed forward. Gunfire felled a few buffalo, and they crashed to the ground. Ghostee jumped over them.

Chunks of wood flew as the surviving buffalo bashed into the castle door and crushed those hiding behind it. With his heart racing, Dayvee guided Ghostee under the arch and ducked low to get through the entryway. He flung his tooth at a Kagard pointing his weapon and hit his arm. His sub-pack and those flowing in threw their weapons.

Bullets ricocheted about the foyer and tore holes into tapestries. The Kagards fell back into the large audience hall. Bullets thunked as they hit the wood of the ornate throne. Drako's group came in the other entrance, then Blake's. The Kagards fell under the barrage of thrown weapons. No more stood to resist them.

Dayvee slid off Ghostee onto his crutches. Horses couldn't get through the other doors into the castle. "Blake, where would they take Tibalt?"

"Probably the North tower. It's narrow with lots of steps, so a few can hold off many. It would be a difficult climb for you. Let me take the Pericards and rush the tower."

Codee arched an eyebrow. Was Dayvee going to let someone tell him he couldn't do it? Even if they'd lose the advantage of speed, he'd manage it somehow. "No. I'll go there with my sub-pack and Reko's group. Drako and Juno, can you show us where?"

Yes, Kayndo, Juno sent.

"Blake, take the Pericards to find Varian. Everyone else split up and secure the rest of the castle."

Boots pounded the stone floors as they rushed to follow Dayvee's commands. Those with Dayvee walked to keep his pace. Drako and Juno directed him as he traversed the endless gray castle corridors. How much farther? Finally, Dayvee came to the steps. Using one stone wall to lean against for balance, he set his teeth and used his crutches to conquer one step at a time, hating the slow pace. The way they were packed into the narrow stairwell made them easy targets.

Companions' voices assaulted his head as reports came in from the groups and his scouts. *Just your tower to secure, and Harthome is ours.*

Blake's been shot in the leg.

Some Pericards are posted inside the castle. Everyone else is returning to the courtyard with any prisoners.

No one's located Varian or the prince.

The Kagards perched on the steps above them came into view. *Now. Castle pigeons fly in the Kagards' faces.* With a flurry of wings, the pigeons covered them, but the Kagards fired their guns blind. Brando yelped, and he grabbed his arm. Dayvee and his friends flung their nails. The Kwin tossed their comeback sticks. Companions growled and, leaping forward tore into them. The steps filled with downed bodies.

Blood had turned Brando's sleeve red.

"Are you okay?" Dayvee asked.

"Yes, it barely grazed me."

He needed to bandage it at least. "Drop back and trade positions with Geno so you can see to it."

Brando frowned, but he fell back. Geno moved up next to Dayvee. He climbed the last several steps and finally reached a landing with a door. Codee tried it. It was locked from the inside.

Dayvee called out, "Tibalt, it's over. We won. Your men are dead or our prisoners. We aren't responsible for the death of your mother, and I don't want to kill you, so come out and surrender."

A clunking sounded as the bar pulled back. Tibalt yelled, "We're coming!"

Dayvee asked, "Who's with you?"

"Varian and two Kagards."

"Okay, come slowly without weapons and your hands in the air!" Dayvee ordered.

Tibalt opened the door and took a few mincing steps out. Varian came behind him, clutching Tibalt's arm and holding a gun to his back. Two burly Kagards pressed close, holding guns up too.

"I'll kill Tibalt—" Varian jabbed the gun into him "—unless you order your people to let us through."

"The man who murdered my parents shouldn't escape." Tibalt threw an elbow into Varian's arm breaking his hold, then Tibalt dropped to the floor.

Varian swung his gun toward Dayvee. Geno lunged in front of Dayvee as the gun fired. The bullet struck Geno, and he crashed back into Dayvee. They both fell to the ground, landing in a heap. Dayvee rolled free and drew his nails to throw, but others' already were landing. Codee's hit Varian's eye, Elayni's slashed his arm, while other weapons slammed into the Kagards.

Jaycee leapt forward, clamping his teeth onto Varian's leg. The other wolves flung themselves at the Kagards.

Guns dropped to the ground as the wolves dragged their enemies to the floor and sprang for their throats. When the companion's drew back, Varian and the Kagards lay dead in pools of blood with their necks torn open.

Tayro fell to his knees beside Geno. He put his mouth over Geno's and blew breath into him.

Dayvee's anguish rose. *No. Please, Kun, no. Don't let Geno die.*

37

Not Better

"Kun can light even the darkest days." ~ Kwutee.

The sky lit in shades of pink, blue, and yellow. Such a beautiful sunrise Kun bestowed. An enormous lump burned Dayvee's throat as he tried to hold back his tears while he rode Ghostee out from the entrance hall into the castle courtyard. His sub-pack bunched close around him, but they were missing one. With a hard look and a lift of his chin, Codee signaled Dayvee to pull it together.

How could he keep his sorrow in check when it overwhelmed him? Jaycee wasn't any help. His grief, as strong as his own assuaged Dayvee. The death howl, their tribute to Geno, still rang in his ears.

Wilee sent, *Codee says complete the task, or Geno's death and all the others will have been for nothing.*

Dayvee couldn't let that happen. He forced his grief down and straightened his face as Ghostee stopped. Their army of supporters milled in front of them and applause bombarded them. Dayvee lifted his arm and pumped his fist.

The clamor was deafening as whistles, animal shrieks, and shouts blended, "Kayndo! Kayndo!"

When they quieted some, Dayvee raised his voice. "This is not my victory, but yours. I'm astounded by the acts of courage I witnessed today as you faced down the ancients' weapons and never hesitated. You took care of one another, me, and our fallen." He shifted his weight. "Gaylo, can you lead us in prayer?"

Gaylo bowed his head. "Thank you, Kun, for allowing us to defeat those who would separate us from You and the Vita." His voice boomed. "Be with us as we celebrate our triumph and mourn our losses." He raised his head.

"Our victory came"—Dayvee's voice broke as his grief rose again—"at a high price. Loved ones died and were hurt. I share your pain and I grieve with you." He choked and drew a breath to calm himself. "Their sacrifices and yours will restore the Vita. I salute you all."

The applause swelled again. His friends clapped too. Dayvee clapped once, but couldn't continue. Taluma would have a chosen king and Varian couldn't harm anyone else, but their victory still felt hollow. Dayvee couldn't rejoice. Not with Geno dead.

He'd want you to finish this, Jaycee sent.

Jaycee was right, as usual. Dayvee touched the wolf's head. Would it be the last time? He might lose him too. His hurt lurched. Focus on something good.

There was one thing that lifted his spirits a little. With Varian dead and the threat eliminated, the Kayndo wouldn't be needed anymore. Dayvee wouldn't have to bear this heavy responsibility. A chosen king and the Kagards would be responsible for meeting any new threats to the Vita. What a relief it would be to have that burden gone. Oh, how he yearned to be just Dayvee. He glanced at Gaylo and clasped both hands together—the signal for the choosing.

Gaylo flicked his hand at his pack members. They outlined a small ceremony ring and placed rocks around it. When they finished, Gaylo entered it. "It is time for a choosing."

Gojo and the White River companions glided in to take positions on Gaylo's left. Jaycee and the other Wolf Mountain companions took Gaylo's right.

As Gaylo explained their history and beliefs, his words brought back the memory of Dayvee's own choosing. "Bring Tibalt forward," Gaylo ordered.

Codee relinquished Tibalt to Blake. With only a small limp betraying his injury, Blake escorted Tibalt into the ring to face Gaylo and the wolves.

The wolves circled Tibalt once, then snarled and bared their teeth. Tibalt backed, and the wolves advanced until he stepped out of the ring where the Pericards took charge of him.

"Tibalt is not worthy of a companion and can't be king," Gaylo said. "The companions will select another."

The wolves trotted into the crowd. They came to the sub-pack. Dayvee's dread rose. Please, don't. He didn't want to be king. They circled Tayro, cutting him off from the rest of them.

Gaylo pointed to him. "Come forward, Tayro."

Tayro's jaw dropped open. He blinked several times as he moved slowly into the ring.

His friends goggled. Why were they all shocked? Tayro should make a good king. He knew the Vita and Taluma's laws. When he told Dayvee he would cut off his legs, he faced his rejection and didn't back down. But why hadn't the wolves selected one of the experienced pack leaders like Leeto or Codee?

Jaycee returned to Dayvee. *Leading Taluma is very different from a pack. Your father or Codee would try, but would be miserable in a city. Tayro will adjust.* Jaycee's high head showed his pride in their choice. *He has strength and resolve now. The deceiver won't find him easily misled again.*

"The companions have chosen Topay to be the king's companion," Gaylo continued. "Jaycee will stay with Dayvee." Relief poured into Dayvee. He wouldn't lose Jaycee. Then guilt stung him. Jaycee would keep suffering with Dayvee because of their bond.

Gaylo put a hand on the shoulder of the pale Tayro. "Do you vow to do your best to uphold the laws of Taluma and defend the Vita, protecting and serving all of Taluma's inhabitants with the help of Topay and Kun?"

Tayro swallowed hard. "I do."

Gaylo let go of Tibalt's arm. "Bring his crown."

Blake limped back into the ring carrying a circlet of burnished wood. Leaves and animals had been carved in it.

Gaylo took it from him and lifted it high. "When the first king wore this crown of wood, it was Taluma's most precious material since the forests had burned. It is a reminder for all of Taluma's people." Gaylo placed the crown on Tayro's head and turned back to the crowd.

"Tayro has been chosen by the companions in accordance with our laws. Will Taluma's citizens give him your loyalty and aid?"

Shouts erupted around the courtyard, and the roar grew with every passing second. "We will!"

Gaylo reached over and took Tayro's arm, raising it high. "I give you King Tayro and his companion, Topay!"

Brando whistled and Dayvee joined his friends in adding to the tumult of applause.

Tayro's hand rose, and they quieted. "Thank you...for your confidence," Tayro's voice quaked, but then strengthened. "We'll try our best not to let you down." He gestured to his companion. "Topay says first we must decide Tibalt's fate."

Blake signaled and Pericards poured into the ring to surround Tayro while Blake himself led Tibalt in again. Good. The Pericards would leave Dayvee alone now, and his friends could go back to just being friends. He wouldn't be restrained by guards any longer.

Tayro stared at the Kagards, then raised his chin. "Topay tells me Tibalt didn't intend evil, but was misled. He isn't strong in the Vita and fears animals." Tayro's gaze traveled over the crowd. "How do you feel?"

"Tibalt's actions caused the torture and death of several people." Tucker's voice rose from beside Tayro. "He's a traitor and should die."

Tibalt had tried to stop Varian from doing more harm to Dayvee. He sure didn't want to see him die. "He thought he was acting in Taluma's interest." He called out. "He wasn't right, but his intentions were good."

"What do you have to say, Tibalt?" Tayro asked.

Tibalt shuffled from foot to foot, then drew himself up. "I let my father and Taluma down when I trusted the wrong person." His shoulder's fell. "Death might be easier than living with the pain of knowing my actions allowed Varian to hurt and kill so many." His voice shook. "I am truly sorry. I'd like to make amends, but I can't undo it, so there's nothing I can say or do that will be enough."

Tayro's eyes bored into Dayvee, "I was misled in the past, and a person I harmed gave me a second chance." Tayro pointed a finger up.

"Kun teaches us to forgive."

Gaylo pointed to Tibalt. "His fear made him susceptible and held him captive to the deceiver. If he faces it, he shouldn't be a threat."

The crowd noise rose again as people discussed it.

Tayro lifted his hand. Quiet fell. "I had a good teacher, who helped me learn to follow the Vita." Tayro glanced at Codee. "Is anyone willing to teach Tibalt not to fear animals like his father wanted?"

Codee gave Tayro a nod, but Drako spoke first. "I told his father I'd teach him, so I'll do it. Since I travel between clans, he'll meet several animals to help him overcome his fears."

"Are you willing, Tibalt?" Tayro asked.

Tibalt glanced at Juno. His lip trembled, but his voice didn't quake. "I'm willing."

"I'm giving you a chance to redeem yourself, but don't make me regret it."

"I won't," Tibalt's sincerity rang out.

"You can go with Drako. Release him, Blake," Tayro ordered.

"Yes, Your Majesty." Blake cut Tibalt's bindings. Tibalt's posture straightened, and he rubbed his wrists. He gave Tayro a bow, then left the ring.

A shadow overheard caught Dayvee's attention. Was it Spiro? No, the bird's wings were bowed at a downward angle. The barred tail, white chest, and black stripe under the eyes identified it as an Osprey winging its way toward him. Unusual for them to be away from water. A voice filled Dayvee's mind.

Kayndo, I was asked by the dolphin clan to bring you a warning.

What is it? Dayvee asked.

Several boats filled with soldiers are coming toward Taluma from the other continent.

Dayvee's breath caught, and a chill ran through him. *How far away?*

A few days.

Tibalt had warned him, but Dayvee had pushed that concern aside. Well, at least it wasn't his problem now. Tayro was king. He reached out for Topay and asked him to pass the message to Topay.

Topay's eyes widened, and he gave a nod to Dayvee. "The Kayndo has informed me that soldiers from the other continent are headed here to invade us. Will you help defeat them?"

"Yes," the crowd shouted.

"We're going to need the Kayndo and all the animals. A Kayndo has authority over kings, so Dayvee will you come forward and lead us?" Tayro asked.

Cackles. Calupi didn't retreat from a threat to loved ones. Tayro needed him. As much as Dayvee wanted the Kayndo's job to be done, it wasn't. Protect the Pack. Defend the Vita. The law couldn't be denied. It screamed at him to do his duty.

Yes, Jaycee sent.

Dayvee stomach knotted, but he directed Ghostee into the ring to join Tayro. Jaycee and the rest of his his sub-pack ringed him. At a signal from Blake another group of Pericards surrounded them again. Ugh.

"Kayndo! Kayndo!" the crowd chanted.

Dayvee raised his hand for quiet. "Today we'll celebrate your victory, welcome our new king, and honor those slain. Tomorrow, we'll make plans to stop the invaders. I'll fight to my last breath."

His sub-pack pressed closer to him, shoulders straight and proud; they shook their fists in the air. "I'll fight to my last breath!" The phrase echoed as the rest took it up, and a huge sea of fists waved above the crowd. The wolves howled. Other animals bellowed their agreement, and cheers resounded from the people.

#

The mid-day sun was bright, birds sang, and butterflies flitted among blooming flowers. All too perfect for a day in which so much blood had spilled. Ghostee and Dayvee led the way, the white horse a beacon in the light, the burial travois behind him. Codee, his friends, and their companions walked beside it. One of his friends didn't walk, but rode in the travois. Graydee crept behind it, ears drooping, tail low. Ghostee picked his way slowly up the hill to the cemetery, reflecting their spirits.

They wove through the paths by the benches and the fountain. Gaylo couldn't have known when he chose this place. Rows of freshly dug graves lay open, waiting in front of the tree that had sheltered Dayvee when he hid from the Kagards. Petals fell around them. Maybe it was fitting that this spot would now harbor Geno.

They had dressed Geno in his ceremony clothes. His forehead held the decorative headband. Below his parted hair, Tayro had drawn the mark of a Calupi, the teeth of a wolf. Kun couldn't miss that Geno was a loyal servant of the Vita. The color Tayro had applied to his cheeks made it seem as if Geno slept. If only he'd awaken.

The procession behind them carried more litters with the bodies of the slain. Dayvee's friends unhooked the travois and placed Geno in front of the graves with the others. The mourners paraded by the bodies, stopping at one or another.

After they filed by, Gaylo cleared his throat. "Since we have so many to mourn, only one will speak on their behalf. Then, with your loved ones tonight, I encourage you to tell their stories, to sing their songs, to honor the sacrifices of those that have gone home to Kun this day."

Gaylo had his list and called each name. Blake spoke for Theron. Codee spoke for Petee, and when Gaylo called Geno's name, Dayvee urged Ghostee forward.

He turned Ghostee to face the crowd. "I'm going to tell you about my friend, Geno. Today, he gave his life for mine. But what I'd like you to know about Geno is that he sacrificed every day to make our lives better. Not just in big ways, but in so many countless small ones.

"This rucksack." Dayvee took it off and held it up. "Geno put on the waterproof coating." He pointed out the bottom corner. "He noticed it was frayed here, so he patched it." He gestured to his crutches, fastened to Ghostee. "He made these for me so I could walk." Dayvee pulled his tooth. "He attached this line so I could retrieve it easily from horseback. I could go on and on. I don't think there's one thing our sub-pack has that Geno didn't fix.

"He didn't talk much, but six words Geno spoke often. 'I thought you might need this', or 'maybe this can make it better.' I never had to ask. He just made it better before you even knew you needed it. He gave me his word he'd have my back. And today, he jumped in front of me to take my bullet."

Fast moving clouds obscured the sun, and the day darkened. Did even Kun mourn Geno's passing?

"Some of you have called me a hero, but Geno was the real hero every day." Leeto would consider it a weakness to cry. Dayvee held back his tears but his friend's faces were wet. "Farewell, our friend, until we see you again. Our hearts and lives will hold a hole until then." Dayvee choked and got it out. "And they're not going to be better."

His friends came and took a corner of the buffalo hide, lowered Geno in the grave, then tossed their corners in to cover him. A mournful howl filled the air as Graydee grieved too. Then all the sub-pack wolves joined in and howled their grief.

Brando took the marker he made for Geno and secured it in the ground at the top of his grave.

The shadows had lengthened by the time the last spoke. Gaylo's voice filled the silence. "Each mourner who's come to show respect may line up, and as you go past, take a handful of dirt from the pile and toss it in the graves."

After everyone went past, all that was left were mounds of dirt in front of the markers.

The mourners milled around for a few minutes speaking to each other. Many thanked Dayvee for making sure their loved ones were honored. Didn't they hold him responsible for their deaths? It didn't matter. He was.

The last of the mourners left. The cemetery, now deserted except for Dayvee and those with him. Graydee lay across the mound that held Geno.

Dayvee couldn't do anything for Geno, but maybe he could for Graydee. *Please, Graydee, don't keep guarding Geno's body. Choose another. That's what Geno would want.*

The packs choosing ceremonies were over for this year, but no pack would make the grieving wolf wait.

I've thought on your words, Kayndo. I know Geno would want me to make it better and keep defending the Vita. I just don't know if I have the strength. I'm so sad.

Oh, Kun, no. How many more must he lose? Tears burned Dayvee's eyes. Guilt and anger ate at him. Too many deaths he was accountable for.

He couldn't keep his glare from Codee. "We bear the responsibility for Geno's death. If you hadn't assigned him, and I hadn't let him come, this wouldn't have happened."

Do you want to make your pack members feel worse? Jaycee sent.

Wilee growled. Red flushed Codee's cheeks. "He wanted to be here. Don't you take the most precious gift Geno could give you and claim it. His life wasn't yours or mine to give, and I won't let you demean it by telling me it was."

Dayvee's chest squeezed him. His skin crawled. He needed to get away. He asked Ghostee to kneel and climbed on. The anger in him was barely contained. "Send my friends home, Codee, and go with. I can't take any more gifts from them, from you, or from Kun."

Run, Ghostee.

Where to?

As fast and far as you can get.

Ghostee raced down the hill, then trotted through the cobble stone streets, his hooves clattering as he wove between people. Dayvee called to the Ursans guarding the gate opening, "Stand aside."

They parted enough for Ghostee to take him through. The sounds diminished as Ghostee opened up into a gallop. Dayvee sucked in fresh air like a man drowning. The trees, the fields, all blurred as they raced by.

Ghostee's breath came labored, and his sweaty flanks soaked Dayvee's pants. *Stop, Ghostee.*

Dayvee slid down, collapsed to the ground, and beat the grass with his fists. He unleashed a torrent of tears, crying for Geno, Graydee, himself, and all those they lost. *Why, Kun? I asked you to keep my loved ones safe. Why have you abandoned me?* He didn't think it possible to shed one more tear. He'd wrung everything out.

Jaycee crookedly loped up. *You can't escape from me.*

Remorse rose in Dayvee. The wolf couldn't lope easily bearing his pain. *I never wanted to escape from you.*

Would you want Geno to live in remorse if you gave your life for him?

Of course not.

He wouldn't want you to either.

Dayvee wiped his eyes with his sleeve. *It's so hard losing him and the others too.*

Jaycee stuck his nose in his face. *Do you still believe the Vita's worth fighting for?*

Yes.

Jaycee's tail wagged. *Then trust in Kun and His plan.*

If this is the plan, it hurts.

You still have to trust Kun and hold onto hope.

Most clanspeople had their hopes pinned on Dayvee. It cost them dearly. Someone else like Leeto might have come to a peaceful resolution. Dayvee wasn't good at being a Kayndo. And what did he have to hope in?

Kun.

How when Kun wasn't listening to him?

You can't give up hope. Codee's tracking you. Bruno says your packmates are hurt that you wanted to send them back. And Brando says the only way to get rid of them is to cage them or kill them.

Somehow Dayvee needed to meet the threats without losing more of his loved ones. He brushed himself off. *I better go to them.* He asked Ghostee to kneel and mounted.

Ghostee was already lathered, so Dayvee only had him walk. Brando cantered up and reined to a stop.

"Where're the others?" Dayvee asked.

"Waiting." Brando frowned. "Did you really want us to go?"

"Yes. No. I don't know. I don't want you to die."

"If we wanted safe lives, we wouldn't be Calupi. We prefer to walk the cliff's edge. Whether we're with you or not, we'll fall off and die—most likely sooner than most. You can't change that. Calupi love adrenaline rushes."

It was true. Dayvee's most thrilling times hunting were when the risk was high. Brando loved fighting in the ring even more when he faced his most difficult foes. And they all vowed to defend the Vita. He couldn't stop his friends from facing danger; they wouldn't be happy as turtles. But he didn't want to be left behind when those he loved died. It hurt too much. Maybe Kun would let him go next.

"I don't think this is about our safety alone." Brando ran a hand through his hair. "You didn't feel trapped until Harthome. Before then, you didn't really want guards, but you hated being separated from your pack more. So why are you shutting us out now? What did we do wrong?"

Dayvee dredged up the reason. When he moaned, they heard. "It's not your fault. It's mine. I'm ashamed I'm so weak." He thought he was out of tears but another fell, and he hated it. "I don't want your pity. I don't want to watch Elayni life mate another or see you fight my battles. I want to hold my head up, but I can't."

"I wondered if that was it. All right—here." Brando handed him his rucksack. "Now, ignore your gifts."

"What?"

"Even though you're the Kayndo and more valuable than all of us, you can't see it. So we're going to do something Calupi. We're going hunting so you'll recognize you have worth."

Could Dayvee even succeed at hunting now? He wouldn't know if he didn't try. His spirits lifted. He sent to all the animals within his mind range. *Tonight I'm not Kayndo but a Calupi hunting, so don't talk to me and do your best to flee.* Dayvee could ignore his gift, but not his duty. His spirits sank. "We can't go hunting. We're supposed to hold the feast and tell the stories of the fallen."

Brando's jaw set. "They'll do it without us."

"What will Codee say about that?"

"He says if you let them, they'll come too. What do you want?"

"The celebration is for Tayro and our victory. They should go back and enjoy themselves, but I won't order them to."

They are coming to join you, Jaycee sent.

Could a Calupi have better friends? Dayvee hadn't appreciated his time with Geno enough. He shouldn't make the same mistake twice. He smiled. *You can pass on that I'm happy to have them, but tell Codee I'm not waiting for the third deer.*

###

Glossary

Andee – Wolf Mountain Pack Calupi

Animal Master – Kayndo

Blake – Pericard Captain of Taluma

Bola – Kwin weapon (rope with balls)

Brando – Dayvee's friend, Calupi of Wolf Mountain Pack

Brodee – Calupi Alpha leader of Big Pine Wolf Pack

Bruno – Brando's wolf companion

Bunjee – Dayvee's adopted younger brother

Cato – Chayla's wolf companion

Chancee – former Calupi of Wolf Mountain Pack, now exiled

Chase – Pericard

Chayla – Calupi of Wolf Mountain Pack in Dayvee's sub-pack

Clay – Milay's former companion

Clunee – Calupi of Wolf Mountain Pack (history writer)

Codee – Dayvee's uncle

Cumback stick – Kwin weapon (boomerang)

Cujo – Kwin weapon (long stick with sharp blades)

Dayvee – Leeto's son and Calupi of Wolf Mountain pack

Dirk – Kagard assigned to protect Tibalt

Drako – Calupi messenger of Wolf Mountain Pack

Dugee – Calupi of Wolf Mountain pack assigned to the Calupi council

Elayni –Dayvee's friend, Wolf Mountain Pack Calupi

Evee – Elayni's wolf companion

Franko – Elayni's father, beta Calupi of Wolf Mountain Pack (trader)

Gaylo – Keeper of the Vita, Calupi of White River Pack

Geno – Calupi of Wolf Mountain Pack in Dayvee's sub-pack

Gojo – Gaylo's wolf companion

Graydee – Geno's wolf companion

Hano – Bunjee's father, Ursan

Harthome – Capital city of Taluma, western continent

Herrick – 1st Alpha of Wolf Mountain pack

Hubert – Kagard Captain Varian appointed

Jaycee – Dayvee's wolf companion

Jerrod – Pericard

JoKayndo – 1st Kayndo (animal master)

Jolay – Codee's mate, Calupi of Wolf Mountain Pack

Jonesee – Brando's father, Calupi of Wolf Mountain Pack

Julee – Franko's second, Calupi of Wolf Mountain Pack

Juno – Drako's wolf companion

Kagard – Kingdom of Taluma's soldiers

Kayndo – Animal Master

Keeli – Brando's mother, former Calupi of Wolf Mountain Pack

Keeno – Kwutee's wolf companion

Kwutee – Keeper of the Vita, Calupi healer of Wolf Mountain Pack

Kun – Creator of Universe, Master and Maker of all things (God)

Law of the Pack – Protect the Pack, Defend the Vita

Latham – Pericard

Layton – King of Taluma, current

Leeto – Dayvee's father, Alpha leader of Wolf Mountain Pack

Luko – Leeto's wolf companion

Marcello – King of Taluma, former (nicknamed the false king)

Miko – Calupi of Wolf Mountain Pack, Former Alpha leader

Milay – Dayvee's mother, Calupi of Wolf Mountain Pack

Nails – Calupi weapon (chakram with several blades)

Nayti – Calupi woman of White River Pack

Neeshi – Nero's wolf companion

Nero – Calupi of Wolf Mountain Pack Calupi, former training leader

Nolan – King of the Kingdom Lucendo on the Eastern Continent of Terra

Pako – Calupi of Wolf Mountain Pack

Pericard – Kagard detachment that protect the king of Taluma

Petee – former Calupi of Wolf Mountain Pack, now exiled

Polo – Petee's wolf companion

Portia – Port city

Razi – Alcoholic beverage

Reed – Botanee Clan member

Reko – Kwin from Grassy Knoll herd

Renay – Calupi of Wolf Mountain Pack

Rodnee – Calupi of Wolf Mountain Pack, Beta leader

Rudee – Calupi of Wolf Mountain Pack

Santo – Bunjee's uncle, Ursan

Shakree – Santo's bear companion

Seemo – King Layton's eagle companion

Serano – Kwin leader of Grassy Knoll herd

Shilo – Reko's horse

Skylay – Milay's companion

Spiro – Dayvee's eagle scout

Sunray – Dayvee's horse

Taluma – The Western Continent Kingdom – (King Layton rules)

Tayro – Calupi of Wolf Mountain pack (Kwutee's apprentice)

Terra – Planet, soil

Theron – Pericard

Tibalt – Prince of Taluma, Son of King Layton

Tinay – Elayni's mother, Calupi of Wolf Mountain Pack

Tobee – Wolf Mountain Pack adult with deformed legs

Tooth – Calupi weapon (knife)

Topay – Tayro's wolf companion

Tucker – Pericard

Varian – Eastern Continent Visitor

Vita – Religious rules and beliefs given to Terrans by Jokanyno

Wilee – Codee's wolf companion

-Acknowledgments-

They say it takes a community to raise a child. It certainly takes a community to put out a book. It wouldn't have been possible without the aid of my incredible team so I want to acknowledge and thank them.

First there's the One who gave me the inspiration and words. My Lord and Savior.

Second is my awesome family and amazing friends who always had words of encouragement. Their belief in me has been unfailing.

Third I want to thank my writer groups for their help. Fantasy for Christ, St. Louis Christian Writers, CIA, and AFCA offered me great advice, critiques, beta reads, contacts, and encouragement.

And I can't forget my editor and proofreader, Nadine Brandes and Stephanie Van Wyk. I shudder to think what my books would look like without their help.

Then there's my cover artist Yvonne Less with Diverse Pixel, cover model Matt Luckey, photographer Katherine Cobert with Cobert Photography, web-site designer Joe Vanderjagt, and my cartographer Ryan Proksch. All of them gave of their time and energy to help me.

Last but not least, I want to thank everyone that reads my books and tells others about them. Your support is really appreciated.

www.ingramcontent.com/pod-product-compliance
Lightning Source LLC
Chambersburg PA
CBHW020224180626
46810CB00006B/2038